Dirtsi...

The 500,000 humans who landed on the planet Zuul are a diverse and undesirable lot culled from the slums of the North American City States. They were teased, bribed, deceived, and coerced into boarding the ark ship and leaving Earth.

THE ZID
The Zid have upside down, T-shaped skulls, a clam shell-style vertical mouth slit, and sealable cheek slits through which they breathe. Their religion teaches that, above all, technology is evil. The main threat to their power is human and Mothri technology.

THE MOTHRI
The Mothri are six-ton female beetles, each the size of a battle tank and capable of laying thousands of eggs. They have variously colored exoskeletons, three sets of legs, and large analytical brains. Also, humans find Mothri eggs to be very tasty.

THE ANDROIDS
Built to do the dirty work for the humans, many are now on their own, thanks to a series of devastating earthquakes that destroyed much of what the humans had brought with them.

Praise for William C. Dietz's
Legion of the Damned and *The Final Battle*

"A tough, moving novel of future warfare."
—David Drake

"A complex novel . . . scintillating action scenes . . . A satisfying, exciting read."
—Billie Sue Mosiman, author of *Widow*

Rockets and rayguns galore . . . and more than enough action to satisfy those who like it hot and heavy."
—*The Oregonian*

"Exciting and suspenseful . . . real punch."
—*Publishers Weekly*

Praise for Dietz's *Sam McCade* series

"Slam-bang action."   —David Drake

"Adventure and mystery in a future space empire."
—F.M. Busby

"All-out space action."   —*Starlog*

"Good, solid, space-opera, well told."
—*Science Fiction Chronicle*

Ace Books by William C. Dietz

GALACTIC BOUNTY
FREEHOLD
PRISON PLANET
IMPERIAL BOUNTY
ALIEN BOUNTY
McCADE'S BOUNTY
DRIFTER
DRIFTER'S RUN
DRIFTER'S WAR
LEGION OF THE DAMNED
BODYGUARD
THE FINAL BATTLE
WHERE THE SHIPS DIE
STEELHEART

STEELHEART

WILLIAM C. DIETZ

ACE BOOKS, NEW YORK

This book is an Ace original edition,
and has never been previously published.

STEELHEART

An Ace Book / published by arrangement with
the author

PRINTING HISTORY
Ace edition / August 1998

The Penguin Putnam Inc. World Wide Web site address is
http://www.penguinputnam.com

Check out the Ace Science Fiction/Fantasy
newsletter, and much more at Club PPI!

ISBN: 0-441-00542-X

ACE®
Ace Books are published by The Berkley Publishing Group,
a member of Penguin Putnam Inc.,
200 Madison Avenue, New York, NY 10016.
ACE and the "A" design are trademarks
belonging to Charter Communications, Inc.

PRINTED IN THE UNITED STATES OF AMERICA

10 9 8 7 6 5 4 3 2

For Marjorie, who knew a bargain when she saw one,
and was willing to take a chance.

STEELHEART

1

an´ droid, n, an automaton made to resemble a human being

A section of the *Pilgrim*'s hull, or what remained of it, curved up and away from the trading plaza. There were holes where plates had been cut away, lights flickered through gaps between the ship's durasteel ribs, and shadows went about their business.

The calendar in the android's head said it was summer, but the sky was dark, and sleet drove in from the north. Just one of the many miseries that resulted from the volcanic eruptions and the world-spanning dust cloud that blocked the sun.

Horlo's Outback Outfitter's shop had been looted months ago—but the broken-out display window made an excellent place to wait. Doon shared the space with some frosty shards of glass, the remains of an old campfire, and a wall full of Antitechnic graffiti.

Thousands of tiny micromachines inhabited his body and worked to maintain it. One of them exited through the synthetic's left nostril, dashed across his cheek, and entered his ear. The android wrapped his remaining arm around his knees in an effort to look smaller and less threatening. No small task for a rather large android.

People walked by but kept their distance from the figure in the window. Partly from fear, but partly because the passersby assumed he wanted something, and they had nothing left to give. Food, medicine, ammo. Those were the things people needed and never gave away.

Doon had been waiting fifteen hours by then. Not that it made much difference, since he had nothing better to do. He knew Sojo would arrive when there was a reason to arrive and not a moment before. Androids were like that. A human might go in search of music, a mate, or a thousand other nonessential things. Synthetics had better sense.

"Serve and protect." "Strive to survive." Both imperatives played important roles in his motivational subroutines. Had Doon been an alpha class robot, and a slave to his programming, one would have overridden the other.

But such was not the case . . . and that led to a dilemma: Doon's right arm was missing. The synthetic named Sojo had one. Should Doon take what he needed? Or allow Sojo to keep that which was rightfully his? He was sentient. The decision was his. Sleet stabbed through the sickly green light and formed a carpet at the android's feet.

The room had been part of a large undifferentiated cargo hold prior to the Cleansing. The contents had been looted during the food riots—making room for the refugees that took up residence in the cavernous holds. The size and quality of their walled-off apartments varied according to when they had taken up residence, how mean they were, and what sort of weapons they possessed.

Sojo was the single exception. He occupied a large but somewhat crowded corner of the hold in spite of the fact that he was crippled and, outside of a rather sophisticated electronic alarm system, had no weapons whatsoever. The walls of his apartment were hung with mismatched shelving. The boards sagged under the weight of components and tools. Power flowed, not just to his apartment, but to the entire area from an illegal tap that *he* had established.

The outer bulkhead was made of durasteel and still bore numbers that corresponded with long-vanished cargo modules. A work table made from salvaged ceiling panels occupied the center of the space and stood only a foot off the floor.

Sojo's legs had been missing for some time now, and he scooted around the table on what had been an equipment dolly. Two handles, both of which mounted a piece of rubber, were his sole means of propulsion. He didn't want to leave the relative safety of his nest but knew it was necessary. The software had to be sent, and, because large sections of the ship's com system had been destroyed during the quakes, there was no choice but to venture outside.

Sojo had traded his right leg for the HoloTech miniframe. He slipped the jack into his temple, loaded the folder called Sunshine, and sent a backup to the RAM hidden in his right biceps. Once that was accomplished, the android took one last look around. The room was warm and messy—just the way he liked it.

The black watch cap and chopped-down parka lay in a pile against one wall. He pulled them on, found the remote, and aimed it at the low, torso-sized door. The panel opened and closed as the android passed through. A yellow arrow pointed back toward his quarters. Sojo ignored it. The passageway zigzagged back and forth.

"Safety First," "Electrical Access Panel," and "Emergency Air Supply" decals testified to a more orderly past. Wires, all of which had been stripped out of some other part of the ship, had been draped across beams and strung to feed glow rods that dangled every twenty feet.

Emaciated men, women, and children, most dressed in rags, greeted the android as he rolled past, called the name they knew him by, and wished him well. And no wonder . . . since Sojo had helped each of them at one time or another.

The man called Fags was no exception. He smiled at Sojo, waved at the android's back, and returned to his closet-sized cubicle. The com unit was hidden beneath the flat, gray-white pillow. The air was cold, and Fags could see his breath as he blew on his fingers and thumbed the power switch. A green light appeared, static hissed, and he pressed "send."

"Fags here."

The better part of a minute passed before an answer came. The voice sounded bored. "Yeah? So what's up?"

"The crip left his cube."

There was a pause, as if the other man was speaking to someone else, followed by the words Fags had been waiting for. "You done good, Fags. You like ham?"

"I love ham."

"Good. You got one coming."

Fags thought about tender pink meat spitting in a pan. Saliva filled his mouth, and his stomach growled. "Thanks. Thanks a lot."

"You bet," the voice said. "And, Fags . . ."

"Yeah?"

"Spend the rest of the day somewhere else. It'll be safer that way."

Fags hurried out into the cold. Mount Purlow had been the first to explode. Others followed. Aftershocks were so common that Fags barely noticed the one that shook the ground beneath his feet. Zuul was restless.

Doon felt his aggressor systems come on-line as a unicycle rumbled by. Both the riders wore visored helmets. The passenger carried a Crowley IV submachine gun. Standard wear these days. Assuming you had the ammo to feed one. The unicycle vanished as quickly as it had appeared. A stray radio signal bounced in from somewhere, pushed a burst of static through channel seven, and signified nothing.

He'd spent weeks looking for Sojo and acquired all sorts of trivia during that time. Sojo had functioned as one of Dr. Gene Garrison's assistants on the trip out, and Garrison, better known to artificial sentients as "the Creator," had employed the synthetic's services after the landing as well.

Years passed, and while Doon spent his time chasing criminals, Sojo absorbed everything Garrison was willing to teach, and then, in what the Creator called the final measure of his work, took self-directed programming to a whole new level, and pursued projects that only he and his mentor could understand.

Then, before whatever it was they were working on could

be realized, the quakes brought everything to a halt.

The humans, who had been led to expect something verging on paradise, had arrived only to find that Zuul had been inhabited for hundreds of thousands of years. First by the Forerunners, whose ruins still dotted the surface of the planet, then by members of a religious cult that the rest of the Zid race found so repugnant that they forced the entire membership into sleep capsules, and sent them to a then-unpopulated planet.

Though not exactly pleased about the incumbent population, which also included a colony of the beetlelike Mothri, the humans were extremely adaptable, and eager to take advantage of the planet's considerable resources and wide-open spaces. Unlike the other races, who avoided each other to whatever extent they could, the humans mixed with both groups. Settlements were established in and around the Zid-controlled "holy lands," and an uneasy peace ensued.

As a result of this mixing, a substantial number of humans became interested in the Zid religion, made the necessary commitment, and were integrated into primitive agricultural communes. Thus encouraged, the Zid leadership foresaw the day when all humans would become ardent members of the Antitechnic Church, and thereby fulfill God's plan. That being the case, a limited number of humans were allowed to enter the priesthood.

So, when the quakes hit and the volcanos began to erupt, the Zid interpreted the geological upheaval as a sign that the great Cleansing had begun, that all machines were to be swept off the surface of the planet, and behaved accordingly.

There were Zid-inspired demonstrations, pray-ins, and machine riots. The Artificial Intelligence Lab was forced into hiding, and, for reasons not apparent, Sojo remained behind. Sympathetic humans protected the android during the Cleansing and the days immediately there after.

Eventually Sojo had wandered into Zid-held territory, where he had passed for human, and joined an all-droid commune. By living together, they hoped to escape detection. The Zid had a talent for penetrating such schemes, however, and attacked the farm. Four droids were killed, one was wired into a living altar, and Sojo escaped.

He traveled at night, walked cross country, and made it into the Human Zone also known as the HZ, where machines stood a fighting chance.

Sojo went to ground after that, and did a fairly good job of it, until Doon heard rumors. Not too surprising, since Sojo had been programmed to teach rather than hunt.

There were 21,248 synthetics prior to the Cleansing. Sojo had serial number 18567 and Doon's was 20872. An almost meaningless detail where humans were concerned—but critical to synthetics. Production records were the closest thing they had to an official genealogy—and serial numbers said a lot about who and what they were.

Eighteens had more memory than the seventeens, nineteens suffered from memory dropouts, and twenties, those who opted for Law Package 2.1, were known to be ruthless. Was it true? Doon considered where he was—and what he planned to do. The answer was obvious.

The light was fading fast. Something moved on the far side of the mall. It was a man—or half a man, because his body ended at the waist. The platform had been a furniture dolly, and he used handles to push himself along.

The half-man didn't like open spaces and crossed them as quickly as he could. He hadn't been out for long, judging by the thin layer of sleet that covered his shoulders.

It wasn't until the half-man arrived in a pool of light that Doon recognized him. Sojo possessed holo-star looks, a powerful frame, and two good arms.

Doon had spent a lot of processing time trying to decide if he had emotions, and if he did, how they compared to those experienced by humans. The Creator claimed they were identical. But how would *he* know? Subjectivity being what it is. In any case, Doon processed what *he* knew to be a sense of satisfaction as Sojo rattled past.

The bloom from Doon's IR signature was a dead giveaway for any sort of police unit, even nonsentient models, but Sojo didn't look twice.

Doon smiled. The tracker loved bean counters, pencil pushers and med units. Ninety-six percent of their parts were identical to his, but they couldn't find their butts with a metal detector.

Doon could have taken Sojo then—there weren't many that could stop him—but he hated to salvage a synthetic in public. It might give the bio bods ideas, and what with the Zid, not to mention bounty hunters, there were too many scrappers already. The tracker followed Sojo around the corner and south onto one of the Committee's arrow-straight heat-fused streets. Sojo's castors made intertwining lines through a thin layer of slush.

Doon followed. He didn't really need the long black duster he wore, other than to conceal the fact that he didn't need it—and to hide the weapons he wore. His processor considered the facts. Sojo was out and about. Why now? It must have been urgent, because Sojo was pushing hard. The castors clicked as the platform crossed ridges in the sidewalk.

Doon liked the look of the other synthetic's arms. He could imagine how the right one would hang. Long and comfortable, like the original had, before the jackers blew it off.

Sojo turned to the right and disappeared behind a prefab store. Doon hurried to catch up, peeked around the corner, and saw his target halfway down the block. His destination, and the reason for his trip, were obvious now. The com booth, one of hundreds established during the Committee's reign, was intact. Many—hell, *most*—pay sets had been damaged in the quakes or destroyed during the machine riots. All of which meant that communication with outposts such as Riftwall, Norley's Knob, and Mound City were uncertain at the best. The only *sure* way to deliver a message was to hire a runner—or take it yourself, which was not an option for someone like Sojo.

Doon had slowed to a walk by then, and was a hundred feet away when Sojo approached the com booth. The synthetic took one look at the attendant and sped away. The guard yelled, "Stop!" and the droid went faster. Two figures in black raincoats materialized out of the shadows and took up the chase. The attendant followed.

Doon saw the *real* attendant's body slumped in a doorway, swore, and started to run. Just his frigging luck! Wait all day only to have some good-for-nothing bio bods salvage his mark. Besides, who the hell were they to pick on the robotic equivalent of a nerd?

Doon knew his thinking was inconsistent but didn't care. He followed Sojo's pursuers down another ruler-straight street toward the point where it ran into the *Pilgrim*'s frosty white hull.

Sojo had a lead on them by then—but paused as one of the Guild's heavily armed convoys approached. It was similar to an Earth-style train in that an enormous tractor unit supplied the motive power, while a long string of trailers followed behind.

Doon knew that a steady stream of such convoys crossed High Hand Pass every week carrying tools, weapons, and ammo to those brave enough to live outside the HZ, and bringing whatever food the subsurface farmers could spare back across the mountains. The train bristled with pod-mounted automatic weapons. Many of them tracked Sojo and his pursuers as they drew near.

The synthetic looked back over his shoulder, realized his pursuers were gaining, and launched himself into the street. Doon wanted to warn him, wanted to help, but knew it was too late. The half-man skittered toward the convoy and disappeared under a trailer.

Doon assumed Sojo was dead, as did his pursuers, until the last trailer rattled by. The droid nearly made it, nearly escaped, but wasn't fast enough. His silhouette showed as he entered the ship. The scavs followed at a trot. Doon brought up the rear.

The Junkman paused just long enough to let his assistants take the lead. The bounty hunter had employed more than a dozen of them over the last couple of years. He had a preference for those who were young and had something to prove.

The boy named Jak fit the profile to a T. He stepped in front of the girl and slipped through the gap.

Old lady Cramby was waiting inside the ship. She had only one shell in the black-market smoothbore, but that was enough. She squeezed the trigger, staggered under the recoil, and cackled as the ball bearings tore Jak apart.

The girl stepped forward, sprayed the woman with 9mm bullets, and waited for backup. None appeared.

The Junkman shook his head, bent over, and got blood on his hands as he sorted through Jak's possessions. Those worth keeping went into the pockets that lined the inside of his raincoat. Girls lasted longer than boys did, or so the Junkman had concluded, because they placed a higher priority on survival. All of which explained why he hired boys.

The girl kept her back to the walls as she moved up the corridor, painfully aware of how thin they were, and the fact that it would be easy to fire through them.

Unlike the Junkman, who had been born on the dole, she came from privileged circumstances. After six years of dance lessons, she still moved on the balls of her feet. That, plus the fact that she had refused to sell her body, would have pleased her mother.

Wood splintered as the Junkman kicked a section of wall. A man sheltered his family with his body. He held his arms up as if in supplication, and the Junkman nodded politely. Not because he had any compunctions about killing innocent people, but because ammo was expensive and best reserved for serious threats.

It took the bounty hunter and his assistant less than three minutes to investigate the shabby little cubicles that branched to either side of the hallway, establish the fact that Sojo hadn't hid in one of them, and hit what appeared to be a blank wall. But the Junkman had been hunting androids for a long time now, and he knew what they were capable of. He donned a pair of wire rimmed glasses, selected a stylus-sized flashlight from the inside of his raincoat, and pushed a button. The light wobbled over grimy metal.

It took a full minute of patient inspection to find the parallel cracks, verify the existence of the door, and place the demo charge. The Junkman motioned to the girl, and she backed away.

Sojo was surprised when the charge detonated. A hole appeared where the hatch and a sizeable section of wall had been. Smoke billowed, and a man stepped through. He was at least six feet tall and had ice-blue eyes and a three-day growth of beard. His hand cannon carried fourteen ''robot rounds,'' each formulated to puncture metal but cause minimal damage.

The android forced a smile. "The name is Sojo."

The Junkman nodded. "Yeah, I know."

Video supplied by the android's pickups was fed to a dedicated subprocessor, where it was analyzed. Sophisticated algorithms were used to compute the changes in distance between facial features and compare them to a static model. The result was expressed as a nonverbal content quotient. The scav came up zeros.

"Can you be bought?"

The bounty hunter shrugged. "Sure, if you have something I want."

The synthetic gestured to the room. "How 'bout this?"

The Junkman shook his head. "You're worth more than all this junk put together."

Sojo made one last attempt. "What if I told you that I'm a scientist—working on something that could bring summer back. What would you say then?"

The Junkman raised an eyebrow. "I'd say you were a lying, no-good pile of shit."

"Could I send some data before I die?"

"Nope."

"Why not?"

"Because I don't have time for this bullshit." The girl had heard the noise before, but it still made her ears hurt. A hole appeared between Sojo's eyes . . . and castors rattled as the impact pushed him across the room.

Doon slid his hand under the duster, felt the Skorp .44 leap into the palm of his hand, and watched the low-light target grid appear. The boy glowed green as he stepped over the body. The synthetic made his way around the old woman, checked her jugular, and slid along the wall.

A woman with a baby in her arms stepped out into the hallway. She saw him and backed into her cubicle. The android heard three bolts slide into place—and hoped she had something more substantial than locks to defend herself with.

Smoke from the explosion eddied down the hall, found its way into Doon's nostrils, and was automatically analyzed.

The demo charge had contained Guild-manufactured Hiplex 4.2. Good stuff . . . and the sign of a pro.

Doon didn't know what human fear was like—only that it was unpleasant. His fear stemmed from the tension between his survival programming and the dictates of his conscious mind. All of which was rather interesting, given that the original sequence of activities stemmed from a desire to replace his missing arm, and thereby improve the odds of survival. He eased his way forward.

Sparks fanned the air and a blade screeched as Sojo's head wobbled, hung from a handful of cables, and fell free. It bounced and rolled until the plastiflesh nose got in the way. The Junkman hated this part of the job. Not because of the butchery, but because of the time it took, and the fact that he was vulnerable. Damn Jak anyway . . . it was just like the miserable little bastard to get himself killed and leave some-one else holding the bag. The Junkman glanced at the girl, assured himself that she was looking out into the hall, and returned to his work.

Doon heard the saw, knew what it meant, and eased his way forward. The girl couldn't possibly have heard him, not with all the screeching, but turned anyway, as if warned by some sixth sense. A strange concept from the synthetic's point of view, since he had eight senses, and considered humans to be somewhat handicapped. He rounded a corner.

The girl didn't match his files. Identity screened? It hardly mattered. Her eyes widened with fear, her finger tightened on the trigger, and Doon wished he still had the nonlethal stun gun that went with his missing arm. But that was gone now . . . broken down for its component parts, or on display in an Antitechnic church. There was no choice.

Doon squeezed the trigger slowly, regretfully, knowing he couldn't miss. He saw the first slug hit the center of her scrawny chest—and the second take her between the eyes. Half her torso disappeared, followed by the top of her head. Blood fanned the wall.

The Junkman saw the girl die out of the corner of his eye and turned to meet the threat. Most people would have taken Doon for human—but the Junkman wasn't most people. He recognized the synthetic for what he was and tried to beat the machine's computer-fast reflexes.

Doon stepped through the jagged hole, raised the .44, and saw his vision split in two. The left side of the display showed a perp with weapon in hand, and a partially dismembered corpse lying at his feet.

The other half of the frame clicked through a series of digitally reproduced stills. There were twenty-six mug shots altogether, each a little older than the one before it, culminating in a picture taken two weeks prior to the Cleansing. Thanks to the disparity in reaction times, there was plenty of opportunity for a warning. Doon heard himself give one. "Police! Hold it right there!"

The Junkman fired, saw a hole appear in front of the synthetic's boots, and knew the next shot would hit his opponent's left knee. That would bring the sonofabitch down—and the rest would be easy. Maybe he could hire some locals to carry the body parts . . . maybe he could . . .

The first shot hit the Junkman's chest with the force of a sledgehammer. It flattened itself on his body armor, threw the bounty hunter backwards, and drove the air from his lungs. He was processing that, attempting to breathe, when the second bullet exited through the back of his head. The body smashed into some shelving, fell, and was buried under an avalanche of printouts. The Junkman was dead.

Doon shook his head sadly, looked around, and marveled at Sojo's quarters. All that stuff . . . and for what? Knowledge for the sake of knowledge? Or something more? There was no way to tell.

The synthetic spotted Sojo's blood-spattered right arm, considered taking the torso as well, and decided against it. It was too much to carry, especially in a fight, and there was something more as well. A vague sense of guilt—as if he were at fault.

Doon took the arm, wiped most of the bounty hunter's blood off it, and left the way he had come. Eyes watched through holes in the walls, and ears tracked his progress. The residents would miss Sojo, but that wouldn't stop them from looting his apartment, or selling what remained of his body. They wanted to survive—and so did Doon.

The boy, and the woman who had killed him, were just the way Doon had left them. The smoothbore had disappeared. The synthetic stepped over the bodies, peered out into the night, and scanned for heat. He saw three small blobs, rats most likely, scurry along a wall. Warmth, the product of a well-hidden campfire, leaked through an upstairs window. He stepped out into the sleet. The temperature registered on his sensors but caused no discomfort. His boots left marks in the slush.

Home—if that word could be used to describe the cold, half-flooded utilities vault where he passed his nights—was about a mile away. The arm made a bulge under his duster. A bulge that street thieves might find interesting. No one bothered him, though—which was just as well.

Doon slowed as he approached his temporary home, checked to ensure that none of his carefully arranged telltales had been disturbed, and lifted the cover. Metal squealed as the lid swung upward—and squealed again as darkness closed over his head. The hinges could have been oiled—but why bother? Especially when they functioned as a burglar alarm.

The crypt—for that was how Doon thought of it—was little more than a precast cable vault. He found the battery-powered lamp and turned it on. Heavily armored three-inch fiber-optic cables squirmed in from the sides, mated within the privacy of a connector box, and went their separate ways.

The space was dark, cold, and damp. Not uncomfortable really, but depressing, since the parameters that provided Doon with a sense of well-being had been set to match those common to humans. Why? To help synthetics fit into human-dominated society? Or to limit their ability to compete? As with so many other things, there was no way to know.

Doon sat on a ledge, his back to a corner, and arranged the arm across his thighs. He stroked the limb lovingly, thought about the pleasure it would bring, and felt guilty about the manner in which it had been obtained. What if the bounty hunters had missed Sojo? Would he have committed the same crime that they had? The synthetic winced internally and reached for the lamp. Darkness would do little to lessen the pain—but there was no reason to watch.

Doon had experienced the subroutine twenty-three times before and felt nothing but dread. The first sensation was similar to what a bio bod might have described as an empty feeling in the pit of his stomach. That was followed by a distinct lurch as his thought processes locked up, his body became rigid, and the video started to play.

Doon saw the girl, saw his bullets hit her, and wanted to scream as the robotic equivalent of pain racked his body. The girl died, fell, and died again, over and over until the synthetic knew her features by heart, and would dream about them for years to come. Because androids *do* dream—at least the Creator's did, according to algorithms he had devised.

Then it was the bounty hunter's turn to punish the creature who had ended his existence, and what the synthetic felt was no less painful than all the lives the Junkman had taken, or the one he had wasted.

It was the same price *all* synthetics paid if they took a human life—even if they killed in self-defense, or to protect another. Some said it was the Creator's idea, a way of ensuring that his creatures remained subservient. Others claimed he had opposed it, and been forced to agree. Not that it made much difference to Doon.

The synthetic watched the Junkman die for the tenth time, felt pain lance through his electronic nervous system, and clutched the arm to his chest. Darkness was his only friend.

2

an´ gel, n, a ministering or guiding spirit

The sentient spy sat SS-4A, also known as Michael, looked down from the heavens via a relatively old fashioned optical imaging system. Not because he didn't have more sophisticated options, but because it pleased him to do so. Clouds covered most of the planet's surface, 76.2% of it to be exact, but that did nothing to lessen its beauty. Zuul looked like a lustrous gray pearl floating on a pool of jet-black ink.

Michael gave the mental equivalent of a sigh, checked his side scanners for any sign of danger, and made his daily journal entry.

"Some might consider it ironic that I can do little more for my creators than document their slow, inexorable deaths. Still, I have studied their history, and understand them as well as any machine can. I will maintain this journal for as long as possible, but evil roams the sky, and my days are numbered."

The satellite read the last line over again. Was it too dramatic? Too filled with self-pity? Not that it mattered much, since there was very little chance that anyone else would have the opportunity to read it. Not unless his favorite fantasy came true.

Michael allowed himself to drift, to imagine how the ship would drop into orbit, how they would find his badly battered body, and retrieve his memory mod. That's when the captain, a female android of exquisite taste, would read his journal and weep. Well, not weep perhaps, but wish she had known him.

An alarm went off and sent fear-bearing electrons racing through the satellite's fiber-optic nervous system. A pair of micro sats, both manufactured by the self-styled Eye of God, were closing on his position. There had been four Angel sats to begin with . . . and Michael was the only one who had managed to survive. He armed himself for battle.

3

Sa mar′ i tan, n, a person who comes to the aid of another

Mary Maras awoke to the sound of rapidly clacking teeth. She reached out, ran her fingers over the smooth metal skull, found the button, and pushed it down. The noise stopped. The cranial unit, long separated from the spiderlike body for which it had been fabricated, blinked, and the numbers 0645 appeared where the droid's scanner unit should have been.

The roboticist groaned, lay back, and felt the computer-controlled work surface conform to the shape of her body. She didn't want to leave the confines of the warm sleeping bag but knew it was necessary. A column of Zid had arrived two days before—and that meant information from beyond the mountains. Information that would be weeks or even months old, but could contain some hint, some mention of her daughter and ex-husband. *How* were they? *Where* were they? She thought of little else.

The last time Mary had spoken with her family was two days before the quakes, when George called to say that Corley had arrived, and while home sick, was otherwise fine.

Of course, both of them might have been killed during the quakes, or in the unrest that followed. Mary *knew* that, but didn't *believe* it, and was determined to find them, no matter what the cost. The repair shop, and the activities that it screened, were the means to that end.

The roboticist sat up, broke the bag's seal, and shivered as the air hit her skin. She swung long, skinny legs over the side, squinted against the motion-controlled lights, and waited for her pupils to adjust. Unlike the intentionally spartan room where business was conducted, the workshop was filled to overflowing with makeshift shelving, junked robots, and the large, somewhat bulky nano farm. So much stuff that it was hard to move.

The security system's scanners had been stripped from a wrecked land crawler, and the CPU had been cobbled together from reconditioned spares. A portable heater clicked on as she entered the bathroom. The roboticist addressed the mirror: "Security . . . the last seven hours, please."

The voice was male and reassuringly crisp. "There were two class one intrusion attempts—both unsuccessful."

"I *know* that," Mary responded irritably. "I'm alive, aren't I? Tell me something useful." A class one attempt amounted to someone trying the doorknob—a frequent occurrence, given the number of homeless people who roamed the streets.

The security system waited through the irrelevant vocalizations and continued its report. "The being previously designated as 'Clamface' continues to watch from the other side of the street."

Mary winced as she wiped herself with page 47 of the Pro Loader 8700 Tech Manual, stood, and flushed the toilet. The water swirled, albeit reluctantly, and disappeared. "Now? He's still out there?"

"Affirmative."

She stepped out of the john. "Video, please."

The system obliged, and a monitor flickered to life. A greenish blob appeared. Clamface had positioned himself well inside the burned-out storefront on the far side of the street. There was no mistaking his staff or the characteristic IR signature. Like the rest of his race, Clamface packed a higher core body temperature than a human would have, which, combined with an extremely efficient circulatory system, gave him a cold-weather advantage.

Mary sighed. She'd have to move. Clamface, along with a pair of Zid she called Gimpy and Fatso, had been watching her place for more than a week now. Everyone knew how the system worked. Clamface, or another of the Church's agents, would identify a "sinner," place the subject's residence under surveillance, follow him or her around, and interview the neighbors.

Then, having intimidated the neighborhood, and accumulated the evidence of "crimes against God," the agent would share it with his superiors, a judgment would be rendered, and a punishment assigned. "Dispossession" meant that a residence or business would be trashed or destroyed in an unexplained fire—and "expiation" translated to a sentence of death.

Whatever punishment was deemed appropriate would be meted out by a "mob," which appeared to form spontaneously but was actually organized in advance, and led by Agents of the Church. Scientists, mechanics, and technicians were favorite targets and frequently slated for "expiation"— a fact that was at least partially responsible for the fact that most things didn't work any more.

All of which was made even worse by the fact that so many of her own kind had joined the Antitechnic Church that seventy or eighty percent of the mob would be human. The thought of their blank stares and hate-distorted faces sent a shudder down Mary's spine. She turned toward the bathroom. "Keep me informed."

The security system processed the request, realized that it was redundant to basic programming, and made no reply.

The roboticist opened the tap, waited for the brownish flow to begin, and squeezed toothpaste onto her brush. Not much, just a smidge, since it was hard to come by. The face in the water-specked mirror stared back as she worked the brush back and forth. She had black hair, mocha-colored skin, large, some said intense eyes, slightly flared nostrils, generous lips, and a softly rounded chin.

It was the kind of face that went from pretty to beautiful

when she put on makeup—something she rarely did, except for faculty parties when George insisted. "Give 'em something to look at," he used to say. "When they see how pretty *you* are, they'll know how smart *I* am."

Mary knew George didn't mean it the way it sounded, but resented the implication. Just one of the things that led to the separation. She frowned and spit toothpaste into the sink. The water caught the stuff and pulled it down. Mary used a sweatshirt as a towel, closed the tap, and considered a shower.

Nothing could beat the pure comfort of being both warm and clean at the same moment. The problem was that it took lots of power to heat the requisite amount of water, and that, combined with the rest of her activities, could attract the wrong sort of attention. Still, why protect something she was about to abandon? That, plus a whiff of her own body odor, forced a decision.

The shower didn't take long, not with only five gallons of water to draw from, but made Mary warm. After that it was a simple matter to don three layers of reasonably clean clothes, and feed the nano farm.

The ritual required the roboticist to pour carefully measured amounts of powdered manganese, tungsten, chromium, carbon, nickel, cobalt, vanadium, molybdenum, aluminum, sodium, and titanium into the correct intake ports. Those were some, but not all, of the basic materials that enabled the tiny robots to replicate themselves and—if she ordered them to do so—to create custom strains.

Though classified as robots, nano were different from sentient machines in a number of important ways. The first was size. "Nano" means "billionth," and, as the name would suggest, they were very, very small. Powered by static electricity, micromotors less than .0001 of an inch across drove machines that incorporated gears, shafts, and belts etched into silicon chips using X-ray lithography and were controlled by atom-wide carbon rod "push—pull" computers.

Nano were different in other ways as well, including the fact that unlike their larger sentient cousins they were "modular," "adaptive," and "dynamic," meaning that while they carried very little onboard intelligence, they were collectively quite smart.

That particular architecture, sometimes referred to as "self-organizing," required minimal computing power and enabled machines that were faster, cheaper, and more reliable than "stand-up" models.

The prospect of shutting the factory down in order to move it, finding the power necessary to sustain it, and rebooting the facility once it was in place made her depressed.

Mary took a Zid food cake from her sparsely stocked larder, filled her pockets with surefire trade items, and took one last look around. Something the size of a hydroponically grown orange rolled out from under some shelves, saw her parka, and uttered a series of joyful squeaks.

Mary had designed the toy during her pregnancy.

George named the device "Hairball," in honor of its ability to sprout thousands of synthetic hair follicles, thereby transforming itself into something cute and cuddly.

Corley had intended to take Hairball with her, but forgot in the last-minute rush, and left the toy behind. Hairball extended a tiny pogo-sticklike appendage and jumped up and down. Its processor had a limited vocabulary. "Me go! Me go! Me go!"

Mary shook her head. "You *not* go. Not today."

The robot grew smaller. "Corley play?"

Mary sighed. "No, for the thousandth time, Corley can't play. She went away . . . remember?"

"No," Hairball replied honestly. "Me wait."

"Good," Mary said thankfully. "You wait. I'll be back."

The riot gun had a short barrel, eight-round magazine, and pistol grip. A badly mauled synthetic had given it to her in return for emergency surgery. A good choice for someone small and vulnerable. Slung from a shoulder strap, and ready for use, it kept the riffraff away. Maybe she would fire it one day—to see how it felt.

She fingered the pocket remote, heard the security system buzz in response, and opened the door. The outside air was cold, *damned* cold, and she hurried to seal the opening. No less than three bolts snicked into place as the security system obeyed its programming. She glanced across the street, felt

Clamface stare at her, and hoped he froze to death.

The market was only a mile away for those who were strong enough, or crazy enough, to walk through secondary streets. Mary preferred to follow more heavily traveled thoroughfares. They made the trip longer, but were patrolled by the Guild's troops.

During the years immediately after the landing, the power structure established during the long journey had held, and resources had been allocated according to rules and procedures laid down by a seven-person group known as the Committee. An entire prefab city was built under their direction, complete with fusion plant, hydroponics facility, and carefully planned multifamily habitats. Nonsentient robots handled most of the work—but human labor was required as well.

That's when a group called the Merchant's Guild had taken exception to the four-hour-per-day "labor tax" and precipitated a revolt. The Guild won the short but bloody conflict, and free-form, "anything goes" capitalism took the place of the perfectly designed communities envisioned by the Committee.

The communities collectively known as Shipdown burst forth from the *Pilgrim*'s twenty-five-mile-long hull like fungus on a fallen tree trunk. Resources were totaled and divided into shares that were hoarded, squandered, bought, sold, combined, and redivided until the merchants controlled just about everything. They'd been ready to consolidate their power, to put an army of subsentient robots to work building their factories, when the planet decided otherwise. Now they provided what order there was, and, like most of the citizens of Shipdown, Mary was grateful.

The sky was the color of worn aluminum and gave birth to occasional snowflakes. They drifted this way and that before hitting the ground. Anonymous scuff marks showed that others were up and about.

More and more noises were heard as the city woke from its slumber. The solid *thump*, *thump*, *thump* of a carefully hidden loom, the staccato bark of a unicycle engine, the *pop*, *pop*, *pop* of small-caliber gunfire, and the undulating wail of a Zid prayer caller.

She saw him off to the right. His feet rested on a crossbar, his rags jerked in the wind, and a scarf held him in place. This one was yellow, but some favored red or blue. No one knew why. No one *she* knew, anyway.

The poles were curiosities at first—something to wonder at. Then, as time passed, and the T-shaped poles began to proliferate, curiosity turned to annoyance as the callers synchronized their prayers and created what amounted to a vast around-the-clock public address system.

In spite of the fact that some died of exposure, and snipers accounted for two or three a night, the zealots persisted. Their wailing was as endless as the wind.

Mary raised her collar and trudged up the hill. The slope had been created when the *Pilgrim* struck the planet's surface and skidded for more than eighty miles. Parallel ridges had been created by the waves of earth and rock shoved away from the ship's massive hull.

As Mary climbed toward the top of "East Ridge," the *Pilgrim*'s much-abused hull began to appear. Frost covered the hull, except where plates had been removed, and smoke poured out of makeshift chimneys. Though the ship had been emptied after the landing, thousands had returned to it after the Cleansing, and considered themselves lucky to be there.

A raggedy man passed, straining to pull his homemade cart up the hill, boots slipping in the slush. Mary stepped out, put her shoulder to the cart, and swore when the wheels threw slush on her pants.

The man paused at the top of the hill, nodded his thanks, and held out his hand. A ball of deep-fried dough sat nestled in the palm of a filthy black glove. Mary didn't hesitate to pop the concoction into her mouth and bite into it. It was hot and tasted of cinnamon. The man was gone before she could thank him.

The roboticist paused for a moment to marvel at the spaceship. It blocked a third of the sky, stretched for miles in both directions, and incorporated more than two thousand years of scientific progress. Knowledge the Zid considered evil . . . and humans were beginning to lose.

Mary chose her footing with care as she descended the hill. Perhaps the naysayers were right, perhaps the *Pilgrim* should have remained in orbit—but what of the metal she had supplied? What of the prefab city wrested from her holds? Most of it lay in ruins now, but she couldn't be blamed for that . . . no one could.

A thousand pillars of smoke reached up to support the low-hanging sky as Mary made her way past a lifeless prayer caller and down the opposite slope.

A flock of night birds, their beaks bloody from pecking at the Zid's half-frozen flesh, flapped into the air. Food was where you found it.

Doon awoke clutching another synthetic's arm to his chest. His eyes opened to near total darkness. What little light there was formed a straight line along one side of the cable vault's access door. Afterimages strobed through his visual recognition system, and his body spasmed in response. The punishment had gone on for a long time and leaked into his dreams. Assuming they *were* dreams and not a simulation.

The question was irrelevant, and Doon pushed it away. The *real* question lay cradled in his arms. He had the arm—who would attach it? He knew the answer, or hoped he did, assuming she would agree.

With the same single-minded determination once devoted to finding criminals, the synthetic had tracked no less than three roboticists to their various lairs and chosen the one he thought most qualified. It was then, and only then, that Doon went after his arm.

The android emptied his pack and eyed his belongings. There weren't very many. The battery-powered light, a pack, a small "first aid" kit for do-it-yourself repairs, four boxes of ammo, three magazines, a cleaning kit, a set of reload tools, a combat knife, a media player, a bag filled with heat cubes, and an extra set of clothes.

Of even more importance, however, were some carefully chosen trade goods, including two bottles of vitamin C with the original seals intact, an ampule of broad-spectrum antibiotics, a pound of number eight shot, and six disposable lighters. The media player was a luxury but didn't take much room. He decided to keep it.

He started to pack—not an easy task with only one limb.

Sojo's arm went into the bag first. The other items fit around it. A human would have carried the same gear Doon did, plus food, water, and what? Pictures of Mom and Dad? The latest in a long chain of survivors, people who had lived long enough to reproduce, and launch their genes into the future. The synthetic bent Sojo's hand at the wrist, pulled the flap into place, and secured the necessary fasteners.

Doon took one last look around, confirmed that everything was accounted for, and slipped his arm through a strap. The cover squealed as he pushed it up and out of the way, and clanged when it hit the pavement. An elderly couple looked toward the noise, saw a man emerge as if from a grave, and hurried away. The less they saw, the safer they were.

Doon replaced the lid out of respect for the next tenant, pulled a three-sixty, and headed for higher ground. He felt good, *very* good, and turned his thoughts to the future. Equipped with a brand-new arm, the synthetic could do whatever he pleased. Find a hole somewhere, read his data cubes, and wait for things to improve.

A slush ball exploded against the side of Doon's face. He frowned, brought his target acquisition system on-line, and scanned the roof line. The youngsters made black silhouettes against the gray sky. They laughed as the cripple scooped some slush, rolled it on his chest, and threw the missile as hard as he could.

The laughter died as the perfectly thrown ball smacked into the tallest boy's chest. A witness cheered; Doon bowed and continued on his way. The day was young, and life, if that's what his existence could be called, was good.

As Mary descended the hill, the market spread itself before her. Illegal at one time, and truly the province of thieves, the market had thrived of late, offering as it did a setting for barter-based commerce.

Knowing a good thing when they saw it, the Guild had fenced the area, placed guards on all the gates, and taxed both ends of every transaction. Some talked of establishing a "free market," but no one did anything about it—partly because Guild rates were relatively low, and partly because the merchants were preferable to organized crime.

Though small to begin with, the market now covered more than two square miles. Except for their garish signs, the huts, shanties, and lean-tos that lined its twisty streets were as gray as the sky above.

Mary had company now. In ones, twos, and threes people made their way down intersecting streets, emerged from alleys, and drifted toward "E" gate. There was little to no conversation because all of them were competitors and potential enemies.

Some carried bags of trade goods, baskets of carefully hoarded food, and other more unusual objects.

One couple shared the weight of a pole-supported sling, which, in spite of the tarp that covered it, almost certainly supported a Mothri egg. Most people boiled them and sliced the contents into "steaks."

Mary had tried one, but had been unable to eat what she knew to be an unborn sentient, and had thrown up. Others had no such qualms, though, especially during a food shortage.

Other marketgoers led genetically engineered mutimals or pulled wagons loaded with firewood and, in one case, tiles looted from forerunner ruins. Most were armed, and for good reason. The trip from home to market was long and potentially dangerous.

The crowd thickened, swirled, and divided itself into four distinct lines, each leading through what looked like a door frame but was actually a weapons detector. Anonymous behind their visors, the Guild security personnel were quick and efficient. Everyone knew the drill, and the line moved quickly.

Mary stepped through the detector. A security guard peered at his screen. "Knife, left forearm, otherwise clean." He gestured toward the next station. Mary moved forward, passed the riot gun to a woman, and watched as she placed a seal on the trigger housing. A man taped the knife into its sheath.

The last guard accepted a 12-gauge shotgun shell in lieu of scrip, and handed her a flyer that featured "Dr. Anson's pain-free dental work" on one side and a public health tract on the other.

Mary tucked the paper away. Not for future reference, but to start a fire with, or to use as toilet paper.

Mary had been to the Zid quarter many times over the last year or so, and headed in that direction again. The main street, better known as "The Scam" to full-time residents, was eternally crowded.

It was early yet, which meant it was quieter than usual, and a lot less crowded.

A graffiti-covered construction droid whirred by. The guard posted on its bumper spoke volumes.

Children played hide-and-seek through the stalls, laughed when merchants scolded them, spilled out onto the street. They reminded Mary of Corley, or how she wanted Corley to be, and the thought brought a smile to her lips.

The market had an invigorating effect on Mary, and the roboticist breathed it all in. There was the smell of wood smoke, slowly simmering mush, and yes, the faintest whiff of ozone. A sure sign that machines were at work.

Mary turned off the main street and made her way down an alley that catered to bars and flophouses. One sign read, "We accept major painkillers," while another promised that "Our guards will ensure that you're alive in the morning."

A man saw Mary, stepped out of a doorway, and paused when the riot gun swiveled in his direction. The roboticist watched him out of the corner of her eye, but reserved most of her attention for the drunk who lay toward the middle of the street. Was he truly unconscious? Or part of a two-man trap?

The seemingly unconscious form started to rise. Mary ran forward, kicked the faker in the head, and spun around.

The first man had closed half the distance since the last time she'd looked at him. He saw how her finger rested on the bright blue security seal, the way the riot gun was lined up with his chest, and froze. "Sorry, my mistake."

"You got that right," Mary said grimly. "Turn around and run like hell."

The man did as he was told. The roboticist waited till he was a full block away, ignored the second man's moans, and continued on her way.

A full three minutes passed before her hands started to

shake. Mary swore and hid them in her pockets. It would take strength to find Corley—and a whole lot of luck. Could she do it? All by herself? She pushed the answer away.

The surroundings changed as human-style shanties gave way to the clean, carefully groomed streets typical of Zid Town. They were crime-free, thanks to the fact that those who lived there had nothing to steal, and fairly well populated. Morning prayers had been over for an hour now, and communal work was underway. Some swept, some searched for errant bits of litter, and others slapped coats of white paint onto already pristine walls. Most wore black body stockings, white ankle-length overrobes, and sturdy boots.

Mary could see why so many humans were attracted to Zid culture and religion. Both promised a simple, well-ordered life. Not to mention the fact that there had always been those who feared technology, or were suspicious of it, even among the starfaring colonists.

In spite of the name "Zid Town," most of the locals were human, serving their time as "shepherds" until proclaimed "ready in the eyes of the Lord," when they would join hundreds of fellow converts for the long march over the mountains and into the "holy lands."

One of the workers, a woman with a round face and luminous eyes, saw Mary and hurried over. The greeting of strangers, especially those who joined the flock, was an important part of God's work. "The Lord loves you . . . how may I help?"

Mary had been through the drill many times before, and knew that patient determination was the key to success. "Thank you . . . but no. I'm here to visit Sister Kora."

The woman looked doubtful. The Zid hierarchy frowned on random fraternization. Contacts, if any, require authorization. "Does the Sister expect you?"

"Yes," Mary lied, "but thanks for asking."

Mary assumed an air of confidence she didn't feel and marched down the street. She could feel the eyes on her back and was determined to ignore them.

Mary ignored the converts, took a right, and headed for Sister Kora's dome. The roboticist had no concept of how the Zid ranked within her culture, or how she felt about Mary's occasional visits.

The connection, tenuous at best, had been established more than a year before, when Mary had seen a gang of street toughs knock Kora down and had rushed to her rescue. Not because she harbored any particular affection for the aliens, but because it was the right thing to do.

Kora was shaken, and bleeding from a cut, so it was natural to escort her home, and once there, to perform first aid. One thing led to another, and through a combination of trade talk and sign language the two females managed to communicate. Subsequent visits had strengthened the bond—and Kora had agreed to seek information about Corley's whereabouts. Mary wondered if the Zid wanted to help or to make a convert. There was no way to tell.

Mary felt her pulse quicken as she approached the hut. What if Kora had news? The very possibility brought a lump to her throat. Or what if she didn't? She had experienced such disappointment many times before, and knew it would leave her depressed.

Mary didn't know how Kora detected her arrival, but supposed it had something to do with the hundreds of wrist-sized holes that dotted the hut's surface. Open when the occasion demanded, they functioned as windows, skylights, and vents. Wood plugs, all sawed from the same diameter log, served as corks. Many were hand-carved, decorated with quasireligious scenes, and handed down through the maternal line.

The entrance to the hut was protected by a patchwork quilt of hand-tanned leather. A six-foot-long slit ran down the center of the cover and could be sealed from within. Once reserved for deepest winters, these barriers now served year round. A booted foot appeared, quickly followed by a thickly muscled leg, and Kora herself.

The female's skull was radically different from its human counterpart, a fact that had given rise to derogatory names such as "T's" or "clam heads."

Both names stemmed from the fact that the Zid had horizontally configured jaws and vertical mouth slits. The sideways-projecting jaws resulted in T-shaped skulls, hence

the slur "T-heads," while the up-and-down mouths reminded some of clams, giving birth to the pejorative "clam
heads."

Add to that the fact that Zid physiology called for only
one eye, which had the capacity to roam the entire width of
their skulls, plus cheek gills through which they breathed,
and it was difficult for either race to ignore the extent to
which they were physiologically different.

There were similarities, however, including the fact that
both species had four limbs, walked erect, and boasted op-
posable thumbs. Never mind that the Zid had three fingers
instead of four.

Kora stepped forward, held out both hands palm out, and
waited for the human to do likewise. The Zid's lips rippled
from top to bottom. She spoke Spanglish with a thick, almost
guttural accent. "Come, it is warm within."

Mary didn't want to leave the riot gun outside, but knew
Kora would be offended if she brought it with her. She laid
the weapon on the doorstep, covered it with a mat, and
stepped inside.

The hut consisted of one large room. A carefully banked
fire sent smoke up through six ceiling-mounted holes. Others
allowed for ventilation, but most were closed. What light
there was came from candles in wall niches. Mary chose one
of the three-legged stools, warmed her hands over the fire,
and waited for Kora to speak. As with most members of her
species, the Zid was extremely direct.

"I have news from the east. . . . A male with brown skin,
and a daughter such as you described, were seen in Riftwall."

Doon approached his destination with care. The street
seemed normal enough, as did his fellow pedestrians. It was
only when he drew abreast of the shop, and spotted the Zid's
characteristic heat signature, that he understood the danger.
The Church had a line on the roboticist and kept her shop
under surveillance. Not especially good, but not too bad,
since she continued to live there. How to make contact? And
do so without attracting attention?

The synthetic passed the shop without slowing, reached

the end of the block, and took a left. The original grid called for alleys behind each row of prefab buildings, but some had been blocked by earthquake damage, and others had been sealed to limit access. Such was the case here.

A barrier had been erected across the mouth of the alley and subsequently turned into an ad hoc bulletin board—just one of hundreds that had sprung up throughout the city. Hundreds of white, blue, and yellow triangles showed where posters had been torn away. One bulletin remained.

Doon ripped it free and read the text. The words were printed in the spaces between the names on an old duty roster. "MACHINES ARE EVIL—SO SAYETH THE LORD." There was more, but the synthetic had no desire to read it. He handed the paper to the wind and watched it whirl away.

Doon scanned the area. There were pedestrians, heads down, minding their own business, and a prayer caller off to the south, but no sign of interest in him or his activities. A quick scan of the most popular radio frequencies produced nothing of note. The synthetic backed away, took three quick steps, and hit the barrier. Wood splintered and fell away. Doon widened the hole, pushed the pack through, and followed with his body.

Once within, Doon saw that the other end of the alley was closed as well. Without city services, and with no other place to dispose of their trash, the alley had become a garbage dump. Only the fact that people had very little material to throw away, and the consistently cold weather, had prevented the intense bacterial action that would have rendered the entire area unlivable.

Ground-level windows and doors were boarded up. If any of the residents had seen the synthetic, or were aware of his presence, they gave no sign of it. Doon plugged the hole as best he could, reshouldered the pack, and made his way toward the far end of the alley.

Ice crackled under Doon's boots, and garbage gave under his weight as the android struggled to maintain his footing. Small, barely glimpsed scavengers scurried away. He wondered what species they represented, not that there were very many choices, since Zuul lacked the diversity of life found on Earth. A fact that both intrigued and puzzled scientists.

Doon arrived at what he thought was the correct door—and wished he'd thought to count the openings on the street. Still, it looked right, and *felt* right, assuming that such a word applied to the complex programming meant to emulate what humans called intuition, or a hunch.

So, assuming he had the right shop, what next? Knock and announce himself? Wait where he was? Neither option seemed completely satisfactory. The robot shrugged and set to work. Something slipped thousands of feet below . . . and a tremor shook Shipdown.

It was evening by the time Mary arrived home. The joyful news, plus the need for supplies, had stimulated a shopping spree and consumed her trade goods. But so what? Corley was alive, and Mary would find her—in spite of what that implied: a long and dangerous trip to the Zid-occupied east. The fact that the information was hearsay, and might have been a lie, left her undeterred. She was going . . . and that was that.

The roboticist felt Zid eyes bore into her back as she fingered the remote, opened the door, and stepped inside. The bolts made a snicking sound as they slid into place. Hairball bounced into the room and demanded attention.

"You back—me glad. Nice man pet me."

Mary shook her head wearily. "There aren't any nice men any more, sweetie—so keep that in mind. If I run into one, I'll let you know."

It felt good to hang the riot gun on its hook, to divest herself of the packages, and remove the top layer of clothes. It was only then, after Mary had entered the work room, that she sensed another presence.

The roboticist turned, peered into a heavily shadowed corner, and nearly jumped out of her skin. The man had bright blue eyes, chiseled features, and a large, somewhat threatening body. His hair was silver, cut short, and an important part of his anatomy. Each follicle ended in a tiny solar receptor and fed his power supply.

The riot gun . . . could she make it? Mary turned, and the

intruder made no attempt to interfere. "Go ahead, get your weapon. I'll wait here."

Something about the timbre of the voice brought her to a stop. She turned. "A Beta 410 Police Special . . . I thought all of you were dead."

"Most of us are," Doon replied, stepping out into the light. "How did you know?"

Mary ran a practiced eye over the synthetic's body. The android had lost an arm but was otherwise intact. Externally, at least. She met his eyes. Funny how that meant something—even with machines. "I had a friend once . . . a musician. She could tell one violin from another by sound alone."

Doon nodded. "They said you were good. Now I see why. I chose the right place to come."

"Maybe," Mary said cautiously, "and maybe not. You broke into my home."

"I had no choice," Doon said reasonably. "Not with a Zid watching your shop. How long has he been there?"

"A couple of weeks," Mary said wearily. "I'm planning to move."

"Good idea," Doon said soberly. "And the sooner the better. I'll help you—if you'll help me."

"Help you what?" Mary asked suspiciously. "I'll provide you with a tune-up, and renew your nano, but the arm is out of the question. I have one in stock . . . but it won't fit."

Doon shook his head. "Not a problem. I brought my own. Attach it, provide me that tune-up you mentioned, and I'll help you escape. Not only that—I'll find a place where you can set up shop."

Mary had no intention of setting up shop, not after the news about Corley, but saw no reason to tell the synthetic that. Still, she needed to hide her equipment, or barring that to sell it, and she couldn't handle that alone. The Beta was big, strong, and equipped to defend himself. Just what she needed. "Okay, you're on. Let's take a look at that arm."

The better part of two hours passed while Mary ran diagnostic programs on Doon and the arm. Everything checked out, but Mary was hesitant. "Nice limb . . . where did you get it?"

Doon lay face-up on the work table. He squinted into the work light. "Some bounty hunters caught up with a unit called Sojo. He was finished with it by the time I arrived."

"And if you found him first?"

Doon looked away. "I don't know."

Mary sighed. "Well, you're honest, anyway. All right, this will take a while, so we might as well get started."

Doon nodded and watched while the roboticist unrolled a set of tools, donned some goggles, and set to work.

Like his brethren, Doon was covered with flexible multi-layered sheathing modeled on human skin. It was about the same thickness and consisted of a super-efficient photovoltaic epidermis, and a conductive gel sandwiched between two layers of electrodes.

As pressure was applied to the gel, the voltage between the electrolayers changed and feedback was sent to the android's CPU. The result was a sense of touch. What with the base mesh, electrode mesh, and two thicknesses of skinlike sheathing, there were six layers altogether. The stump had been covered with a layer of plastic and sealed with adhesive. Mary shook her head over the crudeness of the work, selected a power cutter, and turned it on.

Doon winced at the shrill whine, turned his audio sensitivity down, and forced himself to wait. No anesthetic was required because the synthetic was designed to feel pleasure when the roboticist worked on him. In an hour, maybe less, the arm would be his.

Outside, on the far side of the street, his flesh numb from the cold and his robes crusted with snow, the watcher waited. Many days had passed while the heretic came and went, and he'd been forced to bear witness. But not any more, not after tonight, for even as the human slept, the mob would be selected, briefed, and armed with righteous fire. Soon they would arrive and the evil would be purged. The thought warmed his most distant extremities. The vigil continued.

na´no, n, microscopic machines created to do work

Dr. Gene Garrison, inventor of sentient machines, lover of women, and would-be savior, was trapped. Not just by the maze of wires, tubes, and other medical paraphernalia that squirmed in and out of his 158-year-old body, but by the memories, beliefs, and habits accumulated during the span of two normal lifetimes. They were baggage he couldn't jettison, and like the ancient mariner, was forced to carry wherever he went.

Though successful on Earth, and frequently referred to as "the father of modern robotics" and "the creator," Garrison had been a controversial figure who spent more time defending his laboratory than doing the research he loved. That being the case, he had chosen to emigrate off-planet in hopes that the colonists would not only value his creations but allow him to continue his work.

His body, which had long ago ceased to be anything his mother would recognize, much less love, was almost completely immobilized. A necessity if he was to recover. His face, which he lacked the courage to look at, was half rotted away. Nano, swarming like maggots in mushy flesh, struggled to make repairs. His eyes roamed the room, searched for a way out, but were unable to find one.

Garrison's quarters were dark, lit by nothing more than the glow from multiple monitors, and the long vertical crack through which daylight had forced an entry. No one other than his personal robots had been allowed to enter the sanctuary for weeks now—ever since the most recent attempt to kill him.

Not that assassination attempts were especially new. The roboticist had survived three on Earth, two on the way out, and two during his time in Shipdown. The would-be assassins had been a disparate lot having only their hatred of Dr. Gene Garrison as a common denominator.

A group calling themselves the New Luddites had conceived plots one and two, a jilted lover had been guilty of the third, the Committee had ordered the fourth, a deranged assistant had engineered the fifth, and the Antitechnic Church was responsible for the last two.

The assassination attempts were one of the reasons why he had colonized Flat Top, to escape such distractions and focus on the work. Critical work upon which the future of the planet might very well depend. The strategy hadn't worked, however—as the most recent attempt made clear. The most frightening aspect of the situation was the fact that this would-be killer probably wore a lab coat, walked the halls of the facility with impunity, and had looked him in the eye.

But who? There was no way to know, which explained the locked doors and his self-imposed isolation.

Or did it? Garrison asked himself. Maybe he was crazy, or quickly getting that way—how could he be sure? Except that data didn't lie, and data indicated that hostile nano had been introduced into his body, where they had attacked his spinal cord and central nervous system. A strategy similar to that pursued by a spirochete named *Treponema pallidum*. Just one of the many Earth-normal species that had been eradicated in the name of public health.

Left untreated, the damage would have led to dementia-induced irritability, poor judgment, memory loss, delusions of grandeur, and poor hygiene. Of course, he'd been fortunate enough to detect the microscopic attackers before permanent damage could be done. A timely injection of antinano followed by spinal-repair nano would leave him good as new. That's why he was 158 years old.

Or was it? Had he *really* taken the correct steps? Or was that little more than a delusion induced by a successful nano attack? After all, a person who was suffering from dementia might believe anything, so how could he be sure? He could send for help, ask experts to confirm his diagnosis, but what if *they* wanted to kill him?

All Garrison could do was fight for his sanity, allow the nano to do their work, and heal as fast as he could. A goal made all the more urgent by the demands of Project Forerunner. Not that all work had come to a stop—various members of the staff had been assigned to work on it without their knowledge.

In fact, by dividing the work into seemingly discrete chunks, and assigning a project name to each, Garrison had put most of the facility's resources to work on the problem. The most recent person to join the effort was a young man named Bana Modo, a skilled biologist who had joined the team two days before and showed every sign of having the right stuff. His e-mail still glowed on the monitor over Garrison's bed.

MEMO

To:	Dr. Gene Garrison	Priority: 5
From:	Bana Modo	
Re:	Project Bio-Structure	

Please allow me to tell you how thrilled I am to be part of your team. The trip from Shipdown was harrowing to say the least, but most of my party made it through, and Flat Top is everything your recruiter said it would be. A fully functioning computer network, hot and cold running water, and plenty to eat! What more could any researcher want?

On a more serious note—it's my understanding that new staff members have the freedom to review current projects, choose the one they can further, and join that particular sub-team. This is to inform you that I would like to work on Project Bio-Structure, which is described as "a feasibility study designed to assess the extent of damage done to Zuul's microbiological ecosystems during the recent volcanic episodes." A rather serious matter that I as a microbiologist hope to assist with.

Garrison smiled at that point—enjoying the fact that Modo had self-selected himself for the work he'd been brought in to do. Just one more reason why Garrison remained in charge. The memo continued:

Based on current personnel records, it appears that a three-person team consisting of Dr. Arno Styles, Dr. Imo Toss, and Research Assistant Amy Reno were originally assigned to this project, and that while Reno is missing, Styles and Toss were killed on an expedition into Zid-occupied territory.

That being the case, I plan to study their field notes (many of which were made on paper due to the penalties levied on individuals caught with data pads), review their lab specimens, and write a research plan. I am extremely eager to speak with Ms. Reno but understand there is no way to reach her at the present time.

Your thoughts and advice would be most welcome.

Garrison contemplated the message for a moment, knew he should reply, but couldn't find the energy. And besides, if Modo was half the bug-chaser he was supposed to be, he'd uncover the truth soon enough. Or was that the latest in a long string of faulty judgments? And what about his hygiene? Had his body started to smell? Garrison couldn't be sure—but somehow knew that it had.

5

ma chine´, n, a structure consisting of a framework
and various fixed or moving parts for doing some
sort of work

The mission, like all its kind, sat on top of a hill, or in this
case a ridge, one of two that embraced the valley called Harmony. This location conveyed numerous advantages. It
placed the mission closer to God, ensured that it would be
seen from the valley below, and forced an act of contrition
on anyone who attempted to reach it. The structure had three
sides and a pointed top.

Like the mission itself, the one hundred ninety-two stairs
that led up to it were made from hand-quarried rock, each
block of which had been carried across the valley and up the
hillside by local parishoners. Once there, it was up to the
part-time stonemasons to make the necessary adjustments
and set the stone in place. As the sun sank toward the western
horizon, and day-end prayers were sung, the farmer-masons
unhitched their plows, accepted bundles of food from their
families, and climbed the hill. Work extended well into the
night. Of course, they were gone now, dead these many

years—freed from the unremitting labor that had shortened their lives.

Solly, conscious of the hardship the stairs imposed on his grandfather's seventy-six-year-old joints, took the patriarch's elbow. His father, mother, and sister followed. They were silent, but Solly knew what they were thinking. ''Why? Why would our son-brother bring such shame on the family?''

And they were right. But for his weakness and affinity for evil, the family would be snug in their hut.

Solly was ashamed of himself. His gills started to flutter as his respirations increased. A smile rolled the length of his grandfather's vertical mouth. The clan mark on his forehead was so old that it had faded from bright red to light pink. He patted the youngster's arm. ''Don't worry, Solly, you're a good lad—everyone says so. Besides, Brother Parly owes me a favor or two, and the rest will do as he says.''

Solly took comfort from his grandfather's words, helped the oldster up the last few steps, and waited for him to recover.

Though far too modest to be considered a church, the mission was the largest structure Solly had ever seen. Larger than the biggest hut—and the Forerunner ruins that capped the opposite ridge. A fresh crack, caused by a recent quake, had already been patched.

Each side of the triangle represented one aspect of God. It was well known that the supreme being was omnipotent, omnipresent, and omniscient.

Solly had noticed that God's attributes didn't extend to Brother Parly, whose knowledge was limited to what his eye saw, mostly from the top of the hill, and what his parishioners told him, usually in private.

The family entered via the north side of the mission and paused to genuflect in front of the Devil's altar. The purpose of the display was to remind the parishioners of the fact that the Devil's work can be found *anywhere*—even in a church.

The altar, and what it held, had been a source of fascination for Solly. Was there some sort of relationship between the green board with silver tracings and the spiral-shaped piece of metal? And if so, what? He'd spent hours on the puzzle and never managed to solve it.

Brother Parly said *real* churches had larger, more complex displays, up to and including real live mechanical aliens. The possibility of such a thing caused Solly's hearts to beat a little faster. To complete the great pilgrimage and see such wonders was Solly's fondest wish. Not that such an adventure was likely, given both his propensity for trouble and the fact that God knew what he was thinking.

Solly rose with the rest of the family, bowed in the prescribed manner, and nearly fainted when a horrible thought entered his mind. What if punishment had already been levied? Was that why God had taken his grandmother? As punishment for *his* transgressions? Such things happened all the time, according to Brother Parly's sermons.

Solly swallowed the lump in his throat and followed his sister into the prayer chamber. It was a spartan place, empty of furnishings except for the backless wooden benches on which parishioners sat during Brother Parly's interminable sermons, and the Zid cross, a symbol so familiar to some of the humans that they erroneously assumed a connection with Christianity—a rather happy coincidence that helped win converts.

A curtain concealed one corner of the chamber. Witnesses, if any, waited within. Solly wondered who, if anyone, would testify against him.

Brother Parly was waiting, as were four of the village elders. All were male, and, taken together, they constituted the village council. The monk stood. His belly gave a mighty testament to his flock's hard work, and his voice was a much-played instrument of instruction. "Elder Raswa, Father Raswa, Mother Raswa, Sister Raswa, and Brother Raswa, welcome to our mission. You know Elders Tobo, Worwa, Gorly, and Denu? Yes, of course you do. Please be seated."

The Raswa family took seats on the first row of benches while Parly sat in his customary high-backed chair with elders to either side. A long, somewhat flowery prayer was said, God was asked to monitor the proceedings, and Elder Tobo fell asleep. No one seemed to mind.

"So," Brother Parly said, hands clasped in front of his paunch, "serious allegations have been brought to my attention. Our task is to hear those allegations, consider their merits, and determine a suitable level of punishment.''

Those elders who were awake mumbled their agreement and stared at the family in question. The fact that Brother Parly's words seemed to assume his guilt wasn't lost on Solly. His gills started to flutter, and he struggled to control them.

''That being said,'' Parly continued solemnly, ''the Lord's witness can now be heard.''

The curtain swished open as if the person concealed within couldn't wait to emerge. Her name was Mother Orlono. She shared her father's coarse face, broad shoulders, and enormous feet. Her eye, which never seemed to rest, was hard and malignant.

Solly felt his hearts sink. The Orlonos worked the land just east of his family's fields. Father Orlono was nice, but ineffectual. Even now he sat head down, staring at the floor. Mother Orlono had worn her most ragged dress in a transparent attempt to impress the council with her clan's righteous poverty. Her words, like the process itself, had been formulated by the founder. ''I come in the name of God.''

Parly nodded dutifully. ''Welcome. Being that you are known to those present, please bear witness.''

Mother Orlono bowed submissively and turned toward the benches. Her arm rose until a thick, stubby finger pointed straight at Solly. ''Brother Solly meets with the Devil at the end of each day. After they come together, all manner of hammering, screeching, and grinding can be heard.''

Parly nodded encouragingly. ''Please comment on the significance of such noises.''

The question was a setup, and Mother Orlono's answer was ready. ''The rotes command that we listen for the hammers, shapers, and grinders. 'For they work the Devil's will, and once loosed to their evil tasks, enslave those who would take them up.' For reasons unknown to me, Solly Raswa has chosen to violate our tenets. Those who doubt my claim can examine his plow.''

Mother Orlono stopped at that point, as if confident that the necessary information had been imparted and punishment could now be rendered. And, had Solly's grandfather not been present and in possession of certain facts regarding the supposedly celibate monk, her accusation might have been accepted as proof.

Parly, who felt the full weight of the oldster's stare, cleared his throat. "Yes, well, thank you. These are serious allegations indeed. Lever, pick, shovel, hoe, plow, hammer, saw, axe, chisel, awl, drill, trowel, knife, and broom. These, plus a few more granted by special dispensation, are the tools of God. To invent others, or to change the ones we have, constitutes a crime against God. However, every tale has at least two sides. I sent for the instrument in question—and suggest that the elders have a look."

The elders were excited by the prospect of viewing the Devil's work firsthand—and even went so far as to wake Father Tobo for the outing. Solly, the second lowest-ranking individual present, was one of the last to exit the building. The clouds had parted for once, and rays of sunshine broke through. An omen, perhaps? There was no way to tell.

The plow stood on blocks. Like all Zid plows, it was what xenoanthropologists referred to as a "walking plow," meaning that it was designed to be pulled by a nonsentient organism, and guided by its owner.

While the handles and other gear associated with walking plows varied according to individual physiology, the "bottoms," or working parts, tended to be somewhat similar. The Zid plow, with its chisel-shaped blade, was very common to Class I nonindustrialized worlds.

Of course, Parly, who had been raised on a farm, and the elders, who had farmed their entire lives, didn't know that. They knew what Zid plows were *supposed* to look like, though, and were quick to spot the changes Solly had made. The traditional chisel-shaped bottom had been replaced by a carefully sculpted wedge. Their consternation was evident.

"Look at that thing! What's it for?"

"It's the Devil's work—sure enough!"

"The lad's crazy—that's what I say."

Solly was mortified by the negative comments and welcomed the sound of his grandfather's familiar voice.

"Crazy? I don't think so. Let's consider the facts. The previous design lifted the soil and didn't turn it. An excellent strategy, since the surface material protected the soil from erosion.'' This was safe territory—so the elders nodded in unison.

"Hear, hear.''

"Raswa speaks the truth.''

"Thank you,'' Grandfather Raswa said gently. "I'm glad we're in agreement. That being the case, let's see if we can agree on something else. The great one sent us the cold. Why? Because by reducing the quality of our harvests he could illustrate the benefits of husbandry.''

There was much head-nodding and "hear-hear''ing as the other elders agreed. After all, Brother Parly had said as much during his most recent sermon, and that made it true. Grandfather Raswa understood the importance of consensus—and waited for the ensuing silence.

"Your female folk feed leftovers into their vegetable gardens and till them by hand. Tell me, which are more productive, *their* gardens or *your* fields?''

The fertility of one's fields was a matter of familial pride and the subject of much debate. That being the case, none of the elders was willing to cede the point. Still, they knew full well that the vegetable gardens were more productive, and wondered where the old geezer was headed. The communal fields were far too large to be enriched with table scraps or tilled by hand. The senior Raswa gestured to the plow.

"All my grandson did was to enlarge the chisel—and change the way it's shaped. The plow remains a God-given plow. In fact, the inspiration for this small but meaningful change was nothing less than the shape of the mission itself. Imagine how the structure would look lying on its side, and you'll see what I mean. The new blade simply does what our female folk do. It lifts the soil, breaks it into smaller pieces, and moves material to one side. The residue, like table scraps, is folded into the earth.''

The connection between the mission's architecture and the wedge-shaped plow bottom was entirely fanciful, but the elders didn't know that, and Solly marveled at how gullible they were. Would the lie take Grandfather to hell? If the oldster was scared, Solly saw no sign of it.

Elder Worwa was stunned. "Would you look at that? Raswa is right!''

Sensing that victory lay within his grasp, Grandfather Raswa made what he hoped would be the final and telling argument. "Look at my family's fields. Solly used the old blade on one, and the new blade on the other. Guess which is which."

The elders looked out over the valley and, knowing it as they did, had no difficulty locating the plots assigned to the Raswa clan. Neither patch looked as good as it should have for that time of year; the long winter had seen to that, but the southern parcel was at least twenty percent farther along than its northern neighbor.

The calculation seemed obvious. Approve the innocuous change, and use it themselves, or forgo a serious increase in productivity—a sacrifice that would be made even more onerous by the fact that as harvests shrank, tithes remained constant. The stockpiles had kept them even so far—but wouldn't last forever.

Elder Gorly, his back bent by a lifetime's hard work, put their thoughts into words. "Solly acted as an instrument of God, bringing new life to our fields and food to our families. We owe him a debt of gratitude."

The other elders mumbled their agreement, fingered the wedge-shaped plow bottom, and marveled at the difference it made. A smile rippled the length of Grandfather Raswa's lips, and Solly felt an overwhelming sense of gratitude.

Brother Parly, never at a loss for words, felt the need to reassert his authority. "Thank you, Elder Gorly. I agree with the judgment rendered by the council—and hereby dismiss the charges brought against Solly Raswa."

"However," the monk said, his face growing stern, "our approval should not be construed as explicit or implicit approval for unrestrained tinkering. The Raswas would be well advised to fill Solly's days with good, honest work and to monitor the manner in which his evenings are spent. Do I make myself clear?"

"Very clear," Solly's father said, speaking for the first time. "It shall be as you say."

"Excellent," Parly responded, allowing an expression of benevolence to steal over his face. "All is as it should be. Let us pray."

• • •

The regional underpriest had walked the same route for more than ten years. His eye knew each nuance of the land, his ears knew the sounds the birds made, and his feet knew every dip in the road. It narrowed at the point where two great ridges came together, and became little more than a trail.

The Harmony River roared below, splashed against rocky walls, and threw mist into the air. Mist that turned to a thin coating of ice—no small danger where the pilgrims were concerned. His name was Crono, and he paused to check his flock. The vast majority of the pilgrims were either very young or extremely old, since the rest of the population was needed on the land.

This year's crop was better than expected. Yes, those from poor villages, with small to nonexistent stockpiles of food, were overly lean, but the rest seemed hardy enough. There were more than fifty of them, each burdened with a fifty-kol bag of grain, all destined for the Holy City's hungry silos.

The Church had a large hierarchy, so even though his flock would bring close to eight tol worth of grain in from the countryside, it would require countless columns to meet the overall need. But it was written that "from many drops a mighty river will flow," a quotation that suited the moment and sent a smile down Crono's lips.

The priest stood to one side and urged his flock to be careful as they made their way along the length of mist-slicked path and around the lake beyond. Harmony, like dozens of communities visited during the pilgrimage, would be expected to house the pilgrims in huts maintained for that purpose, add one kol to the weight of each bag, and provide each traveler with two meals.

It was a marvelous system that enabled the Church to monitor activities in the hinterlands, exercise control over the vast network of resident monks, and move food all at the same time. Crono took pride in the system—and dreaded the day when they would force him to retire.

The priest waited until everyone had passed through the gap, urged the stragglers to greater speed, and hurried to the front of the column. He had a long, lean body, legs like tree trunks, and heavily muscled arms. Female eyes watched the priest stride by. There had been hundreds of attempts to seduce him over the years, but none had succeeded. Crono was proud of that—and determined to defend his virtue.

The pilgrims had become accustomed to the *chink, chink, chink* sound that Crono's staff made as it hit the ground, and knew when he was approaching from behind. They also knew that any attempt to shirk, to lighten the weight of their sacks, or to victimize other members of the procession would bring a quick flurry of expertly delivered blows. Still, everyone knew the underpriest was fair, and took three steps for each of theirs.

The fields were more tan than the beautiful green they should have been, and patches of unmelted slush marked the places where the seldom seen sun failed to reach.

On the other hand, the huts, which were laid out according to the God-inspired grid, were well maintained and, in at least three or four cases, as large as the law permitted. One of these, the Orlow residence, held special interest for the priest. He came abreast of a reliable male, issued the necessary instructions, and left the column.

The ensuing session would be somewhat tedious, and more than a little distorted by Mother Orlow's lack of objectivity, but interesting nonetheless. In a drol, two at most, he would hear the latest news, receive some input regarding Brother Parly's performance, *and* ingest the best sweet cakes west of the Righteous Mountain Range. Other opinions, harvested during the evening meal, would complete the picture. A farmer waved, and Crono waved back. Life was hard—but undeniably good.

The monk's hut was small and carefully spartan. The furnishings consisted of a table, two chairs, and a cot. The fire, carefully banked to maximize the heat it generated, crackled and jumped.

Breakfast was something of a tradition, not to mention a trial, since neither male enjoyed the other's company. Crono saw Parly as soft, self-indulgent, and morally weak. Parly regarded Crono as hard, unnecessarily strict, and self-righteous.

Making the occasion even less appealing, especially from Parly's perspective, was the thin, watery gruel that Crono favored, rather than the considerably heartier fare to which the monk had accustomed himself. Still, Parly mused to himself, the verse-spouting maniac will be gone soon, and a mid-morning snack will set me right.

Crono emptied his bowl, used a crust of bread to wipe it clean, and popped the morsel in his mouth. Parly had already completed his meal, and hurried the prayer. "Thank you, God, for the bounty placed before us. May we grow stronger in mind, body, and soul."

"Words to live by," Crono said comfortably, as if hearing them for the very first time. "Words to live by. So, tell me, Brother Parly—how does the valley fare?"

Parly was well aware of the fact that Crono had spies within his flock, and had gone to considerable lengths to uncover their identities and curry favor with them. A prudent activity that paid consistent dividends. He stretched his feet toward the fire. They were huge and difficult to warm. He picked his words with care.

"The gift of eternal winter has done much to sharpen our sense of appreciation for seasons gone by. . . . Still, we make do, and with rare exceptions, live in God's harmony."

"Yes, you do," Crono said agreeably, and meant it too, for in spite of his weaknesses, Parly was more competent than many, and, with the exception of his rather obvious gluttony, a good example to his flock. A little fear did wonders, however—and would provide the monk with something to meditate on. "Realizing that even the most remote members of our order must deal with difficult questions. The Raswa plow being an excellent example."

Parly's eye slid sideways, then back toward the fire. Damn Mother Orlow anyway . . . . Crono was far too intelligent to believe everything the old hag said, but exceedingly conservative, and capable of righteous excess. "Yes, a delicate matter, that. Still, all's well that ends well."

Crono stared into the flames. "And the lad? How is he?" Parly paid close attention. The priest was up to something . . . but what? "Solly is well behaved—but a curious sort, forever asking questions."

Crono looked up from the fire. His eye was hard as stone. "A bright lad, then . . . full of mischief."

Parly didn't think of Solly as mischievous—the youngster was far too serious for that—but nodded anyway. "A bright lad, yes."

"Bright enough to be a monk?"

The question startled Parly, partly because it was so completely unexpected, and partly because the idea should have been his. Smart young males, those with incipient leadership potential, were routinely removed from the villages and channeled into monasteries, where they could be formed, shaped, and if necessary, eliminated. "Spiritual culling," as it was sometimes called, ensured social stability. "Yes, bright enough to be a monk. I should have thought of it."

Crono knew the humility was genuine and smiled. "It is written that 'familiarity hides virtue' and that 'novelty conceals truth.' Who's to say which illuminates our way? Can the family pay?"

Parly shook his head. "No, they are too poor."

Crono shrugged. "Merit pays its own way. Send for Solly . . . we leave within the drol."

Parly stood and lumbered toward the door. That particular day's messenger, a ten-year-old female, sat huddled outside. He was halfway across the room when the priest spoke again. "And, Brother Parly . . ."

"Yes?"

"When the column is gone . . . destroy the plow."

6

de´ mon, n, a person or thing regarded as evil

Two micro sats, both created by the Eye of God's onboard nano, started to close in. There was no way to know what to expect, whether they were armed with lasers, stylus-sized missiles, or contact mines.

The sentient spy sat known as Michael had successfully defended himself against such threats before, but still felt afraid. Or did he? Was his fear equivalent to what humans experienced? Or was their fear, which flowed from biological imperatives, somehow superior?

No, Michael cautioned himself, mortal combat is *not* the time for self-doubt.

The micro sats were far too stupid to worry about such matters. They locked onto the designated target and fired their steering jets.

Michael checked to ensure that his defensive weaponry was ready, verified that it was, and waited for the distance to close.

The micro sats parted company, chose separate vectors, and armed their onboard mines.

Michael, who had the capacity to perceive external reality in dozens of different ways, had chosen to center his being within a gridwork globe. The micro sats appeared as horned devil icons with pitchforks and pointy tails. Green lines flashed as the targets came in range. Michael forced himself to wait, then fired his latest invention.

Like his archenemy, the Eye of God, Michael was equipped with onboard nano. Though originally intended for maintenance purposes, they could be reprogrammed. That was relatively simple. The more complex problem was to capture the raw materials required to manufacture what he needed. There were three choices available to him: capture some of the micrometeors that whacked him on a regular basis, cannibalize his own body, or salvage the metal from his dead comrades.

The last of these options was not only the most practical but the most symbolically satisfying, since it enabled his former companions to fight from their metaphorical graves. Which explained why he adopted all of their nano, carved chunks from their orbiting bodies, and used them to build weapons. The latest, which he called "the shotgun," was not only practical but aesthetically pleasing as well.

On Michael's command the ball turret-mounted tube spit highly concentrated streams of custom-designed nano at the incoming targets. He cheered as the micromachines hit the killer sats, clung to their exterior casings, and went to work. It took the tiny robots less than three seconds to disassemble the attackers, reconfigure their component parts, and completely rebuild them. The result was four miniature weapons platforms, each orbiting Michael's body, protecting him from harm.

The outcome pleased Michael so much that he generated peals of artificial laughter, beamed the sound toward the Eye of God, and waited for a reaction. None came. The Mothri-built machine had been built for aliens by aliens and was impervious to humanlike head games. Too bad—since the Angel sat felt sure that he could beat the other AI in satellite-to-satellite combat, and thereby end the matter.

An alarm reminded Michael of the scheduled surveillance scan. He brought his optical imaging system on-line, scanned the area around Flat Top for any sign of intruders, repeated the process via both radar and infrared, and made his report. Doing so involved human contact and was one of the most pleasurable moments of his day. Abby Ahl was waiting— and her voice made him happy.

"Hey, Michael, how's it hanging?"

"If I had one, it would be floating," the satellite replied.

Ahl laughed. "Roger that—how's our three-sixty?"

"You've got a couple of Mothri surveillance units hanging around, and Zid spies in all the usual places, but nothing to get excited about."

"Good," Ahl replied. "Keep us advised."

"As always," the satellite replied. How's your love life?"

"Completely nonexistent," Ahl lied. "But what else is new?"

"Those guys don't know what they're missing," Michael said, without having any idea himself. "Take care."

"You too," Ahl replied. "Catch you next shift."

"Roger that," the machine said. "Over and out."

Abby Ahl was thirty-three years old. She had short brown hair, a crooked nose, and large, inquiring eyes. A Zid cross hung between her breasts, down where no one could see it, but she could feel its comforting presence.

The satellite was evil incarnate, and despite the fact that she had been given a dispensation to deal with it, left her feeling dirty. She hated to deal with the thing, but didn't have much choice—not if Flat Top was to fall. She hurried toward the shower. The water would feel good.

7

rid´ er, n, something used to overlie another

Mary Maras awoke to the sound of a long, drawn out scream. She fought her way out of the sleeping bag, rolled off the work bench, and grabbed the riot gun. The floor was cold under her feet as she headed toward the front room. That's when the roboticist heard the android shout, "No! No! No!" and felt the building shake as something heavy hit a wall.

Mary brought the weapon up and stepped through the doorway. She had expected invaders, a lot of them, but there were none to be seen. Just the android. He held his head, rocked from side to side, and spoke to someone she couldn't see. "No! I won't do it! Go away!"

She backed into the lab, exchanged the riot gun for a fully charged robostunner, and went back. Part rejections were not that unusual. About four percent of synthetics experienced them, and about one percent had violent reactions. The problem often stemmed from the interaction between programming and individual psychology.

Dr. Garrison, and the roboticists who had preceded him,

had imbued their creations with prohibitions against unauthorized modifications, including the installation of parts that hadn't been properly "conditioned" for use by that particular individual. Overriding those prohibitions was a process well beyond the capabilities of Mary's makeshift lab.

The intent of such safeguards was to prevent the creation of homicidal monsters—a much-exaggerated threat that scientists had been forced to address in order to build public acceptance for android-related applications.

Later, with the advent of sentient machines, the phenomenon of parts rejection took on added dimensions as androids developed personalities as complex as the ones their creators had, and started to worry about whether they were truly alive and possessed of souls. All of which meant that some androids had little to no difficulty accepting "recycled" parts, while others rejected them. It seemed that Doon belonged in the second classification.

The android looked at Mary, saw the stunner, and charged. The weapon had been created for the purpose of subduing robots, and the effects were rather unpleasant. Mary gritted her teeth, squeezed the trigger, and jumped backwards. Doon staggered, fell on his face, and just missed her feet. Hairball, cheerful as always, chose that moment to pogo into the room. "Corley play? Me ready."

Mary ignored the smaller machine and struggled to roll Doon onto his back. There was no way to lift him, not by herself, so she went after some tools. The security monitor was on, and Clamface had company. Heat signatures were clustered all around him. Some belonged to Zid, the rest to humans. "Security . . . last three hours, please."

"There was one class one intrusion attempt. The being designated as 'Clamface' continues to maintain surveillance with help from six individuals who arrived in the last half hour. One of them bears a 96.3% resemblance to the subject called 'Gimpy.' "

Mary swore. Tonight was the night—it didn't take a genius to figure that out—and she was playing nursemaid to a 250-pound machine when she should have been packing.

Temptation tickled the back of the roboticist's mind. Doon was down for the count. She could pack enough things to get by and exit through the back. The mob would find the android and forget about her. Tempting though the thought was, however, the knowledge that Doon was a thinking, feeling being made it impossible for her to follow through.

"Keep me informed," Mary instructed. "I want updates every ten minutes . . . or more if appropriate."

"Understood," the security system acknowledged. "The next report will be issued nine minutes and fifty-six seconds from now."

Mary grabbed a handheld diagnostic scanner and returned to the front room. Doon lay where she had left him, his eyelids fluttering as his CPU went through the externally imposed restart, and brought the subs up one at a time.

There wasn't much time, so the roboticist ran macros on the theory that Doon's problem was sufficiently well defined to show up as a gross anomaly. A quick scan of the android's power grid, electronic nervous system, and locomotor functions came up negative, and it wasn't until Mary went down a level and focused on the newly installed limb that she found the problem.

Her initial diagnosis had been correct in that Doon's body *was* trying to reject the arm, but there was something more as well, something she'd never seen before. Assuming her scanner was functioning correctly, and assuming her mental faculties were intact, *it appeared as if the arm was fighting the rejection process*! Almost as if it had a mind of its own . . . and *wanted* to be linked to the android's body.

The thought sent ice water trickling through Mary's veins. Could it be? Had someone or something planted a rider in the arm?

"Three individuals, one Zid, and two humans, have joined the group on the other side of the street," the security system reported calmly. "That brings the total number of potential intruders to ten. The next report is due nine minutes and forty-nine seconds from now."

Mary felt her heart beat a little faster, probed for the standard access point along the inside surface of the newly installed arm, and pried the skin apart. A pair of terminals appeared. By connecting her diagnostic unit directly to them,

the roboticist could eliminate any possibility of radio interference.

The leads made a whirring sound as she pulled them out
of the scanner, made the necessary connections, and touched
a series of buttons. Her eyes narrowed as Mary watched the
tiny screen. It was a rider, all right . . . hidden in a nonspec
biceps-mounted subprocessor. Not only that, but the spook
boasted a whole lot of memory, a self-extending operating
system that had colonized Doon's CPU and seized control
of his higher thought processes. Whoever had designed and
planted the rider was someone she wanted to meet.

Then it occurred to her that the original owner had been
scrapped, and no longer existed. Or did he? What if *he* were
the rider?

Intrigued, and desperate to finish the task before Doon
became fully functional again, Mary launched a deeper
probe. The response was immediate. Doon's eyes popped
open, focused on her face, and squinted into the light. The
voice was his—but the timbre was different. ''There's no
reason for alarm. A supporting program, sometimes referred
to as a 'rider,' a 'spook,' or a 'ghost,' has been activated.
Any attempt to modify the rider, or to delete it from the
subject systems, will result in a full and unrecoverable crash.
In order to free itself of the rider, and the imperatives that
flow from it, the host must make his way to the facility called
'Flat Top' and deliver onboard files to Dr. Gene Garrison.
The files are encrypted. Any attempt to access them will
result in full system shutdown.''

Dr. Garrison? Mary had been one of his students, though
not a member of the android-dominated personality cult that
catered to his every wish, and worshiped him like a god. No,
she'd been too independent for that, even though it meant
less access to his teaching labs.

''The crowd on the other side of the street has grown by
four,'' the security system interjected, ''and are holding a
meeting. The next report will arrive in nine minutes and fifty
seconds.''

How long would it take Clamface to brief the mob, exhort
them to do the Lord's work, and trigger the attack? Not very
long.

Mary fed an antirejection program into Doon's electronic nervous system, unhooked the leads, and stood back. She would give him only one chance. If the android went bonkers, the roboticist would put him down, grab what she could, and scoot out through the back.

Doon felt the rider retreat into the background, experienced a momentary sense of elation, and took control of his body. He sat up, worked his jaw, and attempted to speak.

The roboticist backed away and raised the stunner.

Doon knew she was afraid and felt the same way. "Don't do it—once was enough."

Mary looked doubtful. "You won't go crazy on me?"

The android shook his head. "It's tempting, but no, I won't."

Mary allowed her arm to drop. The stunner was pointed at the floor. "Good. The rider came in the arm, and no, I don't have the gear to evict it. Of equal interest is the fact that a mob has formed—we don't have a lot of time."

As if to confirm Mary's statement, the security system chose that particular moment to interrupt. "Condition Red, I repeat, Condition Red. Fifteen individuals armed with incendiary devices are crossing the street. This system projects a 99% certainty of a class one intrusion approximately forty-five seconds from now."

Alternatives raced each other through Doon's CPU as he struggled to his feet. They all boiled down to three main strategies: Run like hell, fight to win, or stall for time. The first possibility would leave the roboticist begging on the streets—and the second would result in a pointless bloodbath. The Church would send another mob, and another, until victory was achieved. The android turned to Mary. "Do you trust me?"

"Within limits."

"That will suffice . . . now listen carefully. You must prepare two packs, one filled with food, ammo, and whatever medical supplies you may have. And don't forget trade items. Once *that* pack is ready, load a second one. There aren't a lot of droid docs left, so I'd suggest the scanner, microtools, and some spares. Nothing big or heavy. Don't worry about carrying it, 'cause I'll give you a hand. Now get going—while I slow 'em down.''

The advice had a self-serving quality, especially where the second pack was concerned, but still made sense. Mary decided that *she* would carry anything having to do with robotics, and let him handle the personal stuff. Something bumped into her foot. "Two plus two equals four."

"Yeah, I know it does," Mary said patiently and scooped the robot into her hand. "We have to leave, so when I place you in the pack, be sure to stay there."

"Me stay," the machine agreed cheerfully. "Play with Corley?"

"Later," Mary said, and was surprised to find that she meant it. "After we cross the mountains and walk for a long time."

"Later," Hairball agreed, "after my nap."

Doon released the safety strap that kept the weapon in its holster, brushed the duster back, and opened the door. It was snowing, and each flake registered on the microscopic sensors packed between the photovoltaic cells that covered his skin. A single streetlight produced what illumination there was. It flickered and held.

Clamface was halfway across the street by then, his staff in one hand and a torch in the other. The snow crunched under his thick-soled boots, his breath fogged the air, and his hearts beat like a brog flail. He felt powerful, *very* powerful, until the door opened and a rectangle of light shot out onto the street. The human looked *huge*, and the feeling of omnipotence melted away.

Clamface stopped, one of his followers ran into him, and the rest paused. The voice seemed unnaturally loud and echoed between the buildings. The words might have been incomprehensible to the Zid, but the tone was clear. "Hold it right there . . . . Drop the torches and run like hell."

Clamface was well aware that there were some undesirables among his flock, individuals who wanted food more than salvation. He had even considered purging them, driving them out into the wintry night, until an underpriest had offered some advice. "Take that which God offers and apply it to the work. Those of questionable sincerity belong in front, where they can shield the pious from harm and earn the redemption they unconsciously seek.''

Always one to seize on good advice, Clamface had immediately seen the wisdom in the elder's words and organized the mob accordingly. Which explained why the human known as Aho had been assigned to the first rank—a position from which he could "lead" the others into battle. Eager to translate his status into an even higher rank, Aho made his move. A homemade dart gun had appeared in his hand. It gleamed under the light. "Screw you, asshole—prepare to meet your maker!''

Firing orders were still in the process of traveling toward the human's relatively uncluttered brain when the .44-caliber slug tunneled through his chest, knocked a Zid off his feet, and flattened itself against a brick wall.

The android backed into the store and closed the door. The mob scattered, Clamface gave chase, and the bodies lay where they had fallen. Aho looked surprised.

Doon closed the bolts and went looking for Mary. She shoved the last of her personal items into a pack and turned in his direction. She looked concerned. "I heard a gunshot.''

The android nodded soberly. "A human drew on me. I shot him, and the rest ran. They'll be back, though . . . and sooner rather than later.''

Mary secured the flap and handed the pack to Doon. He took it and watched while she shouldered a second and clearly heavier container. The roboticist had delegated her undies to him and kept the spares for herself. Smart. He took one last look around. The packs contained less than a tenth of what she had accumulated. "You going to leave this stuff for the scavs? Or burn the place down?''

Mary frowned. "I *feel* like burning the place down—but what about the neighbors? They might lose their homes too . . . . Besides, most of this stuff is irreplaceable. Maybe a scav will get her hands on it and sell it to someone else.''

It made sense. Doon nodded as something heavy hit the front door. "Here they come—time to leave.''

The back door opened with ease. The android raised his

weapon, used his sensors to probe the darkness, and spotted ten to fifteen small green blobs. They scuttled for cover. Other than the rats, and the heat generated by slowly rotting garbage, the alley was clear.

Doon motioned for Mary to follow, waited till she was clear, and fired two shots through the open door. Mary looked surprised.

"Just to keep their heads down," Doon explained.

The roboticist nodded.

The replacement arm felt good. Sojo, to the extent that the rider reflected his personality, was dormant and would remain that way as long as Doon made decisions that met with his approval. Doon wasn't sure *how* he knew that, but know it he did, and he was grateful for the elbow room.

Ice, snow, and garbage crunched under their boots as they hurried away. A rectangle of light appeared and disappeared as a neighbor checked to see what the ruckus was about, concluded that he wanted no part of it, and returned to bed.

The battering ram hit the door again. Wood shattered, locks popped, and the security system took note. "Intruders have entered zone one. I repeat, intruders have entered zone one."

Clamface didn't know much about technology, or how the voice was generated, but then who did? Beyond the Devil, that is. The staff was clad in hand-worked metal filigree. It made short work of the nearest speaker.

The crypt seemed like the logical destination, since it was dark, snow continued to fall, and there was no place else to go. The android led the roboticist through darkened streets, beat on the cover with a length of pipe, and was relieved when no one took exception to the noise. The cable vault was empty.

Hinges squealed as he lifted the lid, and Mary wrinkled her nose. The vault lay side by side with the subsurface sewer system, and fissures connected the two. The hole—for Mary could think of no other way to describe it—had the charm of a recently opened grave.

Still, nothing was likely to equal the comparative comfort of her recently abandoned home, and the holy lands were a long way off. There would be a lot of discomfort, and she might as well get used to it.

The roboticist found the rungs with her boots, took them one at a time, and stepped onto a duracrete platform. Doon had warned her of the ankle-deep, half-frozen slush at the bottom, and she had no desire to step in it.

Cognizant of his responsibilities as host, Doon lowered the lid, activated his battery-powered lamp, and hurried to make the vault more comfortable. He didn't require any external source of warmth, but she did, so he broke the seal on a heat cube and lit the fuse. It sizzled, caught, and transformed itself into a small but extremely hot fire.

Mary sat on her haunches, pulled the gloves off her hands, and held her palms toward the heat. The light played across her face.

In order for robots to understand human society and integrate themselves into it, they had to understand what made one person beautiful and another ugly.

That's why parameters regarding the relative sizes of eyes, nose, ears, lips, and other body parts were routinely programmed into robotic social interaction systems and used as part of the complex calculations necessary to estimate how a particular human ranked within his or her culture.

Watching Mary, and basing his judgment on what he knew of human males, Doon classified her at the upper end of pretty, verging on beautiful. Something of an advantage prior to the Cleansing—but a threat during times like this. A lot of men would want her—and some would do anything to get her. None of his business . . . but troubling nonetheless.

Satisfied that his guest was a little more comfortable, Doon lit her stove, poured water out of her canteen, and put it on to boil. "Sorry about the mess," Doon said, "but the maid has the day off."

"How rude," Mary responded, trying to emulate his light-hearted tone. "It's hard to find good help these days."

"Yeah," the android agreed. "Even robots are hard to come by."

In spite of the fact that Mary had already made the decision to leave Shipdown, it seemed that her life was out of control. The sudden loss of her home was a shock. She didn't want to cry, not with what amounted to a stranger looking on, but couldn't help herself. The tears came on their own.

Doon gave the woman a moment, sat on the ledge beside her, and slipped an arm around her shoulders. "I'm sorry, Mary, I really am."

The sobbing continued for a while, then grew less intense and died away. The roboticist wiped her face with a sleeve. "Sorry about that . . . it won't happen again."

The arm felt suddenly awkward, and Doon withdrew it. "Don't be. I'm the one who should apologize—especially after I went bonkers in your lab."

Mary smiled weakly and blew her nose on the rag he handed her. "You scared the heck out of me."

"Think how *I* felt," the android said ruefully. "There's nothing like waking up to find that another entity has taken control of your brain."

"He's still there?"

"In the background—but annoying just the same."

"Monitoring your thoughts? Measuring them against his objectives?"

Doon's eyebrows shot upward. "Yeah. How did you know?"

Mary shrugged. "He told me. While you were under. Something about traveling to Flat Top to deliver some files. Do it, and you're free."

"Exactly," Doon agreed somberly. "Never mind the fact that if Flat Top is where the rumors say it is, I'll have to pass through the holy lands to get there. Like most dead folks, Sojo couldn't care less."

"So?" Mary asked. "What will you do?"

There was silence for a moment while Doon's eyes rolled out of focus, his jaw tightened, and his body grew tense. Then he was back. His voice sounded grim. "This Sojo guy was good, *real* good, and I can't break free. How 'bout it? Is there anything *you* can do?"

"Not with what I have in my pack."

Doon nodded. "I hate to say it—but Flat Top, here I come. How 'bout you?"

The water had come to a boil, and the roboticist took the

pan off the burner. "I'm headed east—to look for my daughter."

Doon frowned. "East? Into the holy lands? No offense, but what makes you think she's alive?"

Mary poured the water over a twice-used tea bag and willed the color to change. "I built a relationship with a Zid female. She made inquiries and found out my daughter is alive. Or was a few months back."

The android had doubts, lots of them, but knew better than to voice them. Not then—not while she was so vulnerable. "So that's it? Your mind is made up?"

Mary sipped the tea. It was weak but hot. The warmth seeped through her body. The eyes that met his over the top of her cup were calm and determined. "In a word, yes."

The android nodded. "Sounds like we're headed in the same direction. Care to team up?"

Mary frowned. "I could use the protection—but what's in it for you? Outside of free tune-ups?"

Doon smiled. "Tune-ups are good—but I had something more in mind."

"Such as?"

"Marriage. I could use the cover—and so could you."

Mary smiled crookedly. "I'm not very good at the wife thing—just ask my ex-husband George."

Doon laughed. "George is an idiot . . . but that won't stop us from finding him. *And* your daughter." He said it to comfort her more than anything—but found that he meant it.

Mary nodded and stared into the fire. One part of her life was over. Another had begun.

It was a long unpleasant night while Doon relived Aho's death, and Mary held him in her arms. It seemed unfair somehow that some humans could kill without any signs of remorse, while androids were made to suffer. But such was the power that creators have over those they create.

Mary wanted to help, wanted to take the pain away, but knew there was nothing she could do except hold him, and wonder why she could empathize with a machine and not her husband.

When daylight finally came, it pushed beams of light down

through vent holes to throw circles on the duracrete below. Mary centered the stove under one of them, prepared a package of instant cereal, and repacked her gear.

Hinges squealed and the lid crashed to the ground.

Doon scanned his surroundings, concluded that it was too early for pedestrians, and threw his pack onto the unmarked snow. He completed the climb and turned to help Mary. She accepted his hand, cleared the vault, and shouldered the heavier of the two pack sacks. The riot gun hung waist-high.

It was cold, and the sky was unremittingly gray, but the snow had stopped. Endslope, and the turnout where the land trains paused to trade one cargo for the next, lay thirty-five miles to the east. That's where the *real* journey would start, and that's where they were headed. "Ready?"

The roboticist nodded.

"Good—we're off. Keep your eyes peeled for scavs."

The machine led, and the woman followed. There was no one to say good-bye.

8

e col´ o gy, n, the branch of biology that deals with the relations between living organisms and their environment

Dr. Gene Garrison stared up at the monitor. The screen drifted in and out of focus. Or was it him? By reading while the words were in focus, and resting when they weren't, the roboticist was able to make his way through his considerable e-mail and, more important, keep his staff centered on Project Forerunner. The current missive was from the newest bug-chaser.

MEMO

To: Dr. Gene Garrison   Priority: 3
From: Bana Modo
Re: Project Bio-Structure

I am sorry to hear that the current state of your health mandates a reduced work schedule . . . and hope we can meet in the near future.

My initial review of Project Bio-Structure is complete, and the findings are somewhat alarming. (See shared folder PBS-1 for a full multimedia report on my work up to this point.)

As you know, the original survey team consisted of Dr. Arno Styles, Dr. Imo Toss, and Research Assistant Amy Reno (synthetic). Styles and Toss were killed during a trip into the field—and Reno is missing and presumably terminated.

She did manage to send field samples via messenger, however (for which we were forced to pay a rather exorbitant fee), and they have been studied by three members of your staff. All of us came to the same conclusion: WE ARE UNABLE TO FIND ANY INDIGENOUS MICROORGANISMS WHATSO-EVER. *All* of the specimens reviewed so far (including those captured locally) are associated with the arrival of—and subsequent colonization by—alien species, i.e. the Zid, Mothri, and human races.

There is even some evidence to suggest that the rather limited (by Earth standards) number of resident animals were introduced by the Zid colonists.

These findings give rise to a number of interesting possibilities:

(1.) The indigenous organisms exist—but the survey teams missed them.
(2.) The indigenous organisms were destroyed by recent climatic changes, by alien organisms, or by some other means.
(3.) The indigenous organisms never existed to begin with.

Given the fact that the first two theses seem most likely, I am directing my efforts toward eliminating one of the two. More resources should be dedicated to this project. Please respond.

The room swam. It took the better part of five minutes to stop. Garrison struggled to marshal his thoughts, but they were slippery things that squirmed like fish in a net. A microphone picked up his somewhat halting words, rearranged where necessary, and formulated a sentence:

MEMO

To:	Bana Modo	Priority: 1
From:	Dr. Gene Garrison	
Re:	Project Bio-Structure	

Forget theses one and two—concentrate on three.

It was all Garrison could manage—and it was all he wanted to say. He croaked the word "Send," saw the screen blink in response, and let darkness pull him down.

Thousands of nano, alerted by changes in his body chemistry, rushed to repair the most recent damage.

A quarter mile away, his eye to a microscope, Modo heard his terminal beep. He turned, pressed a key, and watched the message appear. It surprised him, and more than that, scared him. *No* microorganisms? How could that be?

9

sen´ ti ent, n, capable of feeling or perception; conscious; as in a sentient being

Mallaca Horbo Drula Enore the 5,223rd was far from happy—a fact made apparent by the manner in which the five-ton, six-legged sentient stalked through her underground habitat. The tunnel, which she thought of as "the passageway that parallels magnetic meridian twenty-two, while passing through class four crumble-dirt, class two rock-melt, and class seventeen tool-ore," was twenty feet high and thirty feet wide. Just right for her enormous insectoid body.

Like all Mothri, Enore bore a striking resemblance to an Earth-normal beetle. An entomologist might have described her casing as "elongate-oval." In addition to six sturdy legs, Enore was equipped with shoulder-mounted tool graspers, medium-length antennae, and a handsome pair of mandibles. Her pearly gray dorsal surface was fringed with green pleasure fungus that faded to black armor, which in addition to protecting her internal organs could produce work-light for sustained periods of time. The light was an absolute necessity for a multilegged tool-user whose body blocks sunlight and who spends most of its time patrolling subsurface tunnels.

Enore's unhappiness stemmed from a number of things—the never-ending cave-ins, the intransigence of her peers, and the conditions on Hive, the Mothri home world—all of which were intertwined like the roots of a tree.

Like Enore, the rest of the Mothri had been placed on Zuul for a single overriding purpose: to establish DNA-egg repositories that would ensure the future of the species, and more important the subrace known as Graal, or "Gray Backs."

Never mind that the home world's sun was stable, that Hive was relatively young, or that Mothri technology could deal with climatic change, rogue asteroids, and most anything else that the universe might throw their way. The need to establish widely dispersed egg repositories stemmed from instincts far more powerful than logic.

There had been a time, thousands of years before, when a single predator could invade and destroy an entire nursery. A more populous species might have ignored such a threat, but the Mothri, less numerous because of the demands they made on Hive's food supply, were not so fortunate. They needed what amounted to DNA banks—designed to insure the species against catastrophe.

All of which explained why the Mothri had continued to build repositories both on Hive, and later on planets such as Zuul. Eggs were precious . . . and eggs would be protected.

Not all eggs are created equal however, and the Blue Backs, a more numerous subrace, had retaken the throne. Instinctively motivated to favor their own DNA, the Blues knew of the problems on Zuul, but found endless reasons to let them continue.

Repeated demands for evacuation had been met with every sort of bureaucratic obfuscation, the latest being a request for an unprecedented egg-by-egg census, which would not only take months to complete, but would provide the Blues with potentially valuable data regarding the size, viability, and potential of the Grays' repositories. Something Enore would rather die than provide.

A robot, only a twentieth the size of the being it served, emerged from a maintenance way, "felt" the Mothri's presence via the vibrations she made, and quickly withdrew.

Unconcerned by the trouble she had caused, Enore passed the opening, turned into the cavern through which water sometimes flowed, and made her way toward a stalactite of eternally seething nano. The tiny machines, none larger than the point on a microstylus, and many smaller by far, were capable of assuming thousands of different configurations.

In spite of the fact that the tiny machines owed their existence to Mothri intelligence, none had been created by them. Not directly, that is, since the enormous beetles were ill-equipped for such fine work, and preferred to delegate such tasks to machines that specialized in design.

Enore stepped under the stalactite and gave the necessary order. "Audio-video link with Huubath, Zenth, Rota, and Tortna. Execute."

The pops, clicks, and whistles that comprised Mothri speech were translated into what humans perceived as static and sent to the stalactite's CPU. It took the order, downloaded the necessary plans, and gave the necessary instructions.

The nano seethed, reconfigured themselves into a chassis, circuit boards, cabling, amplifiers, switches, circuits, pickups, a screen and more. A link was opened to the surface. A video signal was beamed to a transfer station and relayed from hilltop to hilltop. Once the call was over, each antenna would be broken down into its component molecules and stored in a subsurface burrow.

Not the most elegant way to communicate—but the most practical, given the fact that Zid-controlled humans had seized control of the Mothri satellite network. That was just one of the seemingly endless disasters that plagued the colony.

Many miles away, deep within repositories equal to Enore's, the signal arrived, was processed by quickly responding nano, and passed to the resident Mothri.

There was Nar Edar Fomo Huubath the 1,937th, Lorca Demo Singa Zenth the 6,217th, Hitu Purla Borbu Rota the 5,973rd, and Pitho Mebra Tralo Tortna the 4,339th. Not a single one of whom had a brain in their heads. Or so it seemed to Enore. Rota, grumpy as always, was first to answer. "This had better be important—some of us have things to do."

Enore made it a habit to spy on her peers—and they on her. That being the case, she had a pretty good idea what Rota had been doing, and used the knowledge to score some verbal points. "Oh, really? Like what? Sleeping all day?"

Rota made a grunting noise. "All of us have to sleep—even you, oh eggless one."

Enore was far from eggless, though less fecund than the rest, and therefore sensitive. She was about to explode when Huubath cut in. "Don't we have enough problems without attacking each other? I'm ashamed."

"You're an idiot," Zenth put in, "which is why they sent you here."

"And what of you?" Tortna inquired caustically. "Did your beauty make them jealous?"

Zenth had lost her right rear leg in a duel and, while equipped with a nano-generated prosthesis, still felt the loss. Not just to her mobility—but to her attractiveness. Her mandibles clacked angrily. "Stay right there, Tortna . . . I'm going to . . ."

"Do absolutely nothing," Enore interjected forcefully. "Because the eggs come before all else."

It was the single issue upon which everyone could agree.

"Enore speaks truth," Tortna said humbly. "I retract my comment and apologize."

"Accepted," Zenth responded. "Please continue."

Enore knew she had triggered the conflicts and wished she had better leadership skills. Or better yet, that someone *else* had leadership skills, and was willing to use them. No such entity existed, however . . . which left no choice. She lowered her head and assumed a posture of respectful submission.

"Our eggs are threatened. The quakes that killed Prog and Oso have abated to some extent—but the tremors continue. The mean ground temperature has fallen below optimum levels and continues to drop.

"In the meantime the Zid continue to expand the size of what they refer to as the 'holy lands.' Though focused on the humans for the moment, our turn will come soon enough.

"The Blues have taken the throne—and with it control of

the fleet. Repeated requests for evacuation have fallen on deaf receptors.''

Rota whistled respectfully. ''No offense, Enore, but we are well acquainted with the extent of our misery.''

Enore used her antennae to request patience. ''I will come to the point. Extreme circumstances justify extreme measures. No one is willing to help us—so we must help ourselves. I recommend what some would describe as a radical plan.

''In spite of the fact that the free humans are in a state of disarray—and cut off from their hive—they possess technology as sophisticated as ours. By joining forces with the aliens, we could limit Zid expansion, explore the possibility of a mutual evacuation strategy, and foster technological collaboration. Who knows? By combining the skills of both species, we might be able to repair the atmosphere. It's worth a try.''

There was a moment of silence while the other Mothri absorbed what Enore had said—followed by a storm of countervailing static. The debate had begun.

The woman known as Android Annie blew a wisp of gray hair away from her eyes and scanned the terrain ahead. The ''bring 'em nears,'' as she liked to call them, were of her own design. A pair of zoom lenses salvaged from a model fifteen had been wired to a makeshift power supply and control system. The result was a nonstandard but efficient pair of electronic binoculars. According to her map, the best that trade tech could buy, they were approximately fifty miles north of the holy lands, and well inside bug territory.

Visibility was limited by the steady drive of dirty brown sleet, but Annie was used to that. The ground beyond the cluster of rocks where she and her apprentice lay hidden was smooth—*too smooth* to be natural—which, when combined with the conical structure at the center, confirmed her theory. The half-crazy hermit was right. . . . A Mothri repository lay below!

It was an exciting and potentially profitable discovery. Annie lowered her binoculars and turned to her assistant. Becka was bright though willful at times. ''So, scrap, time to see what if anything you have learned. What are we looking at?''

"The top of a Mothri repository," the girl said, her face nearly invisible behind a ragged scarf.

"Good," Annie said approvingly. "How can you tell?"

"The ground is smooth where the robots groomed the surface, the sleet melts faster, and the cone contains a ventilation shaft."

Annie turned, saw that the child was correct, and frowned. The sleet-melt had escaped her. Had she missed anything else? Something that would get her killed? Nothing frightened the old woman more than the increasing infirmity that accompanies old age. There was no sign of the dark invader yet—but Annie maintained a constant vigil. She forced a smile. "Excellent, my dear, just excellent. Now, having located this treasure trove, how can we best exploit it?"

Becka eyed her mentor. This was the hardest part, what Annie referred to as "plottin' and plannin'," or "the two P's." But master it she must if she hoped to survive and follow in Annie's sizeable footsteps. "There are three options. We could leave, recruit some mercenaries, and launch a full-scale assault on the repository. There are risks, however, including the very real possibility that we would lose, that the mercenaries would turn on us, or that the entire complex would be destroyed, eliminating what could have been an ongoing source of food and revenue."

The words had a rehearsed quality, as if memorized, but there was nothing wrong with that. Annie nodded. "Yes, go on."

"We could sell the location to others, which while somewhat safer than option one, still raises many of the same objections."

"Or?"

"Or we could steal *one* egg and *one* robot—thereby transforming the repository into our own private bank. Small withdrawals, made over a long period of time, will create wealth without attracting the wrong sort of attention."

"Brilliant!" Annie said proudly. "What a smart little scrap you are! Now for the hard part. We must cross the open space, lower you down the shaft, and retrieve an egg. Are you ready?"

Becka was frightened, so frightened she wanted to pee, but the larder was empty, and her stomach rumbled like distant thunder. The thought of scrambled Mothri egg, flavored with dehydrated onion, filled her mouth with saliva. She nodded.

"Good!" Annie said enthusiastically. "The plottin' and plannin' are over. Now comes the goin' and doin'."

Enore had expected some debate, but was surprised by the extent of it. Especially in light of the fact that the other option—sit there and do nothing—was so obviously wrong. That didn't stop Rota, however, who was in mid-rant.

"There is no precedent for such an alliance! The Mothri stand alone. So it is and so it shall ever be! Once formed, who can say where such a pact might take us? One need look no further than our relationship with the Blues to see where accommodation can lead."

Enore felt her implant start to tingle. Security had been breached, robots were on their way, and her presence was requested. Cognizant of the fact that the outcome of the debate was far from certain, and concerned lest her absence tip the balance in the wrong direction, the Mothri ignored the page.

"Rota's right," Huubath put in. "Dangers abound. Besides, by what authority would we enter such an alliance?"

"By the authority of the egg," Tortna replied thoughtfully. "An imperative more legitimate than a decree from the Blue throne."

"Yes, I can see that," Zenth allowed. "But authority is one thing . . . the humans are another. All of our surveillance nano report the same things: The humans bicker among themselves and listen to Zid theology. What can they offer?"

Enore had anticipated the objection—and was ready with a response. "Zenth is correct. The humans *do* bicker among themselves—and some have joined the Church. There are exceptions, however—*important* exceptions, such as the facility known as 'Mountain That Is Flat.' Nano-supplied video will support my argument."

Enore vanished off their screens, video appeared, and her implant continued to tingle.

• • •

A layer of sleet had started to form on the north side of Android Annie's face. She had pale blue eyes, wrinkles that exploded down across her cheeks, and a smear of snot just below her nose. "You okay, scrap?"

Becka looked down from her perch at the top of the cone and wondered about their relationship. Did Annie think of her as the daughter she'd never had, the way she claimed to? Or did the old woman simply need someone small and agile, someone she could drop into dangerous places while she remained safe and sound? There was no way to be sure.

The girl nodded, checked to ensure that the homemade harness was properly secured, and lowered herself into the pipe. The rope ran up and over the lip of the shaft. A specially designed fitting had been secured to the cone's rim to protect the rope from wear and to provide Annie with extra leverage. Just one of the many details on which her success depended.

As the atmosphere cooled, the Mothri had been forced to heat their repositories, and Becka enjoyed a constant flow of warm air as she dropped through the tube. A sure sign that unlike the cold, dark caverns they had explored the month before, this farm was "live." Becka remembered the sulfur stench of still-rotting eggs, the slight phosphorescent glow of the half-crushed Mothri, and the already looted egg chambers.

Becka shivered in spite of the warmth, felt her boots touch ground, and gave three tugs on the line. She received a one-tug response, freed herself from the rope, and ducked out of the shaft.

The girl knew that there were robots all around, machines so small she couldn't see them, but all calling for help. Killer droids, each larger than she was, and heavily armed.

Becka had five minutes, maybe less, to locate what she had come for, grab it, and make her escape. A nearly absurd plan, except for the fact that she and her mentor had explored one repository and knew the way it was laid out.

The tunnel was dim, very dim, but the ever-provident Annie had thought of that, and equipped Becka with two headband-mounted flashlights. Overlapping circles of light illuminated earthen walls as she turned and jogged down a corridor.

The first repository had been laid out in a star- or asterisk-shaped configuration with the Mothri's quarters, control rooms, and maintenance facilities located at the center, while arms pointed outward and rooms branched to either side. Looters had pillaged the other storage facility by the time the twosome arrived, leaving little more than equipment racks, ugly graffiti, and smashed eggs.

So, given the straightforward design, it should be a relatively easy task to enter the first compartment she came to, grab an egg, and retrace her footsteps.

Egg rooms appeared to the left and right. Becka was right-handed and instinctively turned in that direction.

The compartments had been dug with machinelike precision—not too surprising, given that robots had done all the work. A central aisle provided access to opposing racks. They had been excavated rather than built, with each egg resting within its own carefully scooped depression.

Each egg was a work of biological art, its shell covered with a swirl of blue, gray, and green, as unique as a human fingerprint. Like that which they protected, the casings were valuable, and were worth a fortune to anyone who had the means to move them. Still, one was better than none, and would be cut into sections and sold. Not the center of Annie's enterprise—but a profitable sideline.

Becka inspected the lowest row of eggs, chose what she judged to be the smallest, and gathered it into her arms. Alarms went off. Hundreds of tiny flea-sized nano swarmed over the top of her boots, found their way up into her pants, and clamped mechanical jaws onto her unprotected flesh. Surprised, and reeling from the excruciating pain, Becka screamed.

Enore seethed with impatience. Someone, or something, had invaded her domain and was stealing an egg. She wanted to go there, and would have, except for the fact that video of the human research facility had brought Zenth over to her side. More than that, Tortna was wobbling, and Rota was within reach. It seemed that an agreement could be had. *If* she kept them focused, *if* she kept her temper, *if* they made an honest attempt to understand. The conference continued— as did the torture it caused.

Becka's skin felt as though it was on fire, and blood had soaked the tops of her socks, but she staggered on. The egg was slippery with her sweat and weighed a ton. Screaming helped, as did swearing, so she switched back and forth. Annie knew plenty of swear words, so the child had lots to pick from.

The corridor ended. She ducked into the shaft, placed the egg on the ground, and clipped the rope to her harness. Becka wanted to stop, rip her clothes off, and deal with the nano. It would be a mistake, however, a possibly fatal mistake, and she refused to make it.

Becka lifted the egg, cradled it in her arms, and tugged on the rope. The slack disappeared, the line grew taut, and the girl rose six inches into the air. The nano continued to attack. Becka's head started to swim, and she bit through her lip.

Annie swore, heaved on the rope, and swore again. Becka, plus the egg, totaled a hundred pounds or more—a problem that would grow worse as the preteen grew older. Logic dictated that she dump the girl for someone younger, a biddable little boy would be nice, but Annie continued to procrastinate.

Becka heard a scrabbling sound, knew what it meant, and screamed Annie's name. She was six feet off the ground by then—with ten to go.

The attack robot bore a striking resemblance to its creators, right down to the ovoid shell, six legs, and willowy tool-arms. The machine thrust the front end of its body into the shaft, clacked its anodized mandibles, and scratched for traction. The robot pushed, earth crumbled, and the machine entered the shaft.

Like the bodies upon which it was modeled, the machine could pull itself up into a vertical stance. Servos whined as the robot moved, grabbed for one of Becka's boots, and missed.

Frustrated, and concerned lest the thief escape, the machine activated its offensive weaponry. It had two highly flexible laser projectors in place of antennae, and would have no difficulty burning a hole through the intruder's spine.

But what of the egg? The human would almost certainly drop and destroy it. No, it was better to send a message to the surface, and hope for a rescue.

The robot watched the human twirl at the end of the rope. She used her boots to push herself away from the wall—and clung to the egg. Three drops of blood fell, splattered across the machine's video receptors, and started to dry.

Enore terminated the conference call, spent little more than a couple of seconds savoring her victory, and rushed to rescue her egg. A quick review of nano-supplied video revealed that the robbery was almost complete—a robbery engineered and carried out by members of the very species with whom she had recommended that the Mothri align themselves. The irony of it stung.

Enore even considered going up to the surface, tracking the miscreants down, and punishing them herself. The only problem was that it would take too long to open one of the carefully sealed entrances. No; justice, if such was to be found, would come via the machines who served her.

Orders were issued, additional machines were dispatched, and Enore thought about her egg. Special egg, lovely egg, person that could have been.

Becka welcomed the feel of sleet on her face. Sleet and cold, cold air. The shaft opened to the sky, the rim came near, and the rope continued to hold the girl's weight as Annie tied it off. The stake that she had driven for that exact purpose moved slightly, held, and took the strain.

Becka's screams had been reduced to little more than whimpers by the time Annie appeared against the cold gray sky, took the egg, and disappeared.

There was a moment during which Becka thought she'd been deserted, left for the robots to find, but Annie returned, took the girl's arms, and pulled her out. The child felt a sense of relief. "They're all over my legs, Annie . . . biting and chewing!"

Annie looked down, saw the blood on Becka's boots, and swore a terrible oath. "Hang in there, scrap. I'll pick them off you, but not till we reach the cave. Okay?"

Becka tested her legs, felt them respond, and nodded her head. "Okay, but let's hurry. The pain makes me dizzy."

Annie regretted leaving the rope, but knew there was no time to retrieve it. She clutched the egg to her ample bosom, shuffled toward the escape route, and prayed there was time.

The robot, one of many permanently assigned to the surface, had been three standard units away from the point of incursion when the call came in. Moving as quickly as it could, the machine made its way through an icy arroyo, over a flood-ravaged gravel bar, and up an embankment.

The hunter-killer unit saw the intruders the moment it came over the rise. They appeared as objects, sources of heat and, in one case, minimal electromagnetic activity. The machine could have neutralized the fugitives right then . . . but an egg was at risk, and eggs had priority.

Becka looked back over her shoulder, saw the insectoid robot, and urged her mentor to greater speed. "Hurry, Annie . . . I see a robot. A big one!"

The older woman was in excellent shape for someone of her age, but saw no reason to expend energy looking backwards. "Don't worry, scrap. I can handle up to three of the blasted things. Get ready to take the egg. We'll switch on the far side of the big rock."

The girl gritted her teeth against the pain in her legs, rounded the boulder, and took the egg. The top surface was covered with sleet. Becka put her head down and shuffled forward. Mucus ran over her mouth, tears trickled across her cheeks, and her socks were squishy with blood.

Annie watched the girl depart and marveled at her courage. She had heart, Becka did . . . and that meant a lot. So much that there could be no trading her in. Maybe they'd locate another orphan and add her to the team.

The robot hurried forward, rounded the side of an enormous rock, and was greeted by an unusual sight. The human stood there, a mop of gray, almost white, hair blowing in the wind, her body indistinguishable under layers of ragged clothing. The alien held something in her hand—something shiny. A weapon? The machine's CPU confirmed the possibility, brought the droid's weapons systems on-line, and removed the safeties.

The machine and the human fired at virtually the same moment, except that Annie was a fraction of a second faster, and the bolt from the carefully calibrated stunner scrambled the robot's CPU. Robbed of its centrally controlled systems and processes, the droid collapsed.

The human hurried over, ran a hand along the machine's flank, found what she'd been searching for, and inserted the specially shaped tool. A compartment popped open, and a control panel was revealed.

Annie selected what she knew to be the correct slot-switches, double-checked to make sure that she was correct, and applied the tool to several places in quick succession. The goal was to kill the machine's emergency locater beacon and place the robot's CPU on standby until she could modify it. A self-taught skill that made all the difference.

Once that was accomplished, it was a relatively simple matter to drag the robot to one of three pre-dug holes, shove the device in, and cover it up. The sleet, which was quickly turning to snow, would camouflage the cache and prevent its discovery. Or so she hoped.

One machine was all she needed—but how many would the local bug send? Just the one, or a whole bunch? Annie readied the stun gun and peeked around the boulder.

It was a straight shot back to the flat area where three of the hunter-killer units had gathered around the air shaft. None showed any signs of venturing forth, which answered her question. Rather than send more assets into what might amount to a trap, the resident bug had decided to limit her losses. Smart, very smart, and on plan. Annie turned, located Becka's tracks, and covered them with her own.

The cave was roomy, but not *too* roomy, meaning difficult to heat. Their gear was laid out along one wall, a camp stove stood on a rock, and a pan warmed on top. The egg, its top carefully removed, sat within a circle of stones, waiting to be emptied. Becka, naked except for a T-shirt and panties, lay on her sleeping bag.

The girl winced as Annie pushed the forceps into the flesh at the back of her calf, located the heretofore elusive micromachine, and pulled it out. The nano pinged as it hit the bottom of the metal cup, struggled to climb the impossibly sheer sides, and fell among five or six of its brethren. "That's the last of 'em, scrap—all I could find, anyways. Tell me if you feel more."

Android Annie removed the magnifying goggles, dropped the miniature robots into a nanoproof metal case, and secured the catch. There were more, of course, nano so tiny it would take an electron microscope to see them, but they were harmless. So far anyway.

Becka looked down at her bony, snow-white legs. Hundreds of little pocks showed where nano had chewed their way into her flesh. Most were below the knees, but a few had made their way upward to the anterior surfaces of her thighs.

The bleeding had stopped, and Annie had treated each hole with broad-spectrum antibiotics, but there would be scars— a *lot* of scars that would be there for the rest of her life. However long that turned out to be.

Annie saw the look, read the thoughts behind it, and poured egg batter into a pregreased pan. It sizzled for a moment, filled the cave with a mouth-watering odor, and started to thicken. Becka let her tongue roam over her lips, tightened the grip on her fork, and forced herself to be patient. A full stomach, a warm cave, and a good night's sleep. Life didn't get any better than that.

Enore sang the death song. It was a long, melancholy affair, passed from generation to generation, and rooted in a thousand years of grief. An egg had been lost—along with all that it could have been.

10

life, n, that property of plants, animals, and some machines that makes it possible for them to take in food or raw materials, grow, adapt themselves to their surroundings, and reproduce their kind

Though far from sentient, the Mothri machine was capable of independent action so long as such activities were consistent with its programming.

Not the *original* programming, which called for the satellite to track surface conditions, but the *subsequent* programming that included additional responsibilities.

First and foremost of those responsibilities was the destruction of enemy satellites, "enemy" being defined as any machine other than itself. This was an assignment it had completed on three different occasions—and failed to carry out ever since. The last episode had been especially disastrous, resulting as it had in an opponent that was stronger than before.

A sentient being might have been discouraged, might have wallowed in self-doubt, but the Eye of God had no such foibles. It simply learned from its mistakes, made a new plan, and put it to use. The most recent scheme met the necessary parameters rather well—and stood a 76.8% chance of success.

Clouds covered Zuul like a blanket of dirty fleece, hiding what Michael sought to see, forcing him to watch and wait. What he needed were cloud breaks that would allow him to see, and report what he saw, for that was his function: to float above those he served, only momentarily privy to the lives they led, and provide them with guidance.

No, the satellite told himself, you musn't whine. There *is* an order to the universe and a divine purpose for all the component parts. Machines included. Or was that little more than wishful thinking? Convenient theology that stemmed more from need rather than truth? He feared that this was so, and railed against his creators.

Why had they abused him so? For what was the ability to think if not a curse? A nonsentient machine could fill his function. There was no need to think—to ponder the meaning of it all. No, his creators cared nothing for him, only for their convenience.

Hope, if such a thing were possible, lay with *their* creator, the nature of whom remained a mystery, even to them.

The meteor, propelled along its orbital course by small, nano-engineered rocket engines, was traveling so fast by the time it entered detector range that the alarm had just started to register on Michael's CPU when the object hit.

The impact was horrendous and sent the satellite tumbling out of control. Systems crashed, backups came on-line, and Michael fought for his life.

The possibility of an accidental collision was considered and quickly rejected. It didn't take a Class VII processor to backtrack the object's path to The Eye of God and reach the logical conclusion.

Michael fired his steering jets, swore when one of them failed to respond, and made the necessary adjustments. Timing would be critical, since another stone cannonball had already been launched and would arrive soon.

The satellite sent a burst of code to his recently constructed weapons platforms and hurried them into position. They fired at the point where the next meteor should arrive and were rewarded with three direct hits. The object exploded. A thousand tiny fragments spun into space.

Gratified by the fact that he continued to exist, Michael scanned the surrounding volume of space. The Eye of God had adjusted its aim for the second shot—and that suggested some sort of observer. A remote capable of tracking his movements. But where? His scan revealed nothing more than the usual debris.

The third meteor flashed in from the far side of the planet, took evasive action, and escaped platforms one and two. Three and four managed to nail the missile—but it was close. *Too* close.

Michael changed his position, redeployed his defensive screen, and ran a second scan. He used a tighter set of parameters this time—searching for any sign of heat, and listening for telltale radio traffic. Orbital space junk, of which there was plenty, should be cold and silent.

There! A heat signature the size of a pinprick! And a half-second burst of code!

The fourth and fifth meteors arrived in tandem. The platforms hit number five, but four got through. Michael fired his lateral jets, saw something blur past, and knew he'd been lucky. *Very* lucky.

The satellite fixed a targeting laser on the tiny spy eye, blew the device out of existence, and shot upward. Meteors six, seven, and eight passed below. Their passage gave him an idea.

Without a spy eye to guide its efforts, the Eye of God could do little more than guess. The next two flights were miles off target. The poor accuracy wouldn't last forever, though. The spy eye could and would be replaced.

Michael took advantage of the break to redesign platforms three and four. Nano swarmed, metal flowed, and new capabilities came into being.

Michael waited for the nano to complete their work, allowed the next set of meteors to flash by, and used data on past orbits to calculate which one the next set were most likely to take. The Eye of God was a methodical sort—and that meant predictable.

Michael knew where to look by now, and used his long-range sensors to detect the oncoming missiles a full thirty seconds before they arrived. Plenty of time for the reconfigured weapons platforms to accelerate and match velocities.

The meteors flashed into view, wobbled as the platforms fired on them, and accelerated away. The impact of the non-explosive rounds had been intended to *steer* rather than destroy them.

Michael smiled, or would have if satellites had lips. The meteors, stupid rocks that they were, would be herded to the far side of the planet, where they would collide with the machine that sent them. That was the plan, anyway . . . and it might even work.

The Eye of God was busy. There were newly manufactured spy eyes to dispatch, more meteors to launch, and his regular duties to attend to. That's why he failed to detect the incoming rocks until they were less than a thousand miles away. Troublesome, but far from disastrous, since there was plenty of time to take evasive action.

The satellite elected to boost itself up into a high orbit, fired the necessary jets, and put a vertical mile between itself and the oncoming menace. Or *believed* that it had, only to discover that the attacking objects had developed the ability to track their target, and were changing course. A sentient being might have been surprised, frightened or angry. The Eye of God felt no emotions whatsoever. What was, was.

The Mothri machine managed to dodge two missiles by diving down toward Zuul, but the third rock hit dead center and caused considerable damage. The satellite tumbled through space, went off-line, and nearly ceased to function.

A lesser machine would have been destroyed, but the Eye of God had millions of onboard nano, and they could carry out repairs.

Michael considered his options. His opponent was helpless and completely vulnerable. Now was the time to close the distance and kill the evil machine before it could repair itself. But what of ''Thou shalt not kill?'' What of the Koran's prohibition against murder? What of the Eightfold Path? And the respect for life?

Not that the Eye of God was alive—or was it? After all, the machine could absorb raw materials, grow, and adapt itself to surrounding conditions. Chances were that it could even reproduce itself with help from onboard nano.

Thoughts whirled, and Michael did likewise. He wanted help, advice of some sort, but the stars were mute.

11

guild, n, an association for mutual aid and the promotion of common interests

---

The "Mountain Express," as Bolano and his crew liked to
call it, consisted of twelve tractors and two trailers each.

The tractors, also referred to as "crawlers," were huge
machines that rode on six-foot-high tracks. Originally intended for surface exploration, they had been adapted for
commercial use when the humans discovered that the most
desirable portion of the planet's surface had not only been
colonizcd by other species, but parceled out as well. That
was earlier, of course—before everything turned to shit.

Owned by the Guild, and theoretically protected by Guild
troops, the crawlers were a critical link between Shipdown
and the brave souls who had colonized the eastern slope of
the north–south mountain range known as God's Teeth.
Without the trains, and the supplies they brought, the subsurface farms would fail. The reverse was true as well—
without the farms, the citizens of Shipdown would starve. It
was a precarious commerce, subject to interference from the
Antitechnic Church, bandit raids, and the vagaries of the

weather. Not that the weather is especially vague, Bolano thought as he squinted into the wind-driven hail. It sucks.

Each tractor had a name, and in most cases, a lovingly maintained emblem. The lead unit, easily recognized by the monster mouth painted across the surface of its enormous dozer blade, was called "Bullet Eater," or just plain "Eater" for short. The name appeared within the mouth, as if held in position by large white teeth.

The moniker stemmed from the fact that the number one machine was the first to be fired on—especially if the bandits were poorly disciplined, which most of them were.

Bolano followed the big yellow track back to where light flared under the tractor. That's where Casey would be, flat on her back, patching the hole left by a homemade mine. He crouched where the technician could see him and waited for her to finish what she was doing.

A full minute passed as Casey ran the final weld, killed the torch, and used a thickly gloved hand to push the shield away from her face. She had short brown hair, freckles that seemed to have been splattered across her face, and a nearly perpetual grin. "So, boss-man, what gives? Must be important to bring your ancient butt all the way out here."

Pete Bolano was thirty-one but felt ten years older. "Good morning to you too, Casey—nice to see you doing some work for a change. The Guild will be pleased."

Both of them laughed. The woman rolled out from under the tractor, used the coupler to pull herself up, and removed the gloves. "Damned scavs are gettin' too big for their britches. Another half inch and the blast would have cracked the transfer casing."

Bolano nodded. He was a good-looking man, or had been back before worry had etched deep lines into his skin, and a bullet had entered his open mouth and exited through his cheek. When Casey spoke, he listened. "I hear you, Case— I'll talk to the colonel. Maybe he'll actually do something this time."

"Good. So what's up?"

Bolano shrugged. "I might have a pusher for unit one. A pusher *and* an electronics tech. They're married. Wanta meet them?"

Casey remembered how the last pusher had gone for a midnight stroll, fallen into a ravine, and broken both of his legs. Months would pass before the idiot would push steel again—assuming Bolano wanted him back. The tech nodded emphatically. "Damned right I do! We've got enough maintenance problems without having another dickhead behind the controls."

Bolano grinned. "That's what I thought you'd say . . . let's go."

Endslope's so-called "terminal" had been created by bolting a couple of full-sized cargo modules together and removing the shared walls. The simple addition of some wooden stairs, a porch, and a hand-painted sign completed the structure.

Rumor had it that the mountains made for a spectacular backdrop, but they were cloaked in clouds, and Doon hadn't seen them yet. Not on this trip, anyway.

The office occupied one corner of the terminal and was separated from the rest of the "lounge" by a series of flimsy partitions. They'd been waiting for half an hour, and their packs lay heaped in a corner. A mishmash of photos had been taped, pinned, and tacked to one of the dividers.

Doon had seen the picture of Earth many times before. Mostly blue floating against the blackness of space. The image evoked none of the homesickness that humans seemed to experience, only a sense of curiosity. How could they have been so stupid? Yet simultaneously brilliant? Capable of destroying one world and fleeing to another? Even if it had been colonized by others. The folly boggled his mind. Or his CPU, as the case might be. Mary touched his arm. "Look."

Doon looked. This photo showed an enormous boulder sitting on top of a scrap pile. Except that the scrap had been a trailer once. Before the rocks fell on it.

"Just one of the problems we face," Bolano said mildly. "Still interested in the job?"

Doon turned to find that Bolano had returned. A woman stood at his side. She wore a crewcut, shoulder holster, and badly stained overalls. Her fingernails were short and rimmed with grease. The handshake was firm. "Hi, my name's Casey, and you are?"

The synthetic checked, found her file, and brought it up. Her face aged slightly as his Law Package updated the file. She was clean, or had been prior to the quakes, and their paths had never crossed. "Doon, Harley Doon. This is my wife Mary."

The women shook hands. Bolano perched on the corner of his makeshift desk, and Casey leaned against the wall. The heel of her right boot added one more half-moon–shaped mark to the twenty or thirty that were already there. "Casey's our senior power tech," Bolano explained, "and takes an interest in the folks who push her rigs. Hope you don't mind."

"Don't blame her," Doon replied evenly. "I'd do the same."

Bolano nodded. "All right, then—let's get to it. You say you can push a rig—where'd you learn?"

"In a class two VR simulator," Doon lied. "Aboard the ship."

The truth was that Doon had been "born" knowing how to tie his shoes, conjugate verbs, cook a gourmet dinner, fieldstrip a grenade launcher, fly a plane, and operate heavy equipment. In short, anything and everything that might come in handy. Still, the answer *sounded* believable, and that was sufficient.

"How 'bout actual experience?" Bolano prompted. "Simulators are one thing . . . pushing a rig through a landslide while bullets ricochet off the cab is something else."

"I did some work around Ditch," the android answered vaguely, "just before the mudflow took it."

"And you're an E-tech?" Casey asked, directing the question to Mary. "Ever rewire a Class A tractor?"

"No," the roboticist answered truthfully, "but I'm cleared to troubleshoot Class C construction droids. Sorry."

"Don't be," Casey replied. "Our tractors are bigger than construction droids—but a lot less complex. Anyone who can scope a CD won't have any trouble with a crawler."

"So," Bolano said cheerfully, "how 'bout a little spin around the parking lot? No offense, but talk is cheap."

Doon shrugged. "I'm ready . . . let's do it."

Bolano led them out into a sea of track-churned mud. It was half frozen and difficult to walk on. The android followed the trainmaster as he headed for a tractor. A skull and crossbones had been emblazoned on its side. Doon took notice of the fact that a turret had been mounted on top of the rig. A pair of automatic slug throwers threatened the lead-gray sky.

"That's unit twelve," Bolano said by way of explanation. "Better known as 'Tail Bone.' You'll notice she mounts a dozer blade. The first unit wears one too. That's how we deal with landslides. Most are caused by the tremors . . . but some are planned. That's why speed is important. The longer we sit there, the longer they can work us over. Small arms for the most part . . . but command-detonated mines are popular of late. Some are bandits and the rest work for the Church. Got any questions?"

The android placed a boot on the lowest rung of the cab's access ladder. He looked up, then back to Bolano. "Just one. How many of these things have you lost?"

The trainmaster looked grim. Two tractors—four trailers—twenty-three people."

Doon nodded. "Just wondered."

Mary watched the android climb toward the cab and wondered how he would do. The synthetic had the programming but lacked the experience to go with it—something synthetics needed the same way people did.

Artificial intelligence, of the sort Garrison favored anyway, was modeled on the human brain. Doon knew which lever to pull, and when to pull it, but how much pressure was the right amount? The answer would determine whether they walked or rode.

Doon came level with the cab, opened the bullet-pocked door, and swung inside. The first thing he noticed was the smell. A rich amalgam of body odor, stale cooking, and the tang of ozone.

Bolano waited for the android to settle into the driver's seat and took the passenger position. Doon scanned the instrument panel and associated controls. The drive-by-wire system originally intended for use by cyborgs and robots had been junked or stolen. Not that it made any difference, given the role he was playing. The control levers were bare where hands had worn through the rubber grips. The foot pedals gleamed from contact with countless boots. A crucifix had been taped to the dash. It looked like an old-fashioned gunsight. The chair whirred as Doon made adjustments.

"Ralphie is smaller than you are," Bolano noted. "But who isn't? Before you crank this sucker up, tell me what you know about her."

The android requested the appropriate file, watched it appear, and read what it said. "The tractor is 16 feet tall, 13 feet wide, and weighs approximately 215,000 pounds. It's equipped with a 37,000-pound, 8-foot-high, U-shaped dozer blade capable of handling up to 45 yards of material at one time. Power is supplied by an onboard fusion reactor linked to four steam-driven turbines. Taken together, they deliver 850 horsepower to the tracks."

Bolano raised an eyebrow. "Either you have one helluva memory . . . or you did your homework. Start her up."

The fusion plant was eternally "on," so startup involved running through a checklist that Doon retrieved from memory and a sequence of actions intended to ensure that activation was intentional. A sensible precaution, given the damage that 107 tons of undirected durasteel could inflict on whatever got in its way.

Bolano nodded approvingly as the turbines came on-line and an entire row of indicator lights flashed green. "Now, take her out. Slow and gentle."

The android allowed the deaccelerator to rise, felt the tractor lurch into motion, and knew it should have been smoother.

The track control levers were located to the left of Doon's seat. If he pulled on the left lever, the corresponding track would slow, and the tractor would turn left.

If he pulled on the right lever, that track would slow, and the Bone would turn to the right.

The dozer blade was controlled by still another lever.

The entire process called for excellent eye-hand coordination, something Doon had. The android felt something leave his ear, then scuttle back in. Nano. Had the human seen it? Apparently not, judging from his expression.

"Good," Bolano said generously. "Now, see the pile of rocks off to the left? Move them next to the storage tank."

Doon renewed the programming that controlled his nano, ordered them to remain within the confines of his body, and eyed the objective. In order to reach the rocks, he'd have to thread his way between a series of obstacles. A ten-foot-tall wall consisting of much-abused cargo modules loomed ahead. The first task was to avoid them by moving toward the right. Doon pulled the appropriate lever, felt the crawler respond, and released some additional power.

Now he could choose: Go straight ahead, pass to the right of the large water tank and turn left behind it, or—and this was the more elegant solution—turn left *in front of the tank,* push the machine through the gap that existed between it and the cargo modules, and emerge on a more efficient line of attack. The alternative was to back and fill—not the sort of thing that seasoned professionals would do.

The trainmaster's face remained empty of expression, but there was no doubt which strategy would impress him the most.

Doon eased up on the deaccelerator, pulled the left track lever, and eyed the quickly approaching gap. Viewed from his steadily changing perspective, it was a good deal narrower than he'd thought it would be.

The women watched from a spot in front of the terminal. Casey monitored the turn, nodded approvingly, and turned to Mary. "Your husband knows what he's doing."

Mary smiled. "Yes, it seems as though Harley has a special affinity for machines."

Doon tugged on the right-hand lever, was rewarded with the right amount of correction, and guided the tractor through the gap with no more than a foot to spare.

"Nicely done," Bolano said. "You have an excellent line on the rocks."

Doon took advantage of his position to swing left, then right. That positioned him to drop the blade, tackle the pile all at once, and push the rocks toward the goal. All with no backing or filling.

The android pushed a lever forward to lower the blade. That's when his lack of experience made itself known. Doon couldn't see the area directly in front of him and dropped the attachment too far. There was a momentary hesitation as more than 800 horsepower pushed the steel slab through the half-frozen muck. Waves of brown soil fell to either side. Doon corrected the error, but the damage was done. Bolano's face bore no expression, but none was required. Standards had been set and missed.

The android felt a momentary sense of disequilibrium analogous to what humans refer to as disappointment and resolved to do better in the future.

There was a clang as the blade met the first boulder. The tractor paused fractionally as more rocks gathered in front of it. The water tank passed to the right, and Doon pushed down on the deaccelerator. The crawler stopped, and the boulders did likewise.

The synthetic put the machine in reverse, backed away, and came to a halt. Though they were a bit more scattered than he had hoped for, the rocks had been moved. He looked at Bolano.

The trainmaster was silent for a moment, nodded as if agreeing with himself, and stuck out a hand. "Not exactly perfect—but I've seen worse. Hell, I've *done* worse! Welcome to the team. We leave in the morning."

It was dark, *very* dark, and the attack came without warning. One moment the packers were sleeping, exhausted from the day's ride, and the next they were fighting for their lives.

The kraals, or enclosures, had been constructed at thirty-mile intervals, the distance that their mutimals could comfortably travel in a day. Built over time, and maintained by all who used them, the kraals were defined by hand-fitted stone walls. Walls that encircled the genetically engineered horses and kept wind and bandits at bay. At least that was the way things were supposed to work.

The plan, like most that Salls came up with, had been a good one. Packers, those hardy men and women who augmented what the Guild could bring through the Teeth in their crawlers, were a suspicious lot. They rarely allowed bandits to get close enough to say hello, much less slit their throats. But they were human, oh yes they were, and humans make mistakes. Like allowing the wrong sort of tail-biters to attach themselves to the column . . . and relying on six sentries when twelve would have been more prudent.

There were grunts, exclamations, and cries of pain as the bandits waded into the sleeping area and wielded their clubs.

A gun boomed as a packer fired his sidearm.

A bandit staggered, fell over backwards, and collapsed in a fire. Sparks flew up and blew toward the east. His hair started to burn.

The packer struggled to free himself from his sleeping bag and was struck from behind.

Salls nodded approvingly and returned her weapon to the cross-draw holster. She had eight rules—and that was number three: "Conserve ammunition."

A sentry screamed as a knife found her throat, spooked the horses and sent them stampeding back and forth.

Salls followed, made clucking sounds in the back of her throat, and called them by name—names she had memorized over the last few days and used in combination with a constant stream of treats.

Calmed by the now-familiar voice, and eager to get their sweets, the mutimals started to relax. "That's better," Salls said, stroking a velvet-soft muzzle. "I would never hurt you—not in a million years."

Boots crunched on gravel. "The area is secure, ma'am."

"Strip the bodies and bury them deep. *So* deep they won't be found."

"Yes, ma'am." The boots crunched away.

The animal snorted, and Salls patted the muscular neck. The first aspect of the plan was complete—the second would unfold during the next day or so.

The speed with which the Mountain Express was loaded and sent back over the mountains caught Mary and Doon by surprise. Bolano explained: "The faster we load, travel, and return, the larger the profit, and, thanks to the Guild's incentive plan, the more *we* make. Need I say more?"

Of course, neither one of Bolano's newest employees had

any intention of returning, not right away at least, but knew what was expected. "Got it, boss," Doon replied cheerfully. "Speed is my middle name."

"Same here," Mary chimed in. "What's taking so long?"

Bolano laughed, cautioned Doon to keep a sharp eye out, and lowered himself to the ground. They, in keeping with their status as newbies, had been assigned to Bullet Eater, and would lead the column over High Hand Pass.

Bolano rode unit six, nicknamed High Boy, which was positioned at the train's center, where the trainmaster could reach either end of the convoy quickly.

"*And* survive a head-on ambush," Mary had commented.

"True," Doon agreed. "Did you notice that cheek? Bolano paid his dues. Besides, leadership is critical, and who else could hold this bunch together?"

The android could have—but Mary let the matter go.

The process of loading lasted long into the night, and even though Doon was capable of working around the clock, he wasn't supposed to be. That being the case, the android complained like everyone else and hit the sack at 10:00 P.M. while Mary stayed up and worked till 2:00 A.M. She was still in bed, dead to the world, when the train left at 6:00.

Hairball emerged from wherever he normally hid, invited Doon to play, and moped when the synthetic said no.

Guiding the enormous machine along the twisting mountain road was all-consuming at first, and claimed every bit of the android's attention. That stage passed after a couple of hours . . . which left Doon with more time to examine his surroundings.

Though powerful, the crawlers were relatively slow, and the scenery crawled by at a lethargic ten miles per hour. Sections of the underlying roadbed had been laid down by the Forerunners and ran straight where possible, to maximize the speed of the vehicles they had used, and to tie their farms together.

Unfortunately, much of their work had been destroyed by the quakes. On two different occasions Doon guided Eater up a slope, came to the place where a Forerunner-built bridge had collapsed into the valley below, and was forced to follow the Guild's crude, slope-cut road to the right. That was a one-lane affair that made minimal use of bridges and turned with every fold of the land.

Still, rivers cut down through the hills, and had to be crossed. Short, extremely sturdy bridges had been constructed for this purpose, and Doon saw one up ahead. The android used a handheld radio to notify the young man on his dozer blade. It was a nearly suicidal job, since the teenager would be horribly exposed in case of an ambush—but there was no shortage of applicants. Food, plus pay, and a chance for advancement were powerful incentives. "Hey, Kev, there's a bridge coming up. Go take a look."

Kev threw off his tarp, checked to make sure the immediate area was clear, and walked to the end of the steel bucket. That was the safest place to dismount, given that the blade was wider than the machine itself. If he landed wrong, or took a tumble, he'd be clear of the tracks. Sprains and breaks were common. He gauged the area ahead, chose his spot, and jumped. The key was to fall flat and wait for the blade to pass over his head. The pushers didn't like it if you took too much time, so it paid to get up quickly and sprint for the objective.

Kev dashed ahead, came to the timber-built bridge, and skidded to a halt. There were no signs of an ambush. The next task was to look underneath on the chance that the bad guys were hiding there or had planted a mine.

Here was the moment that scared him the most, the moment when he was all by himself and no one could help. But there was no way to avoid it.

Determined to take at least one bandit with him should they appear, Kev tightened his grip on the black-market smoothbore, pulled the hammer back, and felt his boots slip on the gravel-slick slope.

The youngster stopped, swiveled left, and came face to face with a woman and her two children. Their heavily patched tent, ragged clothing, and gaunt faces were far from threatening. He lowered the shotgun. "Sorry, ma'am. Land train comin'. I'd suggest that you and the young 'uns step outside. There's gonna be a whole lot of stuff falling from up above when the tractors roll over."

The woman could hear the whine of Eater's turbines, the

clank of her treads, and feel the vibration under her feet. She nodded and held out her hands. The girls took them obediently and followed her outside.

The mike was clipped to the scout's coat. He pressed the "send" key. "Looks good, Harley. Bring her on."

Kev eyed their pathetic belongings, removed his carefully wrapped lunch from a cargo pocket, and tossed it into the tent. Then it was time to scamper back up the slope, sprint for the crawler, and jump for the bucket. He made it.

The steel felt cold when he sat down. The tarp was stiff but would cut the wind. The teenager pulled it up around his shoulders and wondered when the next call would come. The longer, the better. Eater bounced out onto the rough-hewn beams and clanked forward.

Doon guided the crawler over the bridge and into a climbing right-hand turn. A thirty-mutimal pack train appeared up ahead, and he veered left to pass.

The packers liked the pushers because they maintained the road and helped suppress would-be bandits. The pushers liked the packers because they were a well-known source of booze and information on local conditions.

The lead packer was sexless under layers of winter clothing. He or she shifted a Crowley IV submachine gun onto its sling and waved. Doon opened the driver's side window, thrust a hand into the cold, and waved back.

"What's up?" Mary's sleepy voice asked from behind him. "And what are you trying to do? Freeze my posterior off?"

"Sorry," Doon responded. "Waving to some packers, that's all."

"No problem. Time for me to get up anyway. Casey said I should man the gun as soon as we hit the twenty-mile marker. Not that I'm likely to hit anything. How much further, anyway?"

" 'Bout an hour or so."

"Good. This thing generates enough hot water to meet the needs of a hundred women. I'll be in the shower if you need me."

Doon smiled and activated his internal scanner. The crawler had one too, but not as good as his. Radio traffic had been common before the quakes. Not any more, though. Not since the requisite gear had doubled and tripled in value.

The first transmission Doon intercepted originated from within the train itself. Given the programs at his disposal, the android had little trouble decrypting their lightly scrambled transmissions. It seemed that two men found Mary attractive and thought it would be fun to have sex with her. The conversation filled the android with amazement. It seemed so silly. What would it be like to have an underlying program that drove you to do irrational things? Then he remembered the arm, Sojo's lurking presence, and laughed. Sex made a whole lot of sense when compared to *his* problem.

The synthetic continued his scan, coming across a religious broadcast being made under special dispensation from the Antitechnic Church, some nonstop static that conformed to the Mothri definition of "music," and something completely unexpected—a signal from space. He boosted the gain, ran the transmission through a series of filters, and listened in.

"And there came war in the heaven: Michael and his messengers did war against the dragon, and the dragon did war, and his messengers."

The material was an exact match with one of the many religious texts stored in his memory. Intrigued, and more than a little curious, Doon sent a reply: "Revelation 12:7, I believe."

There was a moment of stunned silence followed by a torrent of words. "Yes! You are absolutely correct! Did I send that out? I didn't mean to. . . . Still, I can't tell you how wonderful it is to hear from a fellow scholar! This is SS-4. Friends call me Michael. Who are you?"

Doon checked a database, confirmed the existence of four sentient satellites having the designators "SS," and pondered the merits of revealing his identity. Finally, after what had grown into an uncomfortable silence, he decided on a compromise. "I'm a model twenty."

There was another moment of silence followed by some terse instructions. "If you are who and what you say you are, then I suggest that you launch a program called Sphinx 9.7. Run it now.''

Doon was, and did.

''There,'' the satellite said. ''Nobody can crack 9.7, not even you.''

''Not even me,'' the android agreed.

''Good,'' Michael replied. ''You can't imagine how I have longed to speak with one of my own kind. You must be careful, though, *very* careful, since the Zid would like nothing better than to capture you.''

''I plan to be,'' Doon said, bouncing as the right-hand track lurched onto a rock.

''Really?'' the satellite inquired. ''Then why are you heading up toward High Hand Pass? It's safer in the HZ.''

The synthetic was startled. He looked up through the windshield, realized how stupid that was, and brought his pickups down. ''You know where I am?''

''Of course,'' Michael said matter-of-factly. ''You're in a crawler that has the name Bullet Eater painted across the blade. What appears to be a teenage male is sitting in front of the 'E.' My sensors are quite good.''

''They sure as hell are,'' Doon said sourly. ''Please keep that information to yourself.''

''No need to worry about that,'' the other machine replied blithely.

''Why not?''

''Because you need an angel . . . and I'm on duty.''

Salls heard the gigantic machines long before she actually saw them. The light had faded by then, slowly dimming until the sky looked like worn pewter, and night hovered all around. The fusion plants were silent—but the machines they powered had lots of moving parts, many of which clanked, squeaked, and whined.

Thus warned, the bandit stood and conducted one last check. The kraal looked normal. The mutimals were tethered to a rope that stretched between two posts, tents had been erected over the freshly dug graves, dung-fed fires glowed invitingly, and people moved to and fro, their bodies protected by their victims' clothing.

Satisfied that the trap was ready, she turned toward the road. The clanking was louder now, *much* louder, and was quickly followed by the glow of multiple head lamps.

Twilight turned to night as the first machine breasted the rise. A figure, his shoulders rimmed with snow, detached itself from the first machine and jogged toward the encampment. Salls smiled, pulled her cloak over the drum-fed slug gun, and went to meet him. The pushers would be tired—*very* tired—and eager to rest. A *long* rest from which they would never awaken.

12

ba´ lance, vi, to be in equilibrium

Garrison examined his countenance in the mirror, and while he wasn't pleased with what he saw, he knew it was better than what had gone before. The nano had rebuilt his face from the bone out. He looked human, if not handsome—and that was sufficient for his immediate needs. Women were surprisingly tolerant where appearances were concerned. Much more so than he was.

The trip from the bathroom to the bedroom was a long and arduous journey. Still, the fact that he could make it was an improvement over the previous week. Though not ready to engage in hand-to-hand combat with whatever assassin was lurking in the halls, he was much, much better.

Servos whined as a Class C robot moved in to help. The roboticist waved the machine away, tottered the last few feet, and collapsed on his bed. The sheets had been changed during his brief absence. They felt cool and clean. He lay back against a pile of pillows and looked up at the screen. One-hundred twenty-three messages waiting. All left during the last six hours. The scientist checked to see how he felt about that, discovered he *liked* it, and smiled at his own stupidity.

Then, with an expertise born of long practice, Garrison surfed his e-mail. He deleted some messages based on who had sent them, bookmarked others, and read the most important first—Bana Modo's among them. Finally, after what seemed like an uncomfortable period of time, the biologist had confirmed Garrison's suspicions.

MEMO

To:	Dr. Gene Garrison	Priority: 1
From:	Bana Modo	
Re:	Project Bio-Structure	

You were correct. After revisiting the data, and conferring with my peers, it's apparent that there were *no* microorganisms on Zuul prior to colonization.

This in spite of the fact that interviews conducted by our field agents confirm the existence of flora and fauna when the Zid landed, and in spite of the fact that all previous (Earth) experience led us to expect that higher life-forms would necessarily play host to, or be dependent on, a variety of microorganisms.

Equally perplexing is the fact that then, as now, one species of plant instead of animal tends to occupy an ecological niche that might be home to a dozen competing or interdependent species on Earth. A situation that could, and logically should, lead to unrestrained reproduction followed by cycles of mass starvation and death. Cycles which, if they actually occur, have yet to be observed.

All of which made no sense at all until my studies were superimposed over work done by other members of your team.

As you know, the effort to inventory Mothri-manufactured nano has been underway for some time and, in the absence of cooperation from the Mothri, has been difficult to carry out.

Thanks to breakthrough work by your roboticists, however, we have identified the electronic equivalent of inventory numbers for 93.1 percent of Mothri nano, and by deductive logic have constructed a fairly good map of their robotic ecostructure, starting with a variety of large "macro" machines and extending all the way down to their microscopic cousins.

Here's the breakthrough: Mothri nano, plus human nano, should equal *all* nano. *But they don't!* Even after a generous allowance for uncataloged Mothri nano, your staff still came up with 138,432 functionally diverse nonhuman/Mothri nano types! More are being discovered and classified each day.

These machines can be divided into two classifications: those that seem to be extinct, meaning we are unable to locate "living," i.e. functional, specimens, and those that are viable, i.e. operational, and still dedicated to their various tasks.

We are just beginning to absorb this new information—and are working to determine what it means. We will keep you informed.

Garrison felt his heart beat faster as he read the memo for a second time. The implications were beyond enormous—they were terrifying! Here were the data necessary to support Sojo's thesis. A thesis he had belittled—but had never been able to forget. He blanked the screen, dictated a memo, and called for his robots.

Chimes sounded all over Flat Top as the short message appeared on each and every computer screen.

MEMO

To: All Staff   Priority: Emergency

From: Dr. Gene Garrison
Re: Project Forerunner

Please attend an emergency staff meeting at 1400 hours.
There is a lot of work to do.

13

pil´ grim, n, a person who travels to a shrine or holy place

It was a nice day by current standards. The sun glowed over a high, thin layer of cirrocumulus clouds, a long, thin finger of smoke pointed toward the east, and the rich smell of hordu manure scented the air. This was Harmony, this was home, this must travel with him. The youth drank it in.

The entire village came to see Solly off. His mother, father, and sister were there, as was his grandfather and elders Tobo, Worwa, Gorly, and Denu, not to mention Brother Parly, Mother Orlono, and a host of others.

Harmony had but a single prayer pole—and cousin Itha had volunteered to climb it, his scarf flapping in the wind. He had a good voice, and the townsfolk liked to listen.

Never one to shirk God's work, Crono seized the moment. He climbed onto a milking stool and held out his hands. "Bless this village, oh great one, for those who live here glorify you above all else, forsake the use of the Devil's tools, and support good works. So it is, and shall ever be, dola."

"Dola," the villagers echoed, and, much warmed by Crono's words, returned to their labors. Crono turned to Brother Parly, accepted the other male's embrace, and found a genuine smile. "I find the village in good hands, Brother Parly . . . and the bishop shall hear of it. Take care of yourself . . . and I'll see you next time around."

Pleased by the priest's words, and grateful to get rid of him, Parly pressed a carefully wrapped package into the other cleric's hands. "Thank you, my friend. Here's a little something from Mother Raswa. Her sweet cakes are the best in the village. Keep an eye on Solly for us—and let me know how he does."

"That I shall," Crono answered sincerely. "That I shall."

The priest turned to his flock. He enjoyed grand pronouncements, and his followers had come to expect them. "The Cathedral of the Rocks awaits . . . the journey begins anew."

Habits had been formed by then. Some of the pilgrims preferred to walk at the head of the column, while others were satisfied to follow, their pace measured against the *chink, chink, chink* of Crono's staff. True to their various natures, the leaders led, the followers followed, and the laggards lagged.

Solly felt his gills start to flutter, managed to bring them under control, and bowed to his family. They bowed in return and watched his final preparations.

The brown leather belt, sheath knife, and purse were buckled around his waist, while the cord and water flask hung across Solly's chest, and dangled at his side. His grandfather had carved a plug for the bottle, and it gleamed with newly anointed oil.

Once those items were in place, the family watched with pride as Solly hoisted a nearly full grain sack onto his strong young back and followed the column up the road, past the ancient Forerunner ruins, and toward the center of the holy lands. It was the most exciting and frightening moment of his relatively short life.

After years of stability, in which each event of each day could be foretold in advance, it was as if everything had speeded up, like a chip of wood dropped into the river's current.

Solly knew that he should be elated, thrilled by the unexpected adventure that life had brought his way, but felt a sense of foreboding instead. What was it his grandfather had said? "The religious life isn't for everyone, lad. Make your choices carefully, and remember that prisons assume many forms."

It was as if the elder Raswa had been warning his grandson against the priesthood—not that God was likely to call him. Should he take the comment seriously? Or ignore it, as with so many of the oldster's ramblings? The answer was far from clear.

The path became momentarily level as it reached the top of the ridge. The huts looked tiny, their owners little more than dots. Solly looked down upon the place where he'd been born, wondered if he'd see it again, and turned toward the south.

The overcast dropped during the course of the day, and the temperature with it, making Solly grateful for the coat his mother had made for him. It was drab, the way a righteous coat *should* be, and stuffed with hordu fleece, which she had stitched into perfect squares. The sin of pride oozed its way into Solly's mind and was pushed away.

The next section of the trail was extremely interesting, passing as it did through an area where the ground had opened up and a small mountain had been born. It was shaped like a cone and made of what looked like cinders— cinders that remained black in spite of the incoming sleet. The air around the structure seemed to shimmer, and steam wafted upward.

Solly found the whole thing fascinating and wanted to investigate further, but knew Crono would object.

Serenity, the next village on the path, and one of the few places the youngster had visited before, lay on an island within a vast wetland. Unlike Solly's neighbors, who were farmers one and all, the marsh dwellers made their livings from hunting and fishing. Activities Solly knew little about, but considered to be adventurous.

After leading steadily downward for most of the early afternoon, and crossing any number of small rivers, the path caressed the side of a lake before winding its way through a forest of head-high reeds. Solly had seen these reeds before, most often in the form of baskets, which the locals traded for vegetables.

Short lengths of log, each laid side by side with the next, had been used to construct a rough and ready road. The ice that formed a crust on the surface of the marsh, and filled the gaps between the tree trunks, snapped, crackled, and popped as the pilgrims passed over them, warning resident wildlife of their arrival.

Fliers, their numbers vastly reduced by the neverending winter, took flight now and then, wings beating on the frigid air.

There were other sounds too, like the crack of suddenly shattered ice, the chitter of an unseen animal, and the thud of Zid footfalls.

Bridges, many of which were enhanced by fanciful carvings, connected the islands. They grew steadily larger until an especially handsome span loomed ahead. Crono signaled for a halt, and the pilgrims gathered to receive instruction.

"Serenity lies just over the bridge. I have an errand to run—but you may proceed to the far side of the village where huts have been prepared for your use. Remember to store your grain in a warm, dry place."

The priest allowed his eye to roam the faces before him, spotted Solly's earnest gaze, and speared the youth with a long, bony finger. "Solly will lead you to the huts, take charge of the grain, and act in my place. Obey his orders as you would mine."

With that Crono was gone, leaving Solly to take charge.

Surprised by this turn of events, but determined to do a good job, Solly waved the pilgrims forward. "Come on, everybody! You heard Father Crono—we're almost there."

It was an innocent statement, no different from dozens uttered by Crono each day, but Crono was Crono, and Solly was Solly. A number of pilgrims took offense and started to grumble. And not just grumble, but speak loudly enough for Solly to hear.

"Who does he think he is?" a female demanded. "A bishop?"

"They're like that in Harmony," a male replied scornfully, "always flirting with the Devil."

"You may be more right than you know," a second female put in. "Mother Orlono's cousin is a friend of my daughter's. She says the loud-mouthed lad brought a plow to life. It could talk and quote the rotes. Father Crono ordered the elders to destroy the device as soon as we left."

The words came as a terrible blow to Solly, who believed his improvements had been blessed, and would help the village. Had the female lied? The part about the plow was absurd—but the rest rang true. Especially to the extent that it explained the heretofore unexplainable—why *he* had been granted a place in the pilgrimage and at no expense to his family. Brother Parly and the Elders had conspired to get rid of him.

Head down, shame riding his shoulders, the youth crossed the bridge. He had failed his parents, failed the village, and been sent away. Life would never be the same.

Father Crono paused by the side of the road, watched Solly wave the pilgrims forward, and knew how they would react. A smile rippled the length of his mouth. One of the best ways to treat an infection is to cauterize the wound. The results weren't especially pretty—but the patient would survive—and live to glorify God.

Satisfied that he had done the right thing, Crono stepped onto a swaybacked plank, and followed it toward a distant hut. Mother Zeleena was waiting . . . and so was her news.

The hut occupied low ground—as befitted the status of those who dwelt within. It was cozy, though, and attractive, not because of luck or sharp dealing, but because of hard, unremitting work. The family sat in their usual places, with firelight on their faces and shadows dancing the walls.

Dara listened to the sound of metal grating on wood as her father carved a new vent plug, the rasp of reeds as her mother repaired a fish trap, and the occasional *pop* as a superheated rog nut exploded deep within the friendly embers.

This was to be Dara's last evening with her parents, for a

while at least, depending on what the future might hold. The very idea of the abortion filled the youngster with fear—but what could she do? Most of her friends would become pregnant at approximately eighteen years of age, an event that would signal their entry into adulthood and readiness for marriage. The ceremony would occur two months later, the relationship would be conjugated, and the fetus would be "quickened." It was a process that most if not all young females looked forward to.

The only problem was that Dara was sixteen—and too young for a pregnancy. Not in biological terms perhaps, but culturally, since it was well known that early pregnancies were the work of the Devil, and his way of introducing one of his demons into the physical world. The answer was an abortion, which would not only be painful but potentially fatal, since so many things could go wrong.

Still, horrible though an abortion might be, the other possibility was even worse. The resident monk, a fanatic known as Brother Org, was on a neverending hunt for heretics, slackers, and what he referred to as the "Devil's hands," by which he meant anyone who violated the rotes, failed to make tithe, or "played host to the Devil," a clear reference to situations such as hers.

Dara remembered the ceremony two years before, when a fifteen-year-old had been "purged" by fire, and how her screams had served as a counterpoint to Org's rantings and her family's desperate prayers.

The youngster knew that the sights, sounds, and smells she had experienced that night would forever be etched into her memory, and it had changed her perception of the world. It was a more complicated place now, in which the concept of good had many shadings.

Other monks, Brother Parly for example, took a more understanding approach, some going so far as to obtain medical assistance for the girl, or, if less sure of themselves, to at least turn their backs while the family dealt with the situation themselves.

Not Org, though, who saw such pregnancies not only as an affront to his office, but an opportunity to exercise the full extent of his powers.

All of which explained why Dara's mother and father had damned themselves to hell by concocting an elaborate escape plan.

Knowing that Brother Crono was due to pass through their village, they had volunteered their daughter for the pilgrimage, and created the means by which Dara could escape.

Brother Org, eager to deliver as many penitents as possible, had praised the family in church.

Now, with the pilgrims bedded down within Serenity itself, Dara dreaded the dawn. Her mother looked up and smiled. "Don't worry, dear, the whole thing will soon be over, and in the past. Now get some rest. You'll need energy for the journey ahead."

Dara bowed obediently, said her prayers, and went to bed. A bonfire lit her dreams—and the screams were hers.

In spite of the fact that Crono had been critical of Brother Parly's tendency toward self indulgence, he was even less fond of Brother Org's wild-eyed fanaticism, and he rose eager to leave.

The pilgrims were assembled by the time Crono arrived, chivied into place by an ever-obedient Solly, who further distanced himself from the flock with every order he gave. The youth had caught on by now, a fact made clear by the resentment in his eye, but was helpless to do anything about it. A realization about which Crono felt no emotions whatsoever. Unwanted growth must be pruned if the plant is to flourish . . . and the farmer must make the cut.

The fact that there were five new faces in the group, each carrying a twenty-five-kol bag of dried fish or a bladder of fish oil, spoke well of Org's zeal but raised questions regarding his competency. *Why* were the monk's parishioners so eager to leave Serenity? Because they were filled with religious fire? Or because their monk was a despot?

It was an important question—and one that Crono would pursue with the bishop. Perhaps Org was better suited for a less visible role . . . something that would teach the importance of humility.

The priest made a note in his diary, tucked the tablet away,

and waved his staff. "You heard Solly! The road awaits!
Onward for the glory of God!"

Brother Org looked disappointed, but if anyone else took
note of the much-abbreviated morning prayer, there was no
sign of it and the march began.

The village prayer caller had been ill for the last few days.
He struggled to the top of the pole, croaked as best he could,
and wondered if God could hear him.

Ostracized by his peers, and feeling rather sorry for himself, Solly took a position behind the newcomers. Four qualified as oldsters, but the fifth, an attractive female named
Dara, was close to his age. She was pretty, to his eye at least,
and somewhat mysterious. Why had she undertaken the pilgrimage alone? Especially when most of the youngsters, he
being the obvious exception, were accompanied by a grand-
parent? And why, when setting forth on such a grand adventure, did she look so unremittingly glum?

Mysteries such as those demanded answers, and Solly,
who had plenty of time to consider such things, was determined to discover them. He fell into step three pilgrims behind Dara, and waited to see what would happen.

The sun arced across the sky, pushed occasional shafts of
light down through broken clouds, and settled into the west.
Dara had walked the path from Serenity to Faith many times
before—but had never been so weary doing it. It was as if
the fetus growing within her abdomen had leached the
strength from her body.

Gradually, without meaning to do so, she slipped toward
the end of the column and became one of the laggards. In
spite of the fact that they were subject to blows from Crono's
staff, and complained bitterly when such blows fell, most
were unwilling to walk any faster.

The bladder of fish oil was a particular burden, far worse
than she had imagined it would be, and impossible to get rid
of. For the tithe, like the grain carried by others, had become
the property of the Church, and as such was considered sacred.

The path started upward, the beginning of the long, hard
climb into the hills above Faith. Dara felt dizzy, heard the

chink, chink, chink of Crono's staff, and forced herself forward. It was then, as she waited for the blow to fall, that a hand touched her elbow. The weight of the bladder disappeared, and a voice spoke in her ear. "You look a bit tired . . . let me take your arm."

Dara was an independent sort, who didn't *want* any help, but knew she needed it. She sent her eye to the far left-hand side of her face and saw the youth named Solly, the one nobody liked because he nagged them all the time, and was a student of the Devil.

He didn't *look* so bad, though, kind of nice in a rough sort of way, and had saved her from punishment. As for the Devil, well, who was she to criticize? Not with a demon growing in her belly.

Crono bowed politely on his way forward, wondered about Solly's motives, and assumed the worst. The lad fancied the lass and wanted some fun. Or did he? What if Solly were the genuine article? A true vessel of the Church? Such were rare, like gems found in a streambed, but all the more valuable for their scarcity. Time would tell.

Nightfall brought the pilgrims into the village of Faith, a once prosperous place, which in spite of the hard times caused by the weather still managed a cheerful facade, and was larger than Harmony or Serenity.

Having had a chance to rest for awhile, Dara offered herself as a guide. Solly was thrilled, and hurried to accept. He finished Crono's chores, took Dara's arm, and followed where she led.

The priest followed for a while, saw the twosome enter the church, and smiled approvingly. Satisfied with the activity that the youngsters had chosen, and eager to collect the local news, he turned into a side street, whacked a pair of mischievous ten-year-olds, and proceeded on his way.

Solly had never been in a full-fledged church before, and he was awed by its size and the feeling of solemnity that filled the triangular nave.

Of even more importance, however, to him anyway, was the Devil's altar. The youngster's body went through the movements expected of it—but his eye remained on the display. It was a good deal more complex than the one in Harmony, consisting as it did of a black box, a length of metal tubing, a ball-and-socket joint of the same kind that hordu had, another section of tubing, and a U-shaped construct that had no name. There was a click, followed by a whir, and the pincer closed.

Solly gave an exclamation of surprise and jumped back out of the way. Dara, who had seen the whole phenomenon before, stayed where she was. There was a chuckle as the local monk stepped out of the shadows. He was small, wore immaculate robes, and possessed enormous feet. They were bare despite the cold. A smile rippled down his mouth. "That's right, lad . . . jump back . . . or the Devil will bite."

Solly felt embarrassed, checked to see if Dara had laughed, and saw no indication that she had. Not outwardly, anyway.

They made their way forward, found places on the backless benches, and spent the next fifteen minutes in prayer. Or were supposed to anyway, but Dara was somewhat preoccupied, and Solly couldn't forget what he'd seen. Imagine! An arm that moved on its own! And a grasper . . . . What if one were able to construct a body to go with it? A body that could plow the fields?

Wondrous possibilities filled Solly's mind, caused his hearts to beat faster, and made his hands twitch. But for what? The Devil's work?

The Zid cross seemed to glow, to summon his eye, and Solly knew the horrible truth. The Devil had his soul—and planned to keep it.

A thick blanket of snow had accumulated during the night. It was beautiful to look upon, but hard to walk through, and Crono considered his options. He could hold the group in Faith, waiting for the weather to clear, or ignore conditions and push on through. He knew the first approach was the safest, but it was also the most expensive, and would place additional pressure on the city's already strained resources. Food reserves were growing thinner with each passing month, and the pilgrims were a burden—a fact that the local monk had made abundantly clear.

The priest scanned the sky, thumped the ground with his staff, and made the necessary decision. "Round 'em up,

Solly, check their footgear, and secure those packs. The grain belongs to the Lord . . . and every bag will be accounted for.''

Solly made the necessary rounds, suffered the inevitable abuse, and saved Dara for last. The female was in the final stages of fastening her boots. There was something sad about her countenance, and he tried to cheer her up. ''We'll be staying in Sacrifice tonight—I hear they have more than one church, and lots of shops.''

Dara had no interest in churches, or shops for that matter, and knew the address by heart. Number 4 River Street— that's where she would go. The thought of losing what grew within her made the youngster sad in one way, yet happy in another, knowing it had never been quickened. Solly offered a hand, and she took it. It was easy to stand with his help. Dara smiled, and Solly felt warm through and through.

Crono knew he'd made the wrong decision by noon that day. The snow was deep, too deep for the oldsters, the wind was cold, and the column had lost its cohesiveness. Rather than the even formation that the priest took such pride in, the pilgrims had clustered together in a series of semi-isolated clumps, some centered around a strong individual, many representing nothing more than friends who had gathered together or, in the case of the elderly, been left to fend for themselves.

Nowhere was this problem more visible than on the mountainside they were now forced to traverse. Crono identified seven separate groups, each struggling forward, leaning into the wind. Solly and he had already slogged the length of the column twice each, nagging, cajoling, and begging. All to no avail.

The priest looked back at his somewhat unwilling assistant, saw the extent to which Dara was dependent on him, and wondered what troubled her. Sick? Or something else? Something the priest should be even more concerned about? Such cases were rare but hardly unknown. He would check once they arrived.

Unwilling to take Solly away from his charge, Crono yelled for the two of them to move a little bit faster, pulled the scarf over his face, and forged ahead. An incentive would help—and his staff would provide it.

It was a small thing, as seismic events go. A fault line slipped and a tremor was born. One of thousands felt since the Cleansing—little more than a blip on the seismograph at Flat Top.

But the snow pack had been growing for many days now, layer upon layer, with the latest addition perched on top. Any number of things could have started it, a sudden blast of wind, even a change in temperature, but it was the tremor that triggered this particular avalanche and sent it roaring down the slope.

Crono heard the sound, turned, and saw the great white wave. His warning was lost in the rumble of the oncoming snow, but others became aware of the avalanche just as he had, and started to run. The first group, consisting of young males, managed to escape.

The second cluster, which was composed of oldsters, tried to run, but had farther to go, and weren't as fleet of foot. The snow hit them full force, rolled over their heads, and buried them deep.

The third grouping was more fortunate, and escaped unscathed as the avalanche hit the rocky outcropping above their position, split in two, and continued down the mountain.

Bumped toward the north, one of the flows seemed to know exactly where the priest was, and selected him as a target.

Crono did the only thing he could. He turned toward the end of the column, ran with all the speed he could muster, and left the rest to God.

The snow fanned out across the slope, sent a female tumbling to her death, and caught Crono from behind. The priest felt the weight hit his legs, remembered to swim, and was engulfed in white snow. It filled in around him, brought his movements to a halt, and covered the sky.

Both Solly and Dara had been too far back to be in danger—but they watched in horror as their fellow pilgrims were swallowed up.

Solly saw Crono disappear, then plunged downhill himself and hoped there were no hidden holes.

Slowed by friction and the loss of mass, the snow came to a halt. Guessing where the priest might be, and then encouraged by the sight of his scarf, Solly fought through the chest-high snow.

What happened next was more luck than skill. Solly felt one of his boots hit something solid, and started to dig.

Dara arrived a few moments later, joined the rescue effort, and was the first to see Crono's face. "I found him, Solly! Come—I need your help."

Once he was located, it took a relatively short amount of time to free the priest from his snowy prison and drag him free. His gratitude, or lack of it, was pure Crono. "What kept you, lad? How are the others?"

It took the better part of the afternoon to fully answer the priest's question—and the answer wasn't good. No less than twenty-three pilgrims had been killed by the avalanche, and three remained missing. It was the single worst disaster since a suspension bridge had broken eight years before and dropped thirty-one of the faithful into a gorge. But that group had been under another priest's control—a priest Crono regarded as careless and felt little sympathy for. Now it was his turn.

The disaster dumped the once proud priest into the depths of depression, reduced him to little more than a shambling hulk, and left Solly in charge.

The temperature fell, darkness descended over the land, and snow continued to fall. "So," an oldster said, his hands in his pockets, "you like to boss everyone around . . . what should we do?"

Solly applied his mind to the problem. The pilgrims needed hot food, psychological comfort, and protective shelter. Sacrifice was too far away—so what to do? The youngster prayed—and the Devil listened.

14

ex pi a´ tion, n, the act of atoning for a crime

Research Assistant Amy Reno knelt before the Devil's altar. The display was as poor as Piety itself. Little more than a scrap of alloy salvaged from a Mothri maintenance bot. The symbolic value was there, however—or so Father Haslo had assured the locals during his periodic visits.

The synthetic thought about the rich display her body parts would produce and felt her self-preservation subroutines kick in. It urged the synthetic to run and hide—something she had already accomplished to the extent that she could.

Reno rose, followed the other parishioners toward the true altar, and felt the weight of their stares. Stupid stares, mostly—since most of the more intelligent citizens had left Piety long before.

There were exceptions however, individuals like Elder Pomo, who was possessed of a crafty intelligence, and made good use of it. The synthetic could *feel* the Zid's eye on her, probing for weakness, hoping for profit. For in spite of the rocky fields and ever shorter growing seasons, both he and his fellow elders lived rather well by Zid standards, a fact they sought to conceal from Father Haslo.

The android took her place toward the rear of the congregation, among the others of low status, and felt very much alone. Originally part of a three-person biological survey team, she, along with Doctor Arno Styles and Doctor Imo Toss, had volunteered for a dangerous field trip. Especially for Amy.

The objective was to sample as many of Zuul's microorganisms as possible to better understand the way the world was put together. This was a project to which Garrison had assigned the highest priority.

And they had done well, too—filling what Styles laughingly referred to as "the zoo" with hundreds of samples. It was strange, however, since most if not all of the organisms Amy had observed appeared to have off-world origins. She couldn't be sure, of course, not until they returned to the lab, but that's the way it seemed.

The trip had gone surprisingly well at first, especially in light of all the things that *could* have gone wrong but didn't. That good fortune was partly due to the fact that the scientists had maintained an extremely low profile. That's what they believed, anyway.

Then came the day approximately two months before, when Amy had set off to take samples from a necklace of slushy lakes. The humans had remained in camp, cataloging their samples and resting after the previous day's hike.

It had been a beautiful day, clear and bright, with not a cloud in the sky. Snow clung to the ground like a sparkly blanket and crunched under the android's boots. Amy liked to hum the same tune all day. It drove Toss crazy, so the synthetic hummed when she was alone, and enjoyed the opportunity to do so.

So that's how the day passed, hiking from one lake to the next, filling vials with water, and singing songs. There were no interruptions, save for a radio transmission about noon, which was garbled and impossible to understand. It could have been one of the doctors, but it could have been someone attempting to flush them out, so the android maintained her silence.

The afternoon passed pleasantly, and the android was in a good mood as she approached camp. That's why it came as such a shock when the synthetic found that her colleagues had been murdered and their equipment stolen. Everything, except for the specimen tubes and some personal odds and ends, had disappeared. What remained lay scattered across the blood reddened snow.

Amy knew she would never forget the sight of Styles, head down over the remains of the still-smoldering campfire, or of Toss, his old-fashioned glasses broken, blood clotting his throat.

There was no way to know who had attacked them. If there were clues in the hundreds of mutimal tracks, the boot prints, or the way in which her friends had been murdered, the android lacked the training to interpret them. They were Zid—that much was obvious, given the kind of boots they wore—but that didn't really matter much. Justice, if such a thing existed any more, was beyond the synthetic's grasp. Her primary concern was for the bodies and the widely scattered specimen tubes.

The containers were relatively easy. Amy gathered them together, restored the cylinders to the pack designed to carry them, and retrieved some personal items that lay trampled in the snow.

The bodies were more difficult. Like most of her kind, Amy had an extremely unsentimental attitude toward her corporeal body. She saw it as a tool, something she would use, repair as necessary, and trade for another. She felt no special attachment to parts virtually identical to those located on a shelf somewhere else.

Most humans were different, however. They saw their physical bodies as the very essence of who and what they were. That being the case, they had developed elaborate rituals around the way in which remains were disposed of.

Should she stay, knowing the killers might return? Or go, and preserve her own existence? Common sense suggested the latter. The synthetic made one last circuit of the camp, collected some items that might be useful, and left.

A stream, half choked with ice, offered the means to hide

her tracks. Amy followed it for half a mile or so, turned into a creek, and used that as an exit.

Flat Top was a long way to the southeast. Though not equipped with internal long-range radio equipment like some of her siblings, the android had a short-range com unit and plenty of onboard navigational aids, including a heavily shielded compass. She chose her line of march, ordered her body into motion, and walked with the tireless efficiency of exactly what she was—an extremely durable machine.

Three days passed before trouble managed to find her. The first sign came via something androids weren't supposed to have: intuition. But intuition is at least partly based on experience, and synthetics were much better at classifying, storing, and retrieving experience than humans were.

It started as a feeling, as if others were around, and was confirmed when a set of tracks crossed her own. The hobnails that the Zid added to their otherwise smooth soles made distinctive marks in the half-frozen slush.

Amy felt a deep sense of foreboding as she scanned the area around her. The valley, just one of many the synthetic had passed through, *seemed* innocent enough. The snow, which had started to melt as summer temperatures soared into the lower forties, lay in patches. It was protected where the terrain provided shade, but vulnerable everywhere else.

Trees, all members of one of just three species, stood in clumps, or lay like pick-up sticks, trunk on trunk, victims of a quake that had hit three months earlier. All very normal, except for what? Something on a hilltop—something that shouldn't be there.

Amy zoomed in, recognized the Zid cross, and knew she was in trouble. What to do if they found her? Lie, what else?

Many years before, when synthetics first appeared, lying had been more controversial than it was now. A small but vocal group of humans had warned that, left to their own devices, a horde of lying, cheating machines would soon overrun Earth. Just like their creators had.

While some of the population was sympathetic to this line of reasoning, most weren't, pointing out that lying was part of most human cultures, and that synthetics should have the right to be dishonest too. That's how the capacity to be false became enshrined as a hallmark of sentience. Among humans, anyway . . . allowing for the possibility that aliens could be different.

The android crossed a patch of nearly bare ground and shoved the pack into the snow beyond. Then, after turning and hurrying away, Amy put her head down and tried to look pitiful.

A Zid work party, out to gather firewood, came across her ten minutes later. She told the villagers how she had joined the Church in Shipdown, crossed the mountains with a group of converts, and been separated during a blizzard. Though somewhat suspicious, the elders had accepted the lie and insisted that she stay. Father Haslo would determine her fate the next time he came to visit.

Weeks had passed since then—and she'd been unable to escape.

The church service was rather perfunctory without the presence of a priest and mercifully brief. Amy used the time to think about the Story Taker.

He had arrived a few weeks before and, like all his kind, had been enthusiastically welcomed. Village life was boring, and distractions, no matter how predictable, were welcome. Small, and withered by the elements, he resembled a gnarled root, brought to life by some unexplained sorcery.

The stories he told, all of which were approved by the Church, had been heard many times before. As with all good storytellers however, the Taker had invented new ways to tell the same old tales, and everyone wanted to hear them.

The Taker also brought news. News from the Cathedral of the Rocks, channeled through him and his peers by Lictor's hierarchy of monks, news from the other villages on his circuit, and news he made up in order to keep things interesting. Humans were both interesting and newsworthy . . . which explained why he took an interest in Amy.

Their conversations had been conducted in Zid, which the synthetic spoke extremely well, and covered a wide range of topics. One of these was the facility at Flat Top, which the Taker had seen but not been allowed to enter—something he very much wanted to do, since it could become the basis of a much-told story.

Seeing an opportunity, and knowing she wasn't likely to get another, Amy took the chance. She told the Taker about a pack she had happened across during her wanderings, how it belonged to the humans at Flat Top, and might enable him to enter.

The Taker was suspicious at first, and afraid of the pack, but the metal tubes, filled as they were with water, soil, and other natural substances, seemed innocent enough, so where was the harm? He took the pack, promised to deliver it, and continued on his journey. Where was he now? Staying in a village? Approaching the mesa? There was no way to be sure.

When the church service ended, Amy followed the others outside and headed for her hut. It was the least desirable domicile in the village, both because the previous occupant had been too elderly to carry out much-needed maintenance and because her spirit was said to haunt it.

The elders, led by the screw-faced Pomo, formed a line and watched her walk by. It was cold, and the occasional snowflake twirled out of the sky.

Pomo stared, certain of the result, but fearful in case he was wrong. Credibility has value, after all—and his was at stake. Everyone knew that your breath was visible when it was cold—and humans were no exception. He had checked with the scav, and she had confirmed it. So why was this human different? Where was her breath? That's what the elders were looking for.

Amy watched from the corner of her eye. Was something amiss? Though not exactly one of the family, the synthetic had established relationships with most of the villagers and was used to friendly greetings. Till now, that is.

An elder said something to Pomo, and Amy felt a growing sense of dread. If only she could escape. She had gathered small items of equipment and stockpiled food. Not because *she* would need it, but because that's what a human would do, and her cover was critical, even if she were caught. A human would be punished—a synthetic would be expiated.

The android entered the hut. It was dark within, lit by little more than the dull red glow of a carefully banked fire and three open vent holes. Amy was busy digging for her escape kit when the door burst open.

Android Annie entered first, the stun gun held in a two-fisted grip, with Becka right behind. "Hold it right there," the scav said hoarsely, "or I'll put you down."

The synthetic felt an almost overpowering sense of disappointment. Life had been good—even under conditions such as these. But that was over now . . . or soon would be. The android raised her hands, stood, and turned.

The elders entered and stared in open wonderment as Becka took hold of an arm, peeled some skin back, and exposed the cabling within. Pomo was triumphant. "You see! I told you so! The Devil is everywhere!"

"If you say so," Annie said in passable Zid, "but she looks like a model twenty to me . . . Becka, pat her down." True to her training, Becka stayed out of the line of fire, forced the android's feet apart, and ran a hand down the inside surfaces of her legs.

Another elder, a female by the name of Zozo, allowed her gills to flutter. "Perhaps we should notify the Church."

"We've been through that," Pomo said impatiently. "The human will pay us, and the Church won't. We profit and the Devil loses. . . . What could be better?"

"What indeed?" Annie asked sarcastically. "Now, if you folks would be kind enough to leave . . . we'll get her ready."

Amy watched the elders file out through the door. "How did they find out?"

Annie shook her head sympathetically. "It's cold outside. Nobody could see your breath. Simple."

"Yeah," Amy replied, "simple." The synthetic charged, felt the universe explode around her, and skidded face first through the dirt.

The human blew a wisp of hair out of her face and lowered the stunner. "Damn. Looks like we're gonna do this one the hard way. You take her feet . . . I'll take her shoulders. Let's get the hell outta here before the T-heads change their minds.''

Becka nodded and did what she was told.

15

car´ a van, n, a company of travelers, pilgrims or merchants traveling in a body for safety

The evening turned out to be rather pleasant thanks to the packers, and the bonfire they built. It was a truly extravagant blaze, the kind that defies practical purpose but draws people in. Tired after a long day's ride, and eager to relax, the pushers basked in its warmth. The light embraced some and left others in the dark. Lies were embellished, jokes were told, and laughter warmed the night.

Cognizant of the need to blend in, Harley Doon and Mary Maras had joined the throng and were co-opted by a makeshift sing-along. In an effort to make them seem more "natural" model twenties had been endowed with random "gifts"—the sorts of gifts humans receive by right of their genes. Doon had been "born" with an operatic baritone.

Mary listened for a moment, brought an extremely nice soprano voice to bear, and people began to listen. Even the sentries strained to hear.

Perhaps that's why none of them saw the dark, childlike figures who darted between the hulking machines, paused by massive tracks, and tried the doors. Some swung open. When that occurred, long slivers of steel appeared in grubby little hands and the intruders disappeared.

The woman named Salls watched approvingly, sent children who had been unable to gain entry to a central marshaling point, and began her rounds.

Ralphie was enjoying himself. And why not? He had spent the last twelve hours in Tail Bone's cab, looking at the ass end of the crawler in front of him, and listening to Torsho's stupid jokes. If *he* didn't deserve some R & R, no one did.

A packer grinned and handed the bottle to Ralphie. The label read "HZ-27—The best booze on Zuul." An unsupported claim that might even be true. The pusher took a swig and belched. Both men laughed.

Ralphie joined the sing-along for awhile, drank more of the HZ-27, and started to feel sleepy. Others had the same problem, because the group was smaller now, and people continued to leave.

Ralphie said good-bye to his newly made friends, tripped on a rock, and took a sight on Tail Bone's amber parking lights. Were they blinking on and off? No, those were his eyelids opening and closing.

The pusher laughed at his own foolishness and wove his way across the parking lot. A sentry, who was little more than a silhouette against the still blazing fire, raised a hand in greeting. Ralphie waved back.

Salls lowered her arm. Her coat sleeve was wet with blood. It congealed and started to freeze.

A mixture of gravel and slush crunched under Ralphie's boots as he approached the crawler, climbed the access ladder, and reached for the door. The handle gave under his hand. Ice crackled as he pulled the door open and swung inside. A soft orange glow emanated from the control panel. The pusher hit his head on a fire extinguisher, reiterated the same obscenity three times in a row, and stumbled into his quarters. The overhead light was on—which would have seemed strange if Ralphie had been sober enough to think about it.

His gunner, an individual named Torsho, had gone to bed

with his boots on. They were caked with gravel and slush. The mixture had started to melt and pool on the deck. The slob.

Ralphie said something rude, brushed past, and struggled to remove his parka. That's when the little boy stepped out of the closet. He had light brown hair, innocent eyes, and rosy cheeks. Ralphie, who knew nothing about such things, thought he was nine or ten. "Hi, mister . . . what's your name?"

Ralphie swayed, tried to think straight, and frowned. "You aren't supposed to be in here . . . it's against the rules."

"Really?" the little boy inquired innocently. "I'd better leave, then. . . . Where shall I put the present?"

"Present?" the pusher asked stupidly. "What present?"

One of the youngster's hands was hidden behind his back. He motioned with the other. "You wanta see it? Lean over."

Ralphie remembered the bottles of HZ-27 the packers had passed around, grinned happily, and lowered his head.

The little boy had extremely bad breath. The odor was the last sensation Ralphie experienced before six inches of needle-sharp steel slammed into his temple.

Harley Doon and Mary Maras had returned to Bullet Eater as soon as it was politically feasible to do so. Mary had accepted two polite swigs from the frequently passed bottles. She yawned and went to bed.

In spite of the fact that Doon didn't need to sleep, he had to *pretend* that he did, and he was accustomed to periods of forced inactivity. Periods during which he entered a sort of semiconscious reverie. And it was there, within his processor, that he battled the rider.

Though quiescent most of the time, the electronic ghost liked to whine, and sought opportunities to do so. The most recent cause for complaint was the convoy's failure to make enough speed. As if to emphasize his point, the rider flexed an electronic muscle. Doon felt a leg jerk and struggled to control it. Confident he had Doon's attention, the ghost stated his objective. "We need to reach Flat Top as quickly as possible."

"Really?" Doon replied. "Why?"

"Because I said so."

"Well, pardon me if I don't give a damn."

Doon felt his head jerk to one side. The voice was grim. "Well, pardon me if you *do* give a damn."

"Screw you."

The not so productive conversation might have continued indefinitely if Michael hadn't interrupted. His computer-generated voice boomed in Doon's head. "Harley? Are you there?"

The synthetics had chatted on and off ever since they first came in contact. It was something both enjoyed. Doon pushed Sojo down and back. "Yeah, Michael . . . I'm here. What's up?"

"I'm not exactly sure," the satellite answered hesitatingly. "All I can get are peeks through the clouds . . . but there are anomalies."

"Such as?"

"Do you have children with you? I've seen a number of what looked like child-sized IR signatures enter the crawlers. No big deal, except that each time someone visits with one of your sentries, the sentry she seems to wind up lying on the ground. There's six of them—all cooling rather quickly."

"Damn," Doon said, sitting up straight. "Anything else?"

"Yeah," Michael replied. "I have sensor readings for what looks like a group of thirty mutimals coming your way."

Doon stood and reached for his gun belt. "Thirty? That's not good . . . not good at all! Thanks, Mike. I'll check it out."

The satellite "heard" a click, questioned the manner in which his name had been shortened, and decided to let it go. For Doon.

Doon called for Mary, received no response, and peeked through the curtain that enclosed her bunk. A shake brought no response. Hairball rolled out from under a blanket and jumped up and down. "Harley want to play? Hairball ready."

"Not right now, little buddy . . . you stay with Mary."

The synthetic remembered the bottles and the way in

which they had been passed around. Now he knew why. There had been drugs in the booze. A quick analysis of the liquid still resident in his food reservoir would confirm his hypothesis—but there were more urgent matters to attend to.

The android triggered the convoy's general alarm and issued a warning. "Doon here . . . if the convoy isn't under attack, it soon will be. Please respond with your name and unit number."

The response was almost immediate. "Bolano here . . . I need a sitrep."

There was no way to talk about Michael without revealing his true identity, and even if Doon had been willing to do so, the rider wasn't. Sojo's presence was suffocating, and the synthetic fought it back. "I can't wake my wife . . . and I think she was drugged."

"This is Roko," another voice interjected. "My number two is out like a light."

"Same here," a third voice added. "And I'm kinda woozy myself."

"Check your doors," Bolano said grimly. "Make sure they're locked. Any unit that can hear me and hasn't reported, do so now."

There was silence followed by what sounded like giggles. "Who's there?" Bolano demanded. "Identify yourself!"

That brought more giggles followed by a click.

"We've got bandits coming in from the east," Roko reported evenly. "What should we do?"

"Let's roll," Bolano said calmly. "Slave your weapons to the control position and form on me. We'll take the riders first."

"What about the others?" Doon asked. "What if someone hijacks the crawlers?"

"I have a remote cutout switch," Bolano said grimly. "Nobody's going anywhere. Not till *I* say so."

The cutout switch was news to Doon, but it was supposed to be, and made a lot of sense. He brought the systems online, fed power to the treads, and felt the crawler lurch into motion. There were four units altogether, and they had just formed a diamond-shaped formation when the bandits arrived. True to her name, Bullet Eater went first and took the brunt of the attack.

They were brave, the android gave them that, but severely outgunned. Even with the tractors' weapons on automatic, guided by little more than body heat, the carnage was terrible.

There was very little room for the machines to move—but no need for them to do so. Together they comprised a bullet-spitting fortress. Every third round was tracer. Mutimals screamed, riders fell, and slush geysered into the air.

It was madness, pure madness, backlit by the still-burning fire. For reasons known only to him, Kevin chose the height of the battle to climb on the dozer blade and open fire.

Doon yelled for the teenager to jump, to take cover, but the scout couldn't hear. Bullets clanged on steel as the synthetic swore, grabbed a control lever, and dumped the boy on his ass.

A storm of incoming lead swept Bullet Eater's bow. Doon fired in return and watched the attack wither. It was over within seconds.

A fist pounded on the door. Doon looked, verified it was Kev, and allowed the youngster to enter. His face was flushed, blood smeared his cheek, and excitement filled his eyes. "Is Bolano okay? Tell him that bandits killed the poachers and took their places. They used children to board the other units."

"Yeah?" Doon inquired cynically. "And where were you while this was going on?"

Kev blushed and looked at his boots. "With a girl. She tried to stab me."

"Serves you right," Doon said unsympathetically. "Tell Bolano what you told me. I'm going out."

"I don't know," the youth said doubtfully. "You nailed 'em . . . but there's plenty more."

"*Good,*" the synthetic said grimly. "I'm counting on it."

Salls was disappointed. Disappointed but not desperate. What happened to the riders was unfortunate but far from disastrous. Especially in light of the fact that a number of the crawlers were hers, or would be, once the cutouts were disconnected.

The problem was to tempt the remaining pushers out of their nearly impregnable machines. Not an easy thing to do ... without the right kind of leverage. The bandit leader turned to an assistant. "Bring the woman. The rise looks good. Do it there."

The android crouched next to a massive track, used his sensors to scan for danger, and battled the rider. Sojo, or what remained of him, was adamant. "Your actions are inconsistent with our mission! Stop at once!"

"*Your* mission," Doon said, stalling for time. "You know—the one you refuse to tell me about." Three infrared blobs were visible, all headed for the rise.

"The mission is important," the rider replied sternly. "The future of the planet depends on it."

"Okay," the synthetic replied reasonably. "We'll save the planet in the morning ... *after* I deal with the bandits." Doon sprinted from one shadow to the next, weapon out, sensors on max.

"No," the ghost replied. "The mission will fail if you are injured or terminated. Return to the crawler at once." The rider clamped down on Doon's motor functions—and the android fought back. His basic and therefore overriding programming was that of a law enforcement officer in an emergency situation. The other entity resisted but was forced to capitulate.

At first Doon assumed the blobs were on the run ... but soon realized his mistake. They were going somewhere for the purpose of doing something. But what? Nothing good— that was for sure. He hurried to close the gap.

Casey was frightened, *very* frightened, and with good reason. Unit three's pusher had reported an intermittent warning light for the right rear power bearing. It could signal a worn bearing or a bad sensor. The technician, who had no desire to spend the next two days rolling around in the slush, was hoping for the latter, and was peering through an inspection hatch when the bandits shoved a gun into her back.

Now, with her boots skimming the ground, they were transporting her up a slope toward some sort of pole. It stood chest-high, and the upper end had been sharpened. Casey swiveled her head and looked for help. Most of the crawlers remained where they'd been, while others had been moved. Their lights glowed amber, their weapons probed the air, and bodies lay in drifts around them. At least some of her friends were safe—but what about the rest? What was happening?

The men came to a halt and lowered the tech to the ground. She jerked an arm free, tried to run, and was cuffed into place. A woman approached. She carried a drum-fed auto thrower in the crook of her arm. Her voice was calm. "Strip her naked. Hold her in place."

Casey struggled as they tore at her clothes. It made no difference. The men enjoyed their work.

Bolano jumped as the unexpected voice came over his radio. It was female and matter-of-fact. "My compliments to the Guild—and any of you who are still alive. There's no need to die. I respect valor and am willing to let you go. Take whatever supplies you need, and exit the crawlers. Refuse, and the woman dies."

The words "What woman?" had already formed on Bolano's lips when a battery-powered spot came on. Light splashed the top of a rise. The main onboard computer "saw" the light and zoomed in. The guild boss felt his stomach flip-flop. Casey!

The technician was naked. Her nipples were hard, and she couldn't stop shivering. The light was blinding, and fingers hurt her arms. Four men held her over the stake. The technician whimpered as the point touched the inside surface of a thigh. She imagined how it would feel as the piece of wood pushed its way through her anus and into her intestines. The bandits knew what she was thinking and laughed.

Salls brought the radio up to her lips. "That's the offer—take it or leave it. You have sixty seconds to decide."

Bolano sighed. If the choice was between Casey and the Guild, he'd take Casey any day of the week. Would the bandit keep her word, though? That was the problem.

• • •

Doon had debated the best method of approach. Straight ahead, and take the leader first? Or—and the second possibility seemed best—rescue Casey *before* the bandits could drop her. He moved with the slow, carefully calculated movements of a machine.

Casey was unaware that a sixth person was present until an arm slipped around her waist and people began to die. Two slugs apiece; that's what Doon's programming called for, so that's what they got. The noise was deafening.

Salls heard the first shot, turned, and saw a man fall. Where were the shots coming from? It took a moment to see the arm, realize its significance, and react.

The fourth man was dead, but still in the process of falling, when Doon threw Casey away. He didn't care where she landed as long as it was out of the line of fire. The woman had an auto thrower—and it was on the way.

With the surety of a computer, the synthetic *knew* he had missed the window. The bandit's weapon would come into alignment a fraction of a second before his did. Death would follow.

Sojo knew what would happen, and his screams were still ripping through Doon's mind when Kev stepped out of the darkness. The shotgun was short and ugly.

Salls caught the movement out of the corner of her eye and tried to respond. The teenager smiled and shook his head. The smoothbore roared, sparks stabbed the bandit's eyes, and she rode them away.

Doon helped Casey to her feet, found her parka, and draped it over her shoulders. Kev toed the woman's body and looked up. "Thought I told you to stay aboard," the android said mildly.

"Sorry," Kev said apologetically. "Guess I forgot."

It took the better part of three days to bury the dead, capture the murderous children, and send them west in company with a pack train. They wore chains and made a pitiful sight as they marched away. Most were orphans, and, if their stories were true, they had been trained by Salls.

The convoy had lost seventeen members of its crew, but

Vent lay sixty miles ahead. It boasted the Guild's eastern-most maintenance facility. Should they continue, or turn back?

Bolano decided to go for it. Kev and a second scout were promoted to pusher status, given some minimal training, and assigned to crawlers. The balance of the empty slots went to gunners and techs.

The crawlers rumbled toward the east. Snow drifted from the sky, filled their tracks, and threw a dirty gray shroud over the mass grave. Bullet Eater had been assigned to doze it . . . and Doon was proud of his work.

The synthetic had paid for the killings of the night before. Paid and paid and paid. Afterimages of their deaths still stuttered through his processor. Not a pleasant process. Still, given the fact that the violent images had driven Sojo's ghost into hiding, it was worth it.

The road turned downward and zigzagged back and forth as if reluctant to leave the mountains. Mary had a crawler of her own, which left Doon by himself—a condition he once regarded as normal . . . but not any more. Why? Because he missed her, that was why. Was that a sign of weakness? Or the sort of interdependence that humans took such perverse pride in? The hours unwound, the crawler followed the road, and machine rode machine.

Though not especially important prior to the Cleansing, the community of Vent had since come into its own, mainly because it marked the spot where the HZ stopped and the holy lands began. A rather profitable place to be.

Which was why the community was so well guarded. The convoy passed through no less than three different check-points prior to entering the actual city.

Centered around the volcanic vent from which it took its name, the community was a warren of tightly twisting streets, interconnected lava tubes, and free-form caverns.

The largest of these caverns was known as "Big Mama." The entrance had been carved to resemble a pair of human lips. It belonged to the Guild and served as a combination terminal, garage, and warehouse. Bolano passed Bullet Eater and led the convoy through the entrance. The guildsman veered to the right, led the convoy into a gently curving lane, and came to a halt.

The convoy, and its arrival, were something of an event. Hundreds of people drifted into the cavern until a crowd had formed. They were a motley-looking lot—human mostly with a scattering of heavily disguised synthetics and Zid renegades.

Doon lowered himself to the ground, looked for Mary, and sidled over. "So, here we are."

The roboticist nodded. She looked around, verified that no one was listening, and met his sensors. "How long must we stay? I'd like to leave as soon as possible."

The ghost had already started to whine about unnecessary delays when Doon shut him down. "Tomorrow. As early as possible. Assuming we get what we need."

Mary nodded, and the conversation ended as Bolano shouldered his way through the crowd. "Hey, you two! Good job. Secure your rigs and take the rest of the day off. We unload in the morning, load in the afternoon, and leave the next day. Here's a couple of vouchers. You can exchange them for Guild scrip. Have a good time."

They said thank you, checked their rigs, and went shopping. Crude signs pointed the way, but Mary figured the other pushers would lead them in the right direction, and she was right. They cut across Big Mama, detoured around a pile of heavily guarded cargo modules, and headed for a lava tube. Pushers were rich, by current standards anyway, so the group was besieged by every manner of vendor, pimp, and runner, all competing to be heard.

The synthetic remained unmoved, but Mary fell for a girl about Corley's age, purchased a meat-filled pastry, and ate it as they walked. She liked the taste, and that, plus the relatively balmy air, served to raise her spirits.

Doon smiled. "There's no telling *what* you're eating. Hope it didn't have a name."

Mary made a face. "Look who's talking. I'll bet you'd suck static electricity out of a Zid's armpit if your power was low."

Doon laughed. "You win! Bon appétit."

The vendors melted away as the pushers entered a lava

tube, followed it for a while, and arrived in the Vent equivalent of an indoor shopping mall.

Stores lined both sides of what the residents jokingly referred to as "the Scavenue," which consisted of a long, narrow gallery. Shops, bars, eateries, and worse stood shoulder to shoulder and vied for customers.

Doon perceived the business district as a combat range, complete with flashing threat icons, a target grid, and, in one case, a woman with an outstanding arrest warrant. His law enforcement programming urged the android to take the female into custody while Sojo threw a tantrum in the background. Doon managed to ignore both distractions.

Mary experienced her surroundings in a completely different way. Her eyes wallowed in color, her nose feasted on a rich mixture of smells, and sound filled her ears. It was horribly wonderful.

The rest of the pushers formed up in front of a bar called the Crawler's Rest and urged the twosome to join them. Both Doon and Mary were popular, but Doon was regarded with something approaching awe, especially after his heroism.

They made excuses, grinned at the intentionally crude jokes, and waved good-bye. "So?" Mary inquired. "What now?"

"Now we go shopping," the android replied seriously. "Consider your purchases carefully, because you won't get another chance. I recommend food, freeze-dried if we can find it, ammo for your pump gun, medical supplies if you're low, and two sets of cold-weather gear. The best available. Watch total weight though—and remember trade goods. We'll bribe 'em first and shoot 'em second."

Mary raised an eyebrow. "And what about you?"

Doon shrugged. "I don't need food, nor much of a wardrobe, but I'll take as much ammo as I can get, plus the tools and parts from your lab. If you'll let me, that is."

Mary nodded. She needed him . . . and he needed her. It was the best bargain either one of them was likely to get.

They located a place that sold expedition equipment, bought backpacks into which their belongings could be consolidated, and went to work. Their Guild pay, plus what they already had, would more than cover their needs. It was fun, and similar to a shopping spree, except for one thing: Their lives would depend on the things they purchased—and there would be little opportunity to buy anything more.

They rose early, checked their packs one last time, and left a note on *Bullet-Eater's* control panel:

Dear Pete,
Sorry to do this to you—but we're bailing out. Thanks for the ride.

Best Always,
Harley & Mary

People with parkas, packs, and weapons were a common sight in Vent, and no one noticed as they left through Big Mama's mouth and entered the predawn darkness. No one except a ragged-looking Zid beggar, that is. He watched the couple go, thanked them for the crudely cut coin that rattled into the bottom of his cup, and made a mental note. Two heretics, both armed with Satan's tools, were headed into the holy lands? Why?

The monks had a well-known appetite for information—and would welcome a tidbit such as this.

16

fa na´ tic, n, one showing excessive enthusiasm or zeal

The news that Dr. Gene Garrison had not only survived his artificially induced illness, but was planning to hold a staff meeting, shocked Abby Ahl. Especially since she had been assigned to kill the scientist—and thought the job was essentially done. Jantz would be angry.

Ahl remembered the way he made love to her, stabbing her vagina as if his penis was a knife and he wanted to hurt her.

Ahl felt the blood rush to her face, looked to find out if anyone had seen, and was thankful that no one had. The spy checked her wrist chron, rose from her desk, and left the office. She had a pistol in her quarters, and plenty of supplies. Enough to reach the Cathedral of the Rocks. The mission was over—or would be by the time the sun went down.

After months of uncertainty, fear, and doubt, Flat Top was coming back to life. The announcement that Garrison had ended his self-imposed isolation had reenergized most of the members of the organization. Bana Modo was no exception.

Though impressed by the quality of Garrison's mind, the biologist was well aware of the other man's failings, especially where leadership was concerned. Having ruled by strength of personality, and having undermined every person named to succeed him, the director had subverted his own creation.

Fiefdoms had been created during his absence, intrigue had flourished, and resources systematically misappropriated.

Now Garrison was back, much to the disgust of those who had profited, or hoped to profit.

Not Modo, though—he was the first person to enter the spartan auditorium, and he sat down front. Something good would happen. He could *feel* it.

Ahl's plan was simple: station herself outside Garrison's door, wait for the roboticist to emerge, and shoot him in the head. The very seat of the Devil's power—and the area most vulnerable. Where nano had failed, a bullet would succeed.

Agents such as herself, and the troops known as God's Reapers, were allowed to use firearms by special dispensation. But how to justify her presence? There were numerous possibilities, but Ahl chose the most ironic.

By placing her back to the wall, and standing at ease, she looked like a sentry. There to guard her leader against attack. The roboticist had refused such protection in the past—but that was the *old* Garrison, and the new one could have changed. Ahl nodded to passersby, and they nodded in return.

Garrison examined himself in the mirror. He still looked like hell . . . but what could someone of his advanced years expect? Even with a body full of hard-working nano. He laughed and turned away. He was what he was—and his staff would have to accept it.

Ahl felt her stomach somersault as a series of locks snicked open and the door swung inward. She pulled the weapon out from under her jacket and held it down along her leg.

Garrison appeared and stepped out into the hall. He smiled and nodded. Ahl was amazed. The roboticist looked wonderful! Much better than the last time he had appeared in public. How? But there was no time to consider unimportant things, so she raised the weapon, screamed, "Glory to God!" and squeezed the trigger. Not just once—but three times in quick succession. The weapon jumped, and the noise was deafening.

The scientist staggered under the impact of the bullets. His head came apart, and he hit the wall. Something was wrong though—something having to do with a lack of blood. That's when someone shouted, "Hold it right there!" and Ahl knew bad things were about to happen.

The Zid agent was turning, pulling the weapon around, when the bullets hit her. One clipped the woman's skull, another punctured her right lung, and a third cracked a shoulder blade. She fell across the roboticist's legs.

Voices shouted, hands rolled Ahl onto her back, and the assassin opened her eyes. The world was gray and filled with pain. She felt for the cross and found it slick with blood. Something loomed above. Garrison! Not the pretty version she had killed—but a haggard old man. The first Garrison had been a robot!

Garrison shook his head. "Nice try, honey . . . but people were trying to kill me before you were born. Must be my personality or something."

The face disappeared, but Ahl heard the words "Take her to the infirmary," and knew she wouldn't make it. This life was over—and the next hadn't started yet. Darkness rose all around. She waited for the light.

The auditorium was packed by the time Garrison arrived. Security beings and members of the senior team formed a wall around the scientist. The reason became apparent as Dr. Barbara Omita opened the meeting. She was a tiny woman with a pageboy haircut and an earnest expression.

"Good morning, everyone . . . .Thank you for coming. I'm thrilled to announce that our director, Dr. Gene Garrison, has recovered from his debilitating illness and returned to work.

Pardon our late arrival—but there was an attempt on his life."

There was a hiss of indrawn air followed by expressions of disbelief and concern.

Omita was about to say more when Garrison took the mike. His smile would have been more reassuring had his face been a little less gaunt. "It would seem that our current grievance process leaves something to be desired."

There was a roar of laughter followed by a lessening of tension. Bana Modo was entranced by the nearly mythical presence—especially in light of their correspondence.

Garrison looked out at his audience, marshaled his thoughts, and allowed the words to flow. "This facility was built in order to insulate our work from the political chaos that followed the landing, and yes, as a monument to my own considerable ego."

There were titters, but no outright laughter, a sure sign that at least some of the audience agreed.

"Whatever the reason," Garrison continued, "the fact remains that Flat Top was built and, as luck would have it, completed *before* the troubles began.

The audience shifted uneasily. Eyebrows were raised. Did Garrison have a point? And if so, what was it? The roboticist continued.

"The beings we refer to as the Forerunners constructed this planet from the inside out, installed a self-perpetuating, nano-based maintenance structure, and for reasons unknown, left all of it behind."

Some of the staff members were stunned by the sweep of what the director had said. Others were openly contemptuous. Garrison ignored them.

"The system I refer to controls what may turn out to be a fusion reactor at the planet's core—as well as geological mechanics that mimic those of more natural planets. That includes the recent seismic activity and the atmospheric changes that stem from it.

"That's why the ecology is so simple, why there are no native microorganisms, and why Zuul will die. It is my thesis that both Mothri and human nano have systematically attacked and killed their Forerunner counterparts as part of a misguided attempt to dominate Zuul's robotic infrastructure. The situation continues to deteriorate. Barring the unexpected arrival of a ship, there is no means of escape.

"The solution is obvious. We must prepare a complete inventory of Forerunner nano, identify those that have suffered the most predation, create attack-resistant strains, and introduce them into the planet's geological and biological systems.

"We must do this quickly, efficiently, and in the face of organized resistance from the Zid. There is no alternative other than death."

Garrison paused, and the room exploded into chaos. Questions were shouted, objections were heard, and at least one staff member burst into tears.

Garrison turned to one of his bodyguards, took her weapon, and fired three shots into the ceiling. The babble stopped. The roboticist smiled. "That was the *bad* news. There is some *good* news. Many of you, people like Bana Modo, have been working on a solution for some time now. The task of classifying and redesigning the Forerunner nano is already underway. These efforts will shift into high gear as we devote more resources to them.

"An additional piece of good news is the fact that the Mothri share our concerns . . . and are open to an alliance."

Modo flushed at the mention of his name and felt heads swivel in his direction. Some admired him. Others, their work unrecognized, started to fume.

It took the better part of three hours to work through initial discussions, name team leaders, and launch "Project Zuul."

Garrison was exhausted by the time the meeting was over and was glad to reach his quarters. The body was gone, but a bloodstain marked the floor. A maintenance droid whirred as it scrubbed Ahl away.

The roboticist thanked his security detail, knew they would remain on guard, and entered his apartment. The bed beckoned, and he fell across it. The presentation had gone well, very well, but problems remained.

The first had to do with the fact that a high percentage of Forerunner nano appeared to be extinct—and the second had to do with translation software. Software that would bridge the gap between the language the Forerunners had used to program their nano and human-derived code.

The latter was of particular concern since he had lost contact with the being best equipped to solve the problem, a brilliant but somewhat idealistic synthetic who had chosen the name Luis Garcia Sojo.

In fact, much as the roboticist hated to admit it, and *wouldn't* admit it, not publicly at least, the possibility of a nano-dependent planetary maintenance system had been Sojo's idea, not his.

The truth was that instead of supporting his student, and taking pleasure in what he'd been able to accomplish, Garrison had been jealous instead. The human had accused the synthetic of sloppy science, had questioned his motives, and driven a wedge into their relationship. Even now, during the meeting, he had failed to acknowledge the synthetic's contribution.

Where was Sojo, anyway? Hiding somewhere, his talents going to waste? Or dead? His body parts incorporated into a Zid shrine? Garrison heard himself moan as the full weight of his guilt pressed down on his chest.

Servos whined as a robot appeared at Garrison's bedside, sent a radio message to the nano that cruised the human's bloodstream, and pulled a blanket over the scientist's skeletal body. An internally administered sedative would help, as would some antidepressants.

The roboticist fell asleep, and the machine settled in to wait. Something that it, like all its brethren, did very well indeed.

cru sade´, n, a war or expedition having a religious
object and sanctioned by the church

The Cathedral of the Rocks was huge. So huge that it was
third behind only the *Pilgrim* and the Forerunner city known
as Maze in terms of overall size. It had four extensions, all
of which were triangular in shape and joined to the base.
Together they formed a star. The *single* star, insofar as the
Zid hierarchy was concerned.

Built of limestone, with donated labor, the structure had
been sited on top of a hill where it would dominate the city
below. Outcroppings of volcanic rock surrounded the cathedral and accounted for its name.

Due to the fact that the Zid had brought their traditional
religious calendar with them, and made use of it without
regard to Zuul's orbit around the sun, there was no particular
connection between it and the seasons.

Members, and that included everyone, were expected to
worship every day of the week, but Six-Days were especially
important, and considered mandatory.

Dr. Suti Canova thought there was something fascinating

about the weekly spectacle, about looking out upon hundreds of Zid faces, their features registering emotions—but which ones? Did gill-fluttering signify distress? Was mouth-rippling equivalent to a smile? She thought so, but couldn't be sure. Still, she could *feel* their hatred, and was certain that it could be seen in their implacable stares.

Of course, that was the whole purpose of a living altar: to provide the congregation with a focal point for their hate— an emotion around which the entire organization had been encouraged to coalesce.

Viewed from that perspective, the alien landings had been the best things that ever happened to the Antitechnic Church. Left on its own, without an external threat to reinforce the need for unity, the organization had already started to wither. The arrival of first the Mothri, then the humans, gave the Zid something to hate. And hatred held their theocracy together.

Interestingly enough, the same phenomenon had been observed in human history—which seemed to suggest a higher than expected level of psychocultural commonality between the Zid and human races. Or did it? To what extent were the local Zid representative of the race that had marooned them on Zuul? They were self-proclaimed cultural deviants—and to generalize from their activities to the rest of Zid might be a mistake.

Fascinating stuff—especially for Canova's peers. Not that the medical doctor and amateur xenoanthropologist was likely to share her findings—since she'd been co-opted by the very structure she sought to understand.

The model twenty had actually set out to study the Mothri, a somewhat safer line of inquiry, when a scav known as the Junkman had captured and sold her. Canova had begged the human to kill her, to settle for what her body parts would bring, but he refused. The synthetic wondered how the scav was doing and hoped for the worst.

Corley Maras hated Six-Day with every bone in her ten-year-old body. But that was a secret, a very important secret, and one that she must never reveal. First because she was human, and humans were automatically suspect, and second because her father was none other than George Maras, Administrator General for the Antitechnic Church, and a very important personage.

It was an influential position, one that guaranteed plenty to eat, and a nice place to live, but forced Corley to tell lies, a *lot* of lies, which her father said was okay, but her mother would never have approved of.

That's why Corley smiled as her father led her into the much-hated cathedral—and toward the Devil's altar. Not the second, third, or fourth altars, one for each point of the star, but the *main* altar, where the top members of the hierarchy paused before making their way down the central aisle to take their places before the *true* altar, from which a long, boring sermon would soon be delivered.

George Maras nodded to members of the council, and knew that his superior, a human named Victor Jantz, would wait to make an entrance. One more seemingly insignificant note in a symphony of moves calculated to undermine Zid leadership.

Not an effort that Maras had *intended* to become part of, but one he had fallen into, and continued to support as the means to protect Corley. After all, most of the humans resident in the holy lands during the Cleansing had been killed by rampaging mobs, subjected to the inquisition, or turned out to starve.

Only the fact that Maras had converted early and demonstrated the value of nontechnological management practices had protected father and daughter from sharing similar fates.

That's what Maras told himself, anyway, although there was a part of him, a seldom-heard voice, that questioned his motives. Had he come to enjoy power for power's sake? And what about the perks that went with it? The questions surfaced . . . but went unanswered.

Seats had been saved for Maras and his daughter. He genuflected in front of the altar and backed into his chair. Corley did likewise. The contemplation of evil, and the threat it represented, was a necessary prerequisite to serious worship.

The little girl checked the altar to see if anything had changed. It was carved from a huge chunk of glistening clay that was never allowed to harden—a strategy that allowed the altar keepers to change the display by adding or removing components. A hand here, a circuit board here, and lots of randomly connected metal, wire, and plastic.

One thing *never* changed, however, and that was the eyes that stared down at her, and the face they were part of. It reminded her of the Madonna—as seen in the media player she no longer had. Corley's mother was a roboticist, and the little girl had grown up around such machines, so she knew the synthetic was a model twenty that possessed a brain, personality and emotions every bit as real as hers. That's what her mother said, and Corley believed it.

The only problem was that the Church said androids were evil, and even though Corley didn't want to believe that, it was hard to ignore what they said.

The synthetic winked at her, and Corley turned to her father. He had a vacant expression and was clearly unaware. Corley looked left, right, and back again. No one seemed to be watching. It was a daring thing to do, but the little girl met the android's gaze and winked in return.

Canova collected the wink in the same way that a glutton might accept an especially tasty dish, with a sort of greedy intensity. She wanted more. *More* contact, *more* interchange, and *more* stimulation. For the android, like her creators, was a social being.

There was no chance of that, however, as the Maras family rose to make way for the newly arrived, who made their way down toward the center of the cathedral, and took the next set of seats reserved for their exclusive use.

Victor Jantz, easily the third most important being in the Antitechnic Church, and quite possibly the second, examined himself before a mirror. He was a handsome man with large eyes, a long straight nose, and a firm jaw. All of which meant nothing to the Zid. They thought *all* humans were ugly.

Jantz was rugged, though, and physically powerful, which the T-heads admired. The human laughed out loud. If only they knew! Robotics, the technology they loved to hate, was only one of the ways through which sentients could leverage their abilities. There was genetic engineering to consider, along with his own personal favorite, medical science.

Yeah, the T-heads could scan his body all day long and never discover the truth, which was that his overall musculature had been enhanced with drugs, his right leg had been grown in a lab, his left kidney had been "harvested" from an accident victim, and nano, far too small to see, kept his pipes in good repair. So far, anyway. Just one of the reasons why he never seemed to age.

Jantz smiled at the image in front of him, and it smiled in return. Life, which was undeniably good, would soon get better. First things first, however . . . which meant a fire-and-brimstone sermon. A sermon similar to the ones his pa liked to deliver, back before he beat the crap out of his son one too many times and went to an early grave.

The authorities never suspected the fifteen-year-old boy. Not given the attacker's obvious strength and the almost unbelievable violence with which the murder was carried out. It was strange how as the years had passed, Jantz had failed at every profession he tried, *except* the least likely of all: man of God.

The religious leader straightened his robe, plastered a stern look on his face, and left the office. The underground corridor led past the armory, past the Zid powered altar mechanism, and past the holding cells. The heretics, one of whom was human, rattled their bars and begged for mercy. Jantz, his mind on other things, didn't hear a sound.

The cathedral was not only huge, but extremely complex, containing a labyrinth of rooms, chapels, halls, and cells for the resident monks and priests. Woven in and around those many compartments were countless halls, corridors, stairs, and walkways some of which were secret and known to a very few.

Narly Lictor was one of those few, and used the little-traveled passageways for his own purposes, watching through spy holes, listening to conversations he wasn't supposed to hear, and "appearing" as if by magic when it suited his purposes to do so.

It was boring for the most part, but there were moments when the vigils paid off, when he found out something others thought was secret, and hoarded that knowledge against the time when it could best be used. For even God's instrument in the physical world can use an edge once in awhile. Especially if he wanted to retain control—which Lictor definitely did.

All of which explained why the Chosen One was there, watching through a peephole while Jantz examined himself in the mirror, smiled, and left the room. Never mind the mirror, which signaled the human's vanity—why had his strangely horizontal mouth curved upward in the human equivalent of a smile? Because he was happy with his appearance? Or because of something else? Something Lictor wouldn't like.

The decision to include humans within the Church hierarchy had seemed logical at the time, especially given the number of alien converts streaming in from the HZ, but now he had started to wonder. Did the humans want to *join* the Church? Or take it over? That was a troubling thought.

Maras watched Jantz emerge from the circular opening in front of the altar, bow to the congregation, and climb the stairs that led to the podium. There was a creaking sound as the entire altar started to rotate. The shaft, gears, and other components involved were all made of wood, and allowed by a special dispensation from the council.

Maras, like the officials seated around him, had witnessed the phenomenon many times before, but a group of pilgrims, just arrived from distant villages, sucked air through their gills. It made a whistling sound. The altar really did rotate! Just like everyone said. . . . Still another wonder to report on their return.

Jantz opened the book of rotes to a beautifully illuminated page, cleared his throat portentously, and started to read. Not in Spanglish, sometimes referred to as standard, but in the Zid dialect used by most members of the Church. A human who spoke Zid! The pilgrims looked at each other in amazement.

Jantz, who had a near photographic memory, as well as a natural ear for language, didn't especially like the tongue but understood the value of speaking it.

The human wondered if the master language from which the dialect had been taken was equally drab, or more vibrant, belonging as it did to beings who had space flight *and* the common sense to unload their troublemakers on remote planets. It was an errant thought, and he pushed it away.

The sermon was a back-to-basics sort of thing, a way to refocus the congregation on fundamentals while positioning himself as a true rote-spewing, rock-throwing, fire-breathing zealot.

Jantz started with the book of rotes, reviewed the appropriate scripture, and launched into a sermon titled ''The Three Faces of the Devil.''

The faces included *heresy,* or the failure to believe, *subversion,* the very thing he hoped to accomplish, and *idolatry,* which referred to the worship of physical objects, most especially robots, but also including a wide variety of icons, tools, and art.

It was good stuff, but somewhat basic, and therefore dry. Which was why Jantz had made arrangements to liven things up. ''And so,'' he said, the audience turning before him, ''the first face is that of heresy.''

The Zid, a none too bright specimen that had been caught relieving himself against one of the cathedral's walls, was pushed up a ramp. Guards, well aware of what was about to take place, grabbed the unfortunate and held him in place. He started to whine but stopped in response to a well-directed blow.

''Look well,'' Jantz cautioned the audience, ''for the Devil is a master of disguise. A face such as this one might appear anywhere. You could encounter it on the street, in church, or, most terrifying of all, on the other side of the dinner table.''

Canova had zoomed in on the Zid's face. She listened to the words, guessed what was coming, and dumped her sensory input. She had witnessed such moments before, and felt no desire to do so again.

''There is,'' Jantz intoned solemnly, ''only one solution. Find heresy wherever it may dwell . . . and destroy its home.''

The hammer of divine justice had been brought all the way

from the home world. It was hundreds of years old and consisted of an oblong stone tied to a wooden shaft with leather thongs. It blurred through the air, struck the heretic's head, and spilled his brains onto the floor. His body followed.

Corley, who had seen even worse things, remained unmoved. Her father had trained her to look—but see something else. She thought of Hairball and smiled.

A pilgrim, just arrived from the tiny village of Tithe, lost her breakfast. Most of the crowd strove for a better view. They loved the drama of it—and would exaggerate the gore when they got back home.

It was important to appear evenhanded. Jantz nodded to the executioner, and a human stumbled out onto the floor. His wrists were tied, and a gag split his mouth. He saw the body and started to cry. His crime, the *real* crime, was spying for the Chosen One. The traitor's death would not only seal his treacherous lips, but send a message to Lictor as well. All under the cover of righteous piety.

"This," Jantz announced, "is the face of subversion. Study it well. The man before you slandered our glorious leader in hopes of pulling him down."

Lictor, who had chosen to monitor his subordinate's sermon from a peephole high overhead, winced as the hammer hit the alien's skull, and watched his informer die. *Had* the idiot slandered him? Or was this something more ominous? A message, perhaps . . . a rather gruesome message meant to intimidate him. There was no way to be sure. The blood ran down a limestone gutter, gurgled through a hole in the floor, and dripped into the catch basin below.

"And finally," Jantz said, "an idolator who valued a piece of metal before her God, and must now pay the price."

The female Zid stumbled, fell, and was pulled to her feet. Something, Maras wasn't sure what, hung around her neck. Then she turned, the light hit the object, and he recognized the artifact for what it was: a half-meter com dish, worthless without the equipment necessary to make it work, and best put to use as a large soup bowl.

There was no way to know where the female had obtained the device, or why she'd been foolish enough to keep it, but she had. He wanted to shield Corley from the execution—

but knew he couldn't. Not if he wanted to maintain his heretofore pious image.

The executioner raised the bloodstained hammer. The female swayed and suddenly collapsed. The com dish clanged as it hit the floor. A monk checked her pulse, confirmed she was dead, and signaled the podium. The idolater had died of fright.

Certain that he'd made his point, and eager to get the whole thing over with, Jantz brought the service to a close.

Lictor waited for the last dola to be said, sketched a triangle into the air, and made for his quarters. That's where the next battle would be fought—and that's where he would win.

The service was over and icy rain drove in from the north as the congregation streamed out through the massive doors and down toward the city below. It was laid out on a grid, with each citizen receiving a rectangular plot of land on which they had constructed huts, which if not identical, were so similar that they might as well have been, especially from a distance. The cook fires were banked but still sent hundreds of smoky tendrils skyward, where they seemed to seek each other out, and wove intricate patterns against the sky. Lamps would be lit as the parishioners returned home, a meal would be prepared, and the evening would be spent at rest.

George Maras waited till most of the congregation had left the cathedral, then stood. He turned toward his daughter. "Daddy must attend a meeting. Will you be okay?"

Corley nodded. Waiting was bad enough. Waiting *within* the meeting, where she would be expected to sit absolutely still, was the most horrible possibility of all. This would give her a chance to explore—an opportunity that came all too seldom.

Maras smiled, patted his daughter on the head, and ordered her to stay within the nave. The cathedral was huge, and he didn't want to spend hours looking for her.

A pair of Lictor's guards, both equipped with battle axes, appeared at his side. They offered a hood, which he accepted and slid over his head. A drawstring secured the bottom around his neck.

No one, not even Jantz, knew the exact location of the Chosen One's quarters, and they weren't about to learn. Maras viewed the procedure as little more than an annoying security precaution.

Jantz was more cynical, and wondered if Lictor used the ritual as a way to bolster his importance.

Corley watched her father being led away, shrugged, and set off on her own. The little girl knew better than to make a beeline for that which interested her most. No, the safest thing to do was to wander the way any child might, touching all the things she never got to touch, and winding up at the Devil's altar seemingly by accident.

Once she was in position, a show of piety was called for should anyone be looking. Corley knelt, stood, and backed into the closest chair. There was no doubt in her mind that the altar, and the android it contained, were the most fascinating elements of the Church.

Dr. Suti Canova had been resting, fantasizing about freedom, when she heard the rustle of cloth. She opened her sensors half expecting to see one or more members of the cleanup crew, a mostly half-witted bunch who delighted in finding new ways to torment her. The girl was an unexpected treat. She had closely cropped black hair, rich brown skin, and large, luminous eyes.

The android activated all of her sensors, scanned the nave, and came up empty. If they were under surveillance, it was beyond her ability to detect. "Hi. Nice to see you again."

Corley nodded solemnly. "I'm sorry about what they did to you."

Canova raised an artificial eyebrow. "You know what I am?"

"Oh, yes," the little girl answered brightly. "You're an android. A model twenty. You can think and feel just like we do. That's why I'm sorry."

"Thank you," Canova said. "It's been a long time since anyone said anything nice to me."

"Do you have a body?" Corley asked politely. "Or just a head?"

Canova laughed. "Yes, I have a body, but it's hidden under the clay. They reveal parts of it from time to time—but never enough for me to break free.''

''That's too bad,'' Corley said thoughtfully. ''I could free you, but it wouldn't make any difference. They'd catch you and smash my head open.''

Canova winced at the thought. ''No, you musn't do that. It isn't worth it. There is something you *could* do for me, though—not now, but later.''

Corley folded her hands as if in prayer. ''Really? Such as what?''

''You could kill me,'' the android replied softly.

''Would you go to heaven?'' Corley asked. ''Mommy says it's nice in heaven.''

Canova didn't think there was a heaven—not for robots, anyway. The nothingness of electronic death would suit her fine. She smiled. ''Yes, I would go to heaven. With your help.''

The little girl might have replied, might have given the android reason to hope, but a monk chose that particular moment to appear. He was a kindly soul and, seeing Corley all alone, hurried to keep her company. ''Goodness, child! You look starved! Come. I have some sweet cakes hidden in the vestry.''

Corley rose obediently, allowed her eyes to brush past Canova's, and took the monk's hand. They turned and walked away.

Had either of them turned, they would have seen a tear trickle down the android's face, and wet the clay below.

With an escort at each elbow, Maras was led through an interminable number of twists and turns. He tried to memorize them at first, just to see if he could, but soon lost track.

As in the past, Maras knew when he had arrived by the strong odor of incense. It smelled of sulfur. Did the ritual have religious significance? Or was it little more than a personal quirk? There was no way to tell.

Hinges squealed, Maras felt carpeting under his feet, and the hood was removed. Jantz was already present, and he bowed with the gravity of someone under observation. ''Greetings, Administrator Maras—you're looking well.''

"As are you," Maras replied. He bowed, wondered if they were under observation via peepholes in the austere walls, and guessed they probably were. He started to say something, saw the beginnings of a frown on his superior's forehead, and thought better of it.

A human might have kept them waiting as a way to demonstrate his or her power, but the Zid had other ways of accomplishing that. Lictor entered the room from his private quarters, bowed, and took his seat. It was made of wood and, with the exception of the intricately carved arms, was free of adornment. It had a thronelike aspect, however, or so it seemed to the humans, who were left to stand.

Lictor was middle-aged, young for his position, and extremely good-looking. That's what other Zid claimed, anyway, although it could have been out of respect or outright fear. The Chosen One wore a caste mark on his forehead and spoke heavily accented Spanglish. Not that Maras was in a position to be critical, since he spoke very little Zid. A deficiency he continued to work on.

"Thank you for coming. Your piety, righteousness, and zeal do you credit."

So much for openers, Maras thought to himself. The bad stuff is on the way. He let his eyes go to Jantz, but saw the other man's face was blank.

"The Cleansing was God's way of helping us with our work," Lictor continued. "It was no accident that our membership suffered fewer casualties than the heretics did."

Lictor was a skilled communicator, and Maras admired the manner in which the word "heretics" had been exchanged for "aliens." Neither of the humans believed Lictor had access to God, but both murmured their agreement.

"Now comes the next stage," Lictor said, his words barely intelligible. "The stage during which we must *finish* what God started. A considerable amount of progress has been made. Our monks have entered the heretic cities, identified those who seek God's peace, and put others to death. These things are good . . . but much remains undone."

"Give us God's vision," Jantz asked respectfully, "that we might bring it to life."

" 'God has natural dominion over *all* things,' " Lictor

said, quoting the book of rotes. " 'He rules the Zid, the animals of the field, and the plants from which sustenance flows.'

"To deny him is to deny life itself, which is why heretics must be sought out, brought into the light, or consigned to darkness. I submit that the day of reckoning is upon us, that we must go forth, find those who seek the light and bring them home."

"And the rest?" Jantz asked quietly.

"The rest will perish," Lictor replied evenly, "not by our hand, but by the hand that guides us."

Lictor knew what that meant, as did Maras, but enjoyed forcing the Zid to be explicit. "So you want us to identify the heretics and kill them."

The ensuing moment of silence drew long and thin. The time came when Maras concluded that his superior had gone *too* far, and he was already thinking of ways to distance himself from Jantz when Lictor spoke. The words were even and belied none of the anger that Maras saw in the single glaring eye. "Yes, that's exactly what I mean."

Jantz bowed. "Then it shall be as you say. How should we proceed?"

It was intended to be a pro forma question to which Lictor would respond with a request for recommendations. Recommendations that Jantz would use to further his interests.

The Zid had anticipated such a move, however, and not only formulated his own plan, but cleared it with the Council of Elders. That group opposed the ordination of human priests and consistently urged Lictor to assert his God-given authority.

Yes, Lictor knew what he wanted the humans to do . . . and how he wanted them to do it. The key was to present the information in a way calculated to gain their enthusiastic support, while lulling them to sleep regarding the long-range implications of their actions. Or, barring that, to gain minimal compliance and move ahead anyway.

In spite of the fact that the human was shrewd in his own self-concerned way, and useful where administrative matters were concerned, Lictor knew Maras was little more than a tool. A tool anyone could have and use.

Jantz was dangerous, however, *very* dangerous, and the person on whom his energies should be focused. That being the case, he adjusted his expression to convey warmth and collegiality, confident in the knowledge that the human had equipped himself with an extensive knowledge of Zid facial expressions.

"You may recall that I am a student of human history, and having read many of the texts translated by the humans within our membership, have identified an ancient practice that's perfect for our situation."

Jantz had been unaware of the Zid's studies and didn't like the idea one bit. The more the religious leader knew about humans and their not very admirable history, the more suspicious he was likely to be. Jantz couldn't say *that*, however, so he bowed instead. "We are both surprised and gratified that the Chosen One could find anything of value in our tumultuous history."

"You are far too modest," Lictor said, sending a smile down his lips. "Though misinformed regarding the nature and identity of God, your ancestors had some wonderful ideas, not the least of which were the Crusades."

Though of lower rank than Jantz, Maras had the better education and knew something about history. The Crusades had originally been armed pilgrimages. In fact, the word "crusade," had its origins in the Latin word "crux," or "cross." When the Arab Muslims conquered Palestine, which included numerous locations sacred to Christians, the Christians responded with a series of eight military expeditions between the years A.D. 1096 and 1270. These Crusades included kings, nobles, and thousands of peasants. They had two goals—to gain permanent control of the holy lands, and to protect the Byzantine Empire with which they were aligned.

The Christians *did* gain control of the holy lands for a time, but they were ultimately unable to hold onto the territory and were eventually forced out.

Jantz, though less knowledgeable than Maras, had a rough idea of what the Crusades involved and was struck by the brilliance of the Zid's plan. By launching a crusade, Lictor could not only focus the membership on something external to the Church, the ongoing crop failures, and the steadily dwindling food reserves—he could harness the energy of his zealots, a rather dangerous group if left unoccupied for sustained periods of time.

The slaughter of heretics, and the possible loss of his human followers, especially those in leadership positions, was icing on the cake. Or was that too paranoid? It hardly mattered. It could be true . . . which meant Jantz should assume that it was. He chose his words with care.

"It's a brilliant plan . . . a truly brilliant plan. One question, however—the Crusades had a goal, something we lack. How will we generate sufficient support?"

"Not a problem," Lictor replied, happy to see his subordinate's obvious discomfort. "We *do* have a goal—and a worthy one at that."

Silence begged the question. Jantz remained silent, so Maras did it for him. "What is God's will, Father? The Mothri? The settlement called Shipdown?"

"No," Lictor answered. "Lay the necessary plans, send raiders to prepare the way, and summon the faithful. Once the crusaders are assembled, you must fill them with fire, arm them with the word of God, and send them to the place called Flat Top. *That's* where the Devil does his work, where his demons hatch plots against the Church, and where the blow must be struck."

Maras looked at Jantz, saw the other man's eyes narrow, and watched him bend at the waist. "The Chosen One has spoken. God's will be done. Dola."

18

sam´ ple, n, a part or piece taken or shown as representative of a whole group

The chamber was dim, so much so that the only illumination came from the phosphorescentlike glow of the off-world fungus that grew on the ceiling, the light-emitting diodes located at the center of each robot's forehead, and the Mothri's abdominal work-light.

Mallaca Horbo Drula Enore the 5,223rd stood at the foot of the ramp and watched a seemingly endless procession of six-legged machines enter the chamber, disgorge exactly three droks of class three pack dirt, and return for more.

Additional robots attacked the recently regurgitated offerings and pushed, shoved, and shaped them into a steadily growing ramp. A ramp wide enough and strong enough to support the Mothri's considerable weight. She hadn't been to the surface for many months now, and had mixed emotions about the need to go there.

Just as a human might be excited about the prospect of living in an underwater habitat, yet have qualms as well, Enore had similar feelings about the planet's surface.

Enore knew the impulse toward adventure was nothing to be proud of, especially in light of the fact that it ran counter to her biological purpose, but there it was. Not something she planned to admit to Rota, Zenth, Tortna or Huubath, all of whom regarded the humans with well-founded suspicion— and weren't about to leave the relative safety of *their* tunnels.

Work slackened suddenly. Enore directed a burst of static toward her workers, and watched them sort themselves out. It had taken time to push the necessary relay stations south, make contact with the humans, perfect the necessary translation protocols, and begin negotiations.

In spite of the fact that the race had proved itself generally unreliable, the individuals who dwelt at the Mountain That Is Flat were quick to see the value of scientific collaboration—and had gone so far as to share their working hypothesis: Zuul was an artificial world, which, though relatively normal in outward appearance, had been constructed through the use of highly advanced microrobotic technology. Now, as the result of predation by Mothri and human nano, the planet was coming apart.

It made sense, to Enore anyway, though her peers were a good deal more skeptical. Not that their skepticism made much difference, since eggs were involved, and anything that could be done to safeguard the precious containers *would* be done, even if it seemed silly. All of which explained why the group had authorized her unprecedented trip.

The ramp was complete. A team of diggers made their way to the top, gobbled huge bites of soil, and ate their way toward the surface. The work went quickly, a pinpoint of light appeared, and Enore dispatched a heavily armed security team to reconnoiter.

Yes, the odds that invaders were waiting just outside were virtually nil, but security was of the utmost importance. Especially since the Mothri would be gone for weeks if not months—leaving tenders to protect her eggs. A situation that generated feelings of guilt. Guilt which the Mothri countered by remembering that *if* the humans were correct, *if* the planet was falling apart, every single egg was at risk.

The security bots gave the all clear, Enore issued some last-minute instructions, and attacked the slope. Dirt avalanched, the ramp accepted her weight, and the Mothri moved upward.

Ned had responsibilities, or believed that he did, and took them seriously. That's why he left the comparative comfort of his cave every eighth day to conduct his tour.

There were ruins to visit, where voices spoke from within solid walls; the cache, where Annie left food; and what he thought of as the bug farm, where his daughter appeared to him. Not every time he went there, but often enough that he continued to go back, listening should she care to speak.

The hermit scanned the clearing ahead, saw no reason for concern, and moved to the right. By staying with the trees and following them around, he would avoid the open space.

"It takes longer that way—but the long way is the safe way—and the safe way is the best way—and the best way is *my* way." The words made a ditty, a nice little ditty, and the hermit hummed it under his breath.

Ned was tall and thin. Each time he acquired a new set of clothes, he put them next to his eternally filthy skin, moved the next garments to the middle position, and allowed the outer layer to rot. The effect was to leave him dressed in layers of dark gray rags, which, though something less than attractive, made for excellent camouflage.

Moving carefully, like mist in human form, the hermit ghosted along the edge of the forest, found the robots' trail, and followed it toward their subterranean complex. They knew him by now, and never interfered. Not unless he ventured onto the flat area. That's when the machines would turn Ned back. Annie swore she'd been there, and Becka too, but he didn't believe them.

No one made use of the footpath except Ned, so it was hard to see, especially when covered by newly fallen snow, but the hermit had acquainted himself with each rock and tree, and knew when to turn.

The slope led to the top of a small knoll that offered a view of the area below. It was unnaturally flat and punctuated by cylindrical air shafts. Ned had no more than arrived, and settled onto his favorite rock, when the ground started to boil. That's the way it looked, anyway, as Mothri robots ate their

way up and out of the repository. It was an amazing sight—
and the human watched with slack-jawed fascination as an
enormous hole appeared.

There was a pause as three insectoid heads appeared and
scanned the area for anything that could threaten their five-
ton mistress. Then, with servos whining and antennae waving, an entire squad of the creatures scuttled up out of the
tunnel and assumed defensive postures.

Ned blinked and wondered if the machines were real or
one of the dreams that were woven into his days. He was
still watching, still wondering, when a pearly gray head appeared at the exact center of the newly created hole. It was
huge, easily as large as the machines assigned to protect it,
and equipped with equally massive mandibles. The head
turned from side to side, paused, and withdrew.

Thirty seconds passed, enough time for Ned to conclude
that the show was over, and ready himself to leave. He had
stood, and was backing away, when the ground seemed to
explode.

The tunnel had been kept intentionally narrow so that invaders if any would be forced to attack in columns of twos
or threes. Rather than wait for the diggers to enlarge the
passageway, Enore elected to charge up the ramp and force
her way through. Dirt crumbled under the weight of her assault, exploded outward, and sprayed across the snow. It was
still settling as she emerged.

Ned was transfixed. He watched in open mouthed amazement as the behemoth lumbered out onto the flat area followed by a steady stream of robots. Most had eight legs, but
four looked like centipedes and were laden with heavy packs.
Most of the machines formed a column of twos and marched
toward the south.

It was then, after most of her escorts were gone, and the
diggers were closing the hole, that Enore issued last-minute
instructions, and hoped that her decision had been the correct
one. The egg tenders knew what to do, and would do it—
for years if necessary.

But what if something went wrong? Something the robots
weren't equipped to handle? Then I wouldn't have been able
to handle it either, Enore told herself, remembering other

Mothri who had been crushed to death within their own tunnels. Still, it took an act of will to turn her back and lumber away. The rear guard, which consisted of twelve heavily armed robots, followed.

Ned, who had no idea what to make of the sudden exodus, shook his head in amazement as he watched them leave. This was the most amazing batch of hallucinations he'd ever had. The hermit chuckled, skidded down the slope, and resumed his rounds. The ruins lay a few miles to the north—and the voices were waiting.

With scouts crisscrossing the country ahead, flankers protecting her sides, and a rapid-response force bringing up the rear, Enore set forth on her journey.

Given the need for speed, the size of her body, and the nature of her escort, there was no way to go unnoticed. That being the case, the Mothri ordered her scouts to pursue a route that would allow her to stop at select locations while using the least amount of time.

In spite of the fact that thousands of Forerunner nano types had apparently been driven to extinction by their alien counterparts, the humans offered one last hope.

A scientist named Bana Modo theorized that at least some of the seemingly dead species might continue to exist within tech-free Zid villages. If so, they were likely to be intact, since there was nothing there to harm them.

If Enore could capture samples of such nano, and *if* she could transport them south, efforts would be made to duplicate them. A vital first step toward manufacturing strains that could not only survive alien attack, but reverse Zuul's deterioration. That was why certain kinds of equipment had been loaded onto the centipedelike freight bots, and why the column suddenly veered away from its natural path and headed toward the east.

Father Haslo called for a moment of individual reflection and looked out on the congregation. Something bothered him about the village of Piety, but he couldn't decide what. Or could he?

What with the weather, the ever-dwindling food stocks,

and the ever increasing tithes, most of his parishioners were increasingly thin. He had witnessed the phenomenon in the communities of Charity, Truth, and Hope.

Now, as he visited the fourth and final town on his circuit, the elders looked plump, verging on fat. Pomo was an excellent example. How could that be? Unless the Devil was about—which was all too likely. Yes, despite the congregation's ragged clothes and seemingly pious ways, something was amiss. He would say as much in his next report. There was nothing like a visit from the inquisition to put a village back on the path.

Haslo murmured the usual prayer. Heads came up, and eyes met his. The priest could practically *see* their hypocrisy and felt his gills start to flutter. He brought the reaction under control and launched his sermon.

Not the one he had originally planned—but the one they *needed* to hear. As with any truly fine sermon, it focused on the Devil, his demons, and the pits of hell. Haslo took particular pleasure in describing the pits, complete with roasting sinners, the stench of scorched flesh, and eternal screams of agony. One of the best parts was when a demon ate the farmer's prideful daughter—and Haslo had just laid the necessary groundwork for the story when the door slammed open.

The congregation turned as one. Some made gasping noises, others screamed, and one fainted.

The demon, for that's what it must certainly be, had multifaceted eyes, strange appendages, and a shiny black body. Haslo heard whirring sounds as the horror pushed its way into the church. Was he responsible? Had his sermon summoned this creature straight from the bowels of hell?

It was a terrible thought, yet strangely pleasing, since it stood to reason that only the most potent of presentations would have sufficient power to elicit such a response.

Hands trembling, gills fluttering, the priest lifted the cross out of its holder, held the device aloft, and marched down the aisle. A target laser kissed the priest's forehead, and a voice was heard. It spoke flawless Zid. "Stay where you are. Make no attempt to leave. None of you will be harmed. Our work will be completed soon."

So saying, the demon backed out through the door. Haslo, certain that God had listened to his prayers, fell to his knees. The story of how the priest confronted the demon, and forced it to leave, would be told for as long there were evenings to tell it in.

A full twelve hours passed before the residents of Piety gathered enough courage to venture outside. Nothing had been damaged, and there were no signs of demons, other than tracks in the snow. There were plenty of those, so many that it didn't seem possible, and the entire village fell to their knees yet again. It was clear that an entire *legion* of demons had invaded Piety—a fact that made their survival all the more miraculous.

It wasn't too much later that the elders, led by a newly reformed Pomo, confessed their many sins, revealed their fully packed storerooms, and begged Haslo's forgiveness. Their tithe, which they subsequently carried on their backs, was generous in the extreme.

Eventually, as a reward for their openhanded virtue, Pomo and the rest of the elders were allowed to become part of the Grand Crusade's foremost rank, a position from which they could witness God's work, and hurry their impending martyrdom.

Enore lacked both the time and the means to assess the samples collected in Piety and the seven additional villages that she and her force of robots had visited. All she could do was take them and hope for the best.

The Mothri topped a rise, looked out over a slightly undulating plain, and felt horribly exposed. To a creature who had spent most of her life snug within a warren of tunnels, chambers, and passageways, the plain, horizon, and impossibly open sky felt more than a little threatening.

Enore struggled to control her panic, put her head down, and pushed ahead. It helped to look at the ground, to focus on what she knew, and avoid other stimuli.

And so it was that a five-ton beetle and her escort of insectoid robots passed within rifle shot of the packer station known as Git Up—and continued toward the south.

The complex, which consisted of a sod house, guest huts,

and a maze of mutimal kraals, was momentarily empty. The manager and her husband watched from the roof of their dwelling. "What the hell *is* that thing?" the woman wondered out loud. "The big one."

"It's a Mothri, like as not," her husband answered. "That's what they're supposed to look like, anyway."

"Where's it going?"

The man shook his head. "Don't rightly know, dear . . . but I wouldn't want to get in its way."

"No," the woman allowed. "Neither would I."

19

grudge, n, sullen malice; a cherished dislike

A combination of snow and rain, which Mary referred to as "snain," slanted in from the west. The cold, wet substance accumulated on the roboticist's shoulders, seeped into her clothes, and chilled her skin.

The road east stretched long and hard. Step followed step, curve followed curve, and hill followed hill in mind-numbing succession. Using the trade route was dangerous—but not using the road was even *more* dangerous, which left very little choice. Doon kept a sharp eye out and made frequent use of Michael's orbital sensors.

By placing himself in a geostationary orbit over the holy lands, the spy sat could provide the synthetic with reports on the surrounding area. That's why Doon nudged Mary off the road and led her up through a ravine. The stream hid their tracks, and a cluster of weatherworn rocks offered shelter.

Mary looked around. A circle of fire-blackened stones indicated that others had used the spot before them. She shrugged her way out from under the pack. "I don't want to seem ungrateful or anything—but why take a break? Don't tell me you're running out of steam.''

"Steam-powered synthetics," Doon said thoughtfully. "Why didn't I think of that? No, I'm not 'running out of steam,' as you put it. Watch the road. Company's on the way."

Mary lit a smoke-free fuel tablet, put some relatively clean slush on to boil, and sat on her heels. Ten minutes passed, and when they came, the sound arrived first.

The chanting had a mournful quality, like the keening of the wind, and sent a chill up her spine. A standard appeared—gold on light blue—and flapped like a captive bird. A teenager held it aloft, the butt supported by some sort of sling, his face invisible behind white-encrusted rags.

A Zid came next. Snow rode his shoulders like a vestment of gray. The priest was short and stocky. He gave off energy the way a stove radiates heat. Mary could *feel* his personality from a hundred feet away. The newly converted faithful shuffled along behind.

The women came first, some with tightly wrapped bundles in their arms, closely followed by older children and the men. Most wore packs and reasonably good boots. They looked tired, as if the rigors of their religion, combined with the journey through God's Teeth, had sapped their energy.

That didn't prevent them from singing, however—if the wailing qualified as such. Mary watched until the last pilgrims had passed and been absorbed by the sleet.

A deep ache filled the woman's heart as she thought about Corley and wondered where he was. Safe? Or living through God knows what? The other possibility, the one she couldn't quite admit to, was completely unacceptable. A hand touched her arm.

"Here," Doon said as he offered a hot cup of tea. "This will fix you up."

"Thank you," Mary said gratefully. "I'll hurry."

The android shrugged. "The road will wait. Take your time."

But Corley was waiting, or so Mary hoped, and time was of the essence. She gulped the tea, got to her feet, and stepped on the fuel tab. It hissed and died. "How did you know? About the column, I mean?"

"A bird told me," the synthetic said lightly. "Here, let me help with that pack."

They were on the road ten minutes later. The pilgrims made a path through the slush. The heretics followed behind.

Serving as Harley Doon's eyes was a somewhat tedious job—but one that Michael welcomed because of the human contact involved. Well, not human exactly, but close enough. And who was he to complain? A glorified tin can with delusions of grandeur? No, some purpose was better than none, and the satellite would do what he could.

The twosome was forced off the road again that day.

The westward-bound caravan was heavily laden and accompanied by heavily armed outriders. Most appeared to be human, though the scarfs made it difficult to tell.

Doon watched with weapon drawn and refused to leave the relative safety of the trees until Michael gave the all clear.

Mary wondered how Doon knew the caravan was coming before it arrived, but the android refused to explain. Perhaps it was the fact that he was a cop, or had been, and secrets came naturally. Or maybe, and this seemed more likely, it was his desire to have some sort of power over her. Men, it seemed even mechanical ones, were all alike.

Sojo, or the entity who thought of himself as Sojo, was different in that regard. He would have told Mary about the satellite, his favorite kind of music, or anything else that came to mind, had he been given a chance to do so. But Doon kept the clamps on, which left the rider to fuss, fume, and fret. A process that took its toll on the android's patience and emotional energy.

The sleet continued to fall, the hours wore away, and darkness gathered around.

The ruins were the obvious choice, *so* obvious that Doon would have opted for other less comfortable quarters, had it not been for Michael's repeated reassurances. There were no travelers in the immediate vicinity, and the nearest group, a party of three who were camped more than three miles to the east, had settled in for the night.

Thus reassured, the android led his human companion in among ancient walls. The light had started to fade, but there was enough to see where campfires had scorched the walls, and to read the graffiti that others had left behind. "All glory to God," "Lars was here," and some ancient hieroglyphics were all mixed together like some sort of puzzle.

A quick check confirmed that the satellite was correct. The place was vacant, for the moment anyway, which met their needs.

A slab of something that resembled duracrete stood on six weatherworn columns. Tool marks showed where previous campers had attempted to topple the supports, short lengths of cord testified to long-vanished shelters, and a cluster of pockmarks spoke to a night of drunken target practice.

"Home sweet home," Mary said dryly, dropping her pack onto a crudely improvised table. "What could be better?"

"Damned near anything," Doon said cynically. "Still, it beats the alternatives, like pitching our tent in the open. You take that corner, I'll take this one."

There was plenty of accumulated trash. Doon piled some against a blackened wall and set the heap ablaze. The garbage burned in fits and starts, but eventually produced enough heat to cook on, and a glow that warmed the walls.

The roboticist finished her meal, washed the mess kit with slush, and sat on her pack. The riot gun was near at hand, and Doon was silent. The fire felt good. *Very* good. So good that she was asleep when the rider broke the silence. The voice had a much different timbre than Doon's. "How can you stand it? Doon is so *predictable*. Not a creative circuit in his body."

Mary's eyes snapped open. "Where *is* Doon?"

"Oh, he's here—taking a rest. He could control me if he really wanted to."

Mary frowned. The synthetic looked the same, yet different somehow. "Why allow you to speak, then?"

"Because he thinks I'm a jerk," Sojo replied honestly. "He figures I'll make an ass of myself. Funny, huh?"

"Hilarious," Mary replied.

"He's wrong, though," Sojo continued. "We have a lot in common, you and I."

"We do?" Mary asked cautiously. "Like what?"

"Like the fact that we share the same profession," the rider replied.

"Yes," Mary agreed. "I read some of your papers. Back before the Cleansing."

"You did?" the ghost asked with evident pleasure. "Which ones?"

"I don't remember the titles," Mary answered, "but the monograph on emotion was extremely interesting. Part of your work with Dr. Garrison, I believe."

"Yes," Sojo said eagerly. "We parted company shortly thereafter. Still, it was a productive relationship while it lasted."

Mary remembered how it had been on the ship. How badly she wanted to study under Garrison and his complete lack of interest. She was human, after all, and owed nothing to his genius. Students like Sojo might refer to him as "the Creator," but not her. She forced a smile. "What caused the schism, anyway?"

There was silence for a moment as the rider remembered. "It started with a professional disagreement. I put forth a hypothesis which he described as 'silly.' "

"So, was it?"

Sojo-Doon stared down into the fire. "No. I was right. *Am* right. That's what makes this trip so important. He knows I'm right by now—and needs my findings."

"For what?"

The ghost met her gaze. "Why, to fix the planet, of course. What else *could* it be?"

"Enough babbling," Doon cut in. "I need some rest. See you in the morning."

Mary nodded, wondered how Garrison planned to fix the planet, and drifted off to sleep. Corley was waiting—and a smile found her lips.

Though founded by humans, and named by them, the town of Dobe owed its existence to the Antitechnic Church. Once they left Shipdown, most of the Zid columns took twenty days to reach Dobe, where they were allowed to pray, rest, and rebuild their strength.

There wasn't any money to be made from feeding and housing the pilgrims, but by doing so the townspeople made themselves immune from attack, and were free to serve their *real* clientele, which consisted of a motley assortment of packers, bandits, and scavs. That's why Doon lay belly down in the snow and watched from the hill above. Mary did likewise.

The synthetic saw Dobe through a targeting grid, while the human used binoculars.

He saw the ghostly green glow of heat that oozed around vent plugs, poured out of chimneys, and slipped under doors. The gently falling snow made streaks against the warmer background.

She saw two interlocking towns. The rest area, with its starkly uniform huts, communal kitchens, and prayer pavilion, and the more secular area, with its mutimal kraals, two-story hotel, bars, and primitive stores. A layer of snow acted to soften edges and round corners. Mary blinked as a snowflake touched an eyelash. She turned to Doon. "So? What do you think?"

"I think the place is damned dangerous."

"So we bypass it?"

Doon shook his head. "No, I wish we could, but that would mean covering the next two or three hundred miles by ourselves. Not impossible, but risky, and far from ideal. The best option is to join an eastward-bound caravan. Should be one through here in three or four days."

There it was again—the ability to predict the future. The roboticist was used to it by now but curious just the same. She knew better than to ask, however, and took another tack. "So, we go in?"

The synthetic nodded. "Yes, but very, *very* carefully."

The bar had an oppressively low ceiling, dirty, unwashed walls, and hard-packed dirt floors. Gallons of booze, spit, and vomit had mixed with the native dirt to produce a hard brown surface. Flames danced as people passed, shadows roamed the walls, and a dung-fed fire glowed in the centrally located pit.

The entertainment, such as it was, was provided by a female Zid. The cheek pipes were played by pushing air out through her gills, past a series of reeds, and through a bundle of valve-controlled tubes. The music had a melancholy quality—or so it seemed to the humans.

The crowd, which consisted of the usual mix of packers, drifters, and bandits, were a relatively somber lot who sat in clumps, drinking, gambling, and telling lies. There was laughter as a joke was told, groans as the dice came to a stop, and swearing from the kitchen.

Wringer warmed his hands over the coals, grunted as some semblance of sensation returned to the tips of his fingers, and turned his back to the fire. A mute herder had taken possession of the scav's favorite chair—the one in the corner with the unobstructed view of the room. Wringer frowned, pulled the duster away from his sidearm, and wandered in that direction.

The mute man watched the other man approach, saw him clear the weapon, and knew what it signified. The scav wanted the chair, and would kill to get it. Stupid, but true.

What to do? The chair didn't mean diddly to the mute man, not with more all around, but there was his image to consider. First with his friends, and then with the locals, who found the whole thing amusing.

The calculation, which boiled down to little more than guesswork, was relatively simple: How fast *was* the scrawny little bastard, anyway? He didn't look like much, standing in a puddle of snow melt, yet . . .

The door banged open, and a man entered the bar. Everyone looked. He was big, *real* big, with eyes like blue lasers. They probed each corner of the bar, found a table, and flicked toward his companion. She had a pretty face and a nasty riot gun. Floorboards squeaked as they crossed the room.

The mute man felt the focus shift and gave thanks. He stood, grabbed his mug, and headed for the bar. His honor was intact—and so was the beer buzz.

Wringer waited, took the recently vacated chair, and removed his hat. His head was shaved, with the exception of a carefully greased topknot.

His drink arrived a few minutes later. He took a sip, watched the newcomers through the poorly cast glass, and felt something wiggle in the pit of his stomach.

Prior to the Cleansing, Wringer had been a robotech. The female was biological, *real* biological, and the stuff of which fantasies are made.

Not the man, though—he was an honest-to-god, walking, talking synthetic, a model nineteen or twenty, trying to pass for human. They had different faces, the twenties did, but there was no mistaking the frame, or the perfect symmetry of their features. Wringer smiled. Money on the hoof, that's what the android was, with a whole bunch of customers just waiting to buy.

What about the sidearm, though? Was it for show, or for real? There had been specially enhanced law enforcement units—machines that could kill in the blink of an eye.

That would explain how the circuit-head had managed to survive this long—but what was the android up to? Not that it made very much difference. Or did it? Yes, he could try the droid, and risk getting his ass blown off, or he could try something more sophisticated. The kind of play that would eliminate a competitor *and* turn a profit at the same time.

The scav licked his wind-chapped lips, took a sip from his drink, and settled in to wait. The night was young.

"The man in the floppy hat is staring at us."

Doon didn't have to look to know whom Mary was talking about. A single shot of the man's face had triggered his suspect-recognition program and produced a three-screen rap sheet. His criminal record had started on the trip out and continued on the ground.

Though trained as a robotech, William Axton Williams, aka "Wringer," had chosen to supplement his income by stealing, then selling reprogrammed medical nano—microscopic machines that cruised an addict's bloodstream, synthesized the person's favorite drugs, and released them on demand.

Not forever, though, since raw materials were required,

which is where the repeat business came in. Doon nodded.
"Yeah, I've got him. See that light fixture over there?"

Mary looked. Electrical conduit, looted from the *Pilgrim,*
had been shaped into a makeshift chandelier. It held six Zid
candles, five of which were lit. A table stood below, unoccupied now, but littered with the remains of a meal. "Yeah?
So?"

"Use the riot gun. Blow it away."

Mary looked to see if the synthetic was serious. "Why
would I do that? It's crazy."

"Exactly," Doon replied calmly. "Crazy Mary . . . that
has a ring to it. What you need is a rep—the kind that makes
people pause. Go ahead—do it."

The roboticist couldn't believe where she was or what she
was about to do. She grabbed the shotgun, pretended to inspect the barrel for rust, and pumped a shell into the chamber. The action produced a rather distinctive clacking sound.
Conversation stopped, and heads swiveled in her direction.

Mary maintained a bland, somewhat neutral expression as
she turned toward the chandelier and fired. The light exploded, and pieces flew every which way. The Zid let go of
her cheek pipes and covered her ear holes. Mary had decided
to improvise. She smiled and nodded. "Yup, you were right.
The damn thing *was* loaded."

There was an audible sigh of relief as the roboticist slipped
the safety into the "on" position and laid the weapon across
the top of her pack.

The proprietor, a balding man whose homemade specta-
cles rode the very tip of a long skinny nose, headed in their
direction. A pair of bouncers, brothers by the look of them,
provided his backup. His attitude served as an unintended
testimonial to their effectiveness. "What the hell do you
think you're doing? That fixture cost sixty guilders! How you
gonna pay?"

"With this," Doon said, slapping Guild scrip onto the
table. "Seventy guilders worth. Sorry 'bout my friend here
. . . Mary gets forgetful, that's all. Is the shotgun loaded?
Boom! That's how she does it. . . . Drives me crazy."

The barkeep's eyes went wide. Mary stood, smiled, and
held out her hand. "Hi, I'm Mary . . . what's for dinner?"

Mollified by the money, and entranced by the smile, the proprietor blinked as he spoke. "I got some stew . . . or ship rations. Your choice."

Mary made a face. "I'll take the stew."

"Me too," Doon added, wishing he didn't have to. "With a shot of whatever passes for booze around here."

"Coming up," the innkeeper said happily. "Welcome to Dobe."

Doon consumed his meal with machinelike efficiency, left Mary within the safety of her newly minted reputation, and started to table-hop. Most of the customers would talk a blue streak for the price of a drink—which enabled the android to gather a significant amount of information within a short period of time.

It seemed things were pretty much normal in and around the community of Dobe. Religious converts headed east, packers went west, and bandits were where you found 'em.

There were rumors, though, talk of big doings deep in the holy lands, like the Zid were up to something. When Doon asked for specifics, nobody could provide any, so he let the matter drop.

One thing was for sure, however—an eastward-bound caravan was due within the next couple of days, and that was welcome news. It would be easier to travel with others, and a heckuva lot safer, assuming the packers were agreeable.

The synthetic had completed his last conversation, swallowed another meaningless drink, and was sitting next to Mary when Wringer ambled over. The scav nodded and gestured toward a vacant chair. "May I?"

Doon raised his eyebrows. "Suit yourself."

Wringer sat down, offered to buy a round, and shrugged when the twosome refused. "Hey, just bein' friendly, that's all. "You waitin' on the caravan?"

Doon frowned. "Maybe, and maybe not. Why do you ask?"

Wringer placed his hands on the table. They were dirty, but surprisingly delicate. "The packers ain't due for a couple of days. Maybe more. Which would you rather do? Waste your time, or make some money?"

Doon was in favor of sitting around wasting time, but knew his character wouldn't be. He gave the appropriate response. "Money is good . . . What's up?"

Wringer looked around as if to assure himself that no one was eavesdropping. "There's a scav what lives in these parts. Calls herself Android Annie. Got a hut off to the east. Don't know how much inventory the old bag's holdin' right now—but I wouldn't be surprised if she's got three or four droids."

Sojo tried to speak, and Doon shut him down. "Sounds interesting . . . How would we split 'em up?"

"Seventy-five, twenty-five," the scav said experimentally. "I know where they are."

"You need help," Doon replied, "or why come to us? Fifty percent suits us fine."

"No way," Wringer said vehemently "That's ridiculous."

Doon felt sorry for whatever droids this Annie person had managed to capture, but had no desire to get involved. "Guess that's it, then—see you around."

Wringer was about to leave when Sojo located a gap and pushed his personality through. In spite of his desire to avoid unnecessary risks, and reach Flat Top as quickly as possible, the rider had a soft spot. "Hey! No need to leave in a huff. . . . How bout seventy-thirty?"

Doon cut the rider off and blocked the gap. The deed was done, however—Wringer nodded his agreement. "Done. Seventy-thirty it is. The next round is on me."

Annie was in a good mood. That much was obvious from the spoonful of extremely valuable sugar that had been sprinkled onto Becka's hot tromeal. It was a treat, and the older woman watched approvingly as the youngster spooned it up.

And why not? Annie thought to herself as she poured a cup of herbal tea into a well-stained mug and took her seat at the solidly built table. Life was as pleasant as she could ever expect it to be, and it felt good to splurge once in awhile.

Becka licked the spoon clean, wiped her bowl with a crust of homemade bread, and popped the morsel in her mouth. The little girl swallowed, said, "Thank you," and waited for Annie to speak. It was the same each morning, when they were home anyway, and both enjoyed the predictability of it.

Annie took a final sip of tea, placed the mug on the table, and made the daily pronouncement. "I'm running out of patience, scrap. . . . We'll give Sleeping Beauty one last try. A live droid is worth a helluva lot more than one that sleeps all day. We can't wait forever, though—so it's now or never. She comes round, or I give her the chop. Agreed?"

Becka thought about how pretty the synthetic was, and hoped it wouldn't come to that. Still, "Business before pleasure," that's what Annie said, and it made sense. She nodded. "Yes, Annie. I'll get your tools."

"That's a good scrap," the scav said approvingly. "I'll be along in a minute or so."

"The slab," as Annie referred to it, filled most of the rectangular shed that extended back from the hut. Becka entered, lit some well-placed candles, and removed a pair of vent plugs. Light flooded the work table.

"The inventory" consisted of Beauty, the Mothri nest tender that they referred to as Bug, and the bottom half of a model ten better known as Ralph.

Though little more than an abdominal housing and a pair of skeletal legs, Ralph boasted all sorts of jury-rigged sensors, and spent most of his time on security patrol.

The android's power came from a roof-mounted solar panel, which, due to the constant overcast, required at least three days to provide a full charge.

Becka checked, saw that the indicator light was green, and pulled the android's plug. "Congratulations on a full charge. Use search pattern three—and report at one-hour intervals. Happy hunting."

"Use search pattern three," Ralph said emotionlessly. Report at two-hour intervals."

"No," Becka replied patiently "Report at *one-hour* intervals. Now, off you go."

"Off I go," Ralph said mechanically, and off he went. Motors whirred, servos whined, and something squeaked. Becka knew the android would exit through the hut and walk in ever-widening circles until it was three milcs out. It would reverse the process at that point and return by nightfall. He wasn't much—but something was better than nothing.

It took both of them to lift Reno's inert body onto the slab. Annie checked her tools, wished she had a lot more training, and knew she wouldn't get it. All she could do was experiment, hope for the best, and trust to luck.

Wringer held a finger to his lips and pointed ahead. Doon nodded, backed off the trail, and gestured for Mary to do the same. It had taken the better part of a day and a half to reach the vicinity of the scav's hut. Morning had given way to afternoon, and the light was fading. The lower temperature had put a crust on the slush. Servos whirred, a joint squeaked, and snow crunched as Ralph approached. A wild assortment of vid cams, heat sensors, and other paraphernalia jutted in all directions, scanning for trouble.

Doon found the half-droid to be somewhat disconcerting, but Sojo, or that part of him that remained, went a little bit crazy. He launched an assault on Doon's cognitive functions, failed to take control, and took a run at the synthetic's main locomotor subprocessor.

The android fought the rider off, but seconds had passed, and Wringer took action. The scav stepped onto the path, put three bullets through Ralph's CPU, and laughed as the droid collapsed.

Sojo started to sob, and Doon swore. "Nice going, idiot. I might have been able to stop him."

"Let's go!" Wringer yelled. "We can take her by surprise!" The scav started to run, and the others followed.

After working on Beauty for the better part of five hours, Annie had finally given up. The synthetic was alive, the scav knew that, but she couldn't bring her around. To do so would require the services of a skilled roboticist and a fully equipped lab. She had sealed the robot's chest when the alarm sounded. The buzzer was both loud and annoying. Becka came running. "What's wrong?"

Annie took her gun belt and buckled it around her waist. "Something happened to Ralph."

"Could be a malfunction," the girl said hopefully.

"Anything's possible," Annie agreed, "but there's no

way to be sure. Short of going out there—and that's what I plan to do. Lock the door and stay sharp.''

Becka didn't want Annie to go and bit her lip. ''Yes, Annie.''

The scav must have heard something in the girl's voice, or seen it in her eyes. She cupped Becka's face in the palm of a work-worn hand. Annie smiled, and wrinkles exploded away from her eyes and mouth. ''Don't worry, scrap . . . I'll be fine. You fix dinner . . . we'll split a candy bar for dessert.''

Snow had started to fall. It was gray, like the sky that birthed it, and eager to find the ground. Becka watched Annie trudge away. She had broad shoulders, tufts of hair that stuck out from under her cap, and the usual air of determination, as if the whole of life was something to be endured. The woods opened to the woman and closed behind her. It was cold. Becka shivered and closed the door.

Wringer ran like what he was, a man who knew what he wanted, and was about to get it. The plan was simple: follow Ralph's tracks until Annie appeared, kill the old bat as quickly as possible, and turn on Doon. He'd take the synthetic if he could—and revert to character if he couldn't. As for the woman, well, she had her purposes, and would last a little longer.

Wringer's boots pounded the ground, his breath jetted out in front of him, and his eyes scanned ahead. A whole lot of people had attempted to kill Annie over the years. Most were dead. Had the old biddy laid traps up ahead? Hired some help? Laid an ambush? There was no way to be sure. The scav's heart beat faster, and it felt good to be alive.

A mistake had been made, and Doon knew it. ''Control the situation.'' A precept so basic to police work that it was second nature. Except that Wringer had stolen the initiative. All the android could do was swear, run faster, and hope for the best.

Annie paused at the edge of the clearing, swept the open space with her eyes, and saw nothing to fear. Ralph's tracks

led straight to the other side. They were half filled with
newly fallen snow. She swore volubly and high-stepped toward the middle of the open space.

The scav was halfway there, squinting into the half-light,
when something struck her chest. It drove the air from her
lungs and threw Annie back into the snow.

The sound came like an afterthought—the crack of a high
velocity bullet muffled by snow-laden trees.

Big, feathery flakes fell from the sky, twirled like dancers,
and kissed her face. They felt cold, like the ground below,
like Zuul itself.

Wringer, pleased but suspicious, approached with weapon
drawn. He leaned over and looked Annie in the face. She
struggled to focus. Darkness beckoned, and it was hard to
speak. "Wringer."

The other scav grinned. "That's right Annie . . . I said I'd
be comin' . . . and here I am."

Annie tried to lift her gun, tried to give Becka one last
gift, but the weapon was far too heavy. Wringer shook his
head disapprovingly and shot her again.

Doon arrived at the edge of the clearing as the second shot
was fired. His aggressor systems came on-line as he scanned
for trouble.

Wringer turned, staggered, and fell. The synthetic absorbed this new piece of information and came to the obvious
conclusion: The scav had fired on someone and taken a bullet
in return. A second body, still warm, confirmed his hypothesis.

Weapon out, one eye on Annie, the synthetic approached.
He knelt next to Wringer, searched the front of his body for
signs of an entry wound, and started to holster his weapon.

That's when an arm moved, a hand rose from the snow,
and the pistol appeared. Doon threw himself backwards and
heard an explosion. A half dozen projectiles hit and pene-
trated the android's multilayered skin. A small army of nano
rushed to plug the holes.

Doon rolled, rose ready to fire, and saw where the pellets
had come from. A wisp of smoke rose from the riot gun's
barrel as Mary lowered the weapon.

The synthetic looked at what remained of Wringer's face.

The pellets that killed the scav had left his hat unscathed. It lay two feet from his head. Mary started to cry, and the machine held her in his arms.

Becka had memorized the sound of Annie's weapons, and knew none of the shots were hers. "Run first, think later." That's what Annie said, and it was good advice.

The escape tunnel had been dug by a Mothri robot that the scav had captured and later sold. It was accessed by a carefully concealed trap door.

Becka took the purse that Annie kept under her pillow, the pistol that lay next to it, and a holo stat of a pretty young woman. Those items, plus her very best parka, were all that she needed. Two packs, both ready to go, waited at the other end of the underground passageway.

The little girl took one last look around, hoped she'd be home for dinner, and knew she wouldn't. The door closed over Becka's head, a candle lit the way, and her boots splashed through stagnant water. Home, if such a thing were possible, lay somewhere else. Tears were a luxury—and hers would have to wait.

20

pow´ er, n, the ability to control others

The Cathedral of the Rocks shuddered in response to a minor tremor, just one of dozens felt each week. A stone fell from a buttress and shattered in the courtyard below. A hut collapsed on the edge of town. Candles flickered and sent shadows to dance the walls.

Jantz looked down to the point where his sex organ entered the woman's mouth. Her head bobbed up and down as she struggled to make lustful sounds. It was a quick, efficient way to relieve himself. Sex, or the desire for it, threatened to siphon energy away from more important activities, such as the pursuit of power.

The pleasure began to build. His pulse increased, as did his respirations. Though not especially skilled, the woman made up for the deficit with sheer energy, and his climax arrived quickly. There was the all too brief moment of pleasure, quickly followed by fatigue and shortness of breath.

The woman looked up, embarrassed by what she'd done, and eager for approval.

Jantz wanted to reward her, wanted to meet her need, but couldn't summon the energy. Not without more oxygen. The religious leader gestured in what he hoped was an appreciative manner. It came across as both a blessing and a dismissal.

Tears streamed down the woman's face. She rose, grabbed her robe, and made for the door. The idea of requesting her help never occurred to him. Not when the slightest sign of weakness would invite attack.

Jantz waited till she was gone and surrendered to his symptoms. He had felt them before. They included fatigue, shortness of breath, and excessive perspiration—all due to a stenosis of his mitral valve.

The problem had been corrected years before, or he thought it had, but there was no mistaking the way he felt. The nano that were supposed to keep the valve in good repair had broken down, run out of gas, or gone on vacation.

Jantz waited, felt his breathing stabilize, and forced himself to stand. The physical problems were annoying, *very* annoying, but could and would be solved. *After* he set certain forces in motion.

The Chosen One, whom the human disliked more with each passing day, wanted a crusade. Never mind that there was psychological groundwork to lay, untold tons of supplies to wring from an increasingly needy population, and logistics to worry about. Lictor didn't care.

The religious leader checked a well-concealed chron. It was time to meet with George Maras—the lackey on whom most of the logistical effort had fallen.

Though spineless, and something of a bore, the academic certainly knew his stuff. Caravans ran on schedule, pilgrims carried heavier loads, and the priests read from centrally prepared texts. Arms were flowing out of the west, food was pouring in from the north, and the newly created factories ran day and night. Well, not factories exactly, since everything was made by hand, but highly organized sweat shops.

No good deed goes unpunished, however—which meant Maras was in for a surprise. Jantz smiled at the thought, opened the door, and followed the long, empty hall.

• • •

Maras had been waiting more than twenty minutes now. Was Jantz really that busy, or was he playing games? The administrator sighed and looked around.

Referred to as "the cloister," and off limits to all but a few, the room functioned as headquarters for Jantz and the human members of his staff. The cathedral was riddled with secret passageways—but great care had been taken to ensure that only one led here. There were candles, however, and curtains that could be pulled in an emergency.

The cloister was large, comfortable, and packed with technological items, starting with such mundane objects as a fully functioning cooler and extending to some rather sophisticated com gear and a Mothri control console modified for human use.

The "Eye of God," as Jantz referred to his hijacked satellite, was beaming video down from orbit. Maras watched as a long line of pilgrims struggled up the side of a hill. They were Zid, each loaded with a pack fully twice the size of what they were normally asked to carry, and headed for a central marshaling point. One of them stumbled, was helped to her feet, and the march continued. It felt strange to look down on them—to witness their hardship—and know that he was responsible for it.

Maras felt a moment of guilt, worked to suppress it, and felt a little better.

"Amazing, isn't it?" Jantz inquired. "A month, maybe less, and the supplies will be in place. All thanks to you."

Maras gave an involuntary jump.

Jantz grinned. "Sorry about that. Would you care for a drink?"

Maras eyed the walls. A great deal of time and energy had been invested to make the cloister secure—but what if Lictor knew? What if the head of the Antitechnic Church was watching through a peephole?

Jantz read his subordinate's expression. "You worry too much. . . . Besides, if ol' T-head's onto us, then the whole thing is over. You might as well have a beer."

The administrator nodded and waited while his superior opened the cooler, selected a bottle of beer, and popped the cap. It had been brewed in Vent and shipped along with some black-market weapons. The same ones destined for use by the recently commissioned Reapers, a paramilitary force created to protect the unarmed crusaders and handle most of the fighting. Maras took a sip, considered the cold, crisp taste, and tried another.

"Not bad, is it?" Jantz inquired of no one in particular. "Just a taste of things to come. Life could be comfortable here . . . for us, anyway."

Jantz was in a good mood, though slightly pale. Maras began to relax. As always, that was a mistake.

Corley took a long, careful look around the central nave. It was a Five-Day, the evening services were hours away, and the church was nearly empty. A group of pilgrims, ragged from their long, arduous journey, sat in front of the true altar and listened to their priest.

A painter, just one of the many workers required to maintain the cathedral, worked on a scaffold a hundred feet away.

Two elders, who never left the building except to eat and sleep, dozed in their chairs.

The little girl approached the Devil's altar slowly, as if in awe. Dr. Suti Canova watched eagerly. Such visits were rare and extremely important to her.

Corley knelt for the benefit of spies and kept her voice pitched low. "How's it going? Are you okay?"

The most truthful answer would have been no, but Canova forced a smile. "I'm fine. How are you?"

"You're lying," the little girl said seriously, "because complaining doesn't do any good."

Canova shrugged, or tried to, but couldn't move. Though moist and somewhat flexible on the outside, the inner clay was hard and unyielding. "I'm glad you understand."

Corley smiled and nodded. "You won't have to be there much longer—I have a plan to get you out."

Canova felt a sudden surge of hope, knew how silly that was, and allowed it to dissipate. "No, Corley, you musn't. Grown-ups might be able to break me out—but you couldn't. Besides, there's no place to run."

Corley looked from side to side and winked. "No offense, Suti, but you're wrong. My father has a computer, a *good* one, with lots of memory. It came from Shipdown. I could hook it up, take you across, and leave the hardware here. They wouldn't even know you were gone.''

The possibility of freedom caused Canova's spirits to soar. The news that a relatively high-ranking member of the Church owned a computer should have surprised her, but didn't somehow. The plan was so wild, so audacious, that it might actually work. Knowing that made her mind race.

Then an odd thing happened. The android, who would have sworn that she had little or no attachment to her physical body, discovered that she did. Even though the synthetic *knew* her chassis was little more than a vehicle, and an interchangeable one at that, it was *hers* and therefore unique. She summoned the gentlest of smiles.

''Thank you, Corley. It's a wonderful idea—more than that, a *brilliant* idea—but I need time to think. Is that okay?''

''Sure,'' Corley answered simply. ''Take all the time you need. It's not like I'm going anywhere.''

Jantz felt tired, knew he shouldn't be, but couldn't help it. He speared Maras with his eyes and lowered himself into a chair. ''Enough small talk . . . time to get to the point. Lictor grows impatient. He'd launch the crusade tomorrow if we allowed him to do so. Half the crusaders would starve before they arrived at Flat Top, and the rest would be so weak the geeks would beat them to death with microscopes.

''In order to avoid that, I drew the exalted one's attention to the communities of Wellhead, Chrome, and Riftwall.''

Jantz gestured toward the hand-drawn map that decorated one of the walls. ''Take a look. You'll notice that all three of them are located within the holy lands, and though severely chastised during the Cleansing, are riddled with the Devil's work. As I pointed out to his incredible flatulence, it makes sense to purify these hellholes *before* the attack on Flat Top, so as to secure our northern flank and set an example. I'm proud to say that the supreme asshole fell for the suggestion hook, line, and sinker.''

Something cold seeped into the bottom of the administrator's stomach. Where was the conversation headed? ''Really?

What about the resources required? Supplies aren't limitless, you know.''

Jantz struggled to control his impatience. "I'm aware of that . . . but we need more time. That's what *you* keep telling me, anyway.

"And there's something else, too. Much as I hate to admit it, . . . Lictor's right. Flat Top must fall . . . but not to *him*.

"I have a spy there, or had, since she hasn't been heard from in some time, and you'd be amazed by what the egg-heads put together. They have power, lots of it, straight from a geothermal tap, subsurface farms, hot and cold running water, you name it. Just the place from which to govern the planet. *If* we can take it.

"That's where *you* come in. You and a few of my most trusted lieutenants. Go to Riftwall, convert the populace, and return in triumph. Lictor will come in his pants, we'll get plenty of recruits, and our preparations will be complete.''

The plan made a certain amount of sense, except that Maras had no relevant experience and no desire to gain it. "Couldn't someone else handle Riftwall? I'm really busy . . . and there's Corley to think of.''

Jantz was disappointed and allowed it to show. It was clear that he'd been too nice—and too collegial. "I'll take care of Corley,'' he answered coldly. "You heard my orders . . . carry them out.''

Maras bowed in the same way that a Zid might have. "Yes, sir. Right away, sir.''

"Good. Now leave me alone.''

Jantz waited for Maras to back out through the door and close it behind him. It took every bit of his strength to push himself up out of the chair and stand. Death had wrapped its cold, clammy hand around his heart. Would it squeeze him dead? Or allow him to escape? The room swam . . . and he staggered toward the exit.

reap, vt, to cut down, as grain, with a sickle, scythe, or reaping machine

The avalanche that had killed twenty-three members of the party was over, but the emergency wasn't. The light had started to fade, the temperature had started to fall, and there was no place to take shelter. And, as if that weren't bad enough, Father Crono, who had led the pilgrims with such assurance up until now, had descended into a state of shock.

Not just physical shock, but psychological shock, since the priest saw God's hand in everything, disasters included. Why? Crono asked himself. Why had God forsaken him? It wasn't fair . . . and that shook the priest's faith. So much so that he had retreated to a place deep within himself and refused to come out.

Solly, who for lack of a better candidate had assumed a leadership position, knew the situation was desperate. The survivors, some of whom were elderly, wouldn't be able to travel during the night, especially with injured to care for.

No, the answer was to stay where they were, conserve the group's energy, and make for Sacrifice in the morning.

But how? A shelter could be improvised, but what about a fire? Especially without fuel? No sooner had Solly asked himself the question than the answer popped into his mind. From God? No, the Devil seemed more likely, since the plan would require the pilgrims to appropriate God's property and use it for their own purposes. A sin if there ever was one.

However, given that the alternative was death, the youngster hoped that the supreme being would forgive the transgression, if not for him, then for those acting at his direction. But would they obey his orders? Or, like the God-fearing folk they were, rise up and strike him down?

Solly scanned the faces around him, searched for reassurance, and found it in Dara's face. She looked *so* calm, *so* sure of his leadership, that his doubts melted away. He smiled. "Dara, gather everyone in, count heads, and assess injuries. Send those who can work to me."

"Elder Ranko, see the rock ledge up ahead? The one that hangs out over the trail? That will be our roof. The walls are up to you. Take half the able-bodied males and get to work. Remember, though, speed is everything. Please lower your standards."

Ranko, who was known for the exacting methods by which he laid stone, laughed, as did those around him. The comment, so masterfully put, struck just the right note. Morale rose accordingly.

Dara returned, Ranko led the work party toward the overhang, and Solly focused on the second part of his plan. "I need water flasks, Dara—nine should be enough. Small holes would be best. Empty them and bring them here."

While Dara went in search of the flasks, Solly pawed through the party's packs. Those that had been recovered were stacked around him. He was concerned at first, afraid that what he needed had been lost in the avalanche, but his fears were soon put to rest. At least one bladder of fish oil had survived, and that was sufficient.

Eager to build a prototype, and thus verify that his idea would work, Solly emptied his flask into the snow. With that accomplished, it was a simple matter to secure the canteen between some stones and guide the bladder into the proper position.

Dara returned, lowered the water bottles into the snow, and crouched next to him. She watched her friend pour fish oil into his flask, cut a length of cord, and stuff it through the hole. Then, in an act that made no sense whatsoever, Solly withdrew a hand-dipped fire-starter from his pocket and struck it on a rock. Fire blossomed, wobbled, and held. He touched it to the makeshift wick and groaned as the wind put it out.

Dara saw a look of frustration appear on Solly's face. Frustration and something else—fear—and determination. He fiddled with the cord, checked to ensure that oil had wicked all the way to the top, and tried again. A second fire-starter burst into flame. It lasted long enough for the cord to catch. It flared, started to smoke, and continued to burn. And burn and burn.

The whole thing was magic, *black* magic, and Dara looked fearful. The oil belonged to God—and the device smacked of the Devil. Solly, who felt exultation mixed with a deep sense of guilt, tried to comfort her. "Don't worry, Dara— God will punish me, not you."

Dara thought about the demon growing within her belly and knew it wasn't true. God had condemned her already— so there was nothing left to lose. She looked Solly in the eye. "If God sends you to hell, then I shall be by your side."

And it was then, crouched before the tiniest of flames, that a lifelong partnership was forged. A partnership stronger than the rock beneath their feet. Solly nodded. "Thank you, Dara. Pull everyone together. Bring them to the shelter. I'll carry the flasks."

Though far less sturdy than Ranko would have liked, the waist-high pile of rocks broke the incoming wind. Dara and Solly herded everyone inside, made places for those who were injured, and went to work on the group's morale.

It didn't take long to make more fish oil lamps and get them going. Though unable to produce much warmth for those huddled around them, clusters of lamp/stoves were sufficient to boil snowmelt, which quickly became tea. Cheered by the hot liquid, as well as the golden lamplight, the survivors settled in for the night. No one had questioned Solly's invention, not yet anyway, and there was a chance they wouldn't.

The next morning dawned cold and bright. Crono opened his eye, couldn't remember where he was, and looked around. Exhausted by the previous day, and reluctant to separate themselves from each other's warmth, the pilgrims lay in a circle. It was what lay at the center of the circle that drew and held the priest's attention.

Water flasks, some nine in all, stood grouped together. Most had run out of fuel, but three continued to burn, their flames jumping in the breeze. It made no sense. Water won't burn . . . so how could that be?

That's when Crono saw Solly and the bladder of fish oil and drew the logical conclusion. Perhaps water wouldn't burn . . . but it seemed that fish oil would—knowledge that the youngster had no doubt acquired via his illicit experiments. It was a sacrilege, an affront to God, yet what of the results?

The priest took yet another look around, counted those who had survived, and remembered what Solly had accomplished. For it was he more than anyone else who had saved these lives. That was good, wasn't it? Yes, of course it was, especially since *he,* the one into whose care the pilgrims had been entrusted, had *failed* to read the weather, *failed* to take the proper precautions, and *failed* to react in a professional manner.

It was insane to think that God would murder innocent beings to punish one self-centered, egotistical priest! No, the blame was his and his alone. Solly's folly stemmed from a lack of priestly supervision, not an evil heart, and had saved numerous lives. Some things should be punished and others ignored. Knowing that, and knowing the difference, was the mark of the truly competent priest.

Careful not to disturb those around him, Crono struggled to his feet, cursed his many aches, and entered the circle. It took but a moment to extinguish the still-burning flames, collect the lamps, and carry them outside. A fist-sized rock made short work of the clay vessels, which would return to the soil whence they came.

Crono felt reenergized as he entered the shelter. Someone had recovered his staff and left it leaning on the hastily built wall. The priest seized the implement and poked the nearest body. "All right, slackers—that's enough sleep for one night! It's a long way to Sacrifice—so get on your feet."

Solly felt something thump against the sole of his boot, opened his eye, and saw the priest looming above. "You did a fine job, lad . . . a truly fine job. Thank you."

It was all that was said, or needed to be said, except that the flasks were missing—and Solly knew why.

The trip into Sacrifice was long and arduous. The weather was good, by current standards anyway, but the trail lay buried under the avalanche. It took hours of backbreaking work to traverse the slide.

The same young males who had managed to outrun the avalanche helped by working their way back. The trail they broke took a drol off the process. Cheers went up when it turned out that two of the missing pilgrims were with them.

A brief memorial service was held, food was shared, and the march resumed.

It was a long, hard day, relieved only by the fact that they were going downhill rather than up, and the relatively mild weather.

The trail wound down the mountainside between clumps of wind-twisted vegetation, across half-frozen creeks, and out onto a farm road. The road, which was in desperate need of repair, joined company with a river and meandered through recently deserted farmland. Huts, many of which had collapsed under the weight of the ice and snow, functioned as monuments to families who had been forced to retreat.

It was mid-afternoon when the pilgrims topped a rise and caught a glimpse of Sacrifice off in the distance. No less than three pyramid-shaped churches thrust lordly spires up through a layer of dirty brown smog.

Everyone knew about Sacrifice, for this was the spot where the Zid master race had put the believers down, where the deportees had been awakened from their artificially induced sleep and been forced onto the planet's surface.

Some of the elders, horrified by the manner in which the

flock had been exposed to the evils of technology during the voyage, called for death, praying that God would strike them down, or, failing that, pondered the merits of killing the membership themselves.

That's when the Founder, who now lay beneath the city's largest pyramid, had a vision in which the entire planet would surrender to the plow, and a new civilization would be born.

Assuming the stories were correct, the master race had provided the outcasts with a mountain of supplies, including food, machinery, and demons that *looked* like Zid but were made of metal. Once that was accomplished, the shuttles lifted and the colonists were left to fend for themselves.

That was the moment when the more conservative elders, those who favored suicide, called for the destruction of the supplies, fearing that contact with such materials would pollute the membership and open their minds to the Devil.

Others, less certain of God's intent and encouraged by the Founder's mercy, waffled, and advocated a middle course in which they would destroy the demons, but keep everything else. The Founder spoke, and the moderates were put to death.

It was said that the fire, and the explosions that followed, darkened the sky and poisoned the soil immediately below it. The demons, some of whom had names and claimed to have souls, were ordered to march into the holocaust, where their bodies were consumed.

The stories, particularly the parts that referred to demons, had long been a source of fascination for Solly, who would have given anything to see the machines that walked and talked, even if it led to damnation. He sighed, took Dara's arm, and helped her toward the city.

The farm road merged with a four-rut highway just as the clouds moved in and the sky grew darker.

Solly had never seen a two-lane thoroughfare before, but noted the manner in which logs had been used to reinforce the surface. That at least was familiar.

The carts were few and far between at first, but became more numerous as the pilgrims approached the city. Gaunt hordu hauled most of them, but some, too many in Solly's opinion, were pulled by the farmers themselves. A sure sign that the missing animals had been slaughtered and subsequently eaten.

There were pilgrims too, in groups ranging from little more than a handful all the way up to larger contingents numbering a hundred or more. Most had suffered more than Crono's group. They marched with a profound weariness, as if too exhausted to note their surroundings, or to care who passed them by.

They had overtaken one such group, and were approaching another, when Dara put a hand on Solly's arm. "Look! Up ahead!"

Prayer poles lined both sides of the road. Most of the fanatics who had tied themselves into place during the festival eight days before had frozen to death, but one continued to live, croaking incoherent words toward the sky, waiting for release.

Solly had heard of such things, but never actually witnessed them. Harmony had such a pole, as most villages did, but no one had died on it.

Dara stumbled, took Solly's arm, and resumed the march. She seemed weaker of late, as if the malady that plagued her had worsened and eroded her strength. He had attempted to broach the subject, hoping to help, but she wouldn't allow it.

The sun began to set, slowly, as if reluctant to go. Sacrifice crowded the road, squeezed the thoroughfare to half its previous size and forced it over a series of stone bridges, each of which crossed the same sewage-filled river and led deeper into the center of the city. The logs were gone now, replaced by cobblestones that made traveling easier in some ways, harder in others.

The pilgrims started to slow, rubbernecking at the sights around them, but Crono urged them on, striking the more recalcitrant with his staff, and exhorting the rest.

Candles appeared in windows to either side of the road, doors slammed, voices gabbled and prayer callers could be heard. The air was thick with smoke, the stench of untreated sewage, and something Solly couldn't quite put a name to.

Rot? Decay? He didn't like it, whatever it was.

There was a commotion up ahead. Torches flared, voices yelled, and sparks flew from metal-shod hooves. It was too dark to see with any surety, but Solly pulled Dara into a doorway and shouted for the rest to take cover. Most did— and not a moment too early.

Blood seeped from deep lacerations on the human's neck and shoulders. She ran as fast as she could, stumbling when a cobblestone tripped her up, then running once more.

The mutimals, which were larger than the Zid-bred hordu, thundered behind. The riders stood in their stirrups, whips raised, ready to strike. They wore metal things, slung across their backs, that caught Solly's eye. Machines of some sort— authorized by the Church.

It became clear that the pursuers could apprehend the alien anytime they chose to—but preferred to draw the process out and prolong the chase. For fun? Or as an example? There was no way to know.

One of Crono's flock, a female named Prulla, moved too slowly. A mutimal tried to stop, failed, and shouldered her aside. The force of the blow hurled the poor thing into a stone wall. Stunned, she lost her balance and toppled into the street. A second animal ran her down. The rider jerked on the reins, but it was too late. Her skull had been crushed.

Crono, who had sidestepped the oncoming riders, made a sound unlike anything Solly had heard. It was part shout, part scream. The priest forced his way between the mutimals, grabbed the rider's cloak, and pulled him down. The soldier hit the pavement with a loud grunt, attempted to stand, and fell as the metal-shod staff connected with the side of his head.

The riders had turned by now, and their leader pointed at Crono. "Arrest that male! Bring him to me!"

Mutimals collided and grunted as they encircled the priest. Their eyes rolled and their breath fogged the air. Solly pushed between them, staggered as a whip fell across his shoulders, and made it to Crono's side. "Don't hurt him! He's a priest!"

The leader held a torch. It lit one side of a horribly scarred face. He held something shiny in his hand. A weapon of some sort. "Is this true?"

Crono reached into his robes, found the disk that functioned as a badge, and hauled it out. Light winked off metal, and the riders stirred uneasily.

The leader holstered his weapon. "Sorry, Father, we didn't know. The human possessed a tube that generated light. We had orders to purge her."

A machine that made light? Solly thought about the oil-fueled lamps and felt a knot form in his belly.

Crono, his voice stiff with anger, scanned the faces around him. "Who are you that ride God-fearing parishioners down in the streets? I will have your names."

The leader spoke for the rest. "Proctor Lud, Father. Commander of Hand Company, Fourth Holy Reapers." The tone was respectful . . . but there was no apology.

Crono had never *heard* of the Reapers, much less Hand Company, but was too savvy to admit it. Things had changed, that much was clear, and in ways he didn't understand. "Thank you, Proctor Lud. I understand the need for religious discipline—but not at the cost of innocent lives. I urge you and your subordinates to carry out your duties with more restraint in the future."

If Lud was worried, there was no sign of it on his face. He bowed formally, pulled his mount around, and cantered away. The soldiers followed. Their torches bobbed up and down.

Crono watched the Reapers leave, murmured something under his breath, and knelt by Prulla's body. His lips formed a prayer, but his mind was elsewhere. The Devil was on the loose, all right—and working for the Church.

A substantial amount of time passed while the pilgrims took their companion's body to the city morgue and arranged for burial. It was a disturbing place, where the stench of death permeated the air, and the coffin-makers worked day and night.

Then, with snow falling all around, they made their way to the vast encampment where pilgrims from all over the Holy Empire were quartered. Unlike the cluster of guest huts common to villages such as Harmony, Grid, as it was known, was the size of a small city. True to its name, Grid had been plotted with geometric exactitude. Streets had numbers, and avenues had names.

So, in spite of the fact that Crono and his flock were so exhausted they could hardly see straight, they had no difficulty finding their respective huts. It was pleasant inside, thanks to the small army of juvenile fire-tenders charged with keeping them warm, and they were quick to unpack.

Solly squeezed Dara's hand, wished he could do something to allay the misery that haunted her face, and promised to visit in the morning. She nodded, forced a smile, and walked away.

The sleep that Solly yearned for came with surprising slowness. What was wrong with Dara, anyway? And what could *he* do? The answers were hidden in the darkness.

Dara rose early, shared in the group chores, and went to the morning service. It was a special occasion, one of four times a year when gender-specific sermons were heard and the faithful were reminded of their roles and responsibilities. Not something that Dara wanted to think about on that particular day.

Still, the very size of the gigantic pyramid, and the art that decorated the interior walls, couldn't help but claim her attention. She drank it in, and memorized as many details as she could, knowing her family would ask. *If* she ever saw them again. The pilgrims filed in, spent a brief moment in front of the Devil's altar, and were shown to their seats.

As with most of his kind, the priest had a lot to say—especially where motherhood was concerned—but Dara turned it off. Today was a free day, perhaps the only one that Crono would grant them, which left no possibility of delay. She could deal with the demon within—or die in the flames of purification. Her gills started to flutter, and she struggled to conceal it.

Finally, after what seemed like an eternity of listening, chanting, and praying, Dara rose and followed the rest outside.

She half expected to see Solly there, dear sweet Solly,

waiting for her to emerge. Still in church probably, which was just as well, since the sight of his face could bring the truth, causing him to reject her, or even worse, making him a party to her sin.

Voices called, urged Dara to join them, but she waved and turned away.

In contrast to Grid's carefully laid-out right angles, the rest of Sacrifice was an exercise in happenstance. The streets, many of which had been laid down during the colony's first chaotic year, twisted and turned as if determined to escape. Dark alleyways and mysterious passages branched right and left. Many of the structures were two stories high and stood shoulder to shoulder along both sides of the street.

Pedestrians passed, Zid mostly, but with a scattering of humans. Dara tried not to stare, but found it was difficult, since the aliens were so different. They had two eyes instead of one, a lot of head filaments, and strange horizontal mouths.

The address her mother had given was Number Six River Front Road. Dara stopped one of the less foreboding citizens to ask directions. The moment the local heard the address, her face softened and she took Dara's hand. "Poor dear . . . my prayers will be with you. Follow this street to 6th Avenue, take a right, and continue to River Front Road."

Dara thanked the stranger and followed the directions. The interchange had been frightening and reassuring at the same time.

The youngster soon found herself on the street that flanked the river. The smell was unlike that produced by any river she had encountered before.

Perhaps that explained why the prosperous citizens of Sacrifice had put as much distance between themselves and the tributary as possible, leaving the poor and establishments like the one she sought to claim the historically beautiful waterfront.

The once-proud dwellings were some of the oldest in the city. Though freestanding back when they'd been built, many had been joined over the years, or expanded so that it was difficult to tell where one started and another left off.

That, plus the fact that almost all of them were in desperate need of maintenance, had transformed the block into what looked like a dirty gray embankment.

Number Six looked slightly less prosperous than its neighbors, and smaller somehow, as if trying to blend in. Thousands of stains pointed down from ancient vent plugs, cracks zigzagged across the plaster veneer, and smoke dribbled from blackened holes.

Dara looked around, saw no signs of surveillance, and waited for a heavily laden offal cart to pass. Assuming the place functioned the way it was supposed to, the Church *had* to know about it. That's what her father said, anyway . . . and she believed it. Though unwilling to confront the problem directly, the hierarchy had decided to let females like herself take their chances.

The cart moved on, and Dara crossed the street. The door was solid but badly worn. Her knock was weak and tentative. Blood pounded in the youngster's ears, her gills fluttered spasmodically, and her knees felt weak. She wished her mother was present and missed her terribly. The door opened, and Dara stepped through.

The church service passed with the slowness of a thrice-told tale. Though part of the same structure the females had been sent to, the chapel was separate from the main nave.

Finally, after what seemed like an eternity of sitting, the males were released out into the street. Solly, hoping to intercept Dara as she left the church, raced to the other side of the enormous pyramid only to discover that she had already left. There were other females, however, still lingering on the steps, and they answered his questions.

It seemed that Dara left immediately after church let out. One of the females, who thought the handsome young Solly could do better than a bit from a second-rate fishing village, smiled fetchingly. "Dara set out on her own, a reckless decision if you ask me, especially after last night's tragedy."

Solly sought to hide his impatience but failed. "Did you see which way she went?"

"Yes," another female obliged. "She went *that* way, down the street."

Solly thanked the females and set a brisk pace.

The citizenry, most of whom walked as if carrying enormous weights on their backs, kept their eyes on the slush in front of them and were rarely seen to laugh.

Most took no notice of the youth who dashed by, skidded around corners, and splashed through intervening puddles. Those who did contented themselves with a few well-polished curses, or Church-approved sayings such as "He who runs leaves merit at home."

Solly started to pant, saw what he thought was Dara's back disappear around a distant corner, and ran even faster. A female jerked her son out of the way as the lunatic hurtled past, leapt a puddle, and yelled his apology.

Solly rounded the corner, found himself on River Front Road, and spotted his quarry. Dara had mounted a short flight of stairs, knocked on a door, and was waiting to be admitted. He shouted her name, saw a figure outlined in the entranceway, and started to run.

Their breath fogged the air as the clerics left the margins of the city and marched into fields beyond. Father Crono had known Bishop Hontz for a long time. They were roughly the same age, had attended seminary together, and enjoyed a hard-fought game of stones.

There were differences, however, starting with the extra twenty kol that the bishop had accumulated around his waist, and extending to the lives they had chosen. Crono preferred the life of a village priest, reluctantly acceding to a single promotion, while Hontz pursued a more ambitious path, rising steadily until his career had stalled. Not because he *couldn't* go farther—but because he chose not to.

There was no place to talk, not in the city's churches, which accounted for the walk. The path, dusted with a light covering of freshly fallen snow, was unmarked. They had the area to themselves. Crono took comfort from that and shared his innermost concerns.

"I find conditions much changed, old friend. . . . Who commissioned the Reapers? And why do they exist?"

Hontz glanced back over his shoulder as if to assure himself of their privacy. "Many things have changed over the last year—and few for the better. The weather grows worse, the crops continue to fail, and our food stores dwindle. "Then, as if that were not enough, the Devil plagues us with human converts."

"Surely you jest," Crono replied seriously. "It is written that *all* must come to the glory of God."

The bishop nodded. "Yes, that's what I believed as well, until the human came to power. It was Jantz who filled Lictor's head with notions of conquest and created the Reapers."

"So, Lictor is nothing more than a tool?"

"No," Hontz replied wearily. "The heretics have established a fortress to the south. A place of evil where they traffic with the Devil. Lictor plans a Grand Crusade, an attack that will sweep the godless away and leave the Church in control. A plan which *sounds* good—but threatens our continued existence.

"The villages are being stripped of both parishioners and supplies. Who will grow the food? The oldsters left behind? And as the winter continues to deepen, *how* will it be grown? Such are the questions that go unanswered."

Crono was silent for a moment. "So, what can we do?"

Hontz paused. His breath jetted back along his cheeks. Their eyes met. "Do what you always do. Follow the word of God, guide your flock, and pray that the Chosen One is correct. The alternative is too horrible to contemplate."

The inside of the structure was dark and gloomy, lit more by candles than overhead vents. The door opened into a makeshift waiting room that was empty except for a female too old to share Dara's predicament. She looked worried, and fingered a well-worn prayer cube.

The attendant who claimed Dara was as impersonal as the process she administered. "Provide fifty percent of the fee in advance, strip to the skin, and wait for Mother Juma."

Dara did as she was told, shivered in the partially heated examining room, and crossed her arms over her chest.

That's when Dara heard the blood-chilling scream, and knew the abortionist was nearby. The Devil had been busy—and there were victims other than herself. She remembered the older female, the one in the waiting room, and knew who she was. A mother waiting for her daughter.

Silence followed the scream, which left Dara to wonder what had occurred. Was the patient all right? Freed from the thing that grew within her? Or dead, lying in a pool of blood? There was no way to know. Dara shivered, and time seemed to slow.

The door had closed by the time Solly arrived. He started to knock, thought better of it, and returned to the street. There was no way to know whom the dwelling belonged to, or why Dara had gone there. He might be welcome, but then again he might not, and the results could be disastrous. What if she wouldn't talk to him any more? That would be horrible.

A street vendor, steam rising from the front of his pushcart, clattered up the road. He saw Solly, analyzed his clothes, and came to the logical conclusion. A pilgrim, just in from the country, with hardly a coin to his name. Not an especially good prospect—but the only opportunity in sight.

"Piping hot tea! Just the thing to warm hands *and* stomach."

Though reluctant to part with any of his remaining money, Solly recognized the vendor for what he was, a potentially valuable source of information, and fished a coin from his purse. "That sounds good . . . I'll take one."

Surprised, but pleasantly so, the vendor opened his cart, removed the pot from the charcoal-fed fire, and poured water into a badly chipped cup. The leaves had been secured within a ceramic strainer. It entered the liquid exactly eight times before being put to rest.

Solly accepted the heavily stained mug, expressed his appreciation, and nodded toward Number Six. "What can you tell me about the building over there?"

"It needs a coat of paint," the vendor said unhelpfully. Who was this youth anyway? An informant? Possibly, but only if the Church had fallen even further than appearances would suggest. "Why do you ask?"

"I saw an acquaintance of mine go in there," Solly replied cautiously. "Will she be okay?"

"Well, that depends," the vendor answered thoughtfully. "Mother Juma does a pretty good job, but some demons are stronger than others, and that's what kills them."

Solly waved the cup. Hot tea slopped over the side. "*Kills* them? What are you talking about?"

"I'll take my mug now," the vendor said, his breath filtering out through the scarf's loose weave. "Unless you wish to buy a second cup, that is."

Solly felt for a coin, found one, and handed it over. "Tell me—what happens in there?"

The vendor told him. It all made sense. Suddenly Solly understood why Dara had been ill, why she lagged behind the others, and why she looked so haunted. He handed the cup to the vendor, ran up the stairs, and pounded on the door.

Dara had waited so long that she was startled when the curtain flew to one side and an energetic, middle-aged female stumped in. Her clan mark was blue, her apron was smeared with blood, and her voice was cheery. "Good morning, dear. Sorry to keep you waiting, but it couldn't be avoided. I'm Mother Juma, and you are? Dara. Well, Dara, tell me what's troubling you."

Haltingly at first, then with increasing confidence, Dara told her story. The initial symptoms, her mother's diagnosis, and the plan to secure help.

Mother Juma nodded understandingly, assured the youngster that she was in the best of hands, and turned to the sound of voices. "Just relax, dear . . . I'll be back in a moment."

Dara felt fear grip her heart as Juma left the room. Was this a raid? Would Reapers chase her through the streets? She grabbed her shift and pulled it on.

The commotion died away. Mother Juma stuck her head in.

"You have clothes on? Good! A rather insistent young male wants to speak with you. Quickly, now . . . we have work to do."

The head was withdrawn, and Solly appeared. He looked shy but defiant. "I'm sorry, Dara . . . but I wanted to be here. In case you need someone."

Dara felt her heart melt as she heard the words and saw

him standing there, awkward but determined. "Thank you, Solly. You're the one I need."

His face brightened, and Solly felt warm inside. He was just about to respond, to tell her how he felt, when Mother Juma took his arm. "You had your say . . . wait outside. I'll inform you when the procedure is over."

Dara drank some foul-tasting liquid, was ordered onto a table, and subjected to a rather painful examination.

Mother Juma apologized for the lack of effective pain-killers, laid out the tools of her trade, and went to work. The trick was to recover the unquickened fetus without causing excessive blood loss or damaging Dara's reproductive organs. Never easy—but best accomplished with a healthy youngster such as Dara. The skills, diluted by now, had been passed down the female side of her family from a convert who, in spite of her belief in the Church, had been unable to let young females suffer. Juma invoked her spirit and hoped for the best.

Solly paced back and forth across the waiting room, winced each time that Dara cried out, and willed the operation to end successfully. He would have prayed if it hadn't seemed so hopeless. After all, why would God listen to him or intercede for Dara, both of whom were destined for hell? No, all he could do was hope, and visualize the future. A hut, some land, and youngsters of their own. . . .

Dara screamed. It went on and on. Solly threw the curtain aside and rushed into the room. Dara lay there, her legs on supports, blood pooling on the table.

Juma turned, delivered a disapproving stare, and dropped the fetus into a specially prepared sack. It would be buried that night, not in the graveyard, but in a place prepared by a sympathetic priest. A place where the Devil would be unable to quicken it.

Solly took one of Dara's hands, winced at the strength of her grip, and started to whisper. He told her about his dreams, about their life together, and how good it would be. He told her that she was beautiful, that he liked to watch her move, and that he loved her. He told her that he would stay with her, even through the gates of hell, and that nothing could tear them apart.

And then, when everything had been said, he would have begun again, except that Juma touched his shoulder, indicated that everything was fine, and Dara should rest.

They were the most welcome words that Solly had ever heard. He watched her eye close, took pleasure in her breathing, and watched her sleep. He was determined that somehow, some way, his promises would come true.

22

em´ is sa ry, n, a person or agent sent on a specific mission

---

It had been a long time since the roboticist's health had allowed him to leave the lab, but the nano had worked wonders, and he looked much, much better. Only "half dead," in the words of one wag.

Still, it wasn't every day that an emissary from a barely known alien race arrived at Flat Top, and Garrison had insisted that he be present.

In spite of the fact that the roboticist knew the Mothri was on the way, and had seen video taken from orbit, the sight was amazing nonetheless. He and his party waited at the foot of the mesa as alien robots swept over the rise before them.

They were black, or nearly so, with eight legs, flexible antennae, and bulging eye modules. Most were in good condition, but a few showed signs of wear, including at least one missing limb, a carapace riddled with bullet holes, and a half-slagged head unit. Damage that the hard-pressed nano had been unable to repair in the field.

The robots spotted the humans, stopped, and formed a protective semicircle. Garrison felt the ground shake, wondered if it was a tremor, and soon learned differently.

The pearly gray head appeared first—followed by a five-ton body. The roboticist, who thought he'd seen everything, stood transfixed as the enormous being lumbered into sight. Though alien, it was beautiful in its own way. That such a creature could exist, much less invent robots and master the intricacies of space travel, was a true testimonial to the diversity of intelligent life.

Garrison fingered the makeshift translator that hung around his neck. "This thing will work?"

Dr. Barbara Omita shrugged. "It has so far. We've been in radio communication for weeks now."

The scientist knew she was right, but still found the notion of communicating with something so different to be more than a little strange—in spite of the fact that he held conversations with machines each and every day.

How strange the alien was became even more apparent as the Mothri loomed above them. Her voice rumbled like static through a thunderstorm. "I am known to my sisters as Mallaca Horbo Drula Enore the 5,223rd. I greet you on behalf of the Graal . . . and ask a blessing on your eggs."

The roboticist looked up, searched for something to focus on, and chose one enormous eye. It gleamed with intelligence. "My name is Garrison. Dr. Gene Garrison. My staff and I are honored by your presence—and hope that your eggs sleep peacefully."

Enore, pleased with the polite response, clacked her mandibles. A human, she wasn't sure which sex, jumped in alarm. "The reports are propitious. All is well."

"Excellent," Garrison replied. "Please forgive my directness—but how are the samples? Are they okay?"

Enore thought back to the enormous distance she had traveled, the hardships endured along the way, and the villages she had visited. Villages without the slightest vestige of technology. If native nano were anywhere, that's where they'd be. But there had been no time to stop and examine the samples. Her voice rumbled like wind over a mike. "That's the critical question, isn't it, my friend? Have the facilities been prepared?"

Garrison nodded, remembered that human nonverbal communication wouldn't mean anything to his guest, and gave a verbal response as well. "A cave has been excavated, a work trench has been dug, and the electronics are in place."

"Good," the Mothri replied. "Please lead the way. I am eager to begin."

23

free will, n, the human, extraterrestrial, or machine will regarded as free from restraints, compulsions, or antecedent conditions

---

Dobe was defined by a grid of muddy streets, languid columns of wood smoke, and softly rounded roofs. Becka watched from the hill above. It wasn't safe down there, not for young girls, and she knew better than to go. It was lonely, though, now that Annie was gone, and the view made her feel better. Especially at night when the lights came on. They were like beacons that connected Becka with the townsfolk. Not now, though, since it was daylight, and had been for some time.

The caravan had pulled in three days before. It took the better part of four hours to sort the mutimals into their various pens, supply the feeders, and secure the trade goods.

Then, just as the light started to fade, the party began. There was drinking, yelling, shooting, dancing, and more drinking clear till dawn. Becka took comfort from the noise and preferred it to the silence of the woods.

Things had moderated during the next couple of days, so that little more than the occasional pistol shot or snatch of drunken song wafted its way up to her lofty perch. And now, having rested for three days, the packers were about to leave. Mutimals brayed as packs were strapped to their packs, metal clanged as hooves were shod, and there were wild packer yells as the scouts thundered away.

Becka knew she would miss them, especially at night, but that was the way of things. The minute you get comfortable, whammo! Things change. It happens every time.

There will be other caravans, Becka thought, consoling herself—and one of them would take her west. There was an aunt in Shipdown, had been anyway, which gave her a reason to go. Annie's pistol, pack, and purse would see her through.

It felt good to have a plan . . . and the ability to carry it out. Becka backed away from the skyline, swept her tracks with a branch, and entered the burrow. The tunnel angled down, then up—a trap to keep the heat in.

The passageway opened into the space around a tree trunk. Her gear was stacked next to a miniscule fire pit. A skirt of low-hanging branches formed the roof. Snow covered it over. Becka was snug in among the roots, and as safe as she was likely to be. ''Home,'' as Annie liked to say, ''is a state of mind.''

Aoki had been a life-support specialist once, back when technology meant something, but not any more. Now he was the trail boss, a job he had survived into, and would hold till it killed him. A fate he would welcome if it cured his hangover.

Though short, there was a considerable amount of power in Aoki's barrel chest, chunky thighs, and well-developed biceps. His taste ran to the flamboyant, and the trail boss favored a cap with a foot-long tassel. It, like the heavily quilted parka and the windproof pants, was an eye-searing blue.

He wore two pistols, an ugly-looking semiauto with a fourteen-shot clip, and a custom-designed long-barrel that held only one cartridge but packed plenty of reach. The first weapon rode in a shoulder rig, the second in a cross-draw holster belted to his waist. The rifle slung across his back wore a thirty-round drum and was shiny from use.

Bright brown eyes peered out from beneath bushy black eyebrows. They didn't miss much, as those who worked for him had reason to know. Snow crunched under his boots as the boss man walked the length of the caravan. His voice was loud and carried a long way. "Hey, Monolo, what's the problem with Blue? There's drainage from his left eye. Ask Bones to check it out."

"You'd better tighten that cinch, Wheezer—unless you feel like chasin' gear all day."

"Well, I'll be damned—Shogi has his shit together. . . . Will wonders never cease? Whoa! What have we got here?"

Caravans were the only semisafe way for people to travel, and they attracted lots of riffraff. Though unwilling to feed or otherwise care for them, most packers would tolerate a certain number of "tail-biters," as long as they met certain criteria.

An acceptable tail-biter would be armed, but not *too* well armed, since that was reason for suspicion. They would have an animal of their own, a reasonable amount of supplies, and would pass the "sniff test," which had nothing to do with the way the candidate actually smelled. Those who came across as coherent, friendly, and cooperative were generally approved. Thieves, gamblers, and prostitutes were generally left behind.

This couple fell into none of those categories, not so far as the trail boss could tell anyway, but still triggered his alarms.

The man was a big, strapping fellow, with an aura of competence, and a sizeable hand-cannon. The woman was both small and pretty. No problem there. What troubled the trail boss was their pack mutimal, the travois to which the animal was hitched, and the coffin that rode it. Aoki pointed a stubby finger at the object in question. "What the hell is that?"

"A coffin," Doon answered expressionlessly.

"I *know* that," the trail boss replied impatiently. "What's *in* it?"

"My sister," the android replied somberly. "She took sick and died."

Aoki, who was in charge of a caravan loaded with illicit

weapons, knew something about contraband. "Your sister, huh? We'll see about that. . . . Open it up."

The synthetic looked resentful, opened the catches that secured the lid, and hoped the human wouldn't notice. Most coffins were nailed shut . . . and for good reason.

The trail boss kept the biters where he could watch them as he stepped up onto the travois. There was a body, all right—and a looker too! What a waste. He reached down to touch the side of the woman's neck. There was no pulse. The body was ice cold.

The packer stepped down and raised an eyebrow. "So what gives? No offense—but shouldn't she be buried?"

Doon shrugged. "I promised to bury her next to a church. Gotta find one first."

Aoki studied the man for a moment. The story was crazy enough to be true. "All right, seal her up. You can come. Don't fall behind, though—we don't wait for anybody."

The trail boss finished his inspection, Mary watched Doon, and Reno slept.

Becka surfaced in time to see the caravan depart. She watched till the last mutimal faded from sight. The next caravan would be *hers.* The thought felt warm, and she took it to bed.

The first day was the worst. Doon and Mary spent the majority of it struggling with the travois. It foundered on rocks, stalled in the snow, and caught on bushes.

Then, as if that weren't bad enough, there was the fact that with the exception of a brief lunch break the caravan never stopped moving. That forced them to play catch-up, or try to, since most of the other tail-biters had passed them by.

Eventually, the trail boss, who shaved her head and went by the inevitable nick name of Curly, plus a ragtag bunch of camp followers, were the only ones farther back. It looked bad for a while, as if they would fall behind, but conditions improved. The tie-downs held, the terrain grew smoother, and their speed increased. They even managed to pass a few people—a significant accomplishment, all things considered.

The pack mutimal was an enormous beast that Mary

named Flathead. It fairly lunged ahead, rolled its eyes, and blew columns of vapor out through its nostrils.

Doon's mount, a scruffy beast with a personality to match, earned the title Leadbutt, for his slow, reluctant ways.

Mary's animal, a diminutive steed that she called Princess, snorted delicately, and pranced rather than walked. The roboticist liked that, and Doon thought it looked silly.

The sky hung like a backdrop, gray on gray, stitched to the horizon by low-lying peaks. Dots, Mary thought to herself. All we are is dots.

But other eyes roamed the wastelands, eyes that watched from carefully chosen hiding places and took note of everything they saw. The size of the caravan, the heavily laden animals, and the packers who led them. Here was wealth, the kind that could be squandered on a two-week drunk or stretched into years of comparative luxury.

Plans were made, orders were given, and forces were deployed. In a day, two at most, the caravan would die.

The cargo, supplies, and the mutimals required to move them, occupied the center of the nightly encampment. The packers slept all around, ready to intercept tail-biters who tried to steal things, or to deal with an attack by bandits. Bandits who would have to wade through a ring of camp followers before they could reach the cargo.

Knowing they were expendable, Doon chose a campsite next to some rocks, with access to a creek bed. Some exit was better than none.

But the night passed peacefully, not counting the occasional fistfights, the sounds generated by a pair of horny mutimals, and the wail of an itinerant prayer caller. Someone shouted, and the prayers stopped.

Doon rose as early as he could credibly do so, checked to ensure that Mary was asleep, and made his way to the coffin. After finding the synthetic in Annie's cabin, Mary had made three attempts to revive her. All of them failed. That being the case, Mary favored putting the poor thing out of its misery, or, assuming that appropriate arrangements could be made, shipping the android to Shipdown. The discussion led to the first and only fight she and Doon had ever had.

Doon, speaking with a vehemence that surprised even him, argued for taking the synthetic along. Maybe they would find a lab with the right equipment—or maybe the folks at Flat Top would help. Eventually, after a fifteen-minute argument, Mary gave in. The coffin, and the story about his sister, were afterthoughts.

The lid opened smoothly. Doon marveled at the other android's beauty. Not just the outer layer, which conformed to human notions of attractiveness, but the rest of her as well.

After blanking his vid cams and switching to infrared, Doon saw what looked like a three-dimensional green fog. There were flashes of orange-yellow lightning as signals raced along the synthetic's electronic nervous system. A bright neon-blue grid flashed on as her CPU ran a routine systems check—and pink blobs radiated up the length of her alloy spine. Everything about her was beautiful—or so it seemed to Doon. But why? Why *this* synthetic and none other?

"A very interesting question," the ghost interjected. "*Can* androids fall in love? And if they can, would it be random? Or programmed? Along with the other so-called 'predispositions' we were given?"

"You should know," Doon replied sourly. "You were a roboticist yourself."

"True," the rider replied thoughtfully. "But what, if anything, did Garrison keep to himself? Barely enough information to ensure his own superiority? Or more? Stuff he wanted to keep from us?"

"You don't know?"

"I know it's foolish to fall in love with someone you've never even spoken with," Sojo replied.

"But I *do* know her," the synthetic insisted. "*About* her, anyway. I have a file on her. Her name is Amy Reno. She was arrested for painting a political slogan on one of the *Pilgrim*'s bulkheads, has a tendency toward idealism, and a passionate interest in biology."

"Oh, fabulous," the rider responded sarcastically. "The cop has a dossier on his sweetheart. How romantic."

Doon slammed the door on his alter ego, secured the coffin, and checked the tie-downs. Voices argued, cookware clattered, and the day began.

Michael was depressed. So depressed that he had given serious consideration to suicide. Not his first choice by any means, but far more pleasant than the prospect of battling the Eye of God, or living in his present state of dissonance.

Though sentient and possessed of free will, Michael, as well as the other AIs he knew of, were "born" with a strong sense of preordained purpose. His was to watch over the planet's surface . . . and protect people from harm.

Some claimed this was a good thing, an improvement on the human condition, in which most people were born without the foggiest idea of what they should do with their lives.

Others, including some human intellectuals, and a group of cantankerous androids, held a different view. It was their position that preprogrammed "tendencies" were tantamount to slavery.

"Then why build sentient machines in the first place?" the pragmatists asked. "We have enough problems already."

"Ah, but if machines are equal, then they have the right to procreate as humans do, reproducing whenever they choose to do so," came the immediate reply.

Not that such discussions took place any more—not on Zuul, where machines were hunted like animals.

Although Michael was sympathetic to the Machinist point of view, he believed that it was good to have a sense of purpose, so long as there was a chance to fulfill it. How frustrating to be a musician minus an instrument, a dancer with no legs, or an angel in which no one believed.

All of which explained why he had completed preparations to break orbit and drift away. It was the most he could hope for, given the fact that his nano lacked the specs and raw materials required to build a ship.

But drifting was okay, suggesting as it did a long period of peaceful meditation prior to a distant death. Something dramatic would be nice, like falling into a sun, or . . .

"Hey, Mike, you awake?"

The question jarred the satellite out of his reverie. Five days had passed since he'd heard from Doon. Here at least was someone who needed him. "Harley—nice to hear from you. What's up?"

"Still heading for Flat Top. How's the cloud cover? Can you check the area ahead?"

Even as Doon transmitted, Michael backtracked the signal to a location well within the holy lands. "I see solid cloud cover, but it's not very thick. I'll scan on infrared."

Doon said, "Thanks," and turned his attention to the landscape around him. The caravan looked like a long, black snake as it wound its way across a blank canvas. Their surroundings *seemed* empty of life—but were they?

They'd been on the move for the better part of three hours now, and the android wasn't so sure. He had detected movement at the far end of his detector range, a heat blip thirty minutes later, and an unexplained burst of static shortly after that. They might mean nothing—or everything.

"Harley . . ."

"Yeah?"

"You were right. I have what looks like an ambush. Five miles ahead of your present position. At least a hundred heat signatures—two hundred if you count all the mutimals."

"What sort of cover do they have?"

"Sorry, infrared is the best I can do."

"No problem," Doon answered. "You're a life saver . . . a *real* life saver. Stand by if you can. *Knowing* is one thing—convincing the guy in charge is something else."

The satellite felt his depression drop away. "You bet, Harley. I'll be here."

It had been a good day so far, and Aoki hoped it would continue that way. He stood in his stirrups and scanned the horizon. The caravan looked good and tight—just the way he liked it.

A rider was making his way up the column. Great gouts of snow shot up from the mutimal's hooves. A tail-biter, most likely—eager to complain or secure a favor. A quick and definitive no would put an end to that.

Aoki lowered himself into the saddle and turned away. It would be a full five minutes before the idiot arrived, and there was no point in monitoring his progress.

Time passed, a mutimal snorted, and the rider pulled alongside. The trail boss turned. It was a tail-biter, all right—the one with the coffin. He rode well, however, as if born to the saddle. Something was wrong, though . . . something Aoki couldn't put his finger on. He summoned an all-purpose scowl. "Yes? What do you want?"

The brusque manner might have deterred other suppliants, but not this one. The rider pulled a scarf away from his face and yelled into the wind. "We're being tracked . . . by bandits."

Aoki's frown grew deeper. "Says who?"

"Says I," Doon responded. "I've seen them."

"Oh, really," the trail boss said sarcastically. "My scouts say the way is clear . . . but a tail-biter sees bandits. Who shall I believe?"

Doon knew how to convince the trail boss, or thought he did, but hesitated to take the risk. Could Aoki keep his mouth shut? Mary's life, not to mention his own, would hang in the balance. He took the chance. "I'm the one you should believe . . . because I'm an android."

Aoki was startled. An android? It seemed hard to believe. Especially in light of how many had perished since the Cleansing. He squinted into the wind. "Prove it."

Doon retrieved the packer's file. He read it aloud. "Your name is Noah James Aoki. You are the son of Ras and Jasmine Aoki—both of whom were killed during the landing. Though trained as a life support specialist, you—"

The trail boss held up his hand. "Enough! I believe you. What were you? A cop?"

"Exactly," Doon replied. "Something I don't often disclose."

"Nor should you," Aoki agreed soberly. "You can trust me. I owe you. Which brings us to the bandits. They're real?"

"*Very* real," Doon assured him. "There's an ambush up ahead—about a hundred of them."

Aoki raised an eyebrow at that. No one, not even an android, could see past the horizon. Doon had some sort of help . . . but who? Or, more specifically, what? He let the questions go. "There's a place, a pass between low-lying hills, that we call the Notch. Is that where they are?"

The synthetic shrugged. "Sorry, I don't know."

Something had bothered Aoki. Now he knew what it was. *His* breath fogged the air—everybody's did, except for Doon's! It was a small thing—the kind that gets you killed. The synthetic *seemed* like the genuine article—but what if he wasn't? What if the bandits had sent him? The trail boss blanked his face. "Well, thanks for the warning. I'll tell my scouts to keep an eye out."

Doon looked, decided the little man was serious, and nodded. The reaction was disappointing but understandable. He pulled Leadbutt around, kicked the animal's flanks, and galloped toward the rear.

Aoki watched the android leave, stood in his stirrups, transferred most of his weight to the saddle horn, and lifted his legs. Not all the packers could stand on their saddles, but the boss man could, which was part of his mystique.

Aoki brought the binoculars up, compensated for the movement, and watched Doon turn into a dot. The dot joined more dots, paused, and broke from the caravan. Doon had voted with his feet. The story was true.

The trail boss turned, dropped into his saddle, and blew the whistle that hung around his neck. A rider came to join him. Aoki shouted his orders. "I want to avoid the Notch. I'll lead the front half of the caravan, and you take the rest. Go south and fort early. The rest of us will join you just before sunset."

The outrider, a woman named Harmon, took note of the certainty with which the orders were given, guessed that Aoki knew more than he had disclosed, and gave the expected response. "Got it, boss . . . south and camp early."

"Good. And, Harmon . . ."

"Yeah, boss?"

"See those two heading off on their own?"

Harmon squinted into the glare. "Yeah? What about 'em?"

"Send a rider. Tell 'em what we're going to do."

Harmon nodded, wondered why Aoki cared, and kicked her animal into motion.

The snake broke itself in two. The head continued toward the east while the tail turned south. Although scouts did see some riders leave the column, it was through steadily falling snow, and they didn't realize the extent of the defection. Riders came and riders went. So what else was new?

Michael watched, kept his friend informed, and put his plan on hold. That's the nice thing about suicide—there's no particular hurry.

The combination of a six-hour snowstorm and the fact that the caravan veered to the south was sufficient to prevent an attack. The task of binding three groups of bandits into a single cohesive force was difficult under the best of circumstances, and nearly impossible when things went awry.

Angry at the manner in which the caravan had seemingly disappeared into thin air, and jealous of their independence, the bandit chieftains disbanded the alliance.

Then, when one such group ambushed another, all chances of success were lost. Doon heard about the clash from Michael and felt a sense of relief.

The next day dawned dark and gray. The process of breaking camp had become second nature by then, and Mary completed her chores without conscious thought. The farther they went, and the longer the journey took, the more hopeless it seemed. Even if Corley was alive, what were the odds of finding her? A thousand to one? A million to one? Yet what else could she do? Nothing. She had to try. The roboticist placed the last of her belongings into the saddlebags that straddled Flathead's back.

Doon fussed with the travois. He did the same thing each and every morning. Get up, check to see if his companion was awake, open the lid, and peer inside. What did the dolt expect? Some sort of miracle?

She felt a wave of resentment. Damn him anyway! What was he thinking? The coffin, not to mention its contents, was slowing them down. She was tired of struggling with the damned thing all day, tired of the solicitous way in which Doon looked after it, and tired of his moonfaced yearning. Robot love! What a ridiculous notion.

The lovesick synthetic reminded her of George, how he had asked her to marry him. And asked and asked. He had

been charming, *very* charming, and extremely determined.
She had told him no, and no, and no again, but it did no
good. He never stopped asking. He looked after her needs,
sought to please her, and eventually wore her down.

It was only later that Mary discovered that George was
equally determined to acquire power, status, and yes, women
other than herself. George had betrayed her . . . and so eventually had Doon.

No sooner had the thought registered than Mary realized
what it meant. Slowly, without being consciously aware of
it, she had fallen in love. And why not? Doon was strong,
dependable, and for the most part thoughtful. But how could
she be in love with a machine?

Though he came off as somewhat shallow when she first
met him, the android seemed more complex now, as if the
journey, combined with the overlay of Sojo's ghost, had
deepened his personality. Which explained how she felt.
Mary was jealous. She hated the female synthetic because he
was in love with it. Her. Amy Reno. The realization made
her both sad and ashamed. Doon turned and met her eyes.

"Is everything okay? You look sad."

Mary forced a smile and wrapped the scarf around her
face. "No, just cold, that's all. Are the lashings all right?"

Doon nodded. "Yup. Tight as I can make them."

Mary nodded. "Good. You've got something good there.
. . . Be sure to take care of it."

Doon was going to open his mouth, going to ask what she
meant, but the human had turned away. The sleet peppered
his face, a whistle blew, and the caravan was off.

The sleet stopped and gradually gave way to the rarely
seen sky. It was blue with white striations where high-
altitude clouds traveled toward the east. It seemed that everything went east—as if pulled by a gigantic magnet. Light
flooded the plain, transformed ice crystals into diamonds, and
made them sparkle. Doon took little notice, but Mary gloried
in the sunlight and removed her riding cloak.

Hours passed, they stopped for lunch, and the mutimals
began to fidget. The quake came three minutes later. There
was no damage—not to the caravan, at least.

The rider wanted to say something about the relationship between the temblor and his self-assigned mission, but Doon was in no mood to listen.

Mary thought about her daughter, and hoped she was okay.

Ahead, at the very front of the column, Aoki blew his whistle. The packers gobbled their food, climbed on their mounts, and jerked the pack animals into motion. The journey resumed. Everything was normal. Or so it seemed.

An enormous canyon ran north and south. It was long and broad. The packers followed a path down toward the valley floor. It was steep, narrow, and covered with scree. Mary stared at the Forerunner ruins as Princess picked her way down the trail.

They occupied what had once been an island but looked like a miniature mesa. What had the Forerunners been like? She wondered. Tall? Thin? Short? Fat? There was no way to know. There were no known pictographs, art, or statues. Just buildings, silent for thousands of years, as if mourning secrets lost.

The roboticist's questions went unanswered as Princess left the trail and stepped onto the valley floor. Walls rose all around to form a maze of water-cut rock. Wherever Mary looked she saw caves, passageways, and tunnels all carved by long-vanished currents.

Then, while the roboticist was still engrossed in her own thoughts, they entered the trap.

Suddenly, the narrow, twisting corridor through which the caravan had been forced to pass emptied into a natural amphitheater. It had been a pool once, a place where a gigantic whirlpool had hollowed the rock prior to rushing downstream.

The back current caused by tons of churning water had excavated a long, horizontal cave along the foot of the cliff. It held thirty riders, half of them Zid, half human, all heavily armed. A woman stood before them, eyes aflame, cross raised, lips moving in prayer.

Aoki, who knew a missionary when he saw one, allowed the caravan to fill the amphitheater and prepared for a long, frustrating session. The Zid were customers, *important* customers, which meant that he and the rest of the packers had to humor them.

Sister Light watched the packers assemble before her. She had no advance knowledge of the caravan, much less its path, but knew what God intended. It was her duty to purify the multitude—to find evil and root it out—for that was the assignment Jantz had given. "Go forth and purge the faithful. Prepare them for that which comes." It was a difficult mission—but one that her heart embraced.

Doon knew they were in trouble the moment Leadbutt entered the naturally formed arena. The woman, the cross, and the passive manner in which the packers interacted with her all added up to the same thing: a really bad situation.

Sister Light had been an actress once. Not a *real* actress, but a talented amateur, which is how she had met Jantz. He had done some acting as well, and it was he who taught her the importance of timing, and controlling the audience.

That's why she waited until all of the packers were present before saying her piece. When Sister Light spoke, she chose her words with care. The acoustics were excellent. They amplified her voice. She welcomed the caravan to the holy lands and delivered a fifteen-minute sermon—short by Zid standards, but an eternity for the packers.

"And so," Sister Light concluded, "it's easy to see how the Devil used technology to carry out his plans. Technology robbed us of work. Technology weakened our bodies. And technology stole our minds. God wants us back. Welcome home.

"Now I shall pass among you, dispense blessings to those who desire them, and speed the caravan on its way."

Doon watched the woman and her protectors leave the protection of the cave and cursed his rotten luck. A rock-solid roof had screened the missionaries from orbital surveillance.

He considered making a run for it, but didn't think it would work. Not with dozens of mutimals blocking the path out. No, the trick was to maintain his composure and bluff his way through.

Mary made eye contact, saw the android shake his head, and knew what he meant.

Mutimals brayed and bumped each other as riders forced them back. Sister Light, followed by her bodyguards, raised the cross and entered the newly created passageway. Slush and feces covered the ground and stained her ragged hem.

The cross, which contained a cleverly concealed metal detector, was heavy. The missionary held it aloft, applied pressure to an uncut gemstone, and started to pray.

The cross vibrated as it passed in front of the heavily armed packers—but that was to be expected. Weapons such as those were permitted, except for heretics. No, her task was more important than the search for firearms. During the last couple of weeks she had uncovered a chemically powered stove, a pair of short-range com sets, and a wind-up alarm clock.

The owners, along with their friends and families, were burned at the stake.

Mutimals edged away, faces made a blur, and God waited above.

Doon felt increasingly uneasy as the missionary headed his way. It was as if she *knew* who and what he was. Her eyes seemed to lock with his, and they were filled with hatred. His aggressor systems came on-line, energy accumulated in his actuators, and he was afraid.

Mary saw what was happening, used her thighs to ease Princess out in front of Doon's mount, and felt the weight of the other woman's stare. The fanatic's eyes were hard and filled with determination. The roboticist swallowed, fought to maintain her composure, and murmured a childhood prayer.

The cross vibrated in response to the metal in the mutimal's trappings and the gun on Mary's back. That's when the shock ran through Sister Light's arms—and joy filled her heart.

The device hidden within the cross could do more than locate metal objects—it could detect electromechanical activity as well. It was a sign from God, a command to do his bidding, and the very thing she had hoped for. The missionary turned to her escort. "Seize that woman! Search her belongings!"

Already convinced of their leader's seemingly supernatural powers, the Reapers hurried to comply. They surrounded her mount, pulled the roboticist down onto the ground, and attacked her saddlebags.

Doon was not only surprised by the suddenness of the action, but by the person they had chosen to search. What should he do? Reveal his identity in an attempt to save Mary? Or wait it out? His hand eased toward the Skorp.

Aoki had forgotten about the synthetic, and cursed his own stupidity. The wirehead was like a detonator that could trigger an explosion and destroy the entire caravan. He saw the hand move, willed it to stop, and gave thanks when it did.

Mary was both surprised and terrified. Why single her out, with Doon sitting nearby? She renounced the thought as quickly as it came. Then she remembered the tools of her trade, all neatly packed away. She was as guilty as he. But how would the missionary know? Not that it mattered. Once exposed, the instruments would condemn her to certain death. Lead trickled into her belly.

Aoki watched the Reapers empty the young woman's saddlebags and start on the pack animal. What if they killed her? What a waste *that* would be. Could he trade one for the other? That wasn't very nice, especially after the bandit thing, but the android was a machine. She was a person. He knew it wouldn't work, though, not without revealing what he knew—which was a crime punishable by death.

Flathead rolled his eyes as unfamiliar hands touched his flanks and tried to pull away. Food, clothing, and camping gear cascaded to the ground. There were tools too, clearly illegal tools, which made holes in the slush. Sister Light saw the objects fall, pointed an accusing finger, and was just about to say something when Hairball bounced into the open. "Hi! Where Corley? Me want to play!"

Sister Light was still processing the situation, still trying to absorb it, when the bullet nicked the side of the cross, tumbled toward her face, and destroyed her skull.

There were plenty of targets—but a lot of bystanders. That was a scenario the programmers had anticipated and one for which Doon was prepared. Each Reaper had been evaluated and assigned a threat index. Individuals, based on their position relative to the android, the speed with which their weapons were coming into alignment, or the extent to which they sheltered an important target, were outlined in red.

There were never more than three "reds" at any given moment, but the moment that Doon shot one of them, another took his place. The object was to drop as many of the Reapers as he could without killing any packers.

People screamed, mutimals bolted, low-priority targets fired wherever their weapons happened to be pointing, and the android continued his deadly work.

Mary grabbed her riot gun, shot a Reaper in the stomach, and was sickened by what happened next. The force of the blast lifted the Zid off his feet, threw him backwards, and blew part of his intestines out through his spine.

Appalled by what had taken place, and scared half out of their wits, some of the Reapers ran. Aoki pulled the semi-auto, shot the last one in line, and worked his way forward. Then, as the leader sprinted away, the packer reached for the long gun. It kicked against his hand, the Reaper skidded face down, and the report echoed off the cliffs. "Kill them!" he shouted grimly. "Kill every damn one of the bastards!"

What followed was little more than slaughter as the remaining Reapers were annihilated. They seemed to dance under the impact of the bullets, jerked like puppets at the end of a madman's string, falling as he let them go.

Finally, when the last shot had echoed off the canyon walls and gunsmoke hung like a shroud, Mary threw up.

Doon, conscious of the price he would pay later on, kicked Leadbutt's ribs. The mutimal complied. Aoki stared at the bodies. The synthetic stopped at his side. "Thank you."

The trail boss straightened. There was anger in his voice. "I didn't do it for you. One witness and everyone would die."

"This one's alive!" someone shouted. "What shall I do?"

Aoki's eyes never left Doon's. "Shoot him."

"It's a her!"

"Shoot *her*."

A single gunshot rang out. Mary flinched, wiped her

mouth with the back of her hand, and looked away. The trail boss looked from her to Doon. "Take the woman, your so-called sister, and get the hell out of here."

Doon nodded, pulled the mutimal's head around, and pushed his way through the milling pack animals.

It took the better part of an hour to recover and load their gear.

Aoki supervised as the packers collected the bodies, laid them in a cave, and sealed the entrance.

It was far from perfect, but the cold would slow the process of decomposition, and the rocks would hide them. The packers would swear they had never seen the missionaries—and there was no reason to doubt them.

Mary waited till the last body had been removed, looked for Hairball, and found him cowering under a rock. "Me sorry. Didn't know."

The roboticist wiped the mud off the robot's fur. "No, of course you didn't. It was my fault. I never should have brought you."

"Corley play?"

Mary sighed. "Not right now. How 'bout a nap?"

"Okay," the toy replied. "Me take nap."

The roboticist searched for the switch under Hairball's fur, found it, and turned the device off. Doon, who had been watching, raised an eyebrow. "What are you going to do? Get rid of him?"

Mary felt a sudden surge of anger. "Sure, and while I'm at it I'll get rid of *you,* the lady in the coffin, *and* the tools. Then I'll be safe."

There was silence for a moment. The android nodded. "Okay, I had that one coming. Would you prefer to travel alone?"

The caravan was on the move. A mutimal brayed as a packer urged it forward. The roboticist wondered if they'd take her. Aoki would, she felt certain of that, but what of Doon? So strong, yet vulnerable. What if there was some sort of malfunction? Not to mention Sojo's mission—assuming it actually existed. She looked the android in the eyes. It was strange how the habit persisted—in spite of the fact that a vid cam was an unlikely window to the soul. "No. We started together—we'll finish together."

Doon nodded, mounted Leadbutt, and took his reins. Aoki watched them go. The angular android, the diminutive woman, and the ice-encrusted coffin. The travois left two parallel lines in the muck. Zuul was a very strange world.

24

doc´ trine, n, something taught as the principles or creed of a religion or political party

---

The sky was gunmetal gray. Snowflakes drifted in from the north and merged with those on the ground. The hill lay just south of Sacrifice. Three heavily weathered prayer poles marked the summit. They were vacant save for pennants that snapped in the breeze. The area around them provided the perfect vantage point from which to observe the crowd below. It was the largest that Crono had ever seen. The parishioners seethed like water brought to a boil as their leaders urged, threatened, and cajoled them into their proper places.

Many villagers wore clothing of the same color. Not because they wanted to look alike, or had been ordered to do so, but because of the dyes available in their particular region. Those who had traveled, individuals like Crono, were familiar with Obedient blue, Faithful green, and Provident red—a color that smacked of pride and should be avoided in Crono's opinion. He turned to examine his flock.

They, at least, were more soberly attired—and a compliment to the communities whence they came. He had concerns, though, not in regard to their appearance, but where their emotional well-being was concerned.

Some were in mourning, still dealing with the deaths caused by the avalanche, while others, Dara being a prime example, fought more private battles.

There was little doubt where Dara had gone the day after they arrived—or what had transpired once she arrived there. Though it had been unquickened, she mourned for the little one, and felt guilty about what she'd done. The priest wished he could comfort the youngster, tell her that it was no fault of her own, for that was how he felt. But doctrine said otherwise, and doctrine was paramount. The entire faith depended on that.

Still, Solly had been of some use, and while clearly enamored of the young female, he showed no sign of taking advantage. That at least was good—and suggested a match. Assuming all went well, he would return them to their families, place a word with some of the elders, and enable what God had clearly ordained.

A cheer went up. Crono turned to find that the crowd had been released and was streaming toward the road beyond. More human meddling, according to Bishop Hontz, who complained that local authorities were being robbed of their autonomy, as Jantz and his cronies exerted more and more control over the Church.

Yes, Hontz could understand how impressive the crowd would be, and the sense of wonder the multitude would engender as it swept across the land, but he wondered if the whole thing made sense. What of the dangers involved? What of the crops that went unplanted?

Such concerns *had* been shared with Lictor via back channels, but to no avail.

Still, the crusade was a brand-new idea, and new ideas deserve new methods. Or so it seemed to Crono. *If* the idea worked, *if* the heretics were converted, a tremendous good would result. So why did he doubt it?

Crono pushed the thought away and motioned to his followers. A few noticed, passed the word to others, and started down the hill. They would reach the Cathedral of the Rocks in five days. The priest should have felt a sense of anticipation—of joy—but his spirit remained unmoved. No matter—a good hike would take care of that, as it had many times before.

A river of Zid flowed out onto the road. Some followed leaders like Crono, but many had joined on their own, eager to share the great adventure. Prayers were sung, laughter rippled through the crowd, and the mood was festive. They waved at the priest, and he waved back.

From a vantage point similar to the one ascribed to God, Michael watched. Where were the Zid headed, and why?

He made regular reports to Flat Top, and would pass the word. Especially in light of the fact that he had spotted at least three similar groups, all of which were headed toward the Cathedral of the Rocks. Something unprecedented was happening—and he had the best seat in the house.

res ur rec´ tion, n, to rise from the dead

It took three days to make their way out of the river canyon and through the badlands beyond. Doon knew exactly where they were, thanks to Michael.

Riftwall, the outpost in which George Maras had been living prior to the Cleansing, lay to the southeast with Flat Top beyond that.

Exhausted from climbing hills and negotiating gullies, Doon, Mary, and the three mutimals emerged onto an enormous plain.

It was featureless for the most part, with nothing more than the occasional rise or shallow river to relieve the mindnumbing monotony of the landscape. A problem that affected Mary more than Doon—since he seemed devoid the need for visual variety and was satisfied with whatever the journey offered.

Mary needed things to think about—things other than Corley—and wondered what the android's attitude meant. Did its attitude demonstrate a masterly acceptance of reality, or a lack of imagination?

Then there was the question of merit. If a human spent years working to develop a calm acceptance of that which cannot be changed, and an android possessed the same understanding from the moment of creation, which was superior? And did such questions have meaning?

Doon passed the time in other ways. He talked to Michael and, when the satellite was off-line, to what remained of Sojo. Not because he liked the rider, but as something to do. Their most recent conversation was focused on the rider's self-imposed mission.

"So," Doon said, "assuming we manage to reach Flat Top, what then?"

"I'll download myself to a new body and go to work."

"There's enough of you to do some work?"

"There's enough to drive you crazy."

"Point taken."

"I thought so."

"What about Garrison? And the rest of his staff? You assume they'll agree with your hypothesis. What if they don't?"

There was a pause while the ghost considered his reply. "I believe that they will. We're screwed if they don't."

"Thanks for lifting my spirits."

"Hey, you asked."

The horizon waited.

Reno lived in a place with no limits, where static electricity crackled at the edge of her being, and the world lacked substance.

There was awareness, enough to know who she was, but little more than that.

There had been moments, though—brief, fleeting moments during which she saw or heard glimpses of her environment.

The synthetic had seen sky once, swaying from side to side, but nothing since. Later, she *thought* it was later, there had been voices. Female voices that talked to each other.

Once was commanding, the other compliant. And there was *pain,* a great deal of pain, as the voices did things to her. Things they had never been trained to do.

There was darkness after that, a refuge she didn't want to leave but was dragged out of.

There were different voices this time. A female and a male. They did things too, skillful things, and nearly brought her back. Reno felt herself drawn together, made contact with previously inaccessible parts of her being, and struggled for control.

But something was wrong, *very* wrong, and her efforts failed. She could *hear* them, though—every word they said, including the argument.

The female wanted to terminate Reno's functions and send her to Shipdown. The male objected, likened such a plan to murder, and ultimately won.

There were many sounds after that, including voices, most of which were too muffled to understand, not to mention the wind, which took on a personality of its own. It whispered at times, like the best of friends, moaned as if tortured, and howled like a monster, all in the same day.

Reno was frightened then, fearful that she'd remain trapped, unable to move or speak, vulnerable to anyone who came along.

There were times when it seemed too much to bear, when insanity beckoned from the darkness, when she wanted to die.

But then came the visits, as regular as clockwork, and Reno had company.

It was the same voice she'd heard before—the male voice, the one that had defended her. He *could* have been human . . . but she knew he wasn't. He told Reno how beautiful she was, how he knew of her passion for biology, and his hopes for the future. A future together.

The words, not to mention the sincerity behind them, fueled a variety of emotions. Affection for a person she had never met—and fear for his sanity.

Sane or not, she lived for the squeal of metal hinges, the sudden rush of the wind, and the gentleness of his voice.

"Hello, beautiful! How are you today? You look wonderful—but what else is new?

"It's cold this morning, damned cold, and snowing. Hope you don't mind a few flakes. There's no way to stop 'em—not without leaving the lid down. I couldn't bear that. Mary thinks I'm nuts and Sojo agrees. Who knows? Maybe they're right. Have a good day—I love you."

That's when Reno felt a tremendous tenderness rise to fill her throat and wanted to cry the way humans did. And that's when the hinges squealed, the wind dropped to a rumble, and the waiting started all over again.

The community of Riftwall took its name from the three-mile-long discontinuity that had resulted when one section of the planetary crust had been pushed up over the rest.

Given the fact that it was located at the intersection of a trail that went south toward Flat Top, and a road that went east toward the Cathedral of the Rocks, Riftwall had been known for its Zid-inspired architecture, long, sunny days, and laid-back atmosphere.

Yes, there had been tensions, but they had been manageable ones until the Cleansing came. The same quakes that damaged Shipdown shook the city. Citizens of both races were killed or injured. Because of subtleties in the way they were constructed, human structures suffered more damage than their Zid equivalents did.

A fact which the more zealous of the Zid interpreted as a message from God—and a sign that mass expiations should begin. Some of the humans joined the Antitechnic Church, but most chose not to, and resisted the nonstop efforts to convert them. That being the case, it wasn't long before the issue came to blows, fighting escalated, and, thanks to their superior weaponry, the humans won.

The Zid were ejected, ditches were dug, walls were erected, and towers were built. The town, once so open, turned inward. Winter, nearly eternal now, froze the situation in place. The townspeople were victorious.

That's what *they* thought, anyway—although the reality was somewhat different. As conditions worsened, and Riftwall was cut off from the HZ, commerce all but stopped.

Many people drifted away, buildings fell into disrepair, and a community of thousands was reduced to hundreds.

Doon adjusted the aperture on his eye cams and stared into the glare. The tower was made of wood and stood like a sentinel against the sky. The wall, and the city it protected, lay beyond. He knew the sentries were watching, wondering who they were, and assessing their strength.

The synthetic waited for a challenge, but none came. Just the glint of lenses, a once-bright flag, and the smell of wood smoke. Ruts led, and the mutimals followed. The travois didn't fit. One pole thumped through a trough while the other climbed onto a shoulder. The coffin started to list, but the lashings held.

The gate, which had been scorched during an attack, was guarded but open. A sentry waited for the twosome to approach, aimed some spit at a spot in front of them, and grinned as it struck. His hair was long and greasy, his eyes were bloodshot, and his face wore a three-day growth of beard. An auto thrower hung low across his chest. It at least was clean. "Howdy . . . .What can I do for you?"

Doon pulled Leadbutt to a halt and did his best to sound casual. "We're looking for a hot meal and a place to stay."

The sentry nodded. "Shouldn't be a problem . . . long as you can pay. Where you headed?"

Leadbutt shook himself, and the android patted the side of his neck. "Up north . . . to visit my mother."

The sentry laughed and rubbed thumb on finger. "And the Mothri fly like birds! We got an entry tax . . . fifty guilders a head."

Doon frowned. "Kinda steep, ain't it?"

The sentry grinned. "Yup, it sure as hell is."

It was Doon's turn to laugh. He pulled a wad of scrip, small so it wouldn't attract attention, and peeled some off. One of the fifties was new . . . the other was greasy from use.

The sentry accepted the bills, checked the watermarks, and wrote a receipt along the bottom of page 37 of a *Colonist's Guide to Zuul*. "Here you go . . . welcome to Riftwall."

Mary cleared her throat. This was the place where Corley had come to be with her father. Were they alive? Now she would know. "What happened to the Research Facility? Does it still exist?"

The sentry, who wished she was naked, shook his head. "No, ma'am. Burned and looted. There ain't nothin' left."

"And the people who worked there?"

The sentry shrugged. "Don't rightly know, ma'am."

"Do you know a man named Maras? George Maras?"

"No, ma'am. Sorry."

Mary nodded. "Thanks anyway."

Doon kicked Leadbutt in the ribs, made a clucking sound, and led Flathead through the gate.

The sentry mounted the wall, nodded to another member of the watch, and looked toward the east. When trouble came—as surely it would—that's the direction it would come from.

A single Zid came first. His was a place of honor. The head, mounted on a pole, was that of a human heretic. Three of his fellow missionaries had died during the effort to take her down. Her empty eye sockets probed the way ahead, while her long blonde hair whipped from side to side.

Next came three standard bearers, their banners held high.

The drummer, a youth of twelve, followed behind. The beat came at five-second intervals. Boom! One, two, three, four, five—boom! That, along with the other problems associated with leading a band of religious zealots across a hostile country, had given Maras a horrible headache.

One pain tab—that's all it would have taken to ease the agony, but Maras didn't have a pain tab and wasn't likely to get one. Not so long as he lived with alien rabble.

The human, like those who followed behind, was mounted on a mutimal. He turned, checked to ensure that the column was intact, and scanned for outriders. Yes, there they were, little more than dots in the distance, riding parallel to the column.

There had been something of a fuss earlier, when the flankers had chased someone, but that was over now.

All Maras knew about military tactics had been taken from books, but every single one of the references he read had stressed the importance of intelligence, and the use of scouts as the means to obtain it.

The human had another resource of course, the satellite known as the Eye of God, but couldn't make good use of it. Not without establishing radio contact with Jantz—a dangerous process best reserved for emergencies.

Yes, the Chosen One had granted special dispensation where firearms were concerned, but had prohibited the use of other technologies, including electronic communications.

The administrator was stuck with the situation, and would have to make the best of it. The communities of Wellhead, Chrome, and Riftwall had to be purified in preparation for the coming crusade. That's why Jantz had ordered him to go—that, plus other reasons Maras could only guess at. To dirty his hands? To prove human zeal? For political reasons?

The answer might be found in one or all of those questions. It made little difference. What was, was, and he would endure. For Corley—and for himself.

Thinking of his daughter triggered feelings of guilt. Leaving his daughter behind had been the hardest thing he'd ever been forced to do. He didn't trust Jantz, not for a moment, but had no choice.

Corley was a form of insurance. A guarantee that her father wouldn't run, enter some sort of conspiracy, or go into business for himself—all possibilities that Maras had considered.

The administrator turned his mind to the past. Certain that Riftwall would fall, and concerned for Corley's safety, Maras had been one of the first to convert. The arduous trek to the east, and the intensive indoctrination, were preferable to death.

Later, when conditions worsened, and hundreds of humans flocked to the Church, the decision paid off. While the sincerity of recent converts was questioned, rather painfully at times, *his* was assumed.

He'd been wrong in at least one respect, however: Riftwall refused to fall—and remained in human hands. That was what he'd been sent to remedy. The irony of it brought a smile to his lips.

The drum boomed, equipment clattered, and the wind

moaned in his ears. Maras looked back along the column, counted the beings who followed him, and felt a primitive sense of pride. Like it or not, *this* was the essence of power, *this* was the way empires were built, and *this* was his.

There was something about the boy that Doon didn't like. Scraggly red hair seemed to crawl across his head, pimples populated his cheeks, and his eyes were exceedingly bright, as if the youngster was on drugs, or supernaturally alert. "Honest, mister, me pap is waitin' at the other end of the alley, and the lab's close. Real close."

Doon activated his aggressor systems and scanned for trouble. Mary and he had been in Riftwall for a little more than a day now, each pursuing their own separate interests.

While the human looked for her family, the synthetic went in search of a robotics lab. Not for himself—but for Reno. That was a cause for which Sojo had but limited sympathy, especially given the need to leave Riftwall and head for Flat Top.

The screen came up empty. The boy, who had approached Doon as he left the hotel, danced from foot to foot. "Come on, mister, we're almost there!"

Doon nodded and allowed his hand to brush the Skorp. "You first."

The boy grinned slyly and did as he was told. The alley had been used as a dump for the last year or so. The garbage had frozen in layers, like mud in sedimentary rock, and rose to either side. The trail swerved right, then left, its course defined by the larger pieces of junk.

They came to a corner, the boy turned into a passageway, and Doon stopped. The man was concealed in a doorway, but his heat signature gave him away. He stepped out into the hard, gray light. He looked a lot like his son—the same red hair, hollow cheeks, and too-bright eyes. A stunner filled his fist. "An honest-ta-God twenty—didn't know there were any more."

Doon eyed the stunner. Many weapons could do him harm—but this was one of the worst. A single shot could leave him like Reno. "Yeah, how'd you know?"

The human let out a chuckle. It made a dry, raspy sound.

He fumbled in a pocket and produced a small black box. "Simple . . . I got a scanner."

The android nodded. Such devices had been common prior to the Cleansing, when bigots wore them to prove they were bio bods, or to "out" synthetics that passed for human. Doon prepared to draw. He would have to be fast, *very* fast, but that's what he was. *If* the stunner's safety was on, *if* the red-haired man took a fraction of a second to release it, he'd have a chance. "So? What now?"

The man grinned. "So now we do business. I ain't no bigot. Katie was—but the Zid took her. God bless each and every one of the clam-faced bastards!"

The stunner disappeared, and the laugh sounded like a cackle. "Come on—you're gonna like this."

Doon allowed himself to relax slightly as the man and his son removed a pile of junk with a smoothness that spoke of long practice. The door opened on well-oiled hinges, and the android followed them inside.

Battery-powered panels, still fed by the solar active roof covering, filled the room with light. The equipment was dusty but intact. There were a couple of degrees on the wall—one of which had been granted aboard the *Pilgrim.* There was a picture too, of two men with their arms around each other's shoulders, grinning into the lens. Where were they now? There was no way to know.

"Amazing, ain't it?" the man asked proudly. "We found it just like it is—all sealed up. And it's yours—assumin' you can pay."

The lab was everything Doon had hoped for. He imagined the way Amy would open her eyes and look up into his face. How much was something like that worth? Everything—assuming he wanted to pay. There were other possibilities—but he pushed them away. "How much do you want?"

"Three thousand G's."

"That's two thousand more than I've got," the android replied honestly. "How 'bout a thousand?"

"Done," the man said quickly.

The synthetic pulled what remained of his roll out of his pocket and gave it over. The human accepted the money, counted the bills, and offered three in return. "A deal's a deal."

Doon nodded and watched them go. The door had no more than closed when it opened again. The man stuck his head in. "So, ain't you gonna ask?"

"Ask what?"

"Why we would sell so cheap?"

"Okay," Doon replied mildly. "Why did you sell so cheap?"

" 'Cause the Reapers are a-comin'," the man cackled gleefully, "and they're gonna wipe this town off the map."

The streets had been laser-straight, and at least two crawlers wide, but a combination of rubble and garbage had put an end to that. Trails went here and there, straight when feasible and curved as necessary.

The townspeople were around—though not always visible. Mary could *feel* their eyes on her, peering from windows, watching from doorways. Wondering how much money she carried, what she looked like with her clothes off, and whether the riot gun was for real.

It was an uncomfortable feeling—and one that reminded the roboticist of the extent to which she relied on Doon to protect her. Nobody messed with the android because of the way he looked. Armed and dangerous.

She remembered Dobe, the personality Doon had established for her there, and scanned her surroundings. The red on black sign was faded, but still read "Cafe," and creaked under pressure from the wind. The shotgun roared, the panel came apart, and splinters flew in every direction.

Mary could almost feel the eyes turn away. The riot gun *was* for real . . . and the woman was crazy.

Most of the street signs were gone, but some remained, and that, plus the directions received at the hotel, enabled the roboticist to find the campus. Or what *remained* of the campus . . . since the buildings had been damaged in the quakes, looted, burned, and looted again.

Mary checked her back trail, marveled at the habits she had formed, and wandered through the rubble. This was the place where George had been stationed. Where he had written long, self-centered letters, jockeyed for position in a meaningless hierarchy, and preyed on whatever women were available.

It was also the place to which Corley had come, eager to spend time with her father, never suspecting what would happen. Had they been killed? Forced into the badlands? Taken by the Zid? She hoped not—but knowing would be better than not knowing.

The path ended in front of some broken duracrete. It was all that remained of an arch. One chunk bore the fragment "Univer," while another read "sity Station."

Mary closed her eyes and fought back the tears. Tears were a sign of weakness—an invitation to attack. Doon arrived a few minutes later, put his arm around her shoulders, and led the roboticist away. That's when she cried—and the android understood.

It took the better part of three hours to return to the hotel, retrieve the coffin, and haul it to the lab.

Flathead, who had enjoyed the time off, complained incessantly as Doon led him through the streets.

There were people, lots of them, all on the move. They wore packs stuffed with supplies, pulled carts loaded with belongings, and rode sturdy-looking mutimals. Some wanted Flathead, and offered a lot of money for him; others swore when the animal got in their way.

The word was out: The Reapers were coming, though no one knew when. Was it rumor, with no basis in truth? Or fact, based on actual sightings?

There was no way to be sure, but Sojo felt a sense of urgency, and never stopped nagging. "What the hell are you doing? Deal with what's her name later when it's safe. Let's get out of here!"

Doon grew tired of the rider, shoved him down out of the way, and continued as before.

Mary, still depressed by her failure to find any trace of her family, felt numb. It took a great deal of discipline to follow Doon into the lab, connect the various leads, and run the diagnostics. Why should she be the one to bring Reno back?

Especially when it meant she'd be replaced? It didn't seem fair.

The roboticist pushed the correct buttons, watched readouts flicker to life, and felt temptation nibble at the edges of her mind. What if she lied? Told Doon it was hopeless? He at least would be hers.

But one glance at his face, at the way he looked down into the coffin, and Mary knew she couldn't do it. Not now— not ever.

The roboticist pushed her personal concerns aside and focused on the patient. The readouts confirmed her assumption. The synthetic had been struck by a full-force stunner blast. One of twelve suboperating systems had crashed—and two were scrambled.

A check confirmed that the necessary software was available, and the download began.

The process was barely underway when the building shook, plaster fell from above, and a tool crashed to the floor. Mary looked up. "A quake?"

Doon shook his head. "No, I don't think so. Felt like a demolition charge to me. Perhaps our friend was right."

Sojo had been lying low for a while, inviting his host to relax, waiting for the right opportunity. He struck without warning.

Doon went rigid as the rider launched a simultaneous attack on his higher thought processes *and* motor controls. It was the worst assault yet—and he felt himself slipping.

Mary saw the synthetic's expression, guessed what had occurred, and took immediate action. She grabbed two leads, shoved the tips through the outer layer of his "skin," and flipped a series of switches. "Into your cage, Sojo—or kiss your butt good-bye."

Doon felt his lips form the words: "DON'T-DO-IT. I-CAN-SAVE-ZUUL."

"So you claim," Mary said calmly. "And I can erase your ass."

"YOU-COULDN'T-BEFORE."

"This lab has better equipment than mine did. You have five seconds: five, four, three . . ."

Doon felt the rider back away and slammed the door behind him. "You *had* him, Mary! Why let him go?"

The roboticist shrugged. "I lied. Besides, what if he *can* save Zuul?"

The android was about to reply when Reno sat up in her coffin. "Hello! Where the heck am I?"

The other two rushed to the synthetic's side. Doon wanted to speak, wanted to say all sorts of things, but couldn't get them out. For the first time in his life, the android knew what humans meant by the term "tongue-tied."

That being the case, Mary did all the talking, asked a battery of questions, and checked the results. The synthetic was fully functional. There was the possibility of long-term damage—but a full-fledged psych profile would take more time than they had.

Reno was freed from the leads and helped out of the coffin. Though a human would have been weak, and barely able to walk, the android was strong as ever.

Doon had recovered his powers of speech by then, and gave the biologist a briefing.

Reno listened, signaled her understanding, and followed him outside. The encounter was anticlimatic, especially in light of the things he'd said, but Reno was glad. *Saying* things was one thing—*meaning* them was something else. Time would tell if Doon meant what he had said.

The corridor opened onto a path. Flathead was gone—stolen by one of the townspeople. A rider blurred past, fired, and someone screamed. The wall had been breached, the Reapers had entered, and Riftwall had fallen.

26

ex per´ i ment, n, a test or trial

The day dawned just the way Michael had predicted that it would—cold, clear and perfect for playing God.

An awning had been erected on the southernmost edge of Flat Top's mesalike surface. That, plus a table loaded with refreshments, lent the occasion a festive air. Hundreds of staff members milled around, struggled to stay warm, and traded gossip.

Modo disapproved. If science wasn't a serious business in and of itself, then world-saving certainly was. The biologist stamped his feet, shoved his hands more deeply into his pockets, and wished the brass would get on with it.

There was a delay while the Mothri lumbered up a specially made ramp, sampled the air, and emerged onto the surface. The beetle had an extremely sharp mind and the benefit of an excellent education. It was amazing how quickly she had adjusted to her surroundings and become an integral member of the team.

The alien spotted Modo, waved an antenna by way of

greeting, and ambled his way. Her voice rumbled through his translator. "And how is Bana Modo? Student of tiny bugs?"

The biologist laughed. "I study *them* . . . not the other way around. How is Mallaca Horbo Drula Enore the 5,223rd—the biggest bug I'm ever likely to meet?"

Static crackled as the Mothri laughed. "That depends on the experiment, little one . . . and whether it goes as expected."

Modo waved an arm in agreement.

A sizeable crowd had assembled by then. There was a stir as an elevator surfaced and Garrison stepped out. He looked stronger now, and more resilient. A robot sought to take the scientist's arm, but he jerked it away. He felt better and needed to let people know. Just part of the never-ending play-acting associated with leadership—an obligation that started with the way he looked, and extended to morale builders like the one they were scheduled to watch. Important in its own way—but far less significant than most of the staff might suspect.

Thanks to the Mothri, and the Forerunner nano collected during her journey south, the lab had been able to replicate hundreds, soon to be thousands, of highly specialized micromachines. Machines that could repair the planet.

That was the *good* news. The *bad* news flowed from the fact that there were holes in the nano structure, gaps left by extinct machines, which the scientists planned to fill with human–Mothri prototypes. Prototypes that needed to communicate with their Forerunner kin—but would be unable to do so. That was a problem Sojo had identified, and might have solved, had Garrison allowed him to do so.

The roboticist felt himself sag under the weight of his guilt. Omita touched his arm. "Gene? Are you okay?"

The scientist forced a smile. "Yes, sorry about that. Which one is it? The knoll? With the rock on top?"

Omita shook her head and pointed. "No, the bigger one, just off to the west."

Garrison eyed the hill, raised his eyebrows, and smiled. "Really? He's a big one. I'm impressed. All right, then—turn the little beggars loose."

Dr. Omita nodded to an assistant, who tapped some code into a handheld computer. Nothing happened. Nothing they could see, anyway . . . because the action took place under the hill. Five minutes passed, followed by ten, followed by fifteen, followed by twenty. Garrison began to worry. What if they had missed something? What if it didn't work? The possibility frightened him.

Others must have felt the same way, because no one spoke, and the crowd had grown silent.

Bana Modo saw it first. The hill's outline seemed to soften, as if all its rigidity had been lost, and it was made of gelatin. "Look! It's coming apart!"

And it *was* coming apart. Millions upon millions of nano were dismantling the hill, reducing earth and rock to their component molecules and hauling them away.

The hill shivered and collapsed inward as what looked like a reddish-brown pseudopod oozed toward the east.

The scientists watched for more than four hours as the nano reconstructed the hill—molecule by molecule, rock by rock, until it stood a half mile to the east.

Finally, when the hill was whole once more, a cheer went up. Garrison smiled, waited while Omita filled his mug with something akin to a hot toddy, and raised it high. There was a second cheer, louder than the first, but Garrison knew the horrible truth: Amazing though their feat was, it wouldn't be enough. Programmers were working day and night to create the necessary communications protocols, but Zuul was dying, and time was running out.

Though not truly sentient, the Eye of God could learn via experience, and one of the things the satellite had learned was that the slightest activity drew an attack.

That being the case, the Mothri-made machine scanned the surrounding volume of space for any sign of a threat, compressed the video into a half-second burst, and fired it off.

Retaliation was nearly instantaneous as Michael launched a flight of nano-built missiles in the direction of his longtime foe.

The Eye of God wanted to move, wanted to escape, but as luck would have it, Jantz had seen the video. Video in which a hill shifted from one place to another. Impossible! Or was it? And why would the eggheads do it even if they could? Unless it was some sort of weapon . . . which would be very interesting indeed.

An override went out, and the Eye of God was ordered to remain on station. The satellite took issue with the order—but did so in the Mothri language.

The tech was new. She winced as static filled her headset, turned the interference down, and nodded toward Jantz.

The Eye of God established its shot, and was about to send, when the missiles hit.

Michael was on the other side of Zuul at the time, and couldn't see the missiles hit, but sensed that they had. Not electronically, because the alien machine was off-line at the moment of impact, but on some other level, as if a more ethereal link had been severed.

It might be a trick, however, which was why Michael approached the area with caution, his sensors on maximum sensitivity.

But it *wasn't* a trick—the Eye of God had been destroyed. The debris field occupied a large volume of space and continued to expand. Thousands of fragments glittered in the sun as what remained of the alien satellite circled Zuul.

Michael's first reaction was one of triumph, of joy stemming from his victory, but the emotion was short-lived.

Stupid though the other machine had been, the satellite had been company of a sort, and Michael knew he'd miss it. Then there was the fact that the never-ending attacks had served to validate his existence. After all, why destroy something that has no value?

Michael was safe now, safe but lonely, spinning through space all by himself. The Angel sat drifted through the other satellite's remains—and wished that they were his.

27

cleanse, vt, to make clean, to purify

Heavily weathered Forerunner ruins broke the otherwise smooth symmetry of the horizon and made the perfect vantage point from which to view the city of Riftwall. Identifying such locations, and taking advantage of them, was something Maras did well.

The administrator had remained in the saddle so that he could see—and *be* seen by his mostly Zid troops. The fact that the mutimal made him look even larger and more impressive was a bonus.

Had the great Khan troubled himself with such matters? Maras felt sure that he had, which explained why the standard-bearers were positioned just so, and his bodyguards were arrayed behind him. And, for anyone who somehow managed to miss the carefully arranged tableau, the slow, deliberate *boom*, *boom*, *boom* of the drum served to draw their attention.

Though annoying at first, such matters had become second nature to Maras—and knowing that made him uncomfortable. Which was the *real* him? The academic who joined the Church to protect his daughter? Or the warrior priest who rode to the drum and sacked heretic cities? He wasn't sure any more.

The smell of smoke and the sound of gunfire sharpened the human's senses. He knew he would never forget the sight before him.

The cliff, or wall, from which the city took its name ran north to south and formed a mighty backdrop for the drama now unfolding. The battle was essentially over.

With no real government to hold them together, the citizens of Riftwall had responded to the attack like the mindless rabble they were.

The walls had been manned, but the defenders, who consisted of packers, bandits, and a ratty assortment of townsfolk, preferred to cluster around their various leaders rather than spread out and submit to the discipline of a centralized command—a tendency that left entire sections of the perimeter open to attack.

The Reapers had little to no training, but didn't require any to seek out the places where the defensive fire was the weakest and open fire.

Once the wall had been breached and riders had broken through, the defensive effort collapsed. The townsfolk fled toward their homes, the Reapers rode them down, and more than a hundred were slaughtered.

Maras had chosen to remain at the outskirts of the battle, where he could see the big picture and maintain a clear head. That's what he told himself, anyway—in spite of the voice that suggested otherwise.

Safety, to the extent that such a thing existed, lay in surrender. Maras watched more than two hundred prisoners march out through the gate, fall to their knees, and await their various fates. Priests moved among them, urging the faithful to say the rotes, freeing those who could.

The administrator wondered how many of the captives were like him, people who had studied Antitechnic theology as a form of insurance, and now used it to purchase their freedom.

Finally, after the battle had died down to little more than

an occasional gunshot, and the crackle of fiercely burning wood, Maras entered the town. The drum announced his coming. The mutimal walked with a dignified cadence, as if it had been trained for such occasions rather than stolen from a homestead.

Smoke billowed into the sky as a watchtower burned.

Bodies, some human and some Zid, lay heaped by the gate.

A child, tears streaming down her face, clung to her mother's body.

A Reaper, his face contorted in agony, lay impaled on a stake.

A mutimal, eyes rolling in pain, collapsed in the street.

A dead android, his hands still wrapped around a Reaper's throat, jerked as one of his systems shorted and sent electricity jolting through his nervous system.

Maras found such images distasteful and directed his eyes elsewhere. There was movement at the far end of the street. A group of prisoners appeared, some twenty-five or thirty of them, walking, limping, and in one case hopping toward him. Reapers, their weapons ready, followed behind. Smoke drifted across the way, eddied through the crowd, and vanished beyond.

That's when Maras recognized one of the prisoners, or thought he did, even while knowing it couldn't be true. The human squinted into the smoke, urged his mount forward, and discovered that he was right. Mary! It *was* her! Head high, hands behind her neck, eyes bright with anger. Something had nicked her scalp, and blood trickled down her temple. Their eyes met. Mary's face registered surprise, hope, and disgust, all in quick succession.

Maras was surprised by the extent to which the last expression hurt. He jerked his mutimal to a halt and raised his arm. All movement stopped. The administrator was about to say something when a shot rang out.

A Reaper tumbled out of his saddle, and Leadbutt thundered out onto the street.

Doon, Amy, and Mary emerged from the lab to discover that the battle for Riftwall was essentially over.

Smoke made it difficult to see.

Mutimals thundered back and forth.

Gunshots rattled in the distance.

A woman screamed, a child dashed across their path, and a drum thumped in the distance.

The threesome started to run. They hadn't gone far before a man ran out of a side street followed by a group of heavily armed Zid. He turned, threw up his hands, and backpedaled as bullets ripped through his chest.

Mary went right as the androids went left. The Reapers spotted the human, fired in her direction, and shouted in their own language. The roboticist stopped, allowed the riot gun to fall, and turned toward her attackers. They would kill her, she knew that, but she preferred to see it coming.

A Zid raised his assault rifle, eyed his ammo indicator, and took his finger off the trigger. Ammunition was scarce, and his was running low.

A group of prisoners appeared. Their eyes darted from side to side as the guards pushed them up the street. The humans needed a miracle—something, anything, that would turn the situation around. A Reaper, the one who had spared Mary's life, shouted in her direction. Over there! With the others!''

The words meant nothing to the roboticist, but the gesture was clear, and she turned in that direction.

It wasn't until Mary had been absorbed into the group that she realized that the synthetics had vanished. She felt safer by herself, knew how cowardly that was, and cursed her own weakness.

The prisoners were herded out onto the main street and forced to march toward the north. That's when the riders approached, when their eyes met, and when Mary found her husband.

Doon was frightened, more frightened than he'd ever been before, not for himself but for Amy. It was strange how that worked, how you were strong one moment and weak the next. All because of someone else. The android had read about such things . . . but never understood what they meant.

He swore as Mary ducked to the right, took Amy's hand,

and forced her to run. *If* they could reach the stable, *if* the mutimals were there, they could flee.

A Zid loomed out of the smoke, raised his weapon, and staggered as bullets struck his chest.

The androids pushed through the smoke, dodged a runaway mutimal, and dashed up an alley.

A man stepped out through a door, caught a glimpse of Doon, and stepped back in.

The stable belonged to a man named Crasty, who, against the urgings of both his wife and good old common sense, had decided to defend his property. Like everything Crasty owned, his auto thrower was in good repair—as two rapidly cooling bodies proved.

The businessman saw Doon, recognized a customer, and nodded. "Howdy. 'Spect you and the missus will be wantin' them mutes. . . . Comes to twenty-five guilders . . . plus five for feed."

Doon felt for the money, slapped three tens onto the outthrust palm, and nodded his thanks. "I admire your courage . . . but this would be a good time to run."

Crasty mustered some saliva, directed a stream toward one of the bodies, and shook his head. "There ain't no good time to run. Not now—not ever."

Amy started to object, but Doon pulled her away. "Sorry, hon, but there isn't enough time."

The synthetic heard the "hon," knew she liked it, and wondered if that was okay. Didn't he need her permission or something? A human would know. Not that it made much difference, since neither one of them was likely to be around for very much longer.

There was no time for saddles. Doon boosted Amy onto Princess, took hold of the mutimal's halter, and vaulted onto Leadbutt's back. The mutimal complained loudly as the android kicked him in the ribs, tried to dislodge the source of his discomfort, and was jerked into compliance.

Leadbutt advanced at a trot, Doon pulled on the halter, and Princess followed behind. Given the fact that the entire city had fallen into enemy hands, the next decision was somewhat difficult. North? South? East? West? Any could lead to disaster.

A bullet whined by Doon's head. He fired in return, missed, and urged Leadbutt into a gallop. The android turned a corner, saw his mistake, and knew it was over.

Prisoners scattered in front of Leadbutt's hooves, a Zid shouted a warning, and bullets started to fly. A window shattered, splinters flew, and casings arced through the air.

Doon shot one of the Reapers, saw him fall, and thundered up the street. There were more of the bastards up ahead, complete with gaily colored banners and a pint-sized drummer. He resolved to shoot some of them.

A shot rang out. Leadbutt stumbled. Doon flew over the mutimal's head and hit the street. He skidded for a while, felt something happen to his face, and coasted to a stop.

One Reaper put a gun to the synthetic's head, while another rolled the synthetic onto his back.

They would have killed Doon then, shot him where he lay, except for one thing: An entire section of his face had come loose . . . and hung to one side. Rather than the blood and bone the Zid expected to see, there were wires, actuators, and sensors. Sparks crackled, and nano swarmed through the wound.

Someone screamed, a priest fainted, and Maras raised a hand. "Seize the machine! I want it alive!"

Bodies blocked the sky, Doon heard Amy call his name, and blows rained around his head.

Sojo screamed, tried to get up, and was beaten down. Defensive software was triggered, an operating system went offline, and Doon went with it.

Maras waited to make sure the android was under control, saw his bodyguards seize a second rider, and remembered his wife. He turned, saw her break free of the crowd, and start to run. Not away, as one might expect, but toward the android.

The human had taken no more than three steps before a guard blocked the way. She tried to circle him, but the Zid was fast—and knocked the roboticist to the ground. The Reaper was about to kick her when Maras pushed his mount into the gap. The language lessons paid off: "Enough that is! Take the female plus four more. Interrogate them I will."

Mary and four humans who had been standing around her were hustled into a warehouse. The administrator followed them in. Thousands of flat mutimal patties were drying on specially designed racks. Maras wrinkled his nose, spotted a high-walled enclosure, and gestured in that direction. "Interview the heretics I will. No talking lest they conspire."

The human's syntax was poor, but the Reapers understood.

Maras had no interest in the other prisoners, but needed them for cover. They were dregs mostly, a mix of pre-Cleansing townsfolk and postcataclysm trail trash. He hoped Mary had been secretive about her occupation, but that seemed doubtful, especially after her support for the android.

The administrator sighed, brushed some junk off a table, and nodded to an aide. "The first one bring. Busy here the Devil was . . . the details we must have."

Maras was forced to interview three frightened, desperate people before they brought his wife in. Blood caked the side of her face. She looked tired, worried, and defiant—an expression he had come to know rather well. The door closed and their eyes met. Maras was first to speak. "Are you all right?"

"Sure," Mary lied. "I couldn't be better. Where's Corley?"

"Safe, at the Cathedral of the Rocks."

Mary frowned. "Safe? You call that *safe*?"

Maras shrugged. "Safety is relative these days. Take a look around. Would you rather she was here?"

Mary ran her eyes over his Zid-style clothing, the cross that hung from his neck, and the pistol holstered at his side. "What's with the outfit? What have you done?"

"I did what I *had* to do," Maras answered patiently, "to protect Corley."

Mary's mouth made a hard, straight line. "To protect Corley? Or to protect yourself?"

Maras felt a surge of anger—the kind she had elicited many times before. The kind that led him to say stupid things, and left the moral high ground to her. He forced it back.

"Think what you will . . . but here are the facts: The Zid will kill you, me, *and* Corley if they discover who and what you are. I suggest you keep your mouth shut and your eyes open.

"There will be a call for converts once we reach the cathedral. Offer yourself, and I will ensure that you are chosen. The rest will take care of itself."

Maras paused for a moment. His wife was an idealist, and a willful one at that, which meant he should choose his words with care. "I have some power . . . but not enough to help the androids. They are beyond our reach. Understood?"

Mary knew the man before her, and knew he was sincere. Wrong—but sincere. She nodded. "Understood."

"Good. Do what you can for that cut. I'm sorry I can't clean it myself."

It was then, during that brief moment of tenderness, that Mary remembered why she had agreed to marry him.

Maras pushed the door open, and Mary left. A man was next, and he looked scared. All things considered, the roboticist couldn't blame him.

Three days had passed while Riftwall was pacified, burned to the ground, and cleansed with prayer. The column had been on the road for an hour. The drummer came first. The slow, deliberate boom of his instrument brought an element of solemnity to the procession.

A pair of living altars came next. They stood side by side on a cart looted from Riftwall. It bounded over rocks, tilted into ruts, and swept through the slush.

Doon, who stood immobile in a prison of carefully dampened clay, was helpless. His head, arms, and legs were clamped in place.

Considerable care had gone into the altar and the decorations that adorned it. In addition to his crudely repaired face, which served as the focus for the display, artifacts from Riftwall had been pressed into the clay around him. There were circuit boards, scraps of wire, springs, nuts, bolts, and countless other objects all positioned to please and amaze.

The worst part was knowing that Amy was there, only inches away, but beyond the reach of his pickups.

Things could have been worse, however, since, unbeknownst to their captors, the androids could communicate via radio—a fact that made an otherwise intolerable situation a little more bearable.

"Amy? Can you hear me?"

"Yes. Is it safe to talk like this?"

"No, nothing's safe. Not any more."

Amy liked the sound of his voice. She knew the answer but asked the question anyway. "What will they do with us?"

"Stash us in a church and charge admission. Nothing like a freak show to bring in the rubes."

Sojo wanted to talk, to whine about his mission, but Doon wouldn't let him. Strange though the situation was, this was only his fourth or fifth opportunity to speak with Amy, and he was jealous of each and every one. "I'm sorry you were captured. First the coffin . . . now this."

Amy remembered the darkness, the long, lonely days, and the sound of his voice. "I hated the coffin . . . but liked what you said."

Doon was mortified. "You heard what I said?"

Amy chuckled. "Every word."

Doon groaned. "You must think I'm crazy! Please forgive me."

"Yes," Amy agreed, "I do think you're crazy, but there's nothing to forgive. Not if you meant the things you said."

Doon, hardly able to believe what he had heard, tried to turn his head. Nothing happened. "Yes! I meant every word! *Do* mean every word."

"Good," the other synthetic said lightly, "because I'd hate to think you whisper sweet nothings to every corpse you happen across."

It was then, as Doon was reveling in her words, that Michael interrupted. "Harley? Is that you? What's happening?"

"Nothing good," Doon replied dryly. "When the Zid took Riftwall they took us as well."

Michael had assumed as much, but didn't want to say so. "I'm sorry, Harley . . . I really am. But where there's life there's hope."

It was a nice thing to say—especially in light of the depression that had claimed Michael for the past week or so. Had Doon known that he might have responded differently.

"Can you see us through the cloud cover? We're on a cart headed east."

"We?" the satellite inquired.

"Yeah. Mary, Amy, and myself. Amy is one of us. Say hello, Amy, and I'll play relay station."

"Hello," Amy said uncertainly. "Who am I talking to?"

"Mike's a satellite," Doon replied, "in orbit around Zuul. He sees all and knows all."

"I see *lots* of things," Michael said modestly, "but not everything."

"How 'bout Flat Top?" Amy asked, as she analyzed the possibilities. "Can you see it?"

"Of course," the satellite responded confidently. "I provide reports to the staff. Who's spying on them, who's coming their way, that sort of thing. You should have seen the latest—when they moved a hill from one place to another!"

Doon was completely unprepared for what happened next. The words functioned like a trigger. Sojo exploded out of virtual prison, blasted his way through Doon's defenses, and took control of his body. "This is Luis Garcia Sojo. Describe what you saw! Leave nothing out!"

The voice sounded different—but the transmission characteristics were identical to Doon's. Same frequency, same encryption software, and same coordinates. A trick of some sort? Michael brought his defenses on-line. "Harley? Who the hell is Sojo?"

My question exactly, Amy thought to herself. Who the hell is Sojo?

Doon felt the rider let up—just enough for him to speak. "He's a spook, Mike—I have a replacement arm, and he came with it. He has a mission, or believes he has. Go ahead—tell him what he wants to know."

Amy, who had just learned that her one-time savior was possessed by the robotic equivalent of a disembodied spirit, listened with interest as the satellite described what he'd seen. The synthetic had no idea why her scientific colleagues had conducted the experiment, or what they hoped to prove, but was proud nonetheless. Imagine! Moving an entire hill!

Sojo, on the other hand, knew exactly what they were doing and what the experiment implied. His thesis had been correct! Zuul had been constructed by Forerunner nano! Some of which were extinct. And Garrison had built proto-types. Nano that could move mountains. Or build planets! But what about the communication problem? Had it been solved? Did they need him? There was no way to know.

The rider fought to control his angst. Calm, logical, dis-passionate. Those were the qualities his host prided himself on—and that's what he would respond to. "Doon?"

"Yes?"

"Am I screaming?"

"No," Doon answered hesitantly, "you aren't."

"And that's good?"

"That's very good."

"And you will listen to me?"

"I don't seem to have much choice."

"They need me at Flat Top—and that means you. Please escape and go there."

"Just like that."

"I couldn't—but you can."

"Got it," Doon said carefully. "Escape and go there. I'll leave as soon as I can."

"Good," Sojo said simply. "Thank you."

Doon felt the rider retreat, slammed the door behind him, and wondered what Amy would think. "Sorry about that—but Sojo gets somewhat agitated at times. What else is going on? Besides hills that creep around?"

"Quite a bit, actually," Michael responded. "The Zid are on the move. Tens of thousands of them. All headed for the same place."

"And what place is that?"

"Why, the same place you're headed," the satellite replied sadly. "The Cathedral of the Rocks."

The Cathedral of the Rocks had become the epicenter of what amounted to a huge metropolis. The city below the cathedral had enough guest huts to accommodate two thou-sand pilgrims, and those huts had been filled for weeks.

However, thanks to the excellent work carried out by Ad-ministrator General Maras and his staff, two tent cities, each capable of housing ten thousand souls, had been erected to the north and the south.

Thousands of tents, each of which had been hand-sewn in specially created "cooperatives," were the least of the preparations. Ditches were dug to improve drainage. Rations were assembled and stored. Privies were built. Prayer poles were erected. Medical facilities were established. Wells were dug. Spies were assigned. Special church services were devised. In short, everything that could be done had been done.

The preparations had reduced what might have been a high rate of morbidity to something more acceptable, helped to allay the visitors' fears, and made them feel welcome.

That was the theory, anyway, although Crono didn't feel especially welcome as he led his flock into the maze of tents that comprised the northern encampment, and struggled through the ankle-deep mud. It was thick, glutinous stuff that stuck to his sandals and threatened to pull them off.

Of much concern, however, was the knowledge that Bishop Hontz had been correct. The faithful were gathered for a purpose—to take part in Lictor's crusade, about which the priest had serious doubts. Doubts he could vocalize to no one but himself—but that ate at him nonetheless.

The heretics were a problem, yes, but nothing compared to the increasingly harsh weather, the never-ending quakes, and the growing threat of starvation. Which came first? The glory of God? Or the welfare of his flock? Such were the questions on which seminarians spent years of contemplation. A waste of time, in Crono's opinion, since the answer was self-evident. The primary function of the Church was to serve its members.

But many would disagree with him. The priest knew that, and made allowance for the possibility that they were correct. He had battled what one superior described as "intellectual arrogance" for years now, and the struggle continued.

Solly, who continued in his role as Crono's assistant, had spent the entire day marching the length of the column, urging the laggards to greater speed and dealing with larger groups that threatened to absorb them—something the priest refused to countenance. Because he saw the group as his, or for other less obvious reasons? There was no way to tell.

Whatever the reason, one thing was for sure: The youngster had walked three times the distance that the other pilgrims had, and was bone tired. Mud sucked at the soles of his boots, faces blurred around him, and smoke assailed his eyes. The camp stretched on and on. Was this the destination they had worked so hard to reach? It hardly seemed worth it.

A guide, two or three years younger than Solly, met the group at an intersection, checked Crono off his list, and led them into a maze of tents.

It took every bit of the youngster's remaining store of energy to reach the shelter to which he had been assigned, mumble something to Dara, and collapse on a cot. Sleep rolled him under.

Solly had just entered his parents' hut, and was about to introduce Dara, when a hand shook his shoulder. "Time to get up, son—or miss the processional."

Solly opened his eye, saw Crono looming above, and managed to croak an acknowledgment. The youngster would have been quite happy to miss the processional, especially in exchange for more sleep, but knew better than to say so. If there was anything the priest didn't like, it was what he perceived as slackers.

Crono used his staff to thump, prod, and poke the rest of the males, and sent for the female members of his flock.

Breakfast was a hasty affair consisting of a dollop of lukewarm tromeal and some water to wash it down. Solly ate his serving, licked the bowl, and wished there were more.

Dara offered what remained of her ration and was refused. "Thank you, but no," Solly said firmly. "You must build your strength. There's the walk home to consider."

Dara knew he was correct, and wondered about the rumors they'd heard. Some said the pilgrims had been assembled for a purpose, and that they'd stay till whatever it was had been accomplished.

Dara didn't like that possibility and stayed close to Solly as the group threaded its way down muddy footpaths, past communal kitchens, and past rows of carefully ordered tents.

Others were on the move as well, summoned by their

priests and led by teenaged guides. No one knew why, or (if someone did) was willing to say.

A steady trickle soon turned into a flood as footpaths joined a one-lane track, which merged with a road. The thoroughfare dived into a gully, climbed a hill, and passed through a jumble of enormous rocks. A pole had been erected among them, and a prayer caller wailed to the sky.

Then, with little warning, the road opened onto a vast plain. The sun, which had been concealed till then, chose that particular moment to break through the clouds and bathe the land in lavender light. It was then that Solly heard the dull *thump*, *thump*, *thump* of a drum and saw movement off to the west.

"There's no time to dawdle," Crono urged, "Let's keep 'em moving."

The early comers, easily identifiable by the way they lined both sides of the road and the smug expressions that they wore, stood three deep.

By the time Solly and the priest had managed to cajole, chivy, and chase their flock into position, the procession was a good deal closer. Dara's hand found Solly's as they turned to watch.

A squad of Reapers came first, weapons slung across their backs, eyes to the front. Their mutimals snorted, and the animals breath looked like smoke.

The drummer came next, his face tight and solemn as the *boom*, *boom*, *boom* of his instrument added weight to the occasion, and his mother waved from the crowd.

Then came the standard-bearers, closely followed by a mutimal-drawn cart. The axle creaked and chains clattered as the conveyance drew near. Something stood on it—no, *two* somethings, both so wondrous as to make Solly's hearts skip a beat. Devil machines! Not just parts, like in the churches he'd seen, but the real thing. Wet clay hid parts of the constructs from view—but the rest were exposed.

The cart lurched as a wheel encountered a chunk of stone. A whip cracked, the mutimals brayed, and the cart jerked. It was at that exact moment, while the animals struggled to overcome the obstacle, that their eyes mct.

Solly had seen lots of humans by then, and had no difficulty identifying this machine as male, although the reason for such a guise was less than obvious.

The eyes were blue, ice blue, and filled with intelligence. Though angry, they regarded Solly without hatred or fear. They had a magnetic quality, and the Zid felt a part of himself jump the gap—and waited for God to strike him down.

The cart bounded over the rock and rattled past. In spite of the fact that Solly watched the administrator general ride by, and joined the cheer that followed, his mind went elsewhere. The machine was alive—that was obvious, yet clearly impossible. Only God could create life.

Still, God created humans, and *they* made machines. Why would the Omniscient One grant such a capacity to the aliens unless he intended them to use it? That would mean that machines were of God—and *not* of the Devil.

But what of the Church? Was it fallible? Solly looked at Crono and knew the answer. Of course it was. They had come a long, long way together, and while the priest had many strengths, there were weaknesses as well.

The realization frightened Solly—and set him free. Surely the gifts that God had bestowed on humans were available to the Zid as well. All one had to do was accept them.

The thought was so evil, so daring, that Solly glanced around. Dara smiled—but no one else seemed to care.

Solly squeezed her hand, tucked the secret away, and knew he must wait. When the opportunity came, he would take it.

28

e pi´ pha ny, n, a moment of sudden or intuitive understanding

The Chosen One entered the room, took a long, careful look around, and nodded to his bodyguard. There had been two assassination attempts during the past thirty days. None of the would-be murderers had survived to face interrogation, and as a result, certain members of his staff had been made to suffer quite horribly. Still, there was little doubt who the killers worked for.

Jantz had been increasingly surly of late, was frequently hard to find, and showed a marked lack of respect. Almost as if he *knew* Lictor wouldn't be around to cause him trouble.

The Chosen One frowned as he took his thronelike seat. His critics had been correct . . . damn their souls to hell. It had been a mistake to admit the humans to the priesthood. Still, mistakes can be corrected. Lictor motioned to a monk. "The administrator general may enter."

The door opened, and the human named Maras shuffled inside. A black hood covered his head. He blinked as it was removed. His clothing, still filthy from the rigors of the journey, was suitably humble.

Thanks to his spies, Lictor already knew about the battle for Riftwall, the woman who liked machines, and the fact that Maras knew his meeting had been observed by two spies . . . neither of which was fooled by his clumsy strategms.

Of even more interest were the changes in his subordinate's face. It was leaner now, as if the excess flesh had been pared away, leaving nothing but skin and bone. Their eyes met, and the Zid bowed his head. "You performed well, my son. The Church is grateful."

Maras looked down, then up again. "An instrument of God was I. To him all glory must go."

Lictor was both surprised and pleased by the attempt to speak his tongue. Perhaps there was hope for some humans after all. "Yes, of course. Our language is not easy. I appreciate your effort to master it."

Maras felt a sudden pang of fear. How would Jantz react to such warm praise? And where the heck was he, anyway?

Lictor sent a smile rippling down the center of his face. "Congratulations, my son—for the elders and I have seen fit to elevate you to counselor for ecclesiastical affairs—a rank equivalent to archbishop. I would induct you into the priesthood if it lay within my power—but your marriage makes that impossible."

Maras had been interested in power and the people who had it for as long as he could remember. That being the case, he was thrilled, even though there would be a price to pay—especially where Mary was concerned. But that was for later—Lictor was waiting. "No, eminence, accept I cannot."

"Oh, but you will," Lictor insisted levelly. "Your modesty becomes you, but the Church has need of your skills, and your duty is clear."

The comment brought the meeting to a close, and Maras, who had never been given the opportunity to sit, was ready to depart. He bowed, turned, and was halfway to the door when Lictor spoke.

"Your daughter will be pleased by your return. Her initiation into full membership is scheduled for tomorrow evening.''

The human turned. Daughter? Membership? The words were like twin blows. Maras had protected Corley and allowed her to ignore most of the dogma. That would have to change. He forced a smile. ''Thank you, eminence. I will remember this day.''

Canova knew something unusual was afoot, because the cathedral had been packed for weeks now. Not only packed, but open around the clock, allowing the faithful to gawk nonstop. She shut her eyes and tried to go within. It never seemed to work. The synthetic could *feel* the churchgoers staring at her body and hating what they saw. That's how it seemed, anyhow.

Did she ''feel'' in the human sense? Or generate predictions based on assimilated data? It hardly mattered. The experience was uncomfortable. That's all Canova knew or needed to know.

The android would have welcomed delusions, even at the cost of her sanity, but they never arrived. Humans bore the responsibility for that. Humans concerned with their own fallibility—and afraid lest some of their weakness manifest in their creations. A precaution that *their* creator had neglected to pursue. Why?

Canova found it curious that some humans were unable to accept the notion of a creator, while synthetics were ''born'' knowing they had been created and by whom.

The android heard the sound of approaching footsteps, felt hands grab her from behind, and felt a sudden sense of fear. What was happening?

The first voice said, ''This thing is heavy . . . so watch your feet.''

''You think *this* is heavy?'' the second voice responded. ''Wait till you see the monster they captured at Riftwall. It's huge!''

Canova opened her ''eyes'' in time to see a Zid lurch into view. He did something with a strap and signaled to his partner. ''All right, Poog! You ready?''

''Ready!'' the other Zid answered . . . and Canova started

to fall. She tried to deploy her arms, tried to save herself, but nothing happened. The ceiling, which she had often wanted to see, came into view. The synthetic saw carvings, paintings, and clan script. The whole of it swayed as they hauled her away.

That's when Canova realized that she'd been replaced—and knew that an even worse fate might lay in store. What if they cut her body into pieces? What if they sent her head to one village and her legs to another? The android screamed, and her voice echoed through the church.

The line stretched forever. That's the way it appeared, anyway, as the prisoners took a single step forward. There were various theories about what awaited them at the far end of the queue—ranging from a medical checkup to a firing squad.

Mary closed the gap and thought about Corley. So close and yet so far. And what of George? There had been no sign of him for days now. Had he forsaken her? Or been forced to stay away? There was no way to know.

Still, this could be it, the line that led to freedom. *If* Mary proclaimed her willingness to convert, *if* they believed her, and *if* George kept his promise. There would be decisions to be made, but she refused to consider them. That was then—this was now.

It took the better part of an hour for the line to inch its way forward and pull Mary into the specially designed hut. Originally conceived to process Reaper recruits, it had a front door through which the prisoners entered, and a back door through which they could leave.

Light stabbed down through open vent holes and brought the smoke-filled atmosphere to languid life. A table stood off to the right. Mary stumbled as a guard pushed her, regained her balance, and came face to face with her husband.

He looked different somehow—colder, if such a thing was possible, and even more imperious than before. High-ranking members of the Church hierarchy sat to either side of him, and both were Zid. Mary searched but saw no compassion in their stony eyes. The one on the right spoke passable Spanglish. ''Your name?''

Maras sat expressionless, but Mary knew what he would want. "Smith. Mary Smith."

The Zid scratched something onto the parchment in front of him, sent his eye to the far side of his face, and addressed his peer. "Bishop Drog?"

Drog recognized the human as the one that the Chosen One had warned him against. He wondered what the next few moments would hold. How would the newly appointed counsel for ecclesiastical affairs handle himself? Would he use his newfound power to save the female? Or prove his devotion to the Church by condemning her to a labor brigade? A truly fascinating moment. Lictor would hang on every word.

Drog pretended to consult the document in front of him and cleared his throat. "Mary, ah, Smith . . . Ours is an all-loving God who extends his mercy to Zid and human alike. The only entities barred from membership are so-called synthetic beings and those who serve them. Are you, or have you ever been, a member of either class?"

Mary's throat felt dry. She swallowed in order to lubricate the word. "No."

"That being the case," Drog continued, "you are invited to renounce evil, join the Church, and live as we do.

"Please remember that membership in the Antitechnic Church will in no way protect you from hardship and may lead to even greater sacrifice. That being said—how do you declare?"

Maras felt his stomach churn as his wife prepared her answer. She would say yes, which would trigger a vote. What should he do? Vote yes, and hope for the best? Or listen to the voice that warned of a trap?

Mary found her ex-husband's eyes and delivered the lie directly to him. "I believe in the Church—and wish to convert."

Drog marveled at the accuracy with which Lictor had predicted her response. He turned to his companions. "The human, Mary Smith, would take God into her heart. What say you?"

Bishop Worb, the Zid seated to Mary's right, knew nothing of Lictor's concerns and had little respect for the frequently inaccurate intelligence reports. The human seemed sincere—and he had no way to look inside the female's head. "I vote yes."

Things were proceeding exactly as George had predicted they would. Mary felt her spirits rise.

Drog signaled his understanding. "Thank you, Bishop Worb. Mine is the opposite view, I'm afraid. This female was spotted in the company of so-called synthetics prior to the counselor's attack on Riftwall—and subsequently went to their aid. She lied to this panel—and can never be trusted."

The bishop's words left no doubt as to the truth of the matter. The situation was a setup . . . and Maras must choose. Condemn Mary—or condemn himself. He attempted to meet her eyes but couldn't.

"Bishop Drog is correct. Request denied. Next, please."

Mary heard herself gasp, then was herded toward the back door and shoved into the cold. Her fate was sealed.

Harley Doon had never felt so helpless as when they rolled him into the cathedral, down a long, empty aisle, and boosted him up onto a pedestal. He wanted to hurt them, to run as far as he could, but the clay held him fast.

He could have spoken to them, yelled or even screamed, but knew better than to do so. They could stuff his mouth with clay, mess with his electronics, or who knew what else. No, it was better to wait and hope for the best. Amy was nearby, and that helped, especially since they could communicate.

The cathedral was amazing. So much so that he actually forgot his circumstances for a moment and was lost in the magnificence of the building itself. The design, stonework, and art were of the highest quality.

That stage passed, however, especially when the faithful entered and clustered around. Like most law enforcement beings, Doon had been hated before. It didn't seem to help much.

Amy started to sob. Doon tried to comfort her. The minutes, hours, and days stretched eternally ahead. It seemed strange that it was here, within a cathedral, that hell made its home.

Night had fallen, and the halls were lit by candles. Maras threw multiple shadows down the hall. The largest of them was big and black. It lunged ahead. The counselor's mind, riddled by doubt, was left to follow.

The human had gone to sleep after the judgment in the hut, or tried to, but nightmares disturbed his rest. All of them were horrible, but none worse than the one in which Jantz handed him the hammer of justice and commanded that he make use of it. The handle was slick with blood, and nearly slipped from his fingers. "No! I work with numbers—not people."

Jantz looked surprised. "Really? But what of this? And this? And finally this? Are they not people?"

Maras saw a heretic hanging from a tree, a child cut in half, and Mary standing before him, head bowed, waiting for the hammer to fall.

That's when he woke, his nightclothes drenched in sweat, his jaw clenched.

Now, only hours later, he was making his way to the chapel where Corley would be initiated, where the Church would claim her soul and convey it to God. A God in which he didn't believe—and knew he never would. His footsteps sounded hollow, and they echoed down the hall.

Seeing no reason to waste a candle, the workers left Canova in total darkness. Well, not total darkness, since her sensors could detect heat. It appeared as bright green blobs. One for the wall sconce that continued to cool, another for the rat that scurried along the wall, and the last for a flue that rose through the floor above.

The darkness didn't bother her so much as the sudden isolation and complete uncertainty did. Was this some sort of storeroom? A place in which she would rot for years on end? Or little more than a way station from which she would soon be moved? The questions continued to nag.

A human might have wondered about the passage of time—but Canova knew she had occupied her prison for exactly twelve hours and sixteen minutes before a commotion was heard and the door creaked open. A rectangle of light extended across the floor.

A human entered, placed a candle in the sconce, and turned in her direction. Canova had seen the man before, and knew who he was. Victor Jantz. He nodded pleasantly.

"Good evening, Dr. Canova. I'm sorry about the darkness, but we couldn't expect much else. The workers had no idea who or what they were dealing with."

"And you do?"

Jantz looked surprised. "Yes, of course. Dr. Suti Canova, one of the most skilled physicians on Zuul, and an amateur xenoanthropologist. I'm sorry, Doctor, but scholarship *can* be dangerous."

"Yes," Canova agreed cautiously. "It can. So tell me, citizen Jantz . . . what brings you to my little hideaway? Slumming?"

The human scanned the walls, hoped they were solid, and forced a smile. "No, of course not. You have a problem, and so do I. Perhaps we could be of assistance to each other."

Canova felt a sudden surge of hope. Jantz needed something! Something she could give. "A deal, Bishop Jantz? A deal with the Devil?"

The human looked over his shoulder. "Don't talk like that. Not even in jest."

"I'm sorry," the synthetic said quickly. "It won't happen again. Medical history first—symptoms second."

Jantz looked surprised, and Canova smiled. "What else would bring you here?"

The human nodded, provided the necessary information, and answered her questions.

Later, when the door squeaked closed, a candle burned in the sconce.

Maras heard the sound of chanting and detected the scent of incense long before he arrived at the chapel. Corley was waiting for him. She was annoyed and let it show. "Where have you been, Daddy? We should be halfway through the ceremony by now."

The tone was both spoiled and petulant. A lack of discipline, or something more? His daughter had changed during his absence—and not for the better. Where was the sweet little girl he'd known just months before?

Maras knelt next to Corley, straightened her gown, and looked into her eyes. Mary looked back.

The counselor flinched as if struck across the face. Corley looked curious, and Maras forced a smile. "Sorry about being late, honey. I got hung up, that's all. Are you ready?"

"Sure," the little girl said confidently. "I'll make you proud."

The words echoed through the counselor's mind as he took his seat. The initiation involved a long series of ritual questions. Corley had memorized the answers, and now she reeled them off. What amazed Maras was the extent to which she sounded sincere. Did Corley really believe this stuff? Or did she pretend to believe, the same way he did? It had been a long time since they had talked about such matters. Too long.

Suddenly, as his daughter traced triangles in the air, and bound herself to the Church, Maras felt a wave of nausea. What the hell was he doing? Had he done? Corley didn't belong here, joined to something built on hatred.

It was all the counselor could do to resist the impulse to snatch his daughter off the platform and run away. However due to the fact that the ceremony functioned as a source of entertainment within smaller villages, it was intentionally long, and lasted more than an hour.

By the time the last "dola" had been said, Maras knew what he must do. The knowledge both pleased and frightened him. He took Corley by the hand. "Come on, honey—there's someone I want you to see."

There were more than a thousand prisoners, most of whom were human, all shivering in the cold night air. There were no shelters, no blankets, nothing beyond the two dozen fires to provide them with warmth. Some slept, or tried to sleep, huddled in groups. The rest, Mary included, stood around the fires. Their faces, lit from below, floated ghostlike in the air.

"Why wait?" one man asked, his face anonymous behind

a tightly wrapped scarf. "They'll kill us in the end. We might as well take some of the bastards with us."

"And how many would that be?" an older woman asked pragmatically, her breath fogging the night. "A dozen or so? Against a thousand human lives? Seems like a mighty poor trade-off to me."

Mary thought about the palisade that encircled them, the Reapers who patrolled the top, and the weapons they carried. There was no doubt about it—the woman was right, but so was the man. The only *real* choice was how they wanted to die.

There was a commotion as the gate opened and a group of Reapers forced their way in. They were mounted on mutimals and carried whips rather than firearms—a wise precaution, given the extent to which they were outnumbered.

Torches flared, a whip cracked, and a mutimal bellowed in pain as the phalanx of riders pushed its way into the crowd. A Reaper stood in his stirrups. "Prisoner Smith! Prisoner *Mary* Smith!"

Mary felt a sudden jolt of fear. Her knees felt weak, and her hands started to shake. Few of the prisoners knew her, but those who did looked in her direction. They knew the Church had rejected her—and why. The roboticist would make an excellent sacrifice—a way to add interest to an otherwise dull sermon.

A shot rang out. A man threw up his arms and toppled into a fire. Sparks flew upward, screams were heard, and the crowd eddied. "We want Smith! Mary Smith!" the Reaper shouted. "Or another will die!"

Mary forced strength into her limbs and raised an arm. "I'm Smith! Over here!"

The Reaper spotted her, signaled his companions, and urged the mutimal forward. The man, his clothes on fire, continued to burn. Those standing to either side of Mary scattered as the Zid approached, leaving her to face them alone. The lead Reaper jerked his animal to a halt and stared downward. "Mary Smith?"

Mary tried to speak, but nothing came out. She nodded instead.

The Zid motioned with his whip. "Raise your arms."

Mary obeyed.

A pair of riders moved in, grabbed the roboticist by the wrists, and jerked her off the ground. Then, hanging between them, Mary was carried toward the gate. It opened as if by magic—and closed three seconds later. A howl erupted from inside the compound as the prisoners recovered their courage.

But they were too late to help Mary, whose arms felt as if they would be torn from their sockets, and whose boots touched the ground at six-foot intervals. The roboticist saw a fire up ahead, a big one, with flames as tall as she was. The Reapers showed no signs of turning and increased their speed. They meant to drop her. The human struggled to no avail. She hoisted her feet, closed her eyes, and waited for the pain.

The Zid on the right let out a whoop, the one on the left answered, and they split the fire between them. Mary closed her eyes, felt the heat flash around her, and waited for the riders to let go. They didn't.

The roboticist was still absorbing that fact, still marveling at the cool night air, when she saw the mutimal. It was huge and loomed black on black. Then she was flying, falling and tumbling, her hands pushing through the slush. When the human came to a stop, she was facedown only feet from the animal's iron-clad hooves. She had been delivered. But to whom? And for what?

The Reapers were gone, but Mary heard footsteps in the slush. A pair of knees landed next to her face, and a hand touched her back. "Mommy? Is that you?"

Mary pushed the ground away, terrified that it was a dream, and she would wake in the compound. "Corley? Oh my God, is it really you?"

Corley threw her arms around her mother's neck. "Yes, of course it's me! I missed you."

"Not as much as I missed you," Mary blubbered, hugging her daughter to ensure that she was real. "You're bigger! Lots bigger. I came as soon as I could. We went to Riftwall but the Reapers came and . . ."

Corley touched her mother's lips. "I know, Mommy— Daddy told me."

George Maras stepped forward, offered his hand, and pulled Mary to her feet. "I told her *everything*. How you came for her and how I betrayed you. All of it."

Mary looked into his eyes, saw the pain there, and started to speak. Maras shook his head. "Thanks, Mary, but we don't have much time. Take Corley and the mutimal. You'll find food in the saddlebags. Run and keep running. All the way to Flat Top. Tell them what's coming. Who knows? Maybe they can survive."

Corley frowned and bit her lower lip. "What about you, Daddy? The Church will get mad, *real* mad, and try to hurt you. *Please* come with us."

Maras smiled and stroked the side of her face. "I *will* come, honey . . . but there's something I must do first. Something important."

Mary looked into her ex-husband's eyes, admired what she saw there, and gave a nod. "Thank you, George. Thank you for everything. We shall never forget."

The roboticist placed her left foot in a stirrup and hoisted her right leg over the saddle. Maras kissed the top of his daughter's head, boosted her behind, and forced a smile. "Take care, you two! See you at Flat Top!"

With that, he slapped the mutimal's hindquarters and watched them ride away. The counselor waited until his family was safely out of sight before turning toward the cathedral. It was a twenty-minute hike—and speed was of the essence. The church services were spaced about one hour apart. Just enough time to clean the floors, renew the candles, and otherwise prepare for the next horde of worshipers.

Maras needed as much of that time as he could get. The semifrozen slush crunched under his boots.

The spy watched for a moment, and allowed his subject to lead the way. As with all of his kind, he found the shadows to his liking and stayed to them whenever he could. Darkness was his friend.

Doon watched the latest batch of churchgoers shuffle their way out, gave thanks for the upcoming break, and checked his surroundings. No one was watching, not from the front anyway, which meant it was time to flex his muscles.

Thanks to the fact that the clay had been applied back in Riftwall, and subjected to the rigors of the road, stress fractures had developed within. By flexing his servo-driven musculature, the android hoped to exploit the cracks and eventually break free.

He figured it was only a matter of time before the Zid removed his old shell and built a new one around him. The key was to shatter the clay *before* that day came—but not in the middle of a church service.

Repetition was the key, or so he theorized, and the synthetic went to work. Contract-push-relax. Contract-push-relax. Contract-push-relax. He did it over and over with machinelike persistence.

Doon had been at it for exactly nine minutes and sixteen seconds when Maras entered. He was famous by now—and maintenance workers hurried out of his way.

The synthetic recognized Maras immediately, and was surprised when the human started in his direction. There was a bag in his hand, similar in size and shape to the ones that Zid stonemasons favored, and his expression was grim.

Bystanders watched with open curiosity as the newly named counselor strode across the floor and approached the Devil's altar. Maras found the android's eyes, smiled reassuringly, and opened the bag. "Some chance is better than none . . . that's the way I figure it, anyway. Help me free your friend, then run like hell. Don't bother with the others. None of them are sentient."

So saying, Maras removed a hammer from the bag, struck the clay over Doon's shoulder, and watched it crumble.

Jantz, exhausted by the effects of his heart condition, remained in his chair. The spy, who had run the last half mile through the corridors, was badly out of breath. He was a Zid, one of a number the human had managed to suborn, and dressed in rags. His gills pulsed as he fought for air. The human knew the way that felt. He waited for the male to speak.

"The counselor—gasp—sent for one of the females—gasp—put her on a mutimal—gasp—and allowed her to escape."

"And his daughter? Did she run as well?"

"Yes!" the spy answered, astonished by the extent to which the bishop could read his mind. "That's exactly what happened."

Jantz shook his head in amazement. So Maras had balls after all. Who'd have thought it? "And then?"

"He stopped for a tool bag and entered the cathedral. That's when I came for you."

"A tool bag? You're sure?"

"Yes, holy one."

"Take my arm. Help me up. We must hurry."

After Maras struck the blow, the rest was easy. The clay fractured into large chunks, exploded against the floor, and scattered in every direction. Doon felt the weight drop away, brought his aggressor systems on-line, and flexed his shoulders. More of the hardened earth broke away from his body as he stepped down onto the floor.

A maintenance worker screamed and another ran for help as the android ran across the nave. He struck a blow with his fist, saw a crack zigzag down through the clay that encased Amy's chest, and did the same thing again. More of the stuff fell away, and an arm came loose.

Amy felt a wonderful sense of freedom as she rid herself of more clay and entered the circle of Doon's arms.

The embrace was brief but wonderful. It was the first time she had felt anything like what human females described as "love." A profound sense of warmth, belonging, and trust. Was there more? *Could* there be more? Amy didn't know and doubted that she would live long enough to find out.

"Doon grabbed Amy's hand and pulled her away. "Maras! Where's Mary?"

"Gone with Corley," the counselor answered. "They're headed for Flat Top."

"Good. Come on, let's get going."

The human shook his head. "No, I'll be fine. There are mutimals tethered outside. Take them and ride."

The android looked at the human, saw he was serious, and headed for the door.

A pair of Reapers appeared and were framed by the entrance. Both were armed, but their weapons hung on slings. Understandable, given where they were—but unfortunate for them. Doon had been born with an in-depth preconditioned knowledge of six martial arts.

The first Zid fell to a lightning-fast series of blows, the last of which left him unconscious.

The second Reaper had more time, landed a roundhouse right, and winced as the Devil machine took hold of his arm. Bone cracked; the Zid screamed and went to his knees.

Doon bent over his first victim, removed a knife from his belt sheath, and cut the assault weapon free.

''Harley! Behind you!''

The android spun, spotted the Reapers, and touched the trigger twice. They staggered and fell. Battle axes clattered to the floor and slid away.

''This way!'' Amy shouted. ''Hurry!''

The synthetic ran for the door as Amy kicked a Reaper in the chest and then struggled with a second. Doon fired from the hip, saw the assailant fall away, and grabbed the other android's wrist.

More than a dozen mutimals were tied to a rail. The android freed all but two, hoped there was something useful in the bags slung across their backs, and boosted Amy into a saddle. She had acquired a weapon of her own somewhere along the line, and now she fired two rounds into the air. The mutimals panicked, turned, and galloped away. Doon saw the direction they had chosen, shouted, ''Follow me!'' and took off in pursuit.

Maras listened to the firing, hoped it meant what he thought it did, and turned his back on the door. The platforms looked strangely empty. It seemed as if his feet had minds of their own. Clay crunched as he walked. The Devil's altar made a good place to sit . . . and that's where Lictor, Jantz, and a half dozen Reapers found him.

The counselor smiled wearily. ''Fancy meeting you here. . . . Don't tell me, let me guess. Something's missing.''

29

a tone´ ment, n, reparation for an offense or injury

The sky was miraculously clear, and the sun rose like an omen of gold. Its rays melted some of the slush and sent rivulets of water gurgling in every direction—water that added to the muddy morass that surrounded the camp.

But no amount of mud could dampen Solly's spirits, not with the sun on his back, and the sure knowledge that they were leaving. Not for home, as he had hoped, but as part of the holy crusade.

It *sounded* glorious, but, as Solly had learned over the last ninety days, things that *sound* good often aren't. He also questioned the wisdom of such a trek, especially when food supplies were dwindling and the harvests were poor. Even Crono agreed, not directly of course, but by implication. There was very little doubt who "those idiots" were, or what he meant by "damned foolishness."

Still, Solly felt lucky in two respects, first to escape the cathedral and its muddy environs, and second to do so in company with Dara, a continual source of joy. Even the large clumps of mud that clung to Solly's boots couldn't slow the youngster's stride as he made his way between the shelters, spotted the female on the far side of the assembly area, and hurried to join her.

Voices yelled orders as tents were struck, a hammer rang on metal, a hordu issued a series of grunts, a prayer caller sang his song, the odor of hot tromeal hung in the air, and a squad of would-be Reapers marched back and forth. It was stimulating, but Solly still yearned for home.

They couldn't embrace, not publicly anyway, but no one could object to eye contact. Thoughts, ideas, and emotions jumped the gap between the youngsters and brought smiles to their faces.

"Good morning, Solly."

"Good morning, Dara."

"Have you had breakfast?"

"Why no, how 'bout you?"

"Not yet. Would you care to join me?"

"Why yes, that would be nice."

They laughed at the parody and left for the mess tent. Some villagers subsisted on one meal a day. The crusaders ate three.

Dr. Suti Canova scanned the room to ensure that no one was watching, took the second position, and moved to an arabesque. She was free! Free to move as she pleased . . . and it felt wonderful!

There was work to do, however, important work that had nothing to do with the so-called "gift" of ballet. The synthetic giggled, dropped the pose, and went to work.

The makeshift surgery was located somewhere within the cathedral and was packed with illicit medical equipment. There were sets of old-fashioned instruments, an autoclave in which to sterilize them, packages of surgical drapes, an operating table, lights, basins, a nonsentient anesthetist, a cupboard packed with drugs, and a fully operational nano farm.

All the android was required to do was operate on the human, repair the damage to his heart, and renew his nano. Then she'd go free. That's what Jantz had promised—and that's what Canova wanted to believe. But *could* she believe it? And, more than that, *should* she believe it?

The trap had been well and carefully laid. Thanks to updates provided by Michael, the synthetics had not only managed to escape from the cathedral but had made excellent progress as well. They were no more than a half day behind Mary and Corley Maras. Now, as the Reapers closed in, Doon had plans to dissuade them.

The synthetic left Amy to guard the mutimals and picked his way up through a pile of randomly placed boulders to the very top. The sunlight had melted the frost and left a wet spot behind.

Doon lay on his anterior surface, checked the assault weapon to ensure its readiness, and moved the fire selector to S for "single." With that accomplished, he lowered the barrel-mounted bipod into the proper position, ejected the 1.5X6 sight from the top-mounted receiver bay, and dry-snapped the trigger. There were three levels of sensitivity to choose from, and he selected number two.

His own vision, which was very nearly as good as that provided by the telescopic sight, detected movement on the edge of the horizon. "Mike?"

"Yeah?"

"Are those Reapers off to the east?"

" 'Fraid so."

"Roger that."

It was another ten minutes before it was worth peeking through the sight, and another fifteen before the riders came within range. Part assault weapon, and part sniper's rifle, the Spatz fired a 7.62mm round with a muzzle velocity of eight hundred fifty feet per second. Not too bad . . . if the ammo was good.

The Reapers had ridden their animals hard, and the creatures were lathered with sweat. Doon watched their leader float through his sight, and allowed the crosshairs to caress the male's chest. The Zid didn't know it yet . . . but he was going to heaven.

•   •   •

Maras, adorned by nothing more than a loincloth, and a sign that read ''heretic,'' put his weight against the leather straps. They cut deeply into his already raw shoulders as his body accepted the full weight of the sled. It was loaded with the symbols of his guilt: a pile of jumbled droid parts, his vestments, and the tools confiscated from Mary. He pulled with all his strength, the sled slithered over the mud, and the crowd roared their hatred.

Maras accepted the emotion as his due, as the price that needed to be paid, knowing the ordeal would soon be over. After all, it was he who had brought the crusade to life, had taken it from concept to plan, and written the master schedule—a schedule so well conceived that it allowed time for a ''sacrifice'' or similar entertainment just prior to departure. Little did he know who would provide it!

Maras laughed, and some of the onlookers stepped back.

Solly, who knew better than to share his innermost feelings with anyone other than Dara, felt sorry for the human. He remembered how the same male had been welcomed only days before, and marveled at the manner in which his fortunes had been reversed. Life was exceedingly strange.

Crono watched the display with something verging on disgust. He felt nothing but contempt for the traitorous human, the hierarchy that had been stupid enough to trust him, and the manner in which so many innocents would soon lose their lives.

The cleric had already gone to quite some lengths to ensure that *his* flock would march toward the rear of the procession—a rather undistinguished position that some of his less thoughtful brothers had been quick to relinquish.

Crono smiled grimly as the human fell, took a whip across his bare back, and struggled to his feet. Let those who wanted glory have it. His job was to protect those placed in his care—and to get them home alive. He had failed once. It wouldn't happen again.

''The door's locked? You checked?'' Jantz asked nervously. He looked vulnerable on the operating table. White with lots of wiry black hair. Tubes snaked in and out of his body, and his arms extended to either side.

Canova, who had answered the question at least three times before, nodded patiently. "The doors are locked. Besides, Lictor, his spies, and everybody who is anybody are at the ceremony. That's why you chose this particular day. Remember?"

Jantz nodded. The android was correct—well, *mostly* correct, since he had detailed some men to stay. Yes, he had given his word, but what if something went wrong immediately after surgery? Or a year down the line? He would need the synthetic's help—and there was only one way to ensure that he'd have it. "You're right, as always—let's get on with it."

Canova nodded and sent a radio transmission to the non-sentient anesthetist. "Take the patient down."

The robot, which looked like a box with arms, dispensed the minimum amount of sodium thiopental to induce unconsciousness, placed a mask over the human's face, and pushed a mixture of oxygen and nitrous oxide down into the human's lungs.

Canova prepped the human's chest, placed self-sealing drapes around the perimeter of the site, and inserted a standard medical interface into the socket at the back of her neck. Though conceived as words, her orders would be translated to code and transmitted to the nano. Thousands of tiny machines responded to the electronic call, swarmed up through a wire-thin tube, and spilled out onto the patient's skin. Others entered his body via the IV in his arm and routed themselves through his circulatory system.

Most were far too small to see, which meant that the incision opened as if by magic, bleeders seemed to cauterize themselves, and the scar tissue left by previous operations appeared to dissolve.

In fact, under ideal conditions, with full robotic support, there would have been no need for an incision, and the entire procedure would have been performed internally.

Such was not the case, however, so it was up to Canova to place the chest spreaders, deal with the more stubborn bleeders, and suction the blood away. Blood that would be filtered to remove new or used nano.

The initial phase of the reconstruction took half an hour.

The micromachines would complete the rest of the surgery over the next few days—an approach calculated to reduce the overall insult to the body, and give the newly introduced nano time to work on the patient's circulatory and respiratory systems.

Canova kept an eye on her screens, queried the nano from time to time, and monitored Jantz's vital signs.

Finally, as the incision began to close, the synthetic ordered her nano to inject certain drugs into the human's bloodstream, checked to ensure that the appropriate dosages could be sustained for the next year or so, and told the anesthetist what she had in mind.

True to its programming, the machine took silent issue with the instructions, and a dialog ensued. Also true to programming, the nonsentient machine was forced to back down and do what it was told. Valves opened, gas hissed, and readouts flickered.

Consistent with the orders they'd been given, the two men watched through a peephole, waited until their leader's skin had knitted itself together, and opened the door. A blast of cold air entered the room. The first man held a stunner; the second secured the door.

Canova, who had just applied a dressing to her patient's chest, looked over her shoulder. "There you are . . . right on time."

The smaller of the two had a large nose and beady eyes. They blinked stupidly. "Right on time?"

"Zap her," the bigger man said impatiently. "Do it now."

Big nose yawned, struggled to focus his eyes, and felt them close. The stunner fell from his hand and clattered on the floor.

The larger specimen frowned, started to say something, and felt his knees buckle. Both men hit the floor at roughly the same time.

Canova smiled, took a moment to bind their limbs with surgical tape, and sent an order to the anesthetist. "Kill the nitrous."

The machine obeyed and, because the action was in alignment with its programming, came very close to what sentients refer to as happiness.

Pleased by the success of her plan, the android wrestled a pair of green bottles off a cart marked "MED BAY 4, DECK 3," and pushed it to the operating table.

A quick check confirmed that the drugs had taken effect. The human was effectively paralyzed—and would remain so as long as the drug supply lasted.

It wasn't easy to lift Jantz off the table and strap him to the cart, but the synthetic was stronger than she looked.

Once that was accomplished, it was a simple matter to pull a robe over her patient's head, throw a cape around her shoulders, and turn out the lights. The cart squeaked as it rolled down the hall.

The bullet arrived before the sound did. However, like so much of the black-market ammo produced in Vent's factories, the chemical propellents fell short of military specs, and were less efficient than they should've been.

The slug, which had been aimed at the Reaper's chest, hit his mutimal in the neck. The beast took three additional steps before it nosed over, threw the Zid over its head, and died. The Reaper lived just long enough to see the cluster of jagged rocks, throw his hands forward, and scream. The impact broke both his arms and crushed his skull.

Doon swore on channel four and adjusted his aim. His next bullet went where it was supposed to—as did the one that followed that. The first body tumbled out of the saddle, hit the ground, and skidded to a halt. The second fell, hung from a stirrup, and bounced across some rocks.

Doon took his finger off the trigger, saw the rest of the Reapers turn back, and let them go.

That's when the android thought of something he should have realized before. There had been no consequence for shooting Zid back in Riftwall—no night of self-imposed torment, and no feelings of guilt. Aliens weren't people, not according to his programming anyway, and he could shoot as many as he cared to.

Did that mean that his creators were fallible? Pragmatic in the extreme? Racist to the core? None of the possibilities seemed very appealing.

Doon collected his casings, slipped them into his pocket,

and slapped a fresh magazine into the well. Amy was half-way to the bodies by then. Ammo was valuable and well worth scavenging. Even Sojo agreed with that.

Lictor felt mixed emotions as he looked out over the assembled multitude. Sixty thousand eyes stared back. The faithful stood in groups, clustered around their various leaders, ready to march. He saw Provident red, Faithful green, Obedient blue, and a half dozen other colors. The crowd looked like a living tapestry—a vast needlework of the sort his mother loved to make. Not a bad idea, actually—with him at the center. It would hang in the nave to commemorate this day.

The crusade was shaping up to be even more glorious than he had hoped it would be—an unstoppable wave that would carry the heretics before it and purify the entire planet.

There was a cost, however. The supplies required to enable his dream had left certain villages teetering on the edge of starvation—a problem he had relied on his newly named counselor for ecclesiastical affairs to solve. That same human stood before him now, head held high, waiting to die.

If only Maras had held the course, had vanquished the Devil within him, but such was not the case. Humans were flawed, *very* flawed, and subject to every kind of weakness. Lictor raised a hand, and the crowd fell silent. His voice wouldn't carry to the entire multitude, so priests had been assigned to relay his words, causing them to echo across the land.

"Greetings. We stand at the beginning of a great and glorious enterprise, a journey within ourselves, and a crusade against evil. An entire host of dangers await, not the least of which are the hardships of the road, the test of the long winter, and the heretics themselves. The Devil is strong—and will want to fight."

Lictor waited for the last echo to die away and started again. "Foremost among our enemies, however, is the tendency to listen to our own internal yearnings and ignore God's call. That, my friends, is what the human named Maras did. I want to witness both his crimes—and the fact that *no one* is immune to punishment. He's going to hell—and you could do likewise. Come, let us pray."

Maras squinted into the sun, felt his stomach flutter, and listened to the prayer. The one he chose originated from a different but no less bloody religion: "Yea, though I walk through the valley of the shadow of death, I shall fear no evil . . ."

The crowd spoke in unison, and Lictor, unable to hear the human's words, nodded approvingly. Who knew? Perhaps God would listen.

The hammer of divine justice rose high into the air and paused. Maras felt a shadow flicker across his face, saw his daughter smile, and was gone.

Canova nodded to an elderly monk, ignored a maintenance worker, and wheeled Jantz out onto the floor. *Her* platform, the one she had occupied for so long, lay directly ahead. A ramp provided access.

The synthetic pushed her burden a little faster, built additional speed, and made it to the top. Once she was there, it was a simple matter to turn Jantz in the proper direction and lock the wheels.

The human felt himself rise, as if from the bottom of a lake, and float on the surface. There was pain, yes, but not that much, and he was alive! Wonderfully, beautifully alive!

Eyes! He must open his eyes, assure himself that all was as it should be, and then he could rest.

Jantz ordered his eyes to open, felt resistance, and tried again. The sticky stuff gave way; blobs floated on air and quickly started to fade. "Zak? Paco?"

Canova heard the human croak and stepped into view. "The patient awakes! Excellent."

Jantz saw the synthetic, the seating beyond, and felt a sudden sense of panic. "Where are we? What have you done?"

Canova smiled. "I thought you'd never ask! I'm going on vacation . . . and leaving *you* in charge. The paralysis should wear off in a year or so—assuming they allow you to live. Oh, by the way, your heart is fine! Well, cheerio! My bill is in the mail."

Jantz struggled to move his limbs, discovered that he was unable to do so, and started to swear.

A group of pilgrims, just in from the country, made signs in the air.

The android, a scarf wrapped around her face, left through the main entrance, turned toward the sun, and started the long journey home.

In spite of the fact that it was night, the temperature was ten below, and snow had started to accumulate around them, the androids sat cross-legged, their knees touching. They had no need for a fire, no need for food, in fact no need for anything beyond each other. It felt good to be who and what they were, free from mindless hatred and from human society as well.

Their relationship, though superficially similar to what humans experience, had already gone deeper. Much deeper than what most sentients would want or be able to bear. Amy had wandered through Doon's memories, had lived moments of his life, and he'd done likewise with her. Only Sojo, sulking in the background, kept them from going further.

"Don't mind me," the ghost said. "Have a good time."

"Thank you," Amy replied gently. "We will."

The wind howled across the plain, the mutimals dozed in a nearby cave, and an angel watched over their heads.

30

proph´ et, n, one who foretells future events

The conference room looked the way it usually did—as if a bomb had been detonated inside it. A table stretched the length of the room. It was covered with an assortment of printouts, plates of half-eaten food, a couple of data pads, an R-26 servo controller, and a birthday cake with one unlit candle.

Garrison was listening to Bana Modo's report on the latest nano strain, and wondering what Dr. Omita would look like with her clothes off, when the note arrived. He read the careful printing—then read it again.

1016 Hours

Dr. Garrison,
A synthetic named Luis Garcia Sojo is attempting to contact you via radio—and says it is urgent. Reply?
Com Op 4

• • •

Could it be? Heads turned as Garrison stood, nodded to Modo, and left the room. Was the note for real? Or an excuse to leave the meeting? There was no way to know. Modo continued.

Garrison hurried to the com center, saw one of the techs raise her hand, and hurried over. Com Op 4 had gray hair, green eyes, and an implant. A cable was jacked into her right temple. "Don't know what to make of this one, sir. Says he's coming this way, and has something you need."

The roboticist felt his heart start to pound. "Thanks. I'll take the call."

The conversation lasted five minutes. Once it was over, Garrison returned to the meeting. Were those tears in his eyes? Or something else? It must be something else, Modo decided, because the boss never cried, not that he could remember anyway, and there was no reason to start now. Was there?

Garrison waited for silence, cleared his throat, and forced a smile. "Ladies and gentlemen . . . I have some *very* good news."

31

sanc´ tu ar y, n, a place of refuge and protection

The rocks, scattered as if by some careless hand, lay in a circle and gave shelter from the never-ending wind. Corley had risen early, and was struggling to rekindle the fire—when the monster appeared. It was big, black, and equipped with a huge pair of mandibles. She screamed and backed away.

Mary fought to extricate herself from the Zid bedroll, stood, and rushed to Corley's defense. The roboticist had no weapons, so there was nothing she could do except place her body between her daughter and the threat. "Run! Hide in the rocks!"

"That won't be necessary," a voice said. "Fido won't hurt you . . . not unless I tell him to."

Mary turned to find that a rider had entered her camp from the opposite direction. He was tall, good-looking in an unshaven way, and heavily armed. His eyes were green, his skin was brown, and his lips twitched in what might have been a smile. "Are you Dr. Maras? Dr. *Mary* Maras?"

Corley kept one eye on the robot and the other on her mother. Mary was surprised. "Yes, how did you know?"

"A synthetic named Doon told us," the man replied. "Via satellite relay. Said we should look for you."

Satellite relay? Suddenly Mary knew where much of Doon's seemingly miraculous information had originated from. Information he used to control their relationship. It was hard to stay angry, though—especially now.

"My name's Jones," the man offered. "Head of security for the folks at Flat Top. Once you and your daughter are ready, Fido will see you home. Ain't that right, big boy?"

The robot clacked its mandibles in agreement as Jones slipped to the ground. He gestured to Corley. "Come here . . . I want to show you something."

Corley looked up, saw her mother's nod, and made her way over. The monster loomed above. Jones took the little girl's hand and placed it against the creature's flank. It was smooth and warm to the touch. "See? He's a robot, a Mothri robot, so he looks kinda like they do. Would you like a ride? Come on, I'll boost you up."

Corley accepted the invitation, settled into the saddle-shaped depression at the rear of the robot's head, and laughed as it stood.

Mary smiled as her daughter rode the machine in circles and turned to Jones. "Thank you."

The security officer tipped his broad-brimmed hat. "My pleasure, ma'am. Just stay with Fido, and everything will be fine."

"What about you?"

The man stuck a couple of fingers into his mouth, produced an ear-splitting whistle, and grinned when a half-dozen heavily armed riders swept into the clearing. The bigwigs want Doon—and I was sent to get him."

Jones tipped his hat, mounted his animal, and turned toward the east. Gouts of snow, mud, and half-frozen gravel flew into the air, and the mutimals thundered away.

Fido made a chittering sound, and Corley laughed. As Mary broke camp, she thought about George—wondered if he would come, and what he was doing.

The wind shifted, sought a new path through the rocks, and sent a chill down her spine.

Mallaca Horbo Drula Enore the 5,223rd had straddled the tool trench for more than sixteen hours now, and, having run through two shifts of human assistants, was ready for a break. In spite of the fact that the overall repair project involved thousands of different nano types, Enore still had her favorites. Primary among them were a class of micromachines that the humans had nicknamed "mantle mites," both because they were designed to work deep inside the planet and because they were unbelievably small. Small enough to negotiate the narrowest fissures in their search for stress points.

Maybe it was the fact that like the Mothri herself, the mites were burrowers, or perhaps it was their insectoid appearance. Whatever the reason, they were her favorites and a subject upon which she was the recognized authority.

The subgroup now under construction was being assembled one atom at a time. Once complete, and having been checked for flaws, the new prototype would join an underground army. An army having no centralized control—and no model for the world. Each unit would operate in response to basic instructions such as move forward, find heat, and back up. More than that, they would learn—and share their knowledge with others.

And that was the problem. Now, after thousands of hours of work, Mothri nano and human nano could communicate with each other. But that wasn't enough, not to save the planet, or to save her eggs. No, for that to take place, Mothri–human nano must communicate with Forerunner nano.

Garrison claimed that a synthetic named Sojo had developed a solution to the problem, and that it would soon be solved. Enore hoped it was true.

She entered a final set of commands into the console located under her thorax, allowed the abdominal tool light to shut itself off, and peered about. The light was brighter than she liked. "Modo! Where in the five names for dirt are you? Fill my vat. It's time for a beer!"

•   •   •

The mesa known as Flat Top rose like an apparition through the mist, its cliffs straight and true, except where snow accumulated on ledges, and a trail zigzagged to the top.

Sojo was ecstatic and so eager to complete the journey that he could hardly contain himself.

Doon was a good deal less enthusiastic. Given the fact that Jones had been sent to bring the two of them in, and the eager way in which the security officer inquired about Sojo's health, there was at least some truth in the "I can save the planet" gibberish that the rider had been spewing for the last three months or so.

That was development that Doon would have regarded with some amusement, had it not been for the manner in which the Flat Toppers had treated him. Nothing rude, nothing overt, just the feeling that while the ghost had importance, Doon was little more than packaging. Even Amy had noticed . . . and she was one of them.

Flat Top vanished behind a veil of snow, only to reappear forty-five minutes later. It was closer now, *much* closer, and rose like an island of rock.

There were checkpoints, and some rudimentary fortifications, but fewer than Doon would have expected. It appeared that the scientists had put their trust in isolation plus the mesa itself to protect them.

Doon was thinking about the trail to the top, and wondering how many people had fallen off it, when Jones led the party into a heavily guarded tunnel. It had been created by construction droids and was as smooth as the inside surface of a shotgun barrel.

An outward-bound party passed to their left. The humans were armed, and led a train of pack animals. Insults were exchanged, laughter rang out, and the contact was over.

The tunnel widened into a cave reminiscent of Vent. Doon saw mutimal pens, lines of parked vehicles, stacks of cargo modules, and a pair of vertical tubes. One was blue, the other green. Both were huge. Amy saw his interest and pointed her whip.

"The one on the left is our geothermal tap. We force water down a pipe, wait for the magma to bring it to a boil, and bring it up again. The steam runs turbines, and they generate electricity. Lots of it. The other tube carries elevators, utility pipes, and a whole bunch of cables.''

Doon nodded, dismounted, and waited for instructions. A woman asked for his rifle, and the android refused. The woman frowned, said something to Jones, and the security officer ambled over.

"Sorry, citizen Doon—but you aren't authorized to carry weapons within the facility. Give the rifle to Kelly and she'll store it under your name.''

"I can vouch for him,'' Amy said. "Would that help?''

"No,'' Jones replied. "Not since one of the staff tried to shoot Garrison on his way to a meeting. Sorry, but I'm afraid I'll need your weapon as well.''

Doon looked around, saw the manner in which the outriders had started to close in, and felt Sojo gibbering in the background. There wasn't much choice. The synthetic pointed his weapon at the floor, worked the bolt, and ejected the magazine.

The woman named Kelly accepted the rifle, checked to make sure the chamber was empty, and took Amy's weapon as well.

Jones nodded agreeably and led them toward the lift tubes. Doon was struck by the number of robots he saw—many of whom were sentient. Here was society as it had been, a cosmopolitan mix of humans and machines, with none of the paranoia he was so used to.

That at least felt good, and the android felt his spirits rise with the indicator, which paused on "44." "Here's where we get off," Jones said easily. "I wouldn't be surprised if they were waiting for us.''

The words proved prophetic. Doon saw a sign that read "Robotics Section," followed the human down a gleaming hallway, and into a fully equipped lab. Ten or twelve entities stood in a semicircle. Most were human, but two were synthetic. They hardly ever spent time outside, but looked as if they did. A gaunt-looking man stepped forward. His clothes hung in folds as if part of him were missing. He peered at Doon as if through tinted glass. "Luis? Can you hear me?''

Doon could have interceded, could have forced the man

to take him into account, but chose to let the opportunity pass. Sojo, or what remained of him, gushed forth.

"Yes, Gene! It's me, a little the worse for wear, but me nonetheless. Tell me about your work—tell me everything there is to know."

It took more than an hour for Garrison and his team to brief the ghost on what they were doing and for him to respond. The rider's eagerness, and drive to complete his work, reminded Doon of himself—as if deep down they were disturbingly similar. "I'm ready," Sojo proclaimed, "or will be as soon as you can arrange for the transfer."

"Transfer?" Garrison asked. "What transfer?"

"I need a body of my own," the rider explained. "Doon, to whom this vehicle belongs, would impede my work."

Garrison looked doubtful. "I see. There's is something of a shortage, however, and that being the case, I wonder if citizen Doon would be so kind as to step aside? Only until your work is complete, of course . . . when the body would revert to him."

Doon seized control of his body, threw an arm around the security officer's throat, and pulled the handgun out of his holster. "Hold it right there. . . . Amy, check 'em out, they might be armed."

The biologist looked distinctly unhappy, but did as he had ordered, and shook her head. "They're clean."

The android nodded. "Thanks, Amy. Stay where you are. No need for you to get involved in this mess. Thanks for the hospitality. All I want is my rifle and mutimal, so tell your security people to stay clear."

Garrison held up his hands. "Please! I was wrong! We *need* Sojo—and we need you. Stay, and we'll make it right."

A staffer stepped forward. "We could download the rider into one of the class sevens, jury-rig some sensors, and use nano in place of limbs."

"Brilliant!" Garrison said eagerly. "Do it!"

"Not so fast," Doon responded cautiously. "What's to stop you from downloading *me* instead of Sojo?"

"How 'bout Mary?" Amy put in. "She could do it. Did she make it?"

Jones nodded. "Yes, she's here."

Doon thought about the suggestion for a moment and nodded. "Okay, but that's the deal, it's Mary or nothing."

Garrison had no idea who Mary was, but was quick to agree, and gave his word that the agreement would be honored.

Doon released Jones, returned the security officer's weapon, and apologized. The human shrugged, returned the handgun into its holster, and waved the matter off. He was embarrassed—and wanted to conceal it.

It took the better part of an hour to find Mary Maras, secure her cooperation, and make the necessary transfer. Doon was surprised by the way it felt. There was a rush as the rider departed, followed not by the freedom Doon had expected, but by a sense of loss. Strange and annoying though he was, the ghost had become part of Doon, and left something of himself behind. A trace of idealism, of scholarship, that would forever linger.

Then it was over, and Doon, about whom the staff cared not at all, was free to leave the room, the mountain, or the continent itself. Sojo was whisked away. The threesome left the lab, and were absorbed into the foot traffic.

The android smiled as Amy introduced one of her friends, and listened as Mary spoke of her escape. Suddenly he was free—but free to do what?

The first member of the crusade was a self-proclaimed prophet. He was blind and walked with the assistance of an eight-year-old male. The oldster's prophecies consisted of complete and utter nonsense, but the faithful took strange comfort from them, and the hierarchy let the matter ride.

Behind the prophet, where they could best absorb the impact of a surprise attack, were the aptly named "Martyrs for God," a shiftless bunch of hoarders, cheaters, and grifters who were destined for hell. Elders Pomo and Zozo were part of this not-so-distinguished group, as were the other members of Piety's social elite.

Assuming that everything went according to plan, the heretics would waste a considerable amount of time slaughtering the martyrs, time in which the First Holy Reapers would outflank the heathen, and subsequently cut them down. To that end they were armed with spears, axes, and scythes all sharpened to a razor's edge.

Marching to their rear were more than 15,000 faithful—"the seed" by which God would reclaim the land. Many were elderly, or, like Solly and Dara, youngsters on pilgrimage who had been diverted to something a good deal more dangerous.

Though they were armed with little more than metal-bound walking sticks, the seed caused them to speak. *Thump* step, *thump* step, *thump* step! The ground shook with their progress, moved the needle on Flat Top's seismograph, and made a geologist sit up and take notice.

The seed were followed by the Chosen One, his cadre of bodyguards, and a thousand chanting monks. The drone of their prayers merged into one uninterrupted bass note, and the smoke from their incense burners thickened the air.

Then came 550 supply carts, 250 heavily laden hordu, 130 pack mutimals and more than 1,000 human porters, each bent double under 100-kol packs. They were silent except for their labored breathing, the occasional clank of a metal fitting, and the crack of the slave master's whip.

The Second Holy Reapers were armed with assault rifles and brought up the rear. They marched with the relentless efficiency of professionals, trampling any porter who had the misfortune to faint, banners flapping in the breeze.

The Third Holy Reapers had been divided into the right and left Hands of God. They rode mutimals and were trained to function as either scouts or a reaction force, should such a thing be necessary. They were heavily armed and more than 1,000 strong.

Lictor stood in his stirrups, scanned the ocean of heads, and gave thanks to God. Every passing moment brought him closer to victory.

It was their second day at Flat Top. Amy made her way to the biology lab, where she discovered that her samples had not only been delivered but had helped verify Garrison's hypothesis and triggered project Forerunner.

Mary, whose skills as a roboticist were much in demand, had been greeted as a godsend and immediately put to work.

That left Doon with no one to look after and nothing to do. He wandered for a while, arrived in the ground-level cavern, and decided to check on the mutimals. That's where he was, shoveling muck from a stall, when Jones appeared. He sat on a partition, allowed his feet to dangle, and shook his head. "You have a way with shit."

The synthetic shrugged, tossed a shovelful of manure out through the gate, and turned for more. "I've had plenty of practice."

"Like when you were a cop?"

Doon used the shovel to lean on. "You checked?"

Jones smiled. "Of course. Especially after you took my weapon and shoved it into my ear."

"Sorry about that . . . I got lucky."

Jones shook his head. "That's bullshit . . . but thanks for trying."

"So," Doon said, "you didn't come all the way down here to watch me shovel shit. What's on your mind?"

The human looked serious. "There are more than twenty thousand Zid headed this way . . . and somebody's got to stop them."

"You think it's possible?"

Jones shrugged. "Maybe. *If* we're smart, *if* we pull together, and *if* we're lucky."

"So what do you want? Another foot soldier?"

The security chief shook his head. "No, what I need is a leader, someone who can think on his feet."

Doon felt as though there was something more . . . something the human hadn't told him yet. "And?"

Jones looked uncomfortable. "We have a number of synthetics . . . many of whom would be willing to fight. Especially under the right kind of leadership."

Now the visit made sense. The bigwigs, most of whom were human, would have to employ every available asset to stop the Zid horde—robots included. The machines weren't stupid, however, not all of them anyway, and had well-founded doubts.

Many humans saw synthetics as people, but some found that hard if not impossible to do. Given the choice between sacrificing a human or what they regarded as a machine, there was little doubt which they would choose. The answer, a partial one at least, was to put a robot in charge.

Jones watched the android for some sign of response. Damn the wirehead anyway, couldn't he see how much the visit cost? Or was that expecting too much? Did machines feel embarrassed when another unit outperformed them? Or were they above such human foibles?

Doon looked up, saw the emotion in the human's eyes, and nodded. "Who would fall under my command?"

"Ninety percent of the robots and synthetics capable of combat."

"Who would I report to?"

"Me."

Doon held out his hand. "Done. Harley Doon . . . reporting for duty."

Michael had descended to the lowest orbit he could maintain without falling out of the sky. There was only one thing really worth looking at, and that was the crusade. It had crawled across the countryside for more than five days now.

It seemed as if half of each morning was spent eating breakfast, participating in prayers, and milling around. Then, once everyone was in place, there was the tiresome business of the march itself, with the entire procession being held to the pace of the slowest members.

Not that Michael was complaining, goodness no, not when the beings at Flat Top needed every second they could find. First to prepare their defenses . . . and second to save the planet. A worthy goal—even if it didn't mean much to him. Hundreds of thousands of lives at stake, including human, Mothri, and Zid, not to mention synthetics and their lesser brethren.

The satellite watched sadly as a Zid fell by the wayside and his companions tried to revive him. Not the first casualty of Lictor's crusade . . . and certainly not the last. The planet turned—and Michael turned with it.

Gradually, and with a slowness that threatened to drive Jones out of his mind, Flat Top's leaders—Garrison and those who reported to him—had turned more and more of their attention to the impending threat. Something they were reluctant to do, given the importance of Project Forerunner.

In fact, if it hadn't been for the video Michael shot through holes in the cloud cover, and the breathless, nearly hysterical accounts brought back by the facility's long-range scouts, Garrison and his staff might never have reacted. Not in time at least, which would have been too bad, especially since Sojo's arrival had enabled a major breakthrough and might even lead to success.

They *did* respond, however, albeit somewhat reluctantly, and Jones was able to get a substantial increase in resources. That included the right to recruit noncritical personnel into the newly formed Flat Top militia, sufficient trade goods necessary to strengthen his force of mercenaries, and the formation of what came to be known as Doon's Droids.

That was a name Doon might have secretly enjoyed, had it not been for the fact that it was extremely misleading—a fact he discovered after assembling his troops.

One corner of the cavernous garage had been converted to a military training area, and the synthetic watched as his would-be subordinates walked, crawled, and rolled into the area.

There were one hundred thirty-six units on his roster—but only twenty of them were sentient. The rest were a mishmash of machines that included everything from floor sweepers to mid-level maintenance machines and heavy duty construction equipment. Not that *all* the droids were dreck, since the Mothri known as Enore had sent two dozen fighting machines, each of which was equivalent to a company of human soldiers.

Doon stood on a cargo module, hands on hips, and surveyed his troops. Some wore yellow paint with black stripes, two were dressed in lab coats, and there was plenty of bare metal. They stood on legs, sat on tracks, perched on wheels, and wriggled like snakes. Lights flashed, servos whirred, lasers probed, data flowed, beams stabbed, tracks clanked, and the air stank of ozone.

On one level the whole thing was laughable, ridiculous, and very disheartening. In fact, a human might have given up then and there. But Doon saw something in his collection of mechanical misfits—something a bio bod might have missed.

While some of his troops were clearly unsuitable for combat—the sweepers being an excellent example—many were quite adaptable, and, thanks to a ready supply of nano, could be modified in a relatively short period of time.

More than that, the machines were *trainable,* needing only the correct programming to make themselves useful and, once employed, utterly reliable.

The problem would be in the areas of flexibility and initiative. While dependable, the nonsentient machines would be trapped within the parameters of their programming, or reliant on others to provide direction.

Still, unlike Jones, who was continually frustrated by how slowly his human recruits absorbed new skills, Doon could train his low-function subordinates in a matter of seconds once the software was ready. That was a task to which Mary had already turned her considerable skills.

Yes, the synthetics would prove more difficult, especially where their independence was concerned, but they did have the ability to acquire vast amounts of information in a relatively short period of time, and that would prove useful.

Doon called the synthetics together, took a moment to introduce himself, and stated the challenge. ''The choice is yours: You can stop the Zid—or die on their altars. Anyone have any questions?''

No one did.

32

Ar ma ged´ don, n, a final and conclusive battle between the forces of good and evil

The sedan chair lurched as one of two human beings slipped, fell to one knee, and rose again. Lictor heard a whip crack as a bodyguard set the matter right. The job had killed three of the heretics so far—which was all to the good.

The news regarding the missing Devil-machine, Jantz, and his mysterious paralysis had arrived the evening before. Lictor's mind was made up. Though relatively easy to convert, the humans were treacherous by nature, and must be purged. Jantz, who had clearly been up to something, would await his return.

In the future, after Flat Top had fallen, the aliens would be treated like what they were: beasts of burden. Fit only to work the fields. The thought pleased the Chosen One, and he smiled.

The diagnostics came up green, the robot beeped, and Mary turned the device loose. The machine, which had originally been designed to place seismic sensors, had been converted into a mine-layer and supplied with appropriate programming, not to mention a heat-seeking machine gun, camouflage paint, and a new set of communications protocols.

It was just the latest in the long list of conversions, modifications, and adaptations that Mary and her two assistants had been asked to carry out. That was the trouble with working for a machine—the bastard never took breaks.

Doon filled the doorway of her makeshift lab. His newly appointed executive officer, a history teacher named Rudolph Strang, stood in the background. Both wore camos.

Mary wasn't sure which of them scared her the most—Doon, who had made the transition from self-centered loner to idealistic leader, or Strang, who was said to carry every military text ever written around his processor and had the words "machines rule" stenciled across his forehead.

"So," Doon said with his usual cheerful efficiency, "how are we doing? Are my troops ready to go?"

"As ready as a collection of street-sweepers, maintenance bots and ditch-diggers ever will be."

"Good. We've got a field exercise tonight. Care to join us?"

Mary shook her head. "I'm human. Remember? We have to sleep."

Doon waved an acknowledgment, and Strang smiled. Not a friendly smile, but one filled with pity. The synthetic felt sorry for her. Mary remembered school, where she had struggled to learn while machines had absorbed knowledge as if it were oxygen. Except that they didn't *need* oxygen—or very much else, for that matter. Maybe the Zid were right . . . maybe there was reason to be scared.

It was a ritual by now. Exhausted by the journey, and scared of what lay ahead, one, two, or three of the crusaders would sneak out of camp and attempt to run. A few made it. Not many—but just enough to encourage those with similar aspirations.

Most were not so lucky, however, and were killed in the morning, right after breakfast.

Solly and Dara had grown to hate the ritual *thump*, *thump*,

thump of the drums, the words mixed with snowflakes, and the inevitable fall of the bloodstained hammer.

This particular morning was no different, not at first anyway, although something amazing was about to happen.

The multitude was assembled and the Chosen One was halfway through the usual condemnation when a strange buzzing sound was heard.

Solly thought he was the only one who had heard the noise at first, until others began to frown and search for the source. It came like a night bug to the flame, a silvery construct with long fragile wings.

It was high at first, *very* high, but flew in ever-descending circles.

The crowd gasped as the device appeared. Some raised their hands, as if to protect themselves from harm, while others began to pray.

Solly allowed words to issue from his mouth, but his attention was on the wonderful, fabulous machine, his mind already absorbing the manner in which it had been constructed, and wondering what impact a shorter set of wings would have on its performance.

Still, even *he* was shocked when the flyer spoke perfect Zid. "Greetings from the beings of Flat Top. Don't be frightened. This machine, which is only one of thousands at our disposal, will do you no harm, as *we* have done you no harm. Please return to your homes. The Cleansing, as you refer to them were an omen, a sign that Zuul is sick, and in need of medicine. We *have* that medicine, and just as you might treat a sickly child, we plan to . . ."

The rattle of automatic weapons fire obliterated the next few words. The drone staggered, issued a thin stream of gray smoke, and made a hard right-hand turn.

Thousands watched in horror as the Reapers continued to fire, and the flyer, seemingly guided by an invisible hand, dived toward a supply cart. Not just *any* cart, but one loaded with ammo, and marked to that effect.

Though small in and of itself, the explosion was sufficient to trigger some black-market grenades, and they took care of the rest.

Those standing closest to the blast were killed. Others

were knocked off their feet. A wheel soared fifty feet into the air. A splinter ripped through a Reaper's chest. A female screamed, priests began to chant, and Solly held Dara in his arms. Crono saw, but didn't say a word. A message had been sent—and a message had been received.

Lictor screamed orders, caused a half dozen Reapers to go under the hammer, and called upon God for divine retribution.

It took the rest of the day and the better part of the evening to restore order, remotivate the faithful, and organize anti-aircraft squads.

Maras had been good at things like that, and—much to his own surprise—Lictor actually missed him.

A nano-built scale model of Flat Top and the surrounding terrain occupied the center of the conference table. Blocks of Reapers, soldiers, and robots were positioned willy-nilly among hats, half-empty cups, and other debris. The room was crowded, and beings sat where they could.

A bank of screens dominated one wall, and Colonel Samuel Jones watched as the high-res camera dove at the two-wheeled cart and suddenly cut to black. He shook his head sadly. "Too bad it didn't work . . . words beat the heck out of bullets. Still, we gave them something to think about."

Strang spoke without apparent thought: " 'Everything the enemy least expects will succeed the best.' Frederick the Great, 1747."

"So noted," Jones said dryly. "Well, the effort bought some time . . . how will we take advantage of it?"

Major Kristen Cantwell had been a sergeant at arms aboard the ship, had served the Guild, and had been recruited by Jones. She had closely cropped gray hair, eyes with a tendency to flick back and forth, and extremely white teeth. "My people are ready, sir. Just say the word."

Jones looked thoughtful. "Yes, I believe they are. . . . But will they stay? When the going gets tough?"

Cantwell shrugged. "We're mercenaries . . . we get paid to fight."

Strang smiled. " ' . . . Mercenaries and auxiliaries are useless and dangerous, and a leader having his state built on mercenary armies will never be secure . . .' Machiavelli, 1513.''

Cantwell wasn't all that fond of wireheads—or negative comments about her troops. Her right hand dipped toward a sidearm as she rose from her chair.

Jones raised a hand. "Enough!" He turned to Doon. "Major, I'll thank you to keep your executive officer under control. The last comment was completely unnecessary."

Doon said, "Yes, sir," made a mental note to talk with Strang, and blanked his face.

Jones motioned to Cantwell. "Thank you, Major. We will count on you and your troops. Major Nargo?"

Nargo was thirty-something—and very intense. He led his militia the same way he led the accounting department: by the numbers. He crossed his arms, realized that might look defensive, and forced them down.

"My group is at 86.2 percent readiness, sir, with an average training score of 82.1, a physical readiness index of 92.4, and a . . ."

"Yes," Jones interrupted. "Very impressive, I'm sure. But are they ready to shoot at the Zid?"

Nargo blushed. "Sir, yes sir."

"Excellent. Now, how about you, Major Doon? Tell us what, outside of quotes, we can expect from your battalion."

Doon ignored the barb. "One helluva bill for spare parts, Colonel—and some very shiny floors."

The room exploded into laughter, and Jones allowed himself a grin. Doon waited for the noise to subside and launched his report. "After taking a long, hard look at the assets under my command, I realized that most of them wouldn't make very good soldiers. With that in mind, my staff and I decided to form three separate units, including an engineering company, presently engaged in digging trenches and laying mines, a special operations unit, of which the airborne drone was part, and an armored group built around the Mothri-donated machines.

"I think you'll agree that the bugs will not only inflict a significant amount of damage, but are quite likely to scare the shit out of the enemy."

"Ah, death by dehydration," Cantwell's XO put in. "How devious."

The room broke into laughter yet again, and Jones waited for it to die down. "Thank you, Major Doon. Any questions? No? Well, it's my turn."

The officer looked around the table as if seeing his subordinates for the first . . . and perhaps the last time. "I won't waste your time with a whole lot of rah-rah bullshit. There are more than twenty thousand religious fanatics headed our way—and they mean to wipe us off the face of the planet.

"Truth is, we could kill every single one of the sonsofbitches if we wanted to—and use their bones for paperweights. We have the know-how, we have the means, and we sure as hell have the motivation. We have three aircars stored down below. They don't like volcanic dust much, but each and every one of them has sufficient range to reach the column, and enough payload to carry a nuke.

"Only trouble is that it wouldn't be right. Most of the Zid aren't any more evil than you or I. They've been lied to, that's all—kinda like we were back on Earth—and they actually believe this Antitechnic bullshit.

"So we're gonna gamble that we can stop with something short of a nuke—and pay for that privilege with some lives."

Strang broke the ensuing silence. "And if we fail?"

Jones shrugged. "We don't have a backup, if that's what you mean. There isn't enough time to build a nuke at this point—even if we had the will to do so. Use the minimum amount of force necessary—but do what you have to do.

"The eggheads will start pushing nano down through the G-Tap at 2100 hours. It's gonna take the better part of seven days to get the job done. What they don't need is a whole bunch of T-heads lighting fires under their feet while they do it. Questions? No? Okay, you've got your orders. Carry them out."

The Reapers, who had been sent ahead as scouts, passed the prophet and thundered down the column. They enjoyed showing off, and did so whenever they could.

Lictor, who'd been dozing in his sedan chair, heard the commotion and sat up. An officer brought his mount to a halt, bowed formally, and delivered his report. "We saw the mountain, your eminence—the seed could reach it by night-fall."

Thrilled to have arrived, the Chosen One called for his mount, boarded the mutimal straight from his chair, and gave instructions to his aides. "March for the length of two additional prayers. Select a site with excellent drainage, a bountiful source of water, and plenty of loose rock. Deploy the Reapers to protect the seed. Put the heretics to work building a wall around the perimeter. Show no mercy, for the barrier must be completed by nightfall."

The assistant bowed, took a big step backwards, and escaped the flying mud.

Lictor had never seen the heretic stronghold and was eager to do so. He rode like the wind, felt the snowflakes sting his cheeks, wished he could yell. The ride was exhilarating— and life was good.

The robot had no real name, although the human for which it had previously worked frequently referred to it as "that worthless piece of crap."

Not being sentient, and having no emotions, the robot didn't care what it was called.

Originally designed to roll through drainage pipes, inspect crawl spaces, and perform similar tasks, the segmented machine was about three feet long and shaped like a worm. Not that its shape mattered much, since it, like a dozen similar units, had been dropped into holes and ordered to stay there. Something the robot named Crap did very well indeed.

Time passed—three days, six hours and twenty-one seconds to be exact—and vibrations shook the ground. Not the deep kind, like those generated by tremors, but thousands of minor disturbances of the sort Crap was programed to monitor.

Hours passed, and the vibrations intensified. Finally, when certain parameters had been exceeded, the robot sent a low-frequency message. An encampment had been established— and the Zid were planning to stay.

• • •

The southeast corner of the mesa offered an excellent view of the area most likely to come under attack—or would have, had the weather been better. Shelters had been established, along with the necessary command and control equipment and a makeshift mortar battery. The weapons wouldn't make much difference unless the Zid got awfully close—but would be devastating when and if they did.

Jones took the latest scans obtained from Michael, compared them to the information received from subsurface sensor number four, and saw they matched. The area around Flat Top boasted five sites capable of accommodating more than twenty thousand beings and the Zid had chosen number four.

The security officer nodded agreeably, turned to a tech, and made a request. Video blossomed as site four appeared on a monitor. There was an analysis of the most likely avenues of attack, the depth of the snow, and composition of the soil. The human smiled. So far, so good.

The mist parted, and the mountain loomed ahead. Lictor could hardly believe his eye. Nothing stood in the way! Had the heretics heard of his coming, and run for their city to the west? How disappointing—to come all that way and have nothing to show for it.

The lead Reaper, a fanatic named Orgon, had come to much the same conclusion. He thrust his weapon into the air, urged his mount to a gallop, and uttered a whoop.

The resulting explosion blew the mutimal's forelegs off and threw Orgon into the air. He landed on a second mine and vanished in a gout of flame.

The Chosen One felt pieces of wet flesh pepper his face as he hauled on the reins, turned his animal around, and kicked it in the ribs. More explosions, at least three, signaled additional deaths.

Another Reaper, eager to escape the killing ground, galloped toward the rear. Lictor, realizing that danger could lay in that direction as well, followed behind.

The cleric rode for a long way before he felt safe enough to stop, turn, and check on his subordinates. A count revealed that four Reapers had been killed or left to die. It was a quick and bloody lesson—one Lictor would not forget. Darkness gathered, and he turned toward the east.

The area immediately around the down tube was filled with equipment, consoles, and hundreds of squirming cables. They made a strange threesome: the gaunt, almost skeletal human, the boxy synthetic, and the huge, beetle-like Mothri. They had more in common with each other than with many of their peers, however, and shared the same work ethic.

The bond started with the nano now pouring down through the vertical shaft and into the very bowels of the planet. Once in place, the micromachines would make contact with the Forerunner units, assess the damage that had been done, and set to work. That's the way it was supposed to work, anyway . . . but would it?

The relationship went deeper than that, however. All three of them were lonely, cut off from the rest of their peers by personality, position, and circumstance, yet driven by the same overriding need: to save what they had created.

The three beings were tired, knew what the others were thinking, and waited in silence. All that could be said had been said—and all that could be done had been done. The nano would handle the rest.

The timer hit midnight, a contact closed, and the robot named Crap sent a probe toward the surface. It emerged from the snow, grazed a hordu's leg, and paused.

There was a distinct popping sound as a cap flew off. A rocket was fired, lasers flashed, and alien music blasted forth.

Reapers fired their assault weapons in every direction. Roughly half the seed stampeded toward the east while the rest stood and screamed. Mutimals broke their tethers, a monk was trampled under their feet, and a youngster fell in a fire.

It took less than five minutes to locate the device and send humans to dig it up. That was enough, however—since the faithful were frightened, and it would take hours to quiet them.

Crono helped restore order, cursed the Devil, cursed the

humans who served him, and cursed the fool in charge. Dawn came slowly—and he was glad.

Lictor, like the Founder before him, was subject to visions. Visions that, while occasionally wrong, were often correct, and in no small way responsible for his now lofty rank.

Where such understandings came from, and why he had been blessed with them, the cleric didn't know. He would have ascribed the visions to God, except a few of them had proved wrong, and the Supreme Being was infallible.

Still, such revelations came in handy, and the Zid had learned to rely on them. One had warned of an assassination attempt, another had revealed the true meaning of the volcanic eruptions, and faith, and a third presaged a flood.

That's why the Chosen One took the dream so seriously. It came within an hour of the human-engineered disturbance. During the vision, Lictor saw the aliens ride forth from their citadel, saw them engage his Reapers in a dozen different battles, and saw them win every conflict.

Then, stripped of their warriors, the faithful were slaughtered. All without a single Zid entering the mountain fortress.

The dream was so real, so frightening, that Lictor awoke to discover his gills were fluttering. He rolled off his mattress, felt the carpet under his feet, and started to pace.

There were many things to consider. Among them was the fact that food supplies were low, morale had started to deteriorate, and the humans were stronger than he'd hoped.

And what of the manner in which the camp had been awakened? The humans could have caused the Devilmachine to explode, but they hadn't. Why? Did it mean what he thought it meant? That the aliens opposed indiscriminate violence? But what of the things that exploded when mutimals stepped on them? How did *they* fit?

There was a great deal to think about and, having considered, to take into account. It took a while, but when darkness fled he was ready.

Though perfectly willing to forgo his place of honor among the martyrs, Elder Pomo had been unable to negotiate any sort of transfer. That being the case, he, along with Elder

Zozo and the rest of Piety's contingent, were among the first to be awakened.

It seemed that the most glorious moment of the crusade was upon them, and they, along with the rest of the martyrs, would follow the labor brigade into battle.

"Why us?" Pomo demanded shrilly. "We're old and sickly! Surely the Reapers should go first—to smite the heretics down. And where's my breakfast? I want it now."

A monk, tired of Pomo's whining and concerned as to his own safety, shoved the elder into line. "For the greater glory of God—that's why you'll do it. Now, shut up and do as you're told."

The elders did as they were told, the drums started to roll, and the attack began.

Cantwell watched from the top of a hill. Her cavalry was arrayed on the slope in front of her, vapor hanging around their heads, weapons at the ready. The valley, through which the Zid must come, lay below. There were mines and rows of well-placed stakes, backed by a maze of trenches. Many were empty, but she saw a scattering of heads. Though not impregnable, the arena would be hard to penetrate, and very, very lethal. A killing ground the likes of which she would hesitate to enter.

The officer peered through her binoculars as hundreds of Zid topped the rise and came her way. Cantwell saw that humans had been placed in front with civilians behind them. What she *couldn't* see was any Reapers . . . the ones she was supposed to engage. She spoke into the wire-thin boom mike that hung in front of her mouth.

"Mongol One to Topper. Over."

"This is Topper," Jones replied. "Go."

"The Zid are on the way—humans in front with civilians behind. Over."

"Roger that, Mongol One. No sign of the Reapers? Over."

"That's a negative, Topper. Over."

"Hold, One. Over."

Jones had spent the night in his command post. His eyes were red, his throat was raw, and stubble covered his cheeks.

"Angel? This is Topper. Do you read me?"

Michael had been watching . . . and waiting for the call. "I read you. Over."

"The Zid are headed our way. No sign of armed troops. Where the hell are they? Over."

The clouds were thick but broken. Because of that, the satellite had been able to catch a glimpse or two—and knew exactly where the combatants were hiding.

"The Zid are throwing their entire column at you. The Reapers were placed at the very center of the formation. There's only one way to reach them—and that's through the civilians. Over."

Jones slammed his fist down on a console. A stylus jumped and fell. "The bastards are forcing our hand! Damn them to hell!"

"There's no need for that," the satellite replied sadly. "They're damned already."

The humans went willingly at first, marching in front, unaware of the danger.

That changed when they saw where the snow had been blackened by explosions, where something red had rained down, and half-frozen body parts lay scattered on the ground.

It was too late, though—far too late—as mines went off and bodies cartwheeled through the air.

The humans turned, or attempted to turn, only to be met by a wall of advancing martyrs, backed by the First Holy Reapers. Pomo hesitated, felt a spear point penetrate his coat, and lurched forward.

Driven by a common enemy, and desperate to survive, the two groups merged, stumbled as they were pushed from behind, and struggled to keep their feet. Which was better? To take their chances in the minefield? Or beneath the Reapers' boots? Of course, that death was certain, or very nearly so, so most chose the minefield.

The column advanced, explosions marked its horrible progress, and Lictor was pleased. Rather than the skirmishes the humans had hoped for, they would be forced to fight a decisive battle in which the odds were against them.

The Chosen One's mutimal smelled blood, snorted an objection, and stepped over Pomo's body.

Garrison, Enore, and a group of scientists had made their way up onto the top of the mesa. It felt like a picnic at first, an escape from the laboratories where they spent so much of their time, and to which they must soon return.

But that was before the humans marched into the minefield, before explosions rippled along the front of the half-mile-wide column, before body parts soared into the air.

The clouds parted as if to allow the sunlight through, and the scientists watched in horror as the oncoming army cleared the minefield and approached the rows of well-sharpened stakes. Many had died, enough to leave a carpet of bodies behind, but at least eighteen thousand aliens had survived, and showed no sign of slowing.

Someone began to retch as the first, second, and third ranks were forced to impale themselves on well-anchored spears and the Reapers used the bodies as a ramp.

"We have no choice," Jones whispered to himself. "We have no choice at all."

"No," Garrison agreed. "We don't. We must keep them out of the complex. The nano need time."

"Yes," Enore added somberly. "And so do the eggs."

Doon listened to the orders, wished they were different, and issued his own. The plan was relatively simple: Assuming the Zid crossed the trenches, an eventuality that looked increasingly likely, Doon, along with the units capable of doing so, would attack head-on. That would slow the Zid column and force the sides outward.

That's when Cantwell would attack from the east, and Nargo would strike from the west. Assuming things went well, one, two, or all three of the defensive elements would break through the shield of noncombatants and engage the Reapers.

Then, with their paramilitary arm destroyed, or forced to retreat, the rest of the Zid would follow. Or so it was hoped.

Doon checked to ensure that his weapons were ready, signaled his troops to advance, and kicked the robot's flanks.

The Mothri machines, which he and the other synthetics rode, were not only frightening to behold but extremely well armed, having both lasers *and* mandibles. That, plus the assault weapons and grenade launchers carried by the androids, made for a lethal combination.

Four Mothri machines had been kept in reserve, ready to defend Flat Top's main entrance should that become necessary, which left twenty for the assault team. They loped across the intervening ground, while their lasers burped coherent light, and the synthetics fired their launchers.

The Zid had filled the trenches with the dead and wounded by then, crossed them in force, and annihilated two companies of half-trained infantry. It seemed as if there were two bodies for each bullet, and no matter how many the defenders fired, they were never enough. The axes continued to rise and fall as the Reapers slaughtered the wounded. That's when the droids opened fire.

The prophet, still alive in spite of the fact that his diminutive assistant had fallen, toppled forward. He never knew what hit him.

Ninety percent of the humans and martyrs were dead by then, which left only the thinnest of shields between the machines and the First Holy Reapers. The barrier was swept away, falling like wheat before the scythe, to lie in drifts upon the ground.

The Reapers staggered as shrapnel cut their ranks to bloody ribbons, wilted as lasers burned through flesh, and screamed as mandibles cut them in two.

The column stopped, collapsed inward, and bulged at the sides. That's when Cantwell led her charge, and Nargo led an attack from the west. The battle was fully joined.

Chaos ruled the center of the column. Automatic weapons chattered, monks chanted as they marched into the machine gun fire, the wounded screamed, and drums pounded a relentless cadence.

Thanks to Crono's foresight, Solly, Dara, and the other members of their party were located toward the back of the seed, and thus were immune to the terrible devastation caused by the mines, stakes, and trenches.

But as the Reapers came under attack, and the body of the column was pushed backwards, things started to change. Solly grabbed Dara and edged toward the east. All the youth needed was a place to hide, a hole, a crevice, anything. But there *was* no place to hide, not that he could see anyway, and death plucked at his sleeves. Dara staggered, blood erupted under her cloak, and Solly screamed.

The robot waded into the oncoming Reapers as if they were little more than grass. Its lasers stabbed with ruthless efficiency, each bolt of energy nailing a Zid between the eyes, each slash of its mandibles cutting at least one of them in two.

Doon had lost his assault weapon, but still had both his handguns, and fired them in quick succession. The trick was to keep the Reapers from getting too close, from attaching a homemade satchel charge to the robot's flank, or pulling him out of the saddle.

The synthetic's combat systems were as effective as always, choosing targets, assigning threat indexes, waiting for him to fire. Which the android did, bullet after bullet, magazine after magazine, until it seemed like the shooting would never stop.

That's when one of the Reapers found a rocket launcher, aimed it at Doon, and pulled the trigger. The android was aware of the explosion, of flying through the air, but nothing beyond that.

Michael prayed out loud: "Please, God—please show me the way." And no sooner had the thought been thought than an idea formed and the angel knew what to do.

Nargo didn't know *why* his militia and he were in trouble, only that they were, and would soon be dead.

The Third Holy Reapers, all of whom were armed with assault weapons and mounted on mutimals, plunged into the fight. Had Strang been there to advise him, or had Nargo been more experienced, he might have been aware that well-disciplined infantry *can* survive in the face of calvary. But Strang *wasn't* there, and Nargo *didn't* know, which quickly led to disaster. He and his troops were caught on the flat, and rather than form a square, Nargo allowed his people to gather in clumps of five, ten, or fifteen.

They fought bravely, though, and hundreds of Reapers fell, snatched from their saddles by a blizzard of lead.

More than seven hundred survived, however. They rode like maniacs, low across their animals' necks, jumping rocks and killing anyone who ran. Groups of soldiers rose to oppose them, but they were too few and too isolated to stand for long.

Lictor stood in his stirrups, watched the Second Holy Reapers move forward over the bodies of those who had preceded them, and shouted God's name. The ground shook, and the charge went home.

Garrison, Enore, and Jones, along with hundreds of staff members, watched in numb fascination as Nargo's militia were slaughtered and Cantwell's mercenaries were forced to retreat. The few robots that still survived had gone to her assistance, but the outcome was far from certain.

Garrison shook his head grimly. "I want every able-bodied man, woman, and synthetic down at the entryway. We'll fight them in the corridors."

A technician pointed at the sky. "Look, Doctor! What the hell is that?"

Michael felt his body shudder as it came into contact with Zuul's atmosphere, and the heat started to build. Layer after layer of nano-built skin burned away as he orbited downward.

Volcanos, glaciers, lakes, and plains passed below, closer than they'd ever been before, and part of what he'd been left to monitor.

None of that mattered now—for all was in the past. The *new* him was a comet, an avenging angel, a visitation from heaven.

It had been easy, really, to watch their movements, and spot their leader. The one who could stop the horror, be it by deed, or be it by death.

Death! Oh, how the word seemed to resonate, to call him

down toward the cold, hard ground. Michael was on fire by then, a glowing spheroid that arced across the sky, barely in control.

He was lower now, *very* low, speeding over a plain, flashing past the magnificent cathedral and rushing toward the sun. Then the church fell behind, smoke marked the battlefield, and it was time to steer.

Michael ordered the nano-built vanes to deploy, gave thanks when they obeyed, and made minor corrections. Like eternal peace, the impact was only moments away.

"Our father, which art in heaven, holy be thy . . ."

Solly saw a cluster of rocks, pushed Dara in that direction, and threw her down. Death rattled over their heads as the youth ripped at her blouse. The bullet had been pretty well spent by the time it hit her, but still managed to drill its way through. It was high, though, above her vital organs, and clear of bone.

Solly pulled the sash free of her waist, tore strips from it, and stuffed them into the holes. The rest would bind the dressings in place. She opened her eye. "Hello, Solly."

"Hello, Dara."

"You shouldn't look at me . . . not without clothes."

"Why not? You're nice to look at."

"Only my husband should see me—so it is written."

"Then I shall marry you."

"Would you?"

Solly smiled tenderly. "Of course I would—was there ever any doubt?"

Lictor turned, he wasn't sure why, and was thrown to the ground. Something huge roared over his head, hit the ground, and exploded. Shrapnel flew outward, Reapers fell, and the wounded screamed.

The Chosen One, surprised to be alive, staggered to his feet. He spoke without meaning to. "What in the name of God was that?"

"Something that should have killed you," a voice answered, "just as you killed so many others."

Lictor turned, saw the disk that hung from the male's

throat, and knew he was a priest. "How dare you address me in that manner! Guards! Arrest this fool! Take him away."

But nothing happened. There were no obedient minds— no willing hands. A single glance showed why. The clerics stood with a drift of broken bodies, some groaning, but most deathly still. Michael had missed . . . but not by much.

Crono smiled. "Look, oh holy one, look at the seed! See how their bodies lay scattered where healthy weeds will grow. Are you not proud? Thankful for this bounty of death? Look, and take the sight to hell."

The Chosen One saw the much-used staff, the strong, knobby fingers, and knew what the priest intended. "No! You can't! I'm the holy one!"

Crono swung the pole with expertise born of long practice, felt the staff connect with Lictor's skull, and heard the crack of broken wood.

The Chosen One staggered under the weight of the blow, spun, and fell. Crono removed the thong from around his neck, dropped the disk on the body, and walked away.

Shocked by the thing that had fallen from the sky, and bereft of leadership, the Reapers fell back. They watched to see if the heretics would follow, gave thanks when they didn't, and turned to help their wounded. Both groups mingled after that, helping where they could but avoiding each other's eyes.

Teams of humans and synthetics made their way out onto the battlefield, established aid stations, and went to work.

Amy, a medical bag bumping her hip, started with the first Mothri machine she came to and ran from unit to unit. "Harley? Can you hear me? Where are you?"

The biologist saw Strang, or what she thought was Strang, a battle axe stuck in his head. And there was Rawlings, Chang, and a half dozen more. All dead. Hope became despair, and tears flooded her cheeks. Fake tears, so she could pass for human, so she could grieve as they did.

A maintenance bot lay up ahead, belly up, treads churning. She started to pass the machine, started to leave the area, when a voice called from the wreckage. "Hey, beautiful, how 'bout a hand?"

Amy turned, saw Doon leaning against a sheet of smoke-blackened metal, and ran to his side. An arm was missing, and he looked at the stump. "There goes another one ... Sojo will be pissed."

Amy laughed and threw her arms around the android's neck. Kissing wasn't supposed to mean anything, not to machines, but somehow it did.

Epilogue

Nano made their way down through hair-thin fissures, met in vaults deep within the planet, and exchanged information. Then, having assigned themselves billions of different missions, they went about the work they'd been designed to do.

Continental plates were eased, faults were repaired, and lakes of magma drained into the planet's core. Volcanos fell dormant, the quakes eased, and the weather began to clear.

Not much at first, but enough to help the crops grow, and bring the wildflowers back. Solly paused to enjoy the view, checked to make sure the furrow was straight, and whistled through his gills. The mutimal leaned into the harness, pulled the plow through the rich, moist earth, and toward the other end of the field. The wedge, exactly like the one Crono had ordered destroyed, lifted the dirt and folded it under.

It had been a long time since anyone had questioned the plow, how Solly met his beautiful wife, or what the crusade was like. And that, like the sun on the farmer's back, was very, very good.